Hopeless
ELSIE
SILVER

PIATKUS

PIATKUS

First published in Great Britain in 2023 by Piatkus

13

Copyright © 2023 by Elsie Silver

The moral right of the author has been asserted.

A CIP catalogue record for this book
is available from the British Library.

ISBN: 978-0-349-43774-3

Typeset in Fanwood by M Rules
Printed and bound in Great Britain by
Clays Ltd, Elcograf S.p.A.

Papers used by Piatkus are from well-managed forests
and other responsible sources.

Piatkus
An imprint of
Little, Brown Book Group
Carmelite House
50 Victoria Embankment
London EC4Y 0DZ

An Hachette UK Company
www.hachette.co.uk

www.littlebrown.co.uk

Elsie Silver is a Canadian author of sassy, sexy, small town romance who loves a good book boyfriend and the strong heroines who bring them to their knees. She lives just outside of Vancouver, British Columbia with her husband, son, and three dogs and has been voraciously reading romance books since before she was probably supposed to.

She loves cooking and trying new foods, traveling, and spending time with her boys—especially outdoors. Elsie has also become a big fan of her quiet five o'clock mornings, which is when most of her writing happens. It's during this time that she can sip a cup of hot coffee and dream up a fictional world full of romantic stories to share with her readers.

www.elsiesilver.com

For every single reader (and there are a lot of you) who has messaged, emailed, or commented begging for Beau's book.

This one's for you.

Reader Note

This book contains discussions of alcoholism, PTSD, and skin grafting/burns. It is my hope that I've handled these topics with the care they deserve.

1

Beau

I thought pissing my brother off and storming away would make me feel something.

I was wrong.

Even acting like a raging dick when I'm supposed to help a family friend move into their new house feels . . . bland.

As I walk down the main drag in Chestnut Springs, my fingers curl into my palms, nails digging against skin.

I don't feel that either.

I only feel tired.

But not tired enough to sleep.

A train horn blares, and I freeze in place. For years, I've covered the way loud noises startle me, but it's different this time.

You'd expect me to choose either fight or flight, but these days I brace. Pause.

Wait for any emotion to hit. Fear, anxiety, disappointment.

But these days, I feel nothing.

I pivot on the corner of Rosewood and Elm to watch the train puff past. Chugging along. Back and forth. Point A to point B. Load. Unload. Wait overnight. Start over again.

"I am a train," I murmur as I stare at the wheels crushing against the tracks.

I work all day on the ranch because I'm supposed to. I go through the motions. And I hate every second of it.

A woman pushes a baby in a stroller past me and shoots me a confused look. Her expression changes to surprise when she recognizes me. We might have attended high school together, but the same is true for anyone in this town born within a few years of each other.

"Oh, Beau! Sorry, didn't recognize you for a second there."

Probably because I haven't cut my hair in months.

I don't remember her name, so I plaster on a smile. "Not to worry. I'm blocking the crosswalk, aren't I? Here . . ." My arm stretches out to press the crossing button for her.

The woman I can't remember shoots me a grateful grin, hefting a bag up on her shoulder while trying to keep hold of the stroller overflowing with an unnecessary amount of stuff. "Thanks! Nice to see you out and about. You had all of Chestnut Springs worried for a couple of weeks."

My cheek twitches under the strain of keeping my mouth upturned. Yes, I was JTF2, Canada's elite special ops force. Yes, I knowingly missed our transport out to save a prisoner of war. Yes, I was missing in action for weeks and was in rough shape when they found me.

I'm still in rough shape.

People love to talk about it.

You gave us quite a scare.

Try to catch your ride out next time, eh?

I bet you're loving all this attention.

It's when they think I'm not listening that the comments become less tongue-in-cheek and more dagger-in-back.

He looks like he's gonna flip out any second.

Even the therapist couldn't fix him.

What I call stupid, he calls heroic.

I know they all mean well, but the way they express their interest bugs me. Like my getting stuck in enemy territory on deployment has a single fucking thing to do with them. Like I scared people on purpose or just casually decided not to pick up a phone. Civilians can't fathom the shit I've seen, the decisions I've been forced to make.

So I ignore them.

"Gotta love the small-town support," is what I say, because I can't say what I really think. Being the real me—the new me—would just make people uncomfortable.

"Well, you've got it in spades." With a kind nod, she turns and crosses the street.

I blink away, not wanting to follow her but not knowing where I'm going either. The opposite direction, I think.

Which is when my eyes land on The Railspur, the best bar in Chestnut Springs.

It doesn't matter that the sky is blue, and the sun is out on a beautiful summer afternoon. It doesn't matter that I pissed my brother Rhett off. It doesn't matter that a friend needs my help unloading furniture a couple of blocks away.

At this moment, the town bar looks like a damn good hole to hide in.

And a drink doesn't sound too bad either.

"Gary, if you don't slow down, I'm going to take your keys away."

The ruddy-faced older man scoffs at Bailey's warning as I pull up a stool a few down from him. I turn it so one elbow rests on the bar and I'm facing the door. It may be just another small-town bar, but the extensive updates give it an elevated sort of vibe that I like. Western decor fills the space, a wagon wheel chandelier hangs over polished wood floors, and mason jar glassware lends a rustic feel.

"Don't know when you got so lippy," he grumbles, dropping his pint glass away from his mouth. "You barely used to talk to anyone. Now you're bossing me around like a little tyrant all the time."

Shiny, almost-black hair swishes over Bailey Jansen's tanned shoulders. Her back is to us as she bends down to pull glasses out of the small washing machine behind the bar.

"Got comfortable, I guess. And you could use some bossing, old man. Sitting here, harassing me every day."

"I do no such thing. I'm perfectly nice to you. One of the few who is, I reckon."

She spins now, white towel in hand, to point at her only customer in the quiet bar. "You are. And I consider you a friend, which is why I tell you every day you drink too damn much."

Her gaze snaps to mine, dark eyes widening in surprise, like she didn't hear me arrive over the country music and hum of the dishwasher.

"If I stop, you'll be out of work. And maybe even a friend."

Gary is talking to her like he hasn't noticed my presence, but she responds to him without looking away from me. "I can live with that, Gar." She pauses, tongue darting out over parted lips.

Full, glossy lips.

"Beau Eaton. Nice to see you."

The man turns, now alerted to my presence. "Well shit, that is Beau Eaton, isn't it? Big fella, aren't you?" Gary slurs, and Bailey's free hand darts forward to swipe his keys off the bar.

Gary's eyes close and he groans. "Every fuckin' day."

"Yep. Every fuckin' day." She shoves them into her back pocket and then turns back to the washing machine, where glassware has backed up. "Beau, what can I get you? Got anyone joining you? Probably want your favorite couch, yeah?"

I swallow and glance at the couch where my brothers, friends, and I enjoyed many a night out. It feels like a different version of myself sat there. The new Beau sits at the bar with the shy neighbor girl, who wears a pair of acid-wash Levi's better than anyone he's ever seen.

And the sad town drunk.

"Nah, just me today. I'll have whatever Gary here is having."

"A Buddyz Best for the town hero!" Gary slaps his palm on the bar, and I flinch at the sudden noise. At the label. I could crumple under the weight of everyone regarding at me like I belong on some sort of pedestal. Everyone is *always* watching me.

I stare at his weathered hand, flush against the polished wood of the bar top. My eyes close for a beat and I run my tongue along the backs of my teeth to keep from grinding my molars. When I lift my gaze, forcing myself to act casual, Bailey's got her brows drawn tight, dark irises boring into my face as though she has me all figured out. The flat smile I force onto my lips doesn't seem to impress her. In fact, before she turns away to pour me a frothy pint, her head shakes subtly, like she's disappointed.

My gaze trails over her body again, and I rack my brain to remember the last time I saw her. She's always been sweet, shy little Bailey Jansen. Sadly, born into the least respected family in town. Her dad and brothers have dabbled in it all—drugs, prison, theft—and her mom took off years ago.

Worst of all, their land borders ours. I can see it from my house on the ranch, just on the other side of the river, where I've put up a barbed-wire fence, so those assholes know where to turn back around.

But Bailey has always been different in my eyes.

I've always felt bad for her, always felt protective of her from afar. The stares, the whispers. I imagine living in a small town where almost every resident has a story about your family must be fucking brutal. So, I've always been nice to her. I like her—have no reason not to—even though I barely know her.

She's worked at The Railspur for years now, I just ... can't remember how many. Can't decide if enough years have passed for me to notice the way her tank top lifts today, showing a peek of skin on her flat stomach. Or for me to think about the way her perfectly round breasts would fit so well in my hands.

"How long you been working here, Bailey?" I ask, watching her shoulders go a little tense when I do.

She clears her throat. "Just over four years. Started at eighteen."

Twenty-two.

Fuck. I'm thirty-five, which means I was a teenager when—I brush the thought away and drop my eyes as she tosses a coaster down in front of me, followed by a pint of golden lager, white foam spilling over the edge.

"Thanks," I grumble as I swipe a hand through my hair.

6

"Mm-hmm," is all she says.

Bailey is the only person in town who hasn't fallen all over herself to tell me what a hero I am since I got home. She doesn't gawk at me like I'm a rare animal in a zoo.

She works quietly and I try to keep my eyes from straying to her, wondering why she went from chatting happily to shutting down the moment I sat at her bar.

"MIA for two weeks, huh?" Gary starts in, and I see Bailey roll her eyes as she polishes a pint glass to a clear shine.

"Yup."

"How was that?"

Oh, good. The only thing anyone talks to me about anymore.

"Gary!" Bailey's hands fall to her sides and a look of pure shock paints her face.

"What?"

"You can't just ask things like that."

"Why not?"

I can't help it. I chuckle and decide to rescue Bailey from feeling like she needs to save me. "Real warm. Got a nice tan."

The man narrows his eyes, movements a little sloppy. I wonder how long he's been here since it's barely after lunch and he's clearly wrecked. "Heard you got burned. Not the tan I'd be hoping for."

"Ga-ry." Based on the way Bailey enunciates his name, this line of questioning truly horrifies her.

My palm slides across the bar, drawing her attention. "It's okay. Everyone knows about the burns."

She blinks, eyes suddenly a little glassy.

"Really, I'd rather people shoot straight than kiss my ass or tiptoe

7

around me. Why do you think I'm hiding out here in the middle of the day?"

"Because Bailey is the best bartender in town!"

She snorts, lips tipping up as she goes back to polishing a glass. I try to remember if I've ever really seen her smile. I'm not sure I have. She's always busy trying to blend into the background, and I'm only ever here when it's busy. I don't even know if I've ever heard her voice properly until now. There's a melodic tone to it—a gentleness—that's almost soothing.

I'm sick of people talking to me, but it strikes me that listening to Bailey talk might not be so bad.

The first sip of my beer goes down cold and refreshing. And I sigh as it does, feeling a weight come off my shoulders in the presence of the town drunk and the town pariah.

I recognize them as kindred spirits now, a misfit in my own home.

"Third-degree burns on my feet," I announce, since bluntness seems to be the theme here today. "Skin grafts."

"S'okay. You can find some girl with a weird foot fetish who will love that shit."

Bailey props her hands on the edge of the bar and drops her head with a groan. "Jesus Christ, Gary. No more booze."

"So long as your dick is okay." He waves his hand up and down my body. "Face seems fine, wouldn't you say, Bails? You'll be alright, kid. You'll find someone to love ya."

Even drunk, Gary stumbled into a sore spot. I've never considered myself to be vain or obsessed with my appearance. I haven't needed to be. Good genes and having to stay fit for my job have served me well.

Who'd have thought scarred feet would be the thing to skewer my confidence? Fucking *feet*. Like they even matter. It could have been so much worse. I should feel grateful. And yet . . .

Bailey's gaze wanders over my features. And mine does the same with hers. Where the light touches it, her dark hair has a mahogany-like shine. It's silky and smooth, falling in layers from her long bangs at her chin to her shoulder and then further down her back. It doesn't look like Bailey cuts her hair often either. I'm drawn back to lashes so thick and black they remind me of one of those vintage dolls. She's not wearing a stitch of makeup, revealing a light smattering of freckles on her nose.

A warm blush paints her cheeks when she softly replies, "Yeah," and then blinks away.

Her eyes, that one little word—it . . . makes my blood pump faster.

It makes me feel something in a sea of numbness.

My throat bobs as I swallow the dryness in my mouth, trying to push the moment away. Maybe I'm not ready to feel anything after all.

I take another sip and wonder if maybe I'll be able to sleep for more than a few hours tonight if I toss back a couple of pints.

Then I take another sip and swipe a hand over my stubbled chin before I turn to Gary. "Love is the last thing I need. But this beer is hitting the spot. Thanks, Gary."

Talking to him seems safe enough. Safer than talking to Bailey Jansen, who watches me just a little too closely with those big fucking doe eyes.

2

Bailey

It's been two weeks since Beau Eaton snuck into my bar in the middle of the day. Two weeks since I took one look at him and almost dropped the glass in my hand. He's hard to miss with his broad shoulders and tall, well-built frame, and long legs that have him a head above most men who walk through that door. Light brown hair, a little too long, flops over his forehead, the perfect frame for silver-gray eyes. Even slightly unkempt the way he is right now, Beau Eaton is fucking hot. Totally intimidating.

And hot is one thing, but Beau is nice too. And funny.

A true triple threat—or at least he was.

He's never treated me like I'm wearing a scarlet letter on my chest, even when others have. I only know him from the bar, but he's never held my family's reputation against me. He's always offered kind words, a polite touch on my elbow, and a generous tip at the end of the night.

But he's still the town prince, and I'm still the town trash.

He's the hero, and I'm the bartender.

He's an Eaton, and I'm a Jansen.

And yet, he's here every damn day since the afternoon he walked in looking like a caged animal who broke free.

Here every damn day drinking with fucking Gary.

The first day started out sweet enough. He was endearing, if I'm being honest. But for the past two weeks, his presence has slowly morphed from light to dark, gathering itself into an ominous storm cloud.

It's getting to where he's making everyone around him uncomfortable. You can sense the electricity in the air, like lightning ready to strike.

I'm feeling fed up with him too. He's reminding me of my dad or my brothers, and I have sparse patience for that kind of toxicity.

He comes in mid-afternoon and nurses his pints, quietly simmering. I swear I watch his frustration bubble to a boil right before my eyes. His hand stays clamped around the glass, and he takes tight sips from it with white knuckles.

I'm almost positive he's going to shatter it one of these days. He seems too big, too strong, too angry to be squeezing something that fragile so hard.

When people talk to him, he runs his tongue along the backs of his teeth like he's trying to keep from biting them or something.

"So, what'd you do when you spent those two weeks stuck in the desert?"

My jaw clamps at Gary's words. I know he means well, but he's not reading the room right now. Not reading Beau. Must have missed the way he went taut and never relaxed again when a booming thunderstorm rolled through not thirty minutes ago.

11

Yeah, Beau looks ready to burst tonight, but Gary hasn't noticed.

"Tried to stay alive," Beau bites out. There's a tremor in his voice—a quality that reminds me of a dog when they growl at you. It's a warning to back away.

But Gary is too damn drunk to notice.

"They say you missed your flight on purpose to stay behind and save that journalist. That's some real hero complex shit." The words overrun each other, emerging in a sloppy jumble.

Beau just stares at his pint, gazing into the golden liquid. They've already talked about this subject, but alcohol makes a person repetitive. I know because I've spent years studying drunk people. I'm an expert.

"Imagine where your life would be if you hadn't."

My lashes flutter shut because my gut tells me a line exists, and Gary just stepped right over it.

Or right into it.

Beau's thickly corded arm swipes out, knocking both their glasses onto the bar floor. Beer sprays across the smattering of patrons seated nearby, and if not for the music blaring at this point in the night, I'm certain The Railspur would be dead silent as they watch the altercation unfold.

Beau stands so fast his stool topples behind him with a crash. Gary looks instantly terrified. "Imagine where your life would be if you didn't sit here drinking and embarrassing yourself every fucking day, Gary. Ever think about that?"

His chest heaves, the splatter of liquid making the cotton of his T-shirt stick to his clearly defined pecs. Only someone who grew up in the household I did could be smack dab in the middle of a moment like this and be checking a guy out.

Beau isn't my dad, though, and I'm not worried the way I would be if I were in the house I grew up in.

"Beau," my voice comes out clear, not a single waver to it.

"All alone every damn day, a young girl as your best friend. Seems a little pervert—"

"Beau Eaton, shut your mouth and get your ass outside."

His head swivels, gray eyes latching onto mine like he just noticed my presence. Like he didn't expect little Bailey Jansen to be the one barking at him.

He straightens, but I don't care how tall he is.

He doesn't scare me.

Not even when he's like this.

I point to the emergency exit that leads to the patio, and my hand doesn't shake at all. I'm not nervous. I'm pissed off.

Beau turns stiffly, striding around the end of the bar, past the server station, and straight out into the fading light. If I didn't know how many drinks he's had, I wouldn't notice the slight stagger in his steps or the way he leans on the door just a little heavier than necessary.

Before I cut through the small wooden push gate to follow Beau, I glance back at Gary.

"Too far?" he asks, averting his gaze.

My lips flatten against each other. "Yeah, Gary. Too far."

He swipes a hand through his thinning hair and drops his head, hand tapping over the keys he laid on the bar the minute he sat down. "I'll catch a cab."

I respond with a firm nod before shoving out the door onto the darkened patio. The summer storm caused everyone sitting here to flee, their forgotten glasses now partially filled with rainwater.

13

I can still smell the storm. And Beau. Pine and lemon mingle with something deeper, more sensual. Tobacco maybe, like a cigar.

He's slumped against the outer brick facade of the train station-turned-bar. As I approach, he shoves his fists into the pockets of his jeans, chin dropped almost to his chest, eyes fixed on the sneakers he's always sporting.

They feel out of place for him—too white and shiny, too pristine.

"You can't pull that shit in my bar," I say.

He scoffs, still refusing to meet my gaze. "Your bar, huh?"

"Yes, Beau. My bar. My place. The only place in this town where people don't treat me like shit. I bust my ass working here. I bust my ass trying to make customers like me. And behind that wood is *my* bubble. Gary isn't perverted, he's fucking lonely. And he's one of the few people who is consistently kind to me. So, if you think you can waltz into my bar acting like an untouchable asshole and scaring all my regulars away with your antics, you've got another thing coming."

Now his eyes are on me, a little unsteady but narrowed. "Untouchable asshole?"

"Yes." I cross my arms, like they might give me some protection from him. He looks a little wild tonight, a little dangerous—not like the happy-go-lucky guy we all thought we knew before his last deployment.

Silvery light plays off his features, his tan skin and luminous eyes almost glowing as he stares me down. The only thing that moves between us is his chest, rising and falling in time with mine.

But I don't drop his gaze. I'm so over men trying to intimidate me. And it feels wrong on him, so I don't let him have it.

After our staredown moves from a heated moment into awkward territory, he blinks away, jaw flexing.

"Did I embarrass myself?" His voice is all gravel and rumbles over my skin.

"You did. But the good news is your last name is Eaton, so everyone will forgive you and go back to kissing your feet the minute you walk in there and flash them a smile."

"Bailey, what the fuck? Did you really just say that to me?"

"Yes." My head tilts. "Because it's true. All I had to do was be born into my family and everyone looks at me like they're waiting for that part of my genetics to rear its ugly head. Like I'll go from hardworking and polite to a hillbilly criminal mastermind in the blink of an eye just because my last name is Jansen." His brow furrows deeper the longer I talk. "So, yeah. I think you're gonna be fine, even though you embarrassed yourself."

"That's not true."

"What part?"

"People thinking that about you."

"Ha!" The laugh lurches from my throat, sharp and lacking any humor. "That is adorably naive," I say, shaking my head in disbelief.

"Well, I don't see you that way."

I swallow now, eyes flitting away. It's true that Beau has always been kind to me—to everyone. Maybe that's why this new version of him pisses me off so much. "I know." I shoot him a grateful smile. "You're one of the good ones, Beau. That's why you can't keep doing this."

"Doing what?"

"Sitting at my bar and drinking yourself into a sullen stupor every night."

A quiet keening noise escapes him as his head rolls back and forth against the wall, hands coming out of his pockets to scrub at his face. "It helps me sleep at night."

"What?" I can hear my heart pounding in my ears. Somehow, that's not the response I expected.

It's painfully honest.

"The alcohol. It helps me fall asleep. I go home to the ranch and crash. I haven't been sleeping well these days."

My stomach drops at his admission.

"You telling me you drive like this?" My finger waves up and down him, catching on the bulge of keys in his front pocket.

His wide eyes plead with me, desperate and forlorn. I feel monumentally stupid for assuming he was different from Gary. That he'd be in control enough to get himself a cab rather than get behind a wheel in this state.

I was foolish to fall for the chucklehead good-guy act when he's clearly drowning. I can see him sinking right before my eyes. And I want no part in that. I can't afford to be taken down with him.

"Beau." I step forward, right up to him. He tenses, but I'm too pissed off to have many boundaries right now. And I've always felt more at ease around him than most people. He's always had a way of making me feel like that, which is why I don't think twice about shoving my hand into his pocket and wrapping my fingers around his keys.

His body is rigid. His muscles coil, but he makes no move to stop me. The jangle of metal between us has me looking up into his eyes for a sign I've taken things too far.

I angle my face up to his and get caught in his thrall for a moment.

I only see those moonlit eyes and the way his Adam's apple bobs as he swallows.

16

"I'll make you a chamomile tea," I say, breaking the tense silence between us. "Helps with sleep. But you need to promise you won't make a scene like that again."

He nods and drops his head. "I promise."

The tension between us evaporates as he follows me back into the bar. Prying eyes stare at him as he stands, swaying on the spot, like he's going to be the one to clean up the shattered glass.

"Sit your ass down, Eaton," I grumble as I do it instead. The last thing I want to clean up is his blood.

I can tell he's ashamed. And he should be, but I will not pile on his punishment. He's beating himself up just fine already. Instead, I prepare him a steaming mug of tea, wipe up the beer he spilled, sweep the evidence of his outburst into a dustpan, and carry on with my night like he isn't here.

I refill the tea.

He drinks the tea.

We don't talk, but he watches me, spinning the mug between his broad palms. I feel the outline of his keys in the back pocket of my jeans.

Pete, our cook, walks out of the back at 10 p.m. "You all good out here, Bails? Kitchen's closed."

I scan the bar. It's busy for a Monday night, but manageable. We're only open for two more hours anyway. "Yup. All good here," I reply, giving him a brief thumbs up.

Pete returns the motion with a smile and heads out the front doors. He got hired from the city, which means he doesn't automatically hate me. Which makes working with him a breeze.

When I check Beau's tea again, he stops me. "So, he leaves, and you're here alone for the rest of the night?"

I shrug as I take his mug to add water. "Yeah. I'm a shift manager now, so if it was busier, I'd have kept a server on, but I cut her early."

He rests his forearms on the bar, pads of his long fingers pressed together like he needs something to do with them. "But you're alone? You shut down alone?"

Steam rises as hot water pours from the dispenser.

"Correct."

As I slide the mug across the bar top until it bumps into the tips of his fingers, I try to remember how many refills I've done since the tea is looking awfully watery.

I crouch down and rummage through the box of tea on the bottom shelf. The Railspur isn't a big tea place, but I find another bag of chamomile and drop it into the mug, making a mental note to have our general manager, Jake, order more.

When I tie the string around the handle, Beau doesn't move his palms from around the cup, like he's desperate to soak up the heat.

"Does the manager know this?"

"Jake? Presumably. He makes the schedule. Never met the new owner, totally hands-off investor. So as long as the place is making money, I doubt they care either."

His brow furrows. "That's not safe for you. What if something happens?"

My fingertips brush against his hand as I complete the knot.

I peek up now, lifting one eyebrow. "Like some guy pitching a fit and knocking beer all over the place?"

He glares at me, and I try to keep from smirking at him.

With a nonchalant shrug, I answer the question. "I deal with it." *Like I always have.* I've been looking out for myself for as long as I can remember. It doesn't feel like such a hardship anymore. Just reality.

The only thing Beau gives me in response is a hard stare and a grunt.

But he doesn't leave. He drinks tea at my bar for the rest of the night. For two hours, he sits there, keeping watch. And when I kick everyone out at midnight and shut things down, he stays behind, silently guarding me.

"Are you sober?" I ask as he walks me through the darkened parking lot to my car.

"I've been drinking fucking chamomile tea for two hours. I've never been more sober or hydrated in my life."

I suck in a deep breath and pull his keys from my back pocket, holding them out to him on a flat palm. "Don't pull that shit on me again, Beau."

His throat works as he reaches forward and swipes the keys from me. "You're not how I remember you, Bailey."

I let myself smirk now because, of course, we all change. I couldn't stay that frozen, terrified little girl forever.

I wanted to change.

"You're not how I remember you either, Beau."

His eyes shift back and forth between mine, like he's searching for something in them. "What days do you work?"

I snort, glancing down to pull my own keys from my purse. "What days don't I work?"

"Okay, what nights do you work alone?"

"Sunday through Tuesday," I reply, zipping my bag.

Beau nods and says a terse, "Okay," before spinning on his heel and giving me his back, looking every bit the military man he is. Head held high, shoulders perfectly straight.

19

Like he's some sort of knight in shining armor.

One who starts pulling up a stool every Sunday through Tuesday to drink chamomile tea until midnight, so I don't have to close by myself.

3

Beau

Cade: You're coming to the wedding, right?

Beau: It's my little brother's wedding. Of course I'm coming.

Cade: You're not exactly reliable these days. You no-show. And when you do show, you're a miserable asshole.

Beau: I'm only doing my best imitation of you.

Cade: I'm not miserable anymore though. Just an asshole. That's why everyone voted and decided I had to be the one who sent this message.

Beau: Everyone voted? Very democratic.

Cade: Willa says you need to apologize to Winter. She's in the wedding party.

Beau: Willa doesn't run my show.

Cade: You must be new here. Willa runs everyone's show.

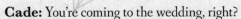

song I don't recognize plays from the speakers, but I two-step anyway. I'm wearing a suit that feels fucking awful, and these dress shoes are rubbing my grafts uncomfortably. Winter Hamilton has one hand on my shoulder and her nose is tipped high as she stares just beyond me. Or possibly at the top of my ear. I'm not entirely sure which.

Dancing with Winter is more uncomfortable than anything going on in my shoes. And that's saying something.

For an entire song, we dance like stiff pieces of wood, ignoring each other. I can see Rhett and Summer dancing too. They look so fucking happy it's hard to watch, but I don't know where to land my gaze. It seems like everyone is watching me. I've got my hands locked in place because I don't want to slide too low or too high on Winter's ribcage. Those are no-fly zones, and based on the way her baby daddy, Theo, is glaring at us, every inch of her might be a no-fly zone.

The music switches over to a slower song and Winter mumbles, "Thanks. That was the junior high dance blast from the past I've always dreamed of."

"Good god, Winter." My fingers tighten. "One more dance."

"Why?" Her head tilts and her blue eyes home in on my face. I feel like I'm in therapy again. Something broken that needs fixing. A specimen for medical professionals to poke and prod and analyze. Between my burns and my brain and my insomnia, I'm like a shrink's wet fucking dream.

I hate that feeling. That expression. Like I'm a big dumb goldfish in a bowl.

"Because I need to apologize to you."

She just shrugs. "No, you don't."

"I blew up at you at a family dinner."

I'd quit seeing all my doctors and wasn't sleeping. I was sore and tired and just wanted to rest for a bit. Winter saw right through it when I dragged her down the hallway to talk. Right through my request for prescription sleeping pills—because over-the-counter ones weren't doing the trick. Her knowing smirk and crossed arms, followed by a calm "no" pushed me over the edge.

I exploded. She didn't deserve it. Everyone heard.

Winter's lips form a slight curve. "Did you? I don't remember."

"Winter," I bite out, annoyed that she's making this so hard for me.

"Beau," is all she responds with as we continue swaying on the wooden dance floor. Over her shoulder, I catch sight of Bailey. Her glossy hair shines like the top of the river, reflecting every light. She's not a guest, but she's tending bar for the reception, and that's good enough for me.

"I shouldn't have done that." My eyes stay on Bailey as I speak to Winter. Focusing on her makes this easier. She's become a calm spot in a mind that is a turbulent storm.

"No, probably not. But you know what, Beau?"

I finally glance down at Winter. "What?"

"We're all human, and we all make mistakes. Especially when we're struggling."

"I'm not struggling."

She snorts and then gives me an exaggerated wink. "Cool. Me neither."

My molars clamp down and I glance back at Bailey. "Okay. Maybe I am."

But I relax when I'm looking at her.

"You sleeping now?"

23

I roll my lips together and consider lying to her. But Winter is so no-nonsense—so not flowery and overly doting—it's easier to be real with her than with the rest of my family. "No. Well, I've gotten on a schedule, and that seems to help a bit." I don't tell her that by *schedule* I mean planning my week around sitting at Bailey's bar drinking chamomile tea. But the truth is, sitting there has given me a purpose, and it feels good.

"Seeing anyone?"

"Like a doctor?"

She nods.

"Nah."

"Why see a professional when we can diagnose ourselves, right?"

I smirk but say nothing.

"A childhood filled with neglect means I learned to survive by not relying on anyone," she says. "Boom. Diagnosed. Saved myself hundreds of dollars. You go."

I curve a brow as I consider what to say next. "PTSD."

"Yeah." Her nose wrinkles as the song nears its end. "So generic. I can see why you wouldn't want to talk to a professional about that."

"Winter, are you making fun of me? I can't fucking tell."

She pats me on the shoulder. "You're big and handsome, Beau. Some people might think that means you're stupid. I think you let people think you are because it's easier that way."

"Wow. Thank you. I'm endlessly flattered, Dr. Hamilton."

"But I know better. You know better. We both know therapy is good but we both don't go. So we're just doing the best we can."

"What does that mean?" My brow furrows, and she steps away at the end of the song.

"Fuck if I know. I've had a lot of champagne to medicate myself

24

through this family event. Have you tried it? It's delicious. At any rate, no hard feelings. Water under the bridge, as they say. But if you need anything, you've got my number."

We shake hands. Then she turns and walks over to Theo, who is eyeing her up her like she might be dessert. That's hard to watch too. So I walk toward someone who isn't.

I'm drawn to Bailey through the crowd like a magnet. Or maybe I've just become the new miserable regular who sits on a stool waiting for her to finish work. Like a sad puppy dog.

But she talks to me like no one else does. About inane things. And sometimes we're just quiet together.

And that quiet is comfortable.

When I lean against the bar, she barely acknowledges my presence. She doesn't need to. She knows I'm here.

"No chamomile tea. But you look like you could use a pick-me-up." She slides a glass of Coca-Cola in front of me, not realizing that *she's* the pick-me-up.

"Thanks," I reply, hunkering down against the bar, preparing myself to emulate what we do at The Railspur. I told my family I'd be at the wedding, and I am. But the truth is, it's overwhelming. It's hot, and loud, and busy in this barn turned event space, and I don't like it.

"How ya doin', soldier?" Bailey asks, propping a hip against the ice well to face me. She crosses her arms and inspects me a little too closely, as if she can sense that something is isn't right.

I stare back at her, absently wondering how many freckles dot her nose. Wondering if they only crop up in the summer or if they linger through the winter. I've never looked at her close enough to notice. There's one just above her lip that I'm pretty sure is always there.

I tear my gaze away and glance at the dance floor, seeing all my family members together. It's nice to see them happy. I put them all through so much. And yet, I take a deep swig of soda, peek back at Bailey, and say, "I'm struggling."

She nods. "Trust your struggle, Beau."

"What does that mean?"

"If we're struggling, we're still in motion, yeah? Heading somewhere better. That's what I keep telling myself anyway."

My chest tightens. I don't want Bailey to struggle.

I'm where I am by choice. She's where she is by birth. It seems profoundly unfair.

But I lift my glass to her all the same. "I'll cheers to that. To struggling together."

She laughs lightly and lifts her drink from behind the bar, clinking her glass against mine. "Less lonely that way, for sure."

It's a simple exchange. Probably nothing noteworthy to the average person beyond two fucked-up people commiserating.

And yet, knowing I have something in common with Bailey makes me feel instantly lighter.

I wish it was her I'd been out there dancing with.

Some people might find the blue sky and the chirping of birds charming. The smell of fresh mountain air and all that. And maybe I'm being ungrateful—that's a distinct possibility—but the charm is all lost on me.

"Beau?"

My older brother's voice cuts into my thoughts as I sit up on the back of a horse, staring over the ridge at a valley of cows who all look the fucking same. They look the same, they eat the same thing every day, they follow each other around almost blindly.

Everything about their existence seems very simple. Boring even.

And yet they all seem happy.

I wish I were a cow. Wish I could find some joy in the monotony of ranch life. Instead, I'm restless and writhing. Trapped beneath the surface of the perfectly manicured façade I slip on for the benefit of everyone around me.

They want me to be okay. And I'm not. Not really. I want them to think I am. But these days? These days, I suck at maintaining my cover.

"Beau!" Cade's voice is real mad now, and I can hear the danger in it. If I were his son, Luke, I'd be trembling in my boots.

But I'm not.

So I turn my head slowly to glance at my brother. "You're dressed like some sort of emo cowboy. Why are you wearing all black on such a hot day?"

He shakes his head in disbelief. "Did you not hear me talking to you?"

I heard my name, but not much else.

"Sorry, just kinda got lost in enjoying the view. Blue skies, the birds chirping." I wave a hand over the horizon. "It's nice."

My brother blinks at me, clearly unsure of what to say next. His eyelashes are so dark, he almost reminds me of a cow with the slow, lazy way he blinks at me.

"Hey, why do cows have such long eyelashes?" I ask, abruptly switching the subject.

His brow furrows in my direction beneath the brim of his cap. "What?"

"Their eyelashes. They're just so damn long. What's the point?"

What's the point of anything?

The words crop up in my head. But they're immediately followed by Bailey's wisdom from this past weekend. And that has my lips tipping up ever so slightly.

Trust your struggle.

So I do. I trust that there's a perfectly good reason my brain needs to know about cow eyelashes.

Cade clears his throat. I'm clearly confusing the hell out of him. And he's doing the thing my family does where they cater to me, no matter how ridiculous I act. Tiptoe around me like it helps me when they accommodate my every whim somehow.

Not like Bailey, who gives me shit at every turn.

"It's just to protect their eyeballs. Dust, rain, insects. That kind of thing."

"Huh." I rest my gloved hands on the horn of my saddle and gaze down at the whole dumb herd of them. "I should have figured that one out. Seems obvious now that you say it."

He hits me with a forced smile, and I stifle a laugh. Cade pretending to be all soft and sensitive is too fucking awkward to take. I wish he'd make a mean joke and threaten to kick my ass.

That would make me feel normal again.

"Ready then?"

Ready.

I stare down at the field. His question is one I've heard before. And yet, it's monumentally different right now.

There's no adrenaline, no thrill, no life-or-death repercussions.

"Oh shit, hang on." I shift in my saddle and reach into my back pocket, pulling my phone out and staring at it like there's a call coming through. All I see is the background picture, which features Luke grinning ear to ear after we threw watermelons out the window of my moving truck. The memory of speeding down a back road, watching them explode on the asphalt, and hearing him squeal with glee never fails to make me smile.

Especially since Cade told us not to.

"Jasper's calling. One sec."

Cade rolls his eyes and mumbles, "Catch up," before urging his mare forward toward the path that leads down into the valley.

"Hey man!"

I'm met with silence. Obviously. Because I'm faking this call.

"Uh-huh." I give Cade a firm thumbs up when he turns back to look at me.

"Right. Oh shit. That does sound important."

Cade has started his descent. He's begun to disappear behind the crest of the hill, but I carry on anyway.

"You sure Sloane can't help you with that?"

Pause.

"Oh. She's in the city, huh? Okay, I'll see what I can do."

I wait several more seconds before adding, "Alright, talk soon." Then, with a light cluck, I urge my horse closer to the edge of the ridge. I can see where Cade has hit flat ground below and the other guys who work for him already waiting down there. I'm hit with a pang of guilt. Guilt that I can't just suck it up and go do the job.

I know I need to stop bailing on everyone. I know I promised to work the family ranch with Cade.

But I can't. I just . . . *can't*.

That knowledge doesn't stop me from feeling like shit when I call down, though. "Hey Cade!" He pulls up and turns in the saddle to glare at me. It's like he knows what's coming. "Just got a call from Jasper! He needs my help. I'm gonna peel out and then try to make it back to wrap up the day with you and the crew."

All he gives me is a nod. He knows I won't be back.

I nod in return before I turn my mount to walk away. Trying to keep my shame at bay.

Once I'm out of earshot, I lift my phone and call Jasper for real. He picks up on the fourth ring. "Workin' hard or hardly workin'?"

I can always trust Jasper to crack me up, razz me a bit. He hasn't taken to smothering me since I got back. In fact, he mostly lets me come to him when I'm ready. Jasper knows trauma. He knows when to push and when to sit back. And he knows how it is to have everyone staring at you, waiting for something to happen, like you're an experiment in a Petri dish.

These days, I feel like I understand him better than ever.

"How'd you guess?" The thump of hooves on the dry ground beneath me rattles my bones, and I can already sense my body starting to relax as I head away from the crew.

"Well, Beau, the only thing reliable about you these days is how unreliable you are."

"Harsh."

He snorts. "But true. You're a big boy. You can take it."

"That's what she said."

He huffs out a laugh, and I can clearly envision the expression on his face—amused but sharp. We've known each other since we were fifteen, practically glued together since he came to live with our family. I don't get much past him anymore.

"So I need you to do me a solid."

He doesn't even hesitate. "Alright."

"If Cade asks, I need you to corroborate my story that you called me away from work because you needed help."

"With what?"

"I didn't say. You pick."

"Okay, I'll tell him I was missing Sloane and that you offered to come dance like a ballerina for me to make me feel better."

"I would if you wanted me to," I deadpan.

He laughs at that. "I know you would."

"Let's say your car battery died and you needed a jump."

"I would never let my battery get old enough to die."

So literal.

"Cade wouldn't know that, though."

He grunts his assent. "It's like we're teenagers all over again. Tricking Cade into thinking we're totally above board."

I chuckle. "The good old days."

That one-liner strikes my friend silent for a beat too long. "There are still good days to come, Beau."

"Of course, I know." I sigh, wanting to end this call before it veers into territory I'm not ready for.

"Is there a reason we're pulling one over on Cade? Planning on telling me where you'll be if you aren't dancing for me or giving my car a jump?"

"Thanks, man. Talk later." I forge ahead quickly before hanging up.

And then I head straight for where the best part of my day always is.

The place that I've come to associate with both peace and purpose.

The stool at the end of Bailey Jansen's bar.

4
Beau

Rhett: Thank you for coming to the wedding.
Beau: Of course. Where else would I have been?
Rhett: Great question. No one knows where you hang out anymore. Only that you disappear and talk to no one.
Beau: I talk to people.
Rhett: You can talk to me too. You know that, right?
Beau: Of course. I know that. Congratulations, the wedding was beautiful. I'm very happy for you and Summer.
Rhett: Thanks. Love you, Beau-Beau. You doing okay? Like really?
Beau: Yeah, I'm great.

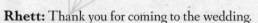

"Have you ever had anal sex?"

As Bailey's sugary voice cuts through the loud music at The Railspur, I spray hot tea from my mouth. My attempt to cover it with my palm only results in me getting soaked. Hot water drips down my forearm and lands on my lap. Pretty sure my eyes have popped right out of their sockets onto the wooden bar top that separates me from sweet, quiet little Bailey Jansen.

Sweet, quiet little Bailey Jansen, who I now spend a good three to four nights a week around.

Sweet, quiet little Bailey Jansen, who just asked me about anal sex like she was asking about whether I take cream in my coffee.

She tosses a rag onto the bar. "Clean that up."

Only Bailey would tell me to clean it up rather than do it herself. That's what I've come to realize about her on these nights I've spent sitting at her bar.

That's what I like about her.

She's not a kiss ass, she's not a pushover, and she doesn't tiptoe around me.

She also might not be as sweet and quiet as I thought.

In a world that feels horribly boring and mundane, Bailey Jansen has proven to be incredibly interesting.

That's why I keep coming back. It's more than just worrying about her being alone.

"Why are you asking me about anal sex?" I mumble as I wipe the bar top and dab off my arm. "And so loudly. People are going to get the wrong idea." I turn, looking around to see if anyone else heard.

Her lips twitch where she stands at the tap pouring a pint, those dark chocolate irises slicing my way from beneath the fringe of her lashes. "People already have the wrong idea about me, Beau."

She turns away, walking down the narrow space behind the bar to the red-haired guy who sits at the opposite end, phone in his hands, eyes down. "Here ya go, Earl," Bailey announces, tossing down a coaster and then the beer on top.

He glances at her but doesn't say thank you. And it irks me.

When she turns back to face me, her eyes are wide, lips drawn back in a cringe. She walks straight at me, holding my gaze, her hips swaying.

She and I have fallen into a comfortable rhythm in the last couple of weeks. One where we talk while I pretend I don't notice how fucking beautiful she is for fear of becoming the weird old creeper who sits here all night.

She props her forearms against the bar right in front of me, a conspiratorial grin on her face. I try not to stare at her breasts pressed against the thin cotton of the frilly off-the-shoulder peasant top she's wearing. But the shimmer in her eyes or the gloss on her lips aren't any less distracting.

"Earl only comes in now and then," she says, flashing white teeth as she peeks back over her shoulder. "But when he does, he *always* watches porn on his phone. And it's *always* anal. I just wasn't sure how common it was. You know?"

"He does *what*?" Alarm bells sound in my mind. I do not know how she can joke about this asshole.

"You heard me." Her lips roll together like she's trying to bite back a laugh, and my eyes follow the motion.

"That's not funny, Bailey. He's watching porn and looking at you. In public."

She rolls her eyes. "As opposed to in private?"

"He's looking at *you*." The muscles in my back tighten. "Thinking about *you*."

She shrugs. "Probably."

"How can you possibly be okay with that?"

34

"I don't usually ask a person's permission before thinking about them while I masturbate."

To cover my shock, I just glare at her.

Bailey sighs and pulls away just a bit. "Listen, I didn't say I was okay with it. But it's kind of funny, or at least I have to roll with it being funny. Because I don't get to pitch a fit every time something makes me uncomfortable." Her fingers tap the bar top. "Welcome to being a Jansen. No one cares if I'm comfortable or not. And if I'm anything short of pleasant, I'm *just like my brothers.*"

The smile she gives me now is full of you're-adorably-naive vibes and I hate this for her. I hate that a town that's been so good to me and my family has been so hard on a girl who didn't ask for the hand she's been dealt.

Beyond her, I see Earl's eyes lift and rake over Bailey's ass.

I guess that's why I find myself up off my stool. Walking down the length of the bar.

Right toward Earl.

He's so engrossed he doesn't even notice me standing behind him. I don't bother looking up at Bailey, because I know she'll be silently begging me not to do this, and I don't want to see that expression on her face.

I don't give a fuck what her last name is.

I clamp a hand down on Earl's scrawny shoulder as I peer down at his phone. Sure enough, there's some blonde down on all fours taking it in the ass with a lot of bright lights and perfect angles.

He startles and clicks his screen off. "Shit! Jesus."

"Earl, I'm Beau."

He licks his lips nervously as he looks back up at me. "Yeah, I know. Beau Eaton."

Bailey snorts a laugh from behind the bar, and from my periphery, I watch her walk away.

"Cool. Great. So, no more porn in public. Yeah?"

"I wasn't—" I cut him off by squeezing my fingers tighter on his shoulder. Hard enough that I hope it hurts.

It feels good.

"You were. I saw. Your lovely bartender saw. We're not going to do that anymore, you got me? You come in for a beer, that's fine. But you're gonna keep your eyes off of her"—I point toward Bailey, who is pretending she's oblivious to what I'm doing—"and your hands where everyone can see them."

"Listen, man, I—"

I drop my voice dangerously low to silence him. "And when you get home and rush to your bedroom to fuck a sock, you're gonna keep her body out of your head and her name out of your mouth. You got me?" I take my hand off the guy and prop my hip against the bar, staring at him to make my point.

"Dude, she's a Jansen. Nobody wanks to a Jansen."

I want to hit him. I vibrate with the itch to shut him up. But that itch . . . is a feeling. And I haven't felt shit in months, which means this feels *good*.

"Pay and leave before I do something I'll regret."

He fumbles with his wallet, tosses a twenty down, and stares at it almost regretfully.

"No change. That's her tip for even tolerating you."

His pale cheeks turn bright red as he stumbles away from the bar. I keep my glare on him as he hustles toward the door with his head down, fingers clasped tightly around his phone.

Fucking pig.

He's gone and I'm still staring. I turn only when I sense Bailey coming up from behind me.

"Ahh," she says, arms crossed under her breasts, the white cotton of her shirt making her tan skin glow. "The Eaton effect." She gives me a smug smile. "If I had that last name, people would ask me *how high* when I said *jump* too."

"No, they wouldn't."

She whips the half-empty pint glass off the top of the bar and turns away. With a shy peek over her shoulder, she adds, "Thanks for what you did back there. It means a lot."

I don't know why such a simple sentence hits me so hard. Her bluntness, her gratitude. I feel like a kid. I almost want to blush.

"It was nothing."

She laughs, soft and melodic, all feminine and amused. "Okay, soldier. Whatever you say."

I'm not a soldier, but I don't correct her. That sense of purpose—even just for a few seconds—felt too fucking good.

So I just drop my head and smile.

"Stop stewing." Bailey doesn't even glance at me as she tips over a spouted bottle of bourbon to fill a shot glass.

"I'm not stewing."

"You are."

I don't feel like arguing with her. To make matters worse, she's right. I am stewing. Stewing over what she said about *The Eaton Effect*. I don't want her to be right. I've always liked Bailey, but over the past several weeks, she's become something of a comfort blanket. A friend even.

She doesn't pester me. She doesn't fawn over me. She makes me tea and lets me be, which is a hell of a lot more than I can say for the rest of the people in my life. Namely, my family, who've made it their job to overstep and inquire about what I'm doing, how I'm doing, and what I'm planning on doing with mind-numbing regularity.

So it irritates me that Bailey can be this fucking great and people can still be so fucking shitty to her.

It even irritates me that part of the reason I sit here four nights a week is because I've developed a totally inappropriate crush on my bartender, like I'm a fucking twenty-year-old bro waiting to make his move.

"Think Earl is rubbing one out right now?" Her lips curve up as she uses the soda gun to fill the rocks glass.

She knows she's pestering me, and it works.

"Bailey."

Now her head inclines in my direction, one eyebrow quirking up. "Beau."

"Don't."

"Just trying to give you something to stew about if you're gonna sit there all quiet and broody."

I scoff and cover my smirk behind the rim of my mug.

This girl.

It's with that mug up over my face that I hear a raucous group of people just outside. A quick glance at my watch tells me it's 12:01— one minute past last call. A glance over my shoulder tells me the only patrons left are a table waiting on their last drinks.

She's walking those drinks over when three men enter, and I can feel Bailey freeze on the spot before I even turn to look at her.

All traces of playfulness on her melt away, the angle of her jaw changing as she sets it.

"Little sis!" Aaron Jansen calls out as he pulls a seat up at one of the round high tops just beyond the bar. "Get us a round on the house."

Bailey keeps her distance but gives her head a little shake, as though that could clear the tension from her body. "Sorry guys, I've already done last call. It's past midnight. That's the rule."

"Come on. What's the point in having a sister who works here if we can't get some special treatment?"

I drop my head low, trying to blend in as an unsuspecting regular. I don't want to start more shit for Bailey, and her brothers and I are *not* on good terms. Not from when we were younger, and not from the time I recently took part in toilet papering their tractor with Cade and Rhett.

It rained that night, and I imagine picking wet toilet paper off of their tractor wasn't a good time. Still, they deserved it. And that was fun.

I smile at the memory.

"Sorry, guys." Bailey approaches her brothers' table with caution, like she doesn't want to get close to them but also doesn't want a scene with the other patrons in the bar. "Not tonight. Management has set later hours for Thursday through Saturday, so try back then."

The oldest Jansen brother, Lance, tips his head back with a groan. "Bailey, come on. We even brought a friend from out of town. Told him you'd take care of us tonight. Seth, this is our little sister, Bailey. Always a bit of a stick in the mud, if you ask me."

My spine straightens, and I glance over my shoulder. The third guy is leering at Bailey in a blatant and unsettling way.

At least I leer at her subtly and beat myself up about it afterward. This guy has no such boundaries.

"Come on, honey. You take care of me, and I'll take care of you."

My heart rate ratchets up a few notches as I continue appraising the situation out of the corner of my eye. The other table of four is pretending not to watch, but it's quiet in the bar tonight, so it's a hard confrontation to miss. When the Jansens roll past, everyone stares because there's usually some sort of spectacle not far behind.

I shift on my stool and use the mug as cover to take another long look at what's unfolding at my four o'clock.

But I freeze at the top of that motion because whoever the fuck Seth is has taken the liberty of sliding his palm over the curve of Bailey's ass, fingers curving inward below her cheek.

I promised her I wouldn't make any more scenes at *her* bar.

But I'm about to break that promise.

Because gawking at her while watching porn is bad enough. But laying a single fucking finger on her without her consent?

That's a death wish.

5
Bailey

I don't know what startles me first. The feeling of an unwanted hand taking a firm grab of my ass or the crash of glass against the floor.

"Remove your fucking hand. Or I'll do it for you." Beau's voice is lower than usual, quieter. More menacing.

I lurch away from the table, shaken, cheeks hot, and realizing shit could be about to go bad. I don't know who Seth is, but if my brothers are here to wine and dine him, chances are he's not a good dude.

All it takes is a few long strides for Beau to be towering over Seth. His lean wrist twists in Beau's impossibly big hand, and a high-pitched squeal spills from his lips.

"Let go!" one of my brothers shouts. I'm not sure which one, because I'm too busy staring down at the heavily corded arm that's extended across my body like a barrier. Protecting me. And his touch is nothing like the hand that was on me before.

His touch soothes.

A screeching sound draws my attention across the bar as chairs drag across the floor. It's my last patrons. They abandon their final round of drinks, dropping their cash and scurrying out. Not wanting to get caught in the crossfire of whatever is clearly about to go down.

It hits me as I watch the situation unfold in slow motion that it doesn't matter if it's one against three. Beau was special forces.

"Let go?" His tone is smooth and eerily unaffected. This clash should feel chaotic, but Beau is the eye of the storm. "I could drop you with one touch."

This man, who's been calmly sitting at my bar night after night, is in his element. His gray eyes, all polished silver, are heated and ... excited.

"Make a single move and I'll snap this fucker's wrist like a twig."

Beau has spent years portraying himself as a happy-go-lucky goofball and it's at this exact moment I realize that was part of his cover. Part of how he protects everyone he loves from the fact *this* is who he is.

Beau is lethal.

"Hey, hey, hey. Relax, relax." Aaron's hands go up like someone is pointing a gun at him. I suppose, given the number of times he's been arrested, it's a natural position for him. "It's all in good fun."

Beau's head tilts. His eyes narrow. He looks every bit the predator he is. And when Seth tries to wind up to hit him, Beau twists his hand incrementally, dropping him to his knees with a wail of pain.

Aaron shifts in his seat, licking his lips, eyes volleying between Beau and Seth. Lance is too fucked-up to react to the situation. I can tell by the size of his pupils, by the way he's slumped against the table like it's the only thing keeping him upright.

I grew up learning to recognize that posture and then hiding from it.

"My idea of fun is breaking this asshole's wrist. How about yours?"

"You already broke it!" Seth wails, losing his menacing demeanor from mere seconds ago.

Beau doesn't even give Seth the gift of his gaze; instead, he keeps his eyes locked on my brothers. "Nah, you're fine. If I broke it, I would have felt it snap. You'll hear it when it does."

"Okay." Aaron shoots me a scowl before getting up and backing away from Beau. He taps Lance on the shoulder, urging him to move. "We're gonna head out. Find another bar."

Beau nods, dipping his chin to an impossibly broad chest, one that barely moves as though he's stopped breathing altogether. "Perfect. I'll walk you fellas out."

And he does. Literally. With Seth's brutalized wrist in his grip, he walks him out like a dog on a leash. My brothers stay ahead of them, checking back over their shoulders with both fear and rage painting their features.

No one has ever walked in acting like they rule the fucking world and then left looking so disgraced.

Looking so *weak*.

Beau tosses them out the big, heavy doors, then yanks them shut and flips the deadbolt.

He turns back around, chin tipped up, shoulders pressed back. "You okay?"

I nod, not sure that I am. "That's going to come back to haunt us," I say, knowing my brothers and how they work. Flying under their radar has been my general tactic until I save enough money to go somewhere beyond their reach. Then I plan to just—*poof*—disappear and never speak to them again.

Out of sight, out of mind.

Beau grins as he walks back toward me. "I know, but it was really fun."

He's always been handsome, but the swagger right now, the glint in his eye . . . the way he leapt to my protection. He's mouthwatering in a way that has heat pooling low in my belly. And for a beat, I let myself stare. I let myself bask in the knowledge he just blew up *for me*.

To protect *me*.

Then I glance away and get to cleaning up. Because fantasizing about Beau Eaton isn't a productive use of my time. Especially when he's so much older, hot enough to turn every head in this town—to set my skin on fire—and a hell of a lot more experienced than I am.

Which, to be fair, isn't hard to be.

To absolutely no one's surprise, I'm too amped up to sleep.

Maybe it was the run-in at the bar. Maybe it's the fact that every time I close my eyes, I see Beau's bulging bicep held out across me, and the ripple of his back muscles through the strain of his T-shirt. I feel the heat and strength of his body, thrown up like a guard rail across mine.

Or maybe it's the loud music blaring all the way from the main house.

Which means my brothers have brought their party home.

I stay away from the main house at the best of times, especially since my dad skipped bail and left town. Now my brothers rule the roost. My dad is a piece of shit, but at least he scared them enough to stay a little in line.

Without him? It's like trailer park mayhem over there.

So I stay far away, living in a seventeen-foot Boler trailer I bought off the side of the road. It's more or less an old shoe box, but I've put some work into it. What I haven't put in is any type of cooling system. Which means it's a sauna right now, even though it's past two in the morning.

The door clangs shut behind me as I step out of the trailer into the hot, muggy night. The light breeze off the river caresses my skin and I sigh, reveling in the feel. Two suspended iron steps bow under my weight as I make my way down them. My flip-flops make that obnoxious slapping noise as I trudge across the grass toward the river.

The river that's just beyond the barbwire fence. On Eaton land.

Not that the fence has ever stopped me. In the dead of night, it's always peaceful and private.

I press down on the top wire, avoiding the barbs, and swing a leg over, clearing the line that separates my family land from Beau's. I know I'm technically trespassing, but I also know that every single Eaton has been nothing but nice to me, even when they've had no reason to be.

Within a few moments, I'm at the top of the embankment, where I kick my shoes off and gingerly head down the steep path sideways. It's easier barefoot. I learned the hard way that flip-flops just twist and turn and trip me up, and the bite of the occasional pebble on the bottoms of my feet doesn't bother me all that much.

I hobble across the wobbly river rocks, shed my clothes, and slip into the darkened water, desperate to cool down. Is it the smartest thing that I do? Probably not. But it thrills me and soothes me all at once. Knowing I'm on a different piece of land than my brothers brings me an odd sort of peace.

"Hooo." The mountain water is cold enough to suck the air right out of my lungs, and I blow out a breath as my feet scrape across the rocky bottom of the riverbed, carrying me further into the gentle flow.

The chilly water whips around every curve of my body. In the spring, the current can become much stronger, but by this point in the summer, it meanders lazily through the town before joining up with the Elbow River.

My arms cut through the water, the smell of silt and pine wafting up around me. That fresh, wet rock scent almost overpowers it all.

Immediately, my body temperature drops, and the internal alarm that can make you panicky when you're overheated stops beeping at me.

After a busy night, it doesn't matter if I'm checked out and lying in my quiet trailer. I *dream* about bartending. Like I'm stuck on some sort of fucking infinite loop.

Bar, drink, till.

Bar, drink, till.

Bar, drink, till.

My body knows the motions and the feelings and the pattern so damn well that I can't escape it.

The river is my reset.

My palm wraps around an offshoot attached to the large log that lies halfway across the river. I grip it and let my body flow back with the icy water.

When I hear the crunching of shoes on pebbles coming from the opposite side of the river, I freeze. I'm fairly hidden, but my heart thunders in my chest at the prospect of being caught. Alone, and in the dark.

I've never encountered a single person down here, so, of course, it happens on a night when I'm already jumpy thanks to my shitty brothers.

The world is silent for a few beats as I try to hold my breath. It's just the soft rush of cool water and the echo of crickets rubbing their legs together.

"Who the fuck is in my river?"

Relief courses through me, and I smile.

Sure, the raspy tone is pissed off, all gravel and steel.

But it's the voice I've come to associate with safety.

And if I had to get caught trespassing naked in a river, I'm glad Beau Eaton is the one to catch me.

6

Beau

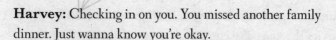

Harvey: Checking in on you. You missed another family dinner. Just wanna know you're okay.

Cade: What Dad is trying to say is that he wants you to stop being a total dickhead and come around now and then.

Willa: What Cade is trying to say is that he misses you and worries about you.

Rhett: What Willa is trying to say is that she thinks you're the sexiest Eaton brother and misses seeing you around because she's stuck living with an ogre.

Cade: Get fucked, Rhett.

Summer: Cade, what Rhett is trying to say is that you'd be sexier with long hair.

Winter: Wrong.

Beau: Oh good, the family chat. Also, I agree with Winter.

Summer: We're just worried about you, Beau. We like having you around.

Beau: Don't worry. I'm fine. I'll make the next one.

The giggle that filters back catches me off guard.

"First of all, it's not *your* river."

I expected it to be one of those Jansen assholes. But no. It's their little sister with the wide eyes that stare at me from the other side of the bar. The one who doesn't take my shit but tolerates my presence. Even when it's stormy.

One reason I can't sleep tonight.

One of many.

"Bailey?"

Her eyes widen as she takes in my bare chest. "How did you know I was here?"

Inky black hair shines under the bright moon as she pushes away from the log she was hiding behind. The water conceals her body, but above that line, my eyes hitch on her shoulders. The way the silvery light hits them—and the fact there are no straps in sight.

I scoff and blink away, not wanting to leer. "I've been a tier one operator for years. If I couldn't pick out a civilian hiding in a river, I'd be dead already."

She bobs in the water, and I drift closer to the edge. The creek must be under twenty feet across here and she's pretty much smack dab in the middle.

I jut my chin out beyond her and shove my hands in the front pocket of my sweats. "There's a pile of clothes on the shore." Her head whips around to confirm, wet tendrils splaying over her slender shoulders. "Your body is disrupting the flow of water." She glances down at herself now, at the way it folds around her in a different pattern than every other stream that passes. "And I could hear you breathing."

Her head tilts to the side, all sass. "You could not *hear* me breathing." Disbelief laces her words.

I like this sassy side of her. Before, when I'd come into the bar with my brothers, she always seemed so beaten down, so startled all the time. She made me want to save her. I just didn't know how.

She's stronger than I remember her, but I wonder if it's all for show. I wonder if we're the same that way.

But I just shrug. "Maybe I could feel you breathing. I don't know how else to explain it. I could just sense it. You hone that sixth sense when your life is on the line."

She stares at me, skin shimmering, reflecting the moonlight. I watch droplets of water roll down the front of her chest to the valley between her breasts.

She seems oblivious to how tempting she looks—to the way she affects me.

"Being able to twist a guy's hand right off his body comes in handy too, I bet."

I shift my gaze from the exposed top swells of her breasts to the river. "If you're looking for an apology for that, you won't get one."

"I'm not."

That has me turning my gaze back to her, trying to figure her out. "How long have you been coming here?"

A soft hum vibrates from her as she taps a finger against her pouty lips. "Trespassing to swim in *your* river? Years now, I guess."

"You know my house is just beyond that embankment?"

"Huh. No. I didn't." I can tell she's lying. "My trailer is just beyond that copse of trees."

"Oh, yeah?" I bend to pick up a rock and pretend I don't know that either.

I guess we're both liars tonight.

"Why don't you live at home?"

She chuckles. "Beau, you've met my family. If you were a tier one operator, I'm sure you can figure it out."

My lips twitch. *Smartass.*

"I like to keep as much distance between myself and them as possible. It's why I work so much. I'm saving up a solid nest egg to get the fuck out of here."

"Yeah?"

She must be able to touch the bottom because she tips her head back, dropping lower into the water to wet her hair again.

"Yeah. I want to travel. Go to school. Pick a spot where I can settle down and not just be the youngest Jansen. A place where no one knows who I am, or where I came from. A fresh start."

I turn the rock over in my hand as I turn her words over in my mind.

A fresh start.

That shouldn't sound as good as it does to me. I shouldn't want to leave this place too. My intense boredom feels like an affront to everyone who loves me, to this beautiful town I call home.

I've seen firsthand what it is to have *nothing.* And here I am, fortunate beyond compare—unhappy to my very core.

I guess that's why I tell her, "You don't need to start fresh. Nothing wrong with this town. You can make it work here."

With her eyes still trained up on the starry sky, she scoffs at me. It's good-natured enough, but it still has me straightening.

"I didn't ask for your opinion."

51

I don't know what to say to that, so I turn and toss the rock downstream to clear some tension from my body. Then I pick up another one.

I wasn't trying to convince her.

I was trying to convince myself.

"You still working at the hospital as a porter?" I ask, grasping at straws that will keep me here with the gentle rush of water and the sound of Bailey's breathing under a blanket of pristine stars. "I remember seeing you there when I still had to go in for appointments."

She hums thoughtfully, drawing my gaze. A sad smirk touches her lips. "I got fired."

My head jerks back. "Why?"

She chuckles now, low and laced with sarcasm. Like something is funny but not *that* funny. "One of my brothers got caught breaking in."

"To the hospital?"

"Yeah. One of the pharmaceutical cabinets in the ICU."

Jesus. Her brothers really are stupid.

"So . . . why did you get fired?"

She spins, limbs sliding through the darkened water. "They accused me of letting him in. Giving him inside information."

Fury bubbles in my gut.

"Did you tell them you didn't?"

She hums again. "I kind of love that you immediately assume I didn't do it. Refreshing."

I scoff, chuck another stone, and duck down like I'm searching for a specific rock, even though in the dark they all look the same. "I know you wouldn't do that."

"Beau, my friend, you are in the minority. Because even with no proof and me denying it, they fired me. I'm not surprised, really. My main disappointment was losing a source of income. I've started cleaning the bar on the mornings that I don't work at night. That's bridging the gap. Barely. But I've been blacklisted pretty much everywhere else in town. No matter how nice I dress, how perfect my resume is, how great my references are, no one wants to hire me."

The injustice of it riles me. She seems so resigned to this being normal. Being okay. Nothing about this is okay. It's all wrong.

"They can't just do that. You need to go back to the hospital and demand—"

"Even if I could get the job back, I don't want to work in a place where people see me that way. Don't you get it? That's how I'm perceived here. The Railspur is the only place that doesn't feel that way, thanks to the fact that none of the workers are local. That's why I'll leave as soon as I've saved up enough to pay a year's rent."

"Why a year's rent? Why not leave now?"

She can't make eye contact with me when she says, "My credit is shot. No one will approve me." Her head shakes before she continues, "Anyway, for a long time, I didn't realize I deserve better. But I do now, and I'm resigned to the fact my last name will always haunt me here."

She keeps saying that and I try not to take it personally. I refuse to accept that this community I've always loved could be so deeply prejudiced against a young girl.

She's wrong.

"It has nothing to do with your last name. Everything to do with you not standing up for yourself."

She barks out a laugh. I recognize immediately that my words were harsh—judgmental—but she parries the blow they might have delivered. This girl is Kevlar.

"For someone who has seen some dark shit, you're sure naive. Living in some sort of magical fairy land over there, Eaton? Why don't you wave your wand, give me a different last name, and we'll put this theory to the test."

The heavy thud of my heart in my chest accelerates, pumping faster as the thrill of a new idea courses through my veins. A new mission.

"Is that a bet?"

"What?" She glides her hands through the water, giving me a confused look.

"That things would be different if you had a different last name?"

"It's not a bet. It's a fact."

"I'll take that bet." My body thrums as this new idea takes shape in my mind. I'd also be willing to bet a therapist wouldn't approve of my plan. But I stopped seeing one a couple of months ago, so nothing is holding me back.

"What bet? For a guy who drinks chamomile tea all night, you seem awfully confused."

"I'll give you my last name and we'll see if people treat you differently."

She goes deathly still. "How?"

"We get married."

There's a pregnant pause. It seems like even the creek stops babbling. And then, "I'm not marrying you. That's insane."

I wave off her words. I'm not accustomed to being rejected. Rejection doesn't factor into my mindset. I usually get what I want, at any cost.

"We'll get engaged. That will give you the promise of becoming an Eaton. We can plan a wedding that never happens."

"Fake engaged?" She sounds incredulous, and I can't blame her. This is a cracked plan. I'm definitely not thinking straight, but I also feel more excited than I have in literal months.

"Yes. We test our theories in public and break up before a wedding ever happens. Obviously."

"Did you spike your tea with something?"

A deep laugh bubbles up out of me. "No."

"Are you high?"

I roll my eyes now. "Bailey."

"Don't Bailey me!" She slaps the water with both hands as she laughs—a high, unhinged sort of squeal. "You're acting insane. Why would *you* want to pretend to be engaged to *me*? Why would you do this?"

"Because it would get my family off my ass about how I'm doing, and where I spend all my time, and all that other overbearing shit they constantly ask me about. And I love a competition. What do I get if I win?"

"I haven't agreed to this yet."

Yet. I'll take that.

Her white teeth drag across her bottom lip as she turns the idea over in her head.

I give her more to consider. "If you're right, you'll get everyone in town off your back for however long it takes you to get out of here. Maybe you can even get another job that pays better."

"People won't believe this."

"Why not?"

"Because you're like town royalty. And you're ... how old are you? You'd never go for me."

55

Wrong.

As soon as the thought springs up in my head, I shove it away. I sidestep every part of myself that knows there's a self-serving aspect to this arrangement.

Every part of myself that knows I don't care about the bet at all. I keep telling myself I am in control when it comes to Bailey.

I *want* to have control.

But I don't.

"I'm thirty-five. And I'd definitely go for you."

Fuck. I shouldn't have said that. I'm losing it tonight, running on the familiar sensation of adrenaline coursing through my veins. Flush with the confidence that the old me possessed.

She tears her gaze away, staring down the river, and a shiver runs through her.

"Shit, you must be cold." I sense her gaze back on me, tracing my outline in the dark. "Why don't you get out?"

"Because I'm not wearing anything."

My heart crashes against my ribs before coming to a screeching halt.

"I won't look."

Her head tilts. "Why don't you get in?"

"Why?"

Her lips twitch. "So I can see what I'm signing up for. Are you husband material, Beau Eaton?"

"Probably not." I smirk. "But if you want to show me yours, I'll show you mine."

She doesn't respond. She just stares. It feels like an entire conversation passes between us in the dark river alley.

Knowing I won't follow through with that challenge, I drop her gaze and turn my back to the water. Cutting the thread pulled taut between us. Not wanting to be that guy. She's vulnerable right now, and my control is horribly frayed.

But I find myself desperately hoping she'll humor me and go for this arrangement. On paper, it seems like she'd get more out of the arrangement.

But off paper . . . I'd be the winner.

Water swishes against her legs as she gingerly makes her way to shore. I wait with bated breath for her to respond.

"Ouch!"

My instincts spin me on the spot to make sure she's okay, and I catch a quick glance of her bare ass. A tan line from where her bikini bottoms must sit. A trim waist and toned thighs. My pulse skyrockets, my dick grows hard, and I turn away quickly, hoping she doesn't realize I saw anything. Her curves are already branding themselves into my brain, and I fail at stopping myself from imagining how it would feel to hold her, grip her ass as I got lost in her. One cheek in each—

"You okay?" My voice comes out thick and strangled as I shut that line of thought down.

"Yeah. Just a sharp rock."

There's a rustle of clothes and then silence.

"You ever going to turn around?" she calls from the other side of the creek.

"I was trying to be polite," I say, propping my hands on my hips as I turn to face her.

She's dressed now, and too far away for me to decipher her facial expression.

"Is that why you already looked at me?"

"I didn't—"

"I saw you. Don't have to be special ops to notice someone whipping around that quickly. You're rusty, Beau Eaton."

"I didn't mean to." I drop my head. "You said ouch, and I—"

"Thought you'd come save me?" Her statement comes out lighthearted, but it hangs heavy between us. Like we both know what this is.

I offered my last name because she looks like she needs someone in her life right now. And, shit, it might be time for me to admit that I need someone too.

I don't address that, though. Instead, I ask, "Are you going to take the bet?"

Her eyes land like heavy weights against my skin. I can't see them clearly, but I swear I can sense her internal struggle.

"I'm going to sleep on it. Meet me here tomorrow night."

"Okay." I nod, fingers squeezing against my hip bones as if that might quell the itch in them.

She turns to walk away, loose cotton shorts creasing under each butt cheek. The ones I'm going to try not to think about while I . . .

"I'll bring a bathing suit next time. Might help with your self-control."

I chuckle to myself.

"Hey, Beau, you never answered my question earlier."

"What question?"

"Have you had anal sex?"

I bark out a laugh. That was not what I was expecting. At all. And I figure, what's the point of lying? "Yeah. Once."

"Did you like it?"

I blink. Wow, okay, just out with it then. Bailey Jansen yelling about anal sex over the creek bed has my boxers feeling outrageously uncomfortable, my dick ready to stand at attention.

"It wasn't the best sex I've had."

I can see the outline of her head nodding. "Yeah. I guess you can't knock it until you try it."

A strangled laugh bubbles up in me. What else am I supposed to do? She's the most confusing combination of innocent, curious, and forthright.

"Goodnight, Bailey."

She turns away with a gentle salute. "Yes, sir."

I almost laugh again. Couldn't sleep before. Probably won't be sleeping after tonight's exchange, either.

7

Bailey

Heavy feet carry me across the lawn, back toward the barbwire fence that divides Eaton property from Jansen property. It seems metaphorical, separating me from what could be a terribly stupid decision. Those sharp little peaks somehow representative of all the ways this bet could come back to hurt me.

I told Beau I needed to sleep on it, but I lay awake in my hot-as-fuck Boler trailer, turning his insane offer over in my mind. I alternated between stressing over going through with the bet and stressing over the prospect of passing it up.

Then I stressed about the fact we didn't set a time to meet up.

I spent most of my day off obsessively cleaning a seventeen-foot trailer that I barely make a mess in. When the smell of bleach nearly overpowered me, I chased myself out of there. Book in hand, I expected to sit by the river and wait for Beau.

But when I hit the riverbank and peer down toward the water . . . he's there. Waiting.

His head snaps up at my approach and our eyes meet from across the water. Unlike last night, I can see him clearly in the sun's fading light. Every hard line. The way his thighs strain against the simple swim trunks he's wearing, the cut line of his quads blending down into his knees.

His white socks and dorky white sneakers.

He nods at me in acknowledgement and my stomach flips.

Sitting there on the shore, thick arms propped on the peaks of his knees, he looks casual, yet coiled and ready to spring into action at any moment. He looks haunted yet at peace.

He looks beautiful.

Too good. Good enough that I could end up standing here gawking at him while my lack of experience flaps in the wind.

So I offer a nod back and forge ahead, clearing my throat and dropping my gaze as I do.

On the path down to the river, my feet lose purchase, but I go with it. Years of taking this path in the dark make doing it in the light feel like child's play. I slide down, still landing on my feet, even though my nails now have dirt stuck under them.

It's when I right myself that I realize Beau has shot up to standing, the tips of his sneakers touching the water.

"You okay?" His voice echoes around us as he projects over the sound of rushing water.

Maybe he's overbearing, but after a lifetime of being ignored or lavished with negative attention, his concern wraps around me like a warm blanket.

I feigned indifference, but I secretly got off on him tossing my brothers and their sketchy friend out of the bar.

His violence doesn't scare me. It should. In most cases, it does.

But with Beau, it feels different. Somehow, his vicious streak soothes me.

And standing here, caught in the snare of his concerned gaze, seeing his chest rising and falling, like he's ready to blast across the river just to check if I'm okay ... I already know what I'm going to tell him.

"We should do it," I call back.

He goes deathly still. "Yeah?"

I nod, taking tentative steps toward the water, trying to act more casual than I feel. "Yeah. But we need to talk about it."

The column of his throat works as he swallows, eyes narrowed in on me, like he can see right through the calm and collected facade I'm trying to put up. I struggle not to let my eyes skate down over his broad chest. Instead, I fixate on the day's final rays of sun and how they hit the thick stubble over his jaw.

"Your place or mine?" I joke, trying to cut the tension.

His gaze drops to the water. "I don't know if I can go in the water. I thought I wanted to, but ... "

My head tilts, urging him to explain.

"The burns. They were infected so badly before. I don't know if I want to chance it."

I've had it in my head he backed down yesterday because I'm *me*. To think the reason he didn't join me in the water was health-related lessens the sting of him turning away.

"Are they healed?"

All he gives me is a shrug. I don't know Beau well enough to push the conversation, so I remove my flip-flops, hooking them through my fingers as I make my way to the log that spans most of the river.

I can feel Beau's gaze latched on to me in an almost

unnerving way, but I keep my eyes cast down as I walk the log like a balance beam.

"Careful," he grumbles when I get about halfway across.

I roll my eyes, but I don't think he sees it. "Been doing this for a while now. I'm fine."

"You crossed to this side of the river?" he asks, catching me in a moment of loose-tongued focus.

Fuck.

I opt to ignore the question, gasping when I step down into the cold water to make it the rest of the way. After treading carefully over sharp rocks, I come to stand beside him, still not making eye contact. I toss my foam sandals down and lift a foot to slide one in, but the rocks shift beneath me, and I find myself tipping.

And then not.

Beau's warm palm captures my upper arm, and he rights me with a deep chuckle. "You can walk that log, but lose your balance putting on sandals?"

When I peek up at him, he's grinning. Right now, he seems more like the carefree man I remember before that final deployment. For a few beats, we get lost in each other's eyes. In the warm light of the golden hour, his take on less of a silver tone, trending more toward the soft gray of the river rocks surrounding him.

He's beautiful almost always. But he's blinding when he smiles.

"Yeah, yeah." My lips twitch and my cheeks heat as I drop my head to slide my feet into the sandals. I try to ignore the fact he still hasn't let go of my arm. His gentle hold brands my skin, and the minute I get those plastic thongs wedged between my toes, I step away, offering him a bright smile in return.

"Wanna come to my place?" he asks. "We can chat there?"

My heartbeat speeds up. "Your place?"

"Yes." He points to where I already know his home sits.

"What if someone sees us?"

He snorts a laugh, scrubbing a massive hand over the stubble on his cheeks. "Well, if you're about to be the future Mrs. Eaton, it would make sense that you'd be at my house, no?"

My tongue darts out over my lips as I shift my focus to the embankment. He seems . . . *happy* about this.

I can't wrap my head around that. It all feels so fucking weird.

"Okay. Yeah."

This time, his hand lands at the base of my neck as he guides me away from the river, fingers so long they curve over my shoulder and dust over the pulse point in my throat.

I can't help but wonder if he can feel my heart rate accelerating, if that was his casual way of checking, or if it was a mistake. I have a sinking suspicion this arrangement is going to leave me overthinking every little touch, every little look.

"Maybe I can make you tea this time."

My laugh comes out a little shrill, his fingers absorbing the vibration in my neck. "I could use something stronger than tea for this conversation."

His hand drops as we walk the path up the embankment. I'm so starved for touch; I wish he'd put it back.

"Well, that's perfect. I've got a couple beers in the fridge that have been ignored. They've got your name on them."

He leads me up the hill and I try not to stare at his ass. But his broad shoulders aren't any less distracting. They flex against the black polyester of whatever workout shirt he's wearing, and they taper down into a perfectly narrow waist. My thoughts drift to what it would be like to prop my legs over them while he buried his head between my thighs. How would that feel?

I remember the way the moonlight hit his bare torso the other night. It's impossible to forget. I wonder how heavy his body would feel over my own. How another person's skin would feel sliding against mine.

I clear my throat and give my head a shake before I ask, "You haven't been drinking at all? Not even at home?"

"No. I'm addicted to chamomile tea now."

It seems like an intrusion to ask if he's sleeping, so I don't. Plus, seeing as how we met down at the river in the middle of the night, it seems like I can make an educated guess.

"Huh," I reply stupidly, before adding, "Good for you."

"Yeah, well, someone I respect told me I couldn't keep drinking the way I was."

The skin on my chest vibrates with the heavy thud of my heart. *Does he mean me?* It could only be me.

"She also told me I'd embarrassed myself and called me an asshole."

I can't stop the shy smile that curves across my lips. "Wow. She sounds really smart."

It's right as we hit the top of the embankment that he turns and glances over his shoulder. "She's pretty too," he murmurs, the golden sky glowing around his silhouette.

He almost freezes me in place with that little addition, but I cover it and roll my eyes with a light laugh. "Cute. Really cute." I gently slap him across the shoulder to cut the tension, not wanting to bask in him and his smooth words for too long.

I remind myself that Beau is older and charming and about to be my *fake* fiancé.

He's always been a flirt—a showboat—and it's nice to get a peek at that side of him. It feels good to be the one who can bring it out in him, but if I'm going to go through with this bet, I'll need to keep reminding myself that we're pretending.

And that Eatons don't mix with Jansens.

"Your house is nice." I spin the cold bottle of beer between my palms. Truthfully, I'm not a beer gal, but this feels like a situation where beggars can't be choosers. "Super modern." I keep my head turned, peering around the open space.

Doesn't suit him if I'm being honest. It's all sharp corners and cold materials. Polished concrete floors. The odd wood beam paired with gray walls. Big floor-to-ceiling windows that face out over the open expanse of land on one side and the creek bed on the other.

"Yeah. After growing up in what felt like a mountain lodge, I built something a little different. Less Old West and more ... " He shrugs from across the table, dipping his tea bag into the steaming mug of water ... over and over again.

It's almost sexual. In, out. In, out.

This fake relationship is going to be painfully long if I can't even deal with the way this man handles a tea bag.

I lick my lips, cross my legs, and take a deep swig of my beer, internally berating myself to get my shit together.

"Fresh. Sleek," he concludes thoughtfully.

"Yes, well. It's very masculine. Just like you." My eyes snap to his. Smug humor graces his every feature. "Fuck. Just ... " I look away, spinning the bottle again, trying not to be overwhelmed by sitting across from him at a small dining table. "I'm nervous. You make me nervous."

"Why?" He doesn't budge, keeping his focus entirely on *me*.

Because I'm endlessly horny, and have you met yourself?

"This situation makes me nervous," I clarify instead of blurting out the first thought that runs through my mind.

For once.

"Okay," he leans back in his chair, appearing so relaxed. I envy his level of confidence. "Let's talk it out. Plan it. Lay it all on the line."

I nod, nibbling at my lip, trying not to let my eyes take the slide back down his body again. "Yes. We need some ground rules."

He leans forward now, elbows propped on the table, mug between his big palms. I stare.

I wish I was that mug.

"No anal sex, Bailey," he deadpans. "I know you're really interested, but I'm just not that into it."

I jolt, eyes about to bug out of my head. My hand shoots up over my lips, and I force myself to swallow the beer in my mouth so I don't spray it all over him. "Oh my god!" I say from behind my fingers. "It was just a question!"

"Yup. A question that no other person has just casually lobbed out to me."

"Well, who else am I supposed to ask?"

"Google?"

I lean back in the chair, groaning as I stare up at the ceiling. "It didn't seem like a weird question in the moment."

Truthfully, I enjoy watching him react. He's so . . . unaffected by me all the time. But when I ask questions like *that*, I get a reaction. It's like proof of life.

"Really?" He's laughing at me now. And who could blame him? He must think I'm nuts.

"No, I just saw the video, and it got me thinking. It was funny. And you seem experienced, so I wanted to know. You could have told me it was personal if you didn't want to answer."

On a chuckle, he says, "Have you had anal sex, Bailey?"

I snort and tip my chin back down to meet his gaze. "I haven't had *any* sex, Beau."

All the humor that laced his body moments ago drains away. I swear I watch it just—*poof*—evaporate.

"Any sex?" He looks incredulous.

"None. Big fat zero. Felt like I should lay that out on the table if we're being honest with each other tonight."

"*How?*" His eyes spark with interest. Not disgust or pity, just ... disbelief. "Aren't you twenty-two?"

"Yes, but I don't know. I just don't go anywhere. The opportunity hasn't presented itself and I don't want to tick it off like an item on a grocery list. And ... who is there? In this town, it's people who wouldn't touch me with a ten-foot pole or people who want to touch me just to say they did."

I hold up a finger like I'm having an *aha!* moment. "In fact, that was the last bet I was unknowingly involved in. So, yeah, I need there to be a very clear plan so nothing gets confused."

So my feelings don't get hurt.

He stares at me for several beats, a glint of steel in his silver eyes. His jaw pops as his teeth grind, and I can't help but notice the way his long fingers flex around his mug, like he's envisioning strangling someone. "We're not going to have sex, Bailey. That's not the point of this arrangement."

I'm slightly disappointed by the conviction with which he conveyed that message. But it also puts me at ease. Honestly, part of what kept me up last night was worrying about how far we'd have to take the act.

And how I'd keep from getting attached if we took it too far.

"Let's just keep anything physical public. Does that work? Has anyone kissed you?"

I give him a droll look, offense flaring in my chest. "Just because I haven't had sex doesn't mean I've been living in a bubble," I bite back. "I just haven't found someone I want to go all the way with. But I want to."

"Bailey." He scrubs a hand over his face. "God. It's like you have no filter around me at all."

I chuckle and glance toward the plush sectional in the living room, envisioning us cuddling there. The weight of his body against mine. The way he might roll me under him and—

The sound of him swallowing is what hits me first. Then him taking a sip of tea. When I finally glance back at him, I can see the amusement swirling in his eyes.

"Shut up."

His lips press together, barely containing the laughter that threatens to spill from him. "I didn't say anything."

I wave a hand over him, my cheeks tugging up as I do. "You might as well have. You say my name like it's a bad word. Or like I exhaust you."

"You're entertaining, Bailey. Possibly even funny. You don't exhaust me. You invigorate me."

"Gee, thanks. Now I feel really fucking young."

He ignores my jab and forges ahead. "Okay, so if you meet this person who you really want to have sex with, you're going to tell me. And we'll break it off."

My eyes close. "I hate this conversation passionately."

He laughs now. It's deep and warm and makes me wonder how I'll ever find someone else I want to have sex with when I'm spending all my time with Beau Eaton.

When my lashes flutter open, I pin him with my glare. "Same for you. If you meet someone who you actually like, you'll tell me."

"That won't happen. But fine."

He sounds so sure.

"Why not?"

"An actual relationship?" He flicks a hand over the table as though swatting a fly away. "You don't see the shit I've seen and still believe a single thing is permanent. I saw the way it crushed my family when I went missing. I don't want to put anyone else through that. Once you've been sent on your way with a shiny new reputation, it'll just be me and my tea. I'll never fall in love, won't let myself."

He holds the mug up in a cheers, but it's not a happy one.

There's a profound sadness—a profound loneliness—about the sentiment, and I don't cheers back.

"When we break up, you have to do something awful," I say.

His brow quirks in question.

"Well, if you dump me, you'll be Poor Beau, who got swindled by the trashy Jansen girl. If I break up with you, I'll be the she-devil who hurt Poor Beau. But if you do something shitty, everyone will forgive you and I'll still get to walk away with my head held high."

"Why do you care? If you're leaving and never coming back?"

I breathe out a heavy sigh that leaves my lungs feeling almost painfully empty. "I'm just so tired of being the bad guy."

"I'll be the bad guy," he says with a firm nod, not needing to think about it.

My chest flutters, but I press on. "How will we convince people it's real?"

A sly grin graces his handsome face as his tongue traces his bottom lip. "Act like we can't keep our hands off each other. Just follow my lead."

"Right." I force my breathing to remain calm at the thought of touching Beau. Kissing Beau. I'm accustomed to hard work, but this doesn't seem like it'll be a real hardship.

What are the fucking chances?

I brush a crumb that doesn't exist off the table. This place is *immaculate.* "Sure. Cool. I could use the practice."

A rough huff of air sounds from his side of the table, and I glance up to see him shifting uncomfortably.

"What about your family?"

His brow drops lower at the mention of the Eaton clan. "What about them?"

"Should we tell them? You all seem so close. Will that bother you?"

Beau drops his gaze and stares thoughtfully at the liquid in his mug. "That's the thing, Bailey. I've been lying to them for years. And they're just now figuring it out, I think."

"What does that mean? Oh my god." I gasp. "You're gay, aren't you? Everything makes so much sense. I'm totally cool with it, by the way."

He chuckles, moving that sly, playful look over my face. "Bailey, I am very straight."

I swallow. "Well, I can see how someone would think you weren't."

His head quirks, his stare unnerving. "Oh yeah? How so?"

I shrug, having to blink away to escape the pressure of . . . *him*. "Never seen you with anyone."

"Been watching me?"

I blow a raspberry and roll my eyes. "Please, everyone in this town watches you."

Strong fingers rap against the table as he fires back, "I've never seen you with anyone, either."

I laugh, because *of course* he's never seen me with anyone. "I suppose my extensive vibrator collection doesn't prove much either, huh?"

He groans and shifts again. "Jesus, Bailey. You always just blurt shit like that out?"

I shake my head, trying to push my embarrassment back down. "Nope. I only seem to blurt stuff out to people I'm comfortable around. So, you. And maybe Gary."

Beau drops his head into his hands, heels of his palms pressing into his eye sockets. "Please tell me you haven't told Gary about your vibrator collection."

I take a swig of my beer. "Don't worry. He was hammered. I doubt he'd remember it."

Beau's head shoots up, an expression of shock painting his face. "Are you joking right now?"

I bite hard on the inside of my cheek. "No. I told him about the one that has all these different vibration settings and the one that has this little suction cup that attaches to the wall. Oh, and the one that straight up looks like a real dick but way, way bigger—" He leans across the table and covers my mouth to silence me.

In response, I hold my hands out, gesturing a good twelve inches as I widen my eyes. I'll never admit it, but his palm against my lips has me fighting the urge to let my tongue trail over his skin. The pressure. The smell of him. My lips move ever so slightly against him, and his hand flies away. Then both come up to cover his eyes again.

Beau's expression has morphed from shock to interest, to ... whatever he's doing hiding behind his palms.

I finally close my slack jaw and let my smile peek out, taking another drink.

The beer doesn't even taste that bad anymore.

"You can't just run around telling creepy old men about this stuff," he says in a strangled voice.

"Give yourself some credit, Beau. You're only thirty-five." His shoulders jump on a chuckle, and I let a laugh slip now. "And for a tier one operator, you sure are gullible."

His head snaps up to me, tips of his ears just a little pink. "Gary doesn't know about your vibrator collection?"

"No, sir." I salute him. "You're the only one."

He scrubs at his face as though he's considering what to say next. "I guess it's fine that I know about your collection. Seeing as how we're engaged now. And I'm not even threatened by the twelve-inch one."

I swallow and parry the joke away like I didn't hear it as I drop my tone. "You sure you're okay with lying to your family just to help me get a job?"

"There's lots I could never tell them. Lots I never will. This is just another one of those things. And I really need ... " He trails off, glancing around the pristine kitchen. It's truly so clean I could eat my meal off of almost any surface. It almost looks like it hasn't been lived in. It's sterile.

" . . . I really need to feel something."

I start in my seat, eyes snapping up to his.

"And honestly?" He scrubs at the back of his neck, lips twisting in a wry grin. "This already feels like the most fun I've had in a long time."

I decide in this moment that if he's not going to bug me about my virginity, I'm not going to bug him about whatever haunts him.

We're both getting something out of this arrangement, and I see the practicality in that. And the practicality soothes me.

It makes sense.

"Okay. How did we meet?"

His jaw works, and I can hear his teeth tapping together. "At the bar. That's the simplest explanation, and also true."

I nod my agreement. "And what's the end date on this deal?"

"Until you're ready to leave. Free and clear. New town, new job. Whatever you want."

"Or until you meet someone real," I add solemnly.

My heart twists because I already know this is going to hurt when it ends. But I also want that for him.

Someone real.

His throat works. "Same for you."

I slide my hand across the table, and he envelops it in his large palm.

We shake. We exchange numbers.

And just like that . . .

I'm engaged.

8

Beau

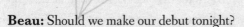

Beau: Should we make our debut tonight?

Bailey: While I'm at work?

Beau: Yeah. I haven't seen you in a few days. We still on? Don't you need to start applying for jobs? The bar would be a simple place to start. Then we can do dinner at the ranch one night.

Bailey: Yeah.

Beau: So, tonight?

Bailey: Sure. Yeah. That's fine.

Beau: Don't be nervous. Gary won't even know what's going on. Just get my tea ready, babe.

Bailey: Can we not do the babe thing?

Beau: Why not?

Bailey: It's just so unoriginal.

Beau: So, not only do I have to be your fake fiancé, but I also have to come up with an original nickname?

Bailey: Correct. It's a new requirement for our deal.

Beau: You drive a hard bargain, Jansen. How many carats on the diamond, fancy-pants?

Bailey: Lol. Four? Five? So big I can barely lift my hand.

Beau: Wow. My girl is high-maintenance. Got it. See you tonight, snookums.

Bailey: Yeah, no. That's not it either.

B ailey has her back to the bar, typing something on the touchscreen computer. Which is why she doesn't notice me sliding onto my regular stool. The one at the end of the bar that puts my back to the wall and gives me a view of the room—and the door.

A way out.

"How goes it, Sweet Cheeks?" Might as well rip the Band-Aid right off.

She freezes in place and Gary's head whips my way.

"The fuck did you just say to her?" Gary's jaw is practically on the floor.

I grin. Yep. This already feels good. I can do this. A show. A mission.

"We're trying out new nicknames."

She turns slowly, and the menacing expression on her face indicates she's going to kill me.

"Why on earth?" The older man sounds genuinely flabbergasted.

"Did Bailey not tell you the exciting news?"

Out of the corner of my eye, I see Gary's brows wrinkle together, but my gaze stays fixed on Bailey. The imaginary nukes she's firing at me do nothing but make me grin back at her. It strikes me that while Bailey is sharp-witted and funnier than I expected, she doesn't know how to have fun. She works too hard. It's like being playful is a privilege never extended to her.

I plan to change that while I have her.

My smile widens to the mega-watt version that has gotten me out of trouble many a time. "We got engaged over the weekend."

"You *what?*"

Bless Gary. He's totally giving off protective dad vibes now. Makes me feel like an even bigger asshole for the things I said to him that night—even though I've made amends.

"Yeah. We've been kind of . . . " Bailey trails off, eyes wide as saucers. Like she's just realized she has to speak about this arrangement aloud. In front of people. "Seeing each other."

Gary's head pivots back and forth between the two of us. Bailey staring at me. Me, smirking back at her, feeling more like myself than I have in a very long time.

It's the thrum of adrenaline in my veins, the camaraderie of being in on something. Having a purpose—a purpose that goes beyond working cows on the family ranch day in and day out.

"That's fast, boy. What are your intentions? She's a lot younger than you. Nicer. A hell of a lot prettier. What are you up to?"

I turn to Gary now, appreciating that he has Bailey's back. It's about time someone did.

"You're not wrong. She's all of those things. But she's also . . . " My eyes slip back to her. She looks fucking terrified. "Brought me back to life. Can't imagine my days without her."

It's not a lie. In fact, every word is true. I don't *only* spend four nights a week sitting here like a loyal guard dog because I hate the idea of her working alone.

I'm not quite that noble.

But I can't bring myself to hold her gaze after I've said it.

"Shit." He scrubs at his wiry gray stubble. "Guess I should have known by the way you're always watching her like you're imagining her with her clothes off. Was gonna tell you to tone down the gawking this week, to be honest."

Well, fuck.

I fall back on my training to keep my face blank, but Bailey coughs like she's got something stuck in her throat. I blink in her direction to see her pretty heart-shaped face painted with both humor and shock.

Once she's composed herself, she says softly, "Gary, please. Beau is a tier one operator. He would never be so obvious."

She sends me a sly wink at the end of her sentence. A dry laugh lurches from me. Sarcastic Bailey never fails to knock me off my feet. And it would appear I'm never living that one down.

"Yeah. My years spent in the special forces impress most people. Bailey though? Bailey just makes fun of me for it."

"You could use someone who is a little less impressed with you," Gary grumbles with a light slur as he takes another drink.

My fingers rap against the top of the bar. "Wow. You're on a roll today."

The man shoots his eyes to the ceiling before they land on my hand and shift to Bailey's. "Hang on. Please tell me you didn't propose to her without a ring. Doubt you need her daddy's permission, but I'll kick your ass if you didn't buy a ring for her."

Bailey's lips twitch, and she props her hands on her hips, looking all smug. She's enjoying watching Gary give me the gears.

Joke's on her, though.

I may not have proposed with a ring, but one quick trip into the city fixed that.

"I proposed with one, but Bailey told me the diamond wasn't big enough and to take it back."

Her foot stomps. "I did not!"

"Gary, you should have heard her. Said something about how she wanted a diamond so big that she could barely lift her arm."

He nods. "That's exactly what she deserves."

"You guys really think I care about that?" She's downright indignant, which is why pulling out the small green velvet box is so damn satisfying.

"I agree with you, Gary." I slide the box across the bar top. "So I went back and got a different one."

Bailey's lips roll together as she regards it, hands still propped on her hips. The tight squeeze of her fingers suggests she's holding herself back from grabbing the ring.

"Well, girl? You gonna show us the goods?"

With a dramatic sigh, Bailey steps forward and swipes the box from the bar. She seems indifferent. Truthfully, she isn't a great actress.

Which is why the way her mouth pops open when she sees the ring for the first time is so damn satisfying. Her cheeks turn pink and her hand quakes, but her eyes stay locked on the platinum ring with a massive teardrop-shaped diamond. Smaller diamonds frame the center stone. Smaller diamonds line the band. It's totally over the top, and I love that for her.

"What is this?"

"A diamond so big your arm will hurt every time you pour a pint."

"It's not real."

Her head shakes and I laugh. "It's very real."

"How much did you spend?" She sounds panicked now. I should have guessed this would freak her out.

"I know a guy. I got a good deal."

"What's a good deal?" Her onyx eyes snap to mine, glistening. "It's too much. It's way, way too much."

She leans across the bar and presses the box back into my hand, so I take it.

But in one quick move, I grab her left wrist and pull the ring from the box. I slide it onto her shaking finger, alarmingly satisfied by how huge it is on her slender digit.

She looks *very* engaged wearing that rock, and it has the caveman inside of me beating his proverbial chest.

Someone should tell him this is fake.

"No, Bailey. It's perfect." I gently stroke my thumb over the delicate bone in her wrist. We haven't really touched yet, and I'm not entirely sure how or where to start. Especially after the virgin confession. It's been a long time since I was one, and I've damn near forgotten what it was like.

When she meets my gaze, she's back to looking alarmed. Worried. She's the shy, awkward girl I remember, not the focused, funny woman she's slowly blossoming into.

"You deserve this."

"And shit, if it doesn't work out, you could pawn that sucker for a pretty penny," Gary adds drunkenly, which makes her laugh.

Then she turns her palm to my wrist and gives me a gentle squeeze to go with her sweet smile. She sucks in a startled breath when I lift her hand and kiss the top of it. Soft, but longer than is necessary. I keep my eyes on hers, giving her a look I shouldn't.

A look that stills the air between us.

When I wink at her, she turns the prettiest shade of pink and yanks her hand back like she's touched something scorching hot. Then she gets back to work. And I spend the entire night drinking chamomile tea and watching patrons gawk at the massive rock on Bailey's finger. They're too stunned to ask questions but too impolite to look away.

Every time she catches someone staring, I see the corners of her mouth twitch before she presses her lips together and averts her gaze.

And that right there makes the ring worth the ridiculous price tag. I've saved my money for years and was never sure what I wanted to spend it on.

This seemed like a worthy investment.

I shoot up in bed, ready to fight, but the sheets tangled around my waist stop me. For a moment, panic engulfs me. I need to run, need my legs to move, but they betray me, leaving me helpless. I've mussed my bedding in a way that makes no sense unless I was flat-out wrestling with it. My pillow is damp with sweat, and my skin is slick with it.

My feet burn like I've just walked over the flames.

Every fucking time, it's 2:11 a.m.

"Fuck." I flop down, pressing the heels of my palms into my sockets as I focus on stabilizing my breathing.

The dream is always the same.

I have the same urge to fight, to run, to spring into action, but my body fails me, and I end up crawling or dragging myself. I'm always in the desert. Micah is always there, on the brink of death.

And I always feel like I need to save him.

It's irrelevant that I *did* save him. My brain takes me back to that feeling of pure helplessness, the eternal high alarm with no reprieve. While we were camped out in that cave for two weeks, I suppressed those emotions, but they haunt me now.

I kick the sheets off. Even with air conditioning, I'm sweltering. Since I found Bailey in the river that night, I fantasize about dipping into the cold water and cooling this phantom burning sensation that feels all too real. I fantasize about relaxing enough to feel safe while doing it.

I'm drawn to the river now. I keep finding myself down there, not exactly remembering the path I took or when I arrived.

Maybe it's the water. Maybe it's the dark.

Maybe it's Bailey.

Regardless of what it is, I head there again tonight. I don't even bother with socks. As I make my way down the path to the shore, my feet feel like they are on fire, the freshly grafted skin rubbing against the fabric inside my shoes.

When I get almost to the bottom, I'm not alone.

Across the creek, against the riverbank, sits Bailey, in the same frilly white cotton dress she wore at work tonight. Her cheek rests on a balled-up sweater that covers the crest of her bent knees. Her arms are wrapped tightly around her shins. Like she's trying to be as small as possible.

In the moonlight, I can see her ring gleaming.

"Bailey?" I call her name, even though I already know it's her.

Her head snaps up, body going rigid. Then her hand flies up, one finger to her lips, giving me the international symbol for *shut the fuck up.*

I'm instantly on high alert, my heart rate skyrocketing back to the level it was after my recurring nightmare. I prowl down the rest of the hill, making as little noise as possible on the rocky shore. When I get to the water and look over at her, her eyes are wide. Body still.

I'm about to say something, but she taps her finger against her lips again.

Her signal draws my eyes down to the water. My white sneakers toe the water line.

Logically, I know my feet have healed. I've been given the go-ahead to swim—to live my life—but I just haven't been able to let go of the anxiety.

All at once, I'm faced with the question of what I want more. To get to Bailey? Or hang on tight to my anxiety?

It's not a question I need to think about for long. I'm not sure I think at all before I'm wading into the cold waterway to get to her, not caring about myself at all in the process.

Very on brand for me. It's why I am where I am.

Unlike Bailey, even at the deepest point, I can touch. So I walk, trudging through the water until I come out dripping on the other side. Bailey's gaze latches onto my feet as I stride toward her.

I try to ignore the chafing from the terry-like material inside the Adidas shoes. But as soon as I drop down onto the silty ground next to her and lean my back against the embankment, I rip them off.

In the dark, the burns appear less angry. They're mottled, a little twisted at the seams where the newly grafted skin meets the old skin, but less red, shinier now.

It's the first time I've been barefoot around someone new.

"I thought you said they weren't healed yet," Bailey whispers, eyes tracing my feet propped on the sandy ground.

"I lied. I've just been too shit-scared to take the fresh feet for a spin in dirty water."

Her face turns, lifting up to mine. "Why tonight?"

I shrug and wiggle my toes on the loose ground. It feels good to get them out of those fucking compression socks and hot shoes. "I had a good reason to get across the river."

She swallows loud enough for me to hear.

"What's going on, Bailey?"

She turns away now, like she's too embarrassed to face me. "My brothers."

My spine goes rigid.

She holds her left hand up, diamond glinting, and wiggles her fingers in front of us. Her voice comes out in a resigned hush. "They heard about the ring through the grapevine, I'm assuming from someone at the bar. I heard them talking about pawning it as I was heading down here for a swim. They came to knock on my door, so I hid behind a tree until they went inside, then I bolted to the river."

"I'm going to kill them."

Bailey's responding smile is sad. "They aren't worth it. And that would fuck with your hero status in town."

I wave her off. "It'd be fine. No one would care." I say it without thinking, with no regard to how it might feel to her. I say it because it's true—and that's the worst part.

The words land and I hear her grunt when they do. A soft thud, like a limb hitting the dirt in front of me.

"I'm sorry." My shoulder presses against hers, but she doesn't nudge me back.

"Don't be. It's true."

"I don't know if I'd say—"

"Beau, stop. The whole cheery, rose-colored persona you fake does nothing but annoy me. I've always seen past it. The way you switch from all happy-go-lucky and goofy to stern and uneasy. The way your face drops when you stare off into space for a beat too long. I do it too, and maybe that's why I see it. But honestly, don't bother around me. It's almost offensive. It's okay to not be okay."

My chest aches. I feel the cracks in it, the fault lines of all the hurts I've suffered, all the bad shit I've seen, all the things I mostly rationalize or tuck away. They come roaring back to the forefront in the presence of someone who doesn't care if I get lost in them for a minute.

"You're not going back to sleep at your trailer," I say, not wanting to acknowledge what she's just said to me. Instead, I fall back on what I do best: taking care of people.

"Wasn't planning on it."

"What were you going to do?"

Bailey shrugs. "Probably just sleep here."

"By the river?"

"Yeah." Her response is nonchalant as she tugs the sweater down over her head and settles in.

My brow furrows as I take in our surroundings. The warm air carries the scent of wet rocks. I can hear the crickets chirping above us. See the moon reflecting on the water. Feel the supple press of Bailey's body beside mine.

I could insist that she come back to my house. I could insist I go back to hers.

But this doesn't seem like a bad place to spend the night.

"Okay." I shift closer, deciding that—fuck it—I'm going to sling an arm over her and tuck her against me. I can't remember the last time I held someone who wasn't on the brink of death. Someone who I just wanted to hold.

This time, she doesn't flinch when I touch her. Without Gary and everyone else in the bar watching us, she doesn't act unnatural at all.

"What are you doing?" she asks, but her body doesn't resist. Her small frame melts right into mine without a single complaint.

"Holding my fiancée, duh," I say, thumbing the diamond on her finger.

She snorts a laugh to cover for the way she's cuddling into the shelter of my arm. She can't be cold, but there's something desperate in the way she presses herself against me. "Okay. Fine. Is this practice?"

Practice.

One simple word shouldn't make me hard. But somehow *practice* does it. It fills my head with many things that Bailey and I could practice. The things I could show her.

"Yeah, Baby Doll. It's practice."

Silence descends between us. Tension builds.

And then, "Hey, Beau?"

"Yeah?"

"Not that one, either."

I laugh. And then we don't talk. We don't need to.

We sit on the riverbank, side by side. Both of us practicing being okay with not being okay—together.

9

Bailey

Lance: Where you at? Come have a drink.
Aaron: Yeah, we came looking for you, but you weren't home.

I wake up held tight against something hot and hard. I rub my cheek against cotton, wanting to nuzzle back into one of the best sleeps of my life. A soft breeze fans over my cheek, and before long, I realize my pillow has . . . a heartbeat.

I freeze as my eyes snap open. The early morning sky has taken on a pale blue hue, and I realize that mine and Beau's "practice" lasted all night long.

We're clinging to each other. My cheek against his heart as he curls himself around me. Top arm caging me in like a shield.

I might as well be a teddy bear getting snuggled by the hottest super soldier of all time.

Correction: *my fiancé.*

My chin dips down, and I turn carefully in his arms, reveling in the heat of him against my back as I stare down at the diamond adorning my ring finger. It's too much. It's way too fucking much. Not only does it not belong on a girl like me, but it's further proof that Beau doesn't understand the way my world operates.

Nice shit gets stolen. End of story.

I don't get nice shit. I wasn't made for it. And it wasn't made for me.

As soon as I'm done basking in the feeling of being held, I'll tell him. I'll force him to take the ring back. I'll sit him down and make him understand that although we have an agreement, there is still a line in the sand between us.

One where—

He shifts, smacking his lips in an almost child-like way as his top leg hooks over me and pulls me closer while he . . .

Grinds his massive morning wood into me.

Now I really freeze on the spot.

A real man is pushing a real boner into *me*.

I've thought about this nonstop. What I'd do. How it would feel. I've *dreamed* about this.

Being a twenty-two-year-old virgin makes me sound . . . wholesome somehow. Living in my head is a whole different story. Because, yeah, I'm a virgin, but I'm not desperate to hang onto my V-card. In fact, I'd say I'm eager to get rid of it.

I mean, have you seen my dildo collection? My YouPorn search history? A silicon vibrator I pretend is Jensen Ackles snagged my hymen years ago.

Nah, I'm not saving shit. I'm horny as hell with no one I like enough to work that energy out on. I am desperate to—

"Sugar tits, are you pressing your ass against me?"

My hips shoot forward, and I squeak as I scramble to create space between us. "You can't call me sugar tits," is what I come back with as I turn to face him, palms on my hot cheeks like it might cool them down. Or maybe like I have a rewind button there. That would be ideal.

Beau props his arm behind his head and grins at me. "That's the part you draw issue with?"

I sniff, tipping my nose up, refusing to let my mortification make me feel small. I have years of practice holding my head up high when I should be embarrassed. I reach down to straighten my skirt.

"I was just lying here, keeping you safe. Sleeping. Quietly minding my business. And you were grinding against my—"

"Stop!" My hand shoots up, a physical barrier to cut him off. "Just stop. I was asleep," I lie.

Beau grins bigger, like he knows I'm full of shit. And fuck, he looks beautiful. There's sand in his hair, stubble on his face. His tan T-shirt has ridden up just enough to show a peek of bronzed abs.

"I didn't even know I was doing it," I say, attempting to weave the truth into what I'm thinking must be a very transparent lie.

He waggles his eyebrows at me.

"Ugh! Stop! You pressed your gigantic boner into me first!"

He laughs as he rolls onto his back, hands scrubbing over his face, which does nothing but make his forearms ripple.

But it's the sound of his laughter that gets me. It's warm and full. It vibrates through my body. It makes my stomach flip. It hits me with a jolt of lust right between my legs.

"Why are you laughing? This isn't funny. It's awkward as hell."

"It's funny because if you know that, you weren't sleeping."

Shit.

I brush the sand off myself, making a show of it to avoid having to look at Beau and his stupid, knowing smirk. "Well, if you know it, you were awake too," I argue back.

"Yeah, but I was groggy. I haven't slept that well in months. My body was celebrating."

When I peek at him, he winks, and I'm a pile of nervous mush all over again.

"What's your excuse?" he teases, still laid out flat on his back. It strikes me as an especially vulnerable position for a man like him.

I kneel at his side, taking in what has to be close to six feet, four inches of solid muscle.

His body is a well-honed machine.

I imagine it propped over mine. Thrusting.

"I'm horny," I blurt, deciding I'd rather not lie. What's the point? He sees through it anyway.

His gray irises latch onto mine for a few beats. I expected him to laugh, but he just stares at me.

"What? Is that so alarming to you? Is it because I'm a woman? I'm twenty-two, and I swear I'm almost at the point where I'd fuck anyone just to try it out."

He groans now, hands back on his face. "Bailey."

When my eyes trace lower, I can see his length straining against his shorts. With his eyes covered, I casually hold my hand out to compare sizes.

For science.

"You can't fucking say things like that to me."

"Why not?" I snort, a thrill racing through my body when I

realize his dick is longer than my hand. "We're engaged. I'm practicing, remember?"

"What are we practicing right now, exactly? Other than making my dick so hard it might burst?"

I nod, staring at his penis and feeling very mature and matter-of-fact about it. No, this is good. *Normal.* "We're practicing talking about sex. I'll need to be open about it one day when I do it, right? So I might as well get comfortable talking to a man about . . . " I flail my hand around as I search for the right words. "Bodies. I should get comfortable talking about bodies. Seeing bodies."

"Yeah?" He replies from behind his hands. "Then tell me about how wet you are right now."

That brings my train of thought to a screeching halt.

He drops his hands from his face, now wearing an expression I don't recognize. His eyes have gone dark, almost titanium, growing more turbulent the lower they travel. "Lose the sweater and let's see if your nipples are hard."

My mouth drops open, but I don't respond.

"You want to practice talking about sex? Let's practice." His raspy voice vibrates across my skin like a touch. Somehow, his cock fills even more of his shorts.

I hesitate for only a second before I reach down and peel the sweater off, keeping it clutched in my lap. My fingers dig into it, using it as a shield for his question about . . . lower.

When I glance down, my hard nipples are pointing straight at him through the thin cotton bodice of my dress, like my body is screaming, *This one! Do this one!*

He seems momentarily surprised by my boldness before the expression slips away.

Then he growls, "Fucking knew it." His tongue darts out over his lips, but he makes no move to change his position or reach for me.

I chance another look at his crotch and watch him reach down to adjust himself, a quiet groan escaping me as I do. My brain spirals. How must that feel? Taste? He does it so casually, with such surety.

I bet he fucks like that too. Like he just *knows* he's good at it. No bumbling. No stuttering.

I bet Beau Eaton knows how to handle a woman's body like a pro.

"Are you wet, Bailey?"

Boom, there's the proof.

A shiver races down my spine, and my eyes flutter shut. I squeeze my thighs together and press my sweater down harder over my lap, feeling the way my pussy slides as my hips twist ever so slightly.

"You are, aren't you?"

I keep my eyes closed because I don't know if I can handle seeing him right now.

"Tell me."

I pant, my body going hot. It's too much. Talking about sex is one thing, but I feel like I might combust. And the fact of the matter is, this seems like seriously blurring whatever lines Beau and I have laid out. I know I'm going to have to touch him—kiss him—but that's in public. That's for show.

Whatever this is right now? It's none of those things.

It's private. It's intimate. And considering the fact that no one else is here . . . it's not for show.

I push to standing and finally meet his gaze, one that's now laced with confusion. "The only thing I'm telling you is that I'm going to go back to my trailer and get cleaned up so I can apply for jobs."

His chest rises and falls, and he catches up to whatever whiplash

I just put him through. But he doesn't fight it. He blinks and his eyes clear, like we both just experienced a possession and are coming back to reality.

He props his hands against the ground and rights himself, unfolding long limbs as he comes to stand before me—towering over me.

He stares down at his feet, toes wiggling on the sandy ground. In the morning light, the damage to them is clearly visible. The skin stretched just a little too tight. Smooth spots. Bumpy spots. Spots that are redder, spots that are whiter. Just past the bridge of his feet, it swaps back to smooth, regular skin.

A border. One side holds all the pain, but if you cover it up? It's like nothing ever happened.

I want to ask questions, but I don't. Nothing worse than people rummaging through your trauma just so they can rubberneck.

I know the sensation, and I won't subject Beau to it. If he wants to tell me his stories, he will.

He notices me staring, and he winces. I recognize the look on his face because I've experienced it.

Embarrassment.

I feel inclined to snap him out of it.

My gaze falls to the dog tags around his neck. I reach for them, the bumps in the chain sliding through my fingers, but his eyes stay trained on his feet.

I give the chain a tug, startling him out of his moment. "Don't do that."

"Do what?" His brow furrows.

I tug again, pulling him closer. "Don't play stupid. And don't be ashamed."

I try to step back, to give myself space, because the way he's staring at me right now is disarming. But his big hands move fast, shaping my waist and gripping me.

Immobilizing me.

The low morning sun is blinding white over the tops of the trees, and I swear it gives him an otherworldly effect as he glares down at me.

He drops his head and brushes his nose against my cheek. My head tilts, and my fingers grip the tags tighter, tongue darting out over my lips.

Is he going to kiss me?

Our lips are almost touching, but I'm too stunned to move.

"Shame?" He hums the word but doesn't press closer. I feel the warmth of his breath against my damp lips, the rumble of his deep baritone over my throat. "Rich coming from the girl who just refused to answer my question about her—"

I push away from him, chest heaving like I've just been on a run. My nostrils flare as I try to pull myself together. *Again.*

Composing myself, I brush at my dress and steer the conversation in a different direction. "Okay, well, I'm going home. I'll see you around." I give him a drive-by smile, one that feels forced and is only turned on him for a beat as I look around myself, settling on the ground like it's super interesting.

"What about your brothers?"

He snaps my attention back up to him with the question and I wave him off. "Nah. They'll be sleeping off last night. Without Dad around, they don't even pretend to stay in line."

He assesses me a little too closely. His jaw pops, which suggests he doesn't believe me or doesn't like the answer. The edge of anger emanating from him makes me nervous.

"Okay, well—"

"We need to tell my family soon. Would be weird for them to find out from someone else."

"I'm off tonight. We could ... "

"Okay. I'll see what I can pull together and let you know."

He's all business now. Except for the leaf stuck in his hair. My cheeks tug up at the sight.

I expected to feel uncomfortable around Beau, uncomfortable with this deal. But I don't. I practically showed him my nipples, and now we're standing here chatting like normal grown-ups who can easily talk about sex and bodies.

"Great. Well ... " I rock on my feet, searching for a way to end this conversation, not sure where we go from here. "Thanks for the ... practice." The word comes out on an awkward laugh, and I shake my head at myself, dropping my gaze again.

Only to see that the swelling in his shorts is still there.

This is fake, fake, fake.

Suddenly, I feel a lot less grown-up. I feel giddy and uncertain, and like I need to get away so I can squeal into a pillow and over-analyze every single thing that has happened in my life for the past few days.

So, I dart to the barely there path I've created up this side of the bank because I need to put a little space between Beau and his big dick and me.

A low chuckle caresses the back of my neck.

"Bailey, we're going to need a lot more practice if we're going to pull this off."

"Why's that?" I call over my shoulder, refusing to turn back to him.

"Because if you act all jittery around me, no one is going to believe we're madly in love. And I need them off my ass."

I bark out a laugh. This entire thing is *ridiculous*. "Well, just don't ask me if my pussy is wet in front of them." I hit the top of the embankment and feel more in control now that I've got room to breathe. Hands on my hips, I stare down at him, huffing lightly, sucking in the fresh morning air. "Then we should be fine."

That mischievous smile pops up on his face again, but it's not all play—there's an edge of danger to it too. "But it will be, right?"

"No. Because this is fake, remember?"

He stretches now, hands behind his head, grinning like the Cheshire Cat. "You faked those hard nipples real well, sugar tits."

I have most certainly bitten off *way* more than I can chew.

And all I can think as I stare down at this beautiful, broken, confusing man is . . .

What the fuck have I done?

10
Beau

Beau: Dinner tonight at six. All set with the fam.

Bailey: Okay. I'll have to walk over.

Beau: Why?

Bailey: I have a flat tire.

Bailey: Actually, four flat tires.

Beau: I'm coming over. Right now.

Bailey: Why?

Beau: Because four flat tires aren't an accident. No one just randomly gets four flat tires.

Bailey: Not sure my brothers will like an Eaton driving onto the property. Don't come here. It's not safe for you.

Beau: Bailey, I don't give a fuck what they like.

I drive onto the Jansen property like I own the fucking place. I'm going to play it cool enough not to freak Bailey out, but I want to smash something. The rage that's always in me simmers too close to the surface for comfort.

My palms twist on the steering wheel of my truck as I run through what I plan to say to her in my head, so I don't come off like an overbearing asshole.

I drive past the main house, a bit shocked by the neglect. Every side displays chipped paint, while cardboard slabs secured by duct tape cover some windows.

Tattered clothes are hanging on a line, and I wonder how long they've been there. Beer cans litter the yard, concentrated around a large burn barrel just steps from the back door.

Too fucking close to the house to be safe. Idiots.

I knew this property was a dump, but seeing it firsthand—knowing Bailey grew up in this squalor—makes something in my chest twist.

She deserves so much better than this. She shouldn't have to hide in the fucking riverbank from her own flesh and blood or worry about the people she should trust most in the world stealing shit from her.

I keep driving past the shithole her brothers call home, heading toward the river in the general direction of where I know she must live.

I weave through the treed lot, over the dry bramble that collects in the wheel ruts that lead me further back into their property. There's clearly been zero maintenance.

Rage bubbles up, hot splatters of it lashing me.

When I turn the corner, it's replaced by cold focus. The focus

I pulled upon overseas. The kind that let me kill people and carry on relatively unscathed because I knew I did what had to be done to survive.

Bailey sits on the metal step of her trailer, wiping at her tear-swollen eyes.

I step out of my truck and turn on the spot, taking in what appears to be a sprinkling of her belongings all over the dirt ground.

Clothes, makeup, jewelry, papers.

When I finally come to face her again, she's holding a stuffed horse that looks so well loved it's coming apart at the seams.

Except it doesn't need to anymore. There's a slash down the side of it. Bailey's eyes lock with mine while her hands continue trying to shove the stuffing back into it.

I don't even need to ask her what it means to her. The small brown horse shows all the wear and tear of being a comfort to a little girl who, no doubt, has had little comfort in her life.

"Who. Did. This?" I bite out, my voice a low growl.

Bailey blinks frantically. "It's fine. I'll clean it up. I left my trailer unlocked when I fled last night. They got in." She hiccups and hits me with the saddest smile, then tosses the stuffed horse into the plastic garbage bag at her feet. She can't even watch herself do it. Her chin turns up, and she shifts her gaze in another direction.

I flinch. The sight of her throwing it away hits me low in the gut. It winds me.

"It's just stuff. I can replace it." Her eyes fill again as she stares over at her small truck. Despite its worn appearance, I imagine the old Ford Ranger handles the wild road that leads to her trailer well enough. Or it did. Right now, it sits on its rims, black rubber draped over the circular shape, spilling onto the ground, beyond deflated.

"It's just that—" She presses the back of her hand against her lips as her voice breaks. "I can't afford this right now."

I itch to grab her and squeeze her, but I'm worried I might break her right now. She's too fragile, and I'm too heated.

The sight of her crying makes me want to hurt someone.

Probably her brothers.

"Bailey, I don't mean to overstep, but with the amount you're working, why can't you afford this? You shouldn't have to pay for it, obviously, but . . . "

She stands and starts swiping things off the ground, looking more angry than defeated now. "Because I'm an idiot. That's why. My brothers charge me astronomical rent, so I—"

I hold a hand up. "Sorry, what? They charge you rent to live here?"

Her face flames. "Basically, I pay the mortgage on the property. Or the re-mortgage."

"Why are you the only one paying for anything?"

"I don't know."

"Bailey . . . "

"What, Beau?" she screams, turning to me. "You think I don't know how fucked-up it is? I can't rent anything in town because no one will approve me. I'm trying so hard to fly under the radar. I'm trying so hard to start fresh. And then there's this part of me that feels guilty for it—like I owe them something. Like I don't deserve to start over. Like how could I possibly think I'm better than the rest of my family and I deserve more than this?" She gestures around herself. "This is first-class living compared to what I grew up in."

The explosive outburst steals her breath. Steals mine.

Her hands cover her face and then push up through the silky

hair I spent the night with my nose pressed into. The smell of the cool rocks and something minty in her hair wrapped around me all night long.

"I'm just so tired," she says, her voice small and wrung out. Her shoulders droop, and a tear races down her golden cheek. "I work hard to rise above it all, but I am so, so tired of struggling."

Again, my hand itches. This time, to wipe the tear away.

I don't bother resisting anymore. With three long strides, I'm standing in front of her. I tug her in, one arm around her shoulders, one hand palming the back of her head, and press her against my chest.

Because I can't handle staring into her sad fucking eyes.

I expect her to cry, but she doesn't. She relaxes in my arms, melting against my torso, just like she did all night long.

Like she feels safe enough to be tired around me. To let her guard down.

I want her to have that all the time, which is why I say what I came here to say in the first place, even more sure of myself than I was before. "You're not fucking living here anymore."

"I can't just—"

"I'm not having my fiancée live here."

"Beau." Her voice chides me, but her body softens further.

"What, Bailey? No one will believe I'd be okay with you staying here. Just rationalize it that way."

My arms tighten around her, a little firmer now. She's not breakable.

"What about my tires?"

She sniffs and I rub a comforting palm over her head, smoothing her hair. "I'll take care of it. I'll take care of it all."

"I haven't moved it anywhere in years. Are you sure it's okay?"

Bailey is buckled in safely beside me but won't stop staring out the back of my truck.

At where I have her trailer hooked up.

Because she's not fucking living there anymore.

She refused to move into my house with me, so I made her my neighbor.

She stood there with her hands on her hips and her jaw hanging down to her feet while I took it upon myself to hook her trailer to the hitch of my truck and take it out of that hellhole.

Those dumbasses slashed the tires on her truck, but not on the trailer. And I used that to my advantage.

"Bailey, it's fine. I'm going slow and it's not far." I have my window down, the sound of the plastic garbage bags fluttering in the wind as we drive.

"I'm sorry." She faces the front again and slouches down into her seat.

"For what?"

"Being the most high-maintenance fiancée in the world."

I snort at that. "You are so far from high-maintenance, it's not even funny. You slept on the ground with me last night."

A soft smile touches her lips as she looks out the window. "Yeah, I liked that, actually."

I nod firmly. "Same. I wasn't lying when I said it's the best I've slept in months. No pills. No alcohol. Just hard ground, fresh air."

And *her*. The only thing that's come close to working.

Silence cloaks us as we pull into Wishing Well Ranch. I was

supposed to be helping Cade today. Once I got out of the army, I planned to be his right-hand man. That's what I told everyone I'd do.

Although I grew up here, I failed to realize something ... I'm not a rancher. I don't care about the cows. I don't find joy in working the land.

My brother wakes up every morning dedicated to running the family ranch.

I wake up every morning dreading it.

But I hate the idea of letting them all down. So I get up and do it. Bailey and I are alike that way, doing things we don't like to support our families the only way we know how.

My family is just a hell of a lot nicer than hers. A hell of a lot harder to let down.

"Alright, sugar tits." I break the silence by cracking a joke. "Where should I build your castle? Facing the river?" I gesture out the same way my house faces. "East for sunrise? West for sunset? The world is your oyster."

"But your house is *right* there." She points at the modern house, probably a mere thirty feet away.

"Yep."

"I told you I wasn't going to live *with* you."

"This isn't living with me. It's living adjacent to me."

"It's really close. Too close." Her arms cross and her eyes narrow.

"I think it's the perfect distance."

Her jaw flexes as she bites down on her teeth. "It's my house, and I say it's too close. How about there?" She points at a copse of thin birches in the distance.

"Fuck no."

"Why not?"

"It's too far away."

"It's just far enough."

"Why would two people in love live in separate houses that far apart from each other on the same property?"

It's not safe is what's really running through my head. In light of today? In light of last night? It would take too much time for me to reach her if something went wrong over there. I wouldn't hear the noise. See the lights.

I might as well sleep at her front door like the guard dog I am at this point.

She stares at me, and it's not in anger. It's more like I can see her brain whirring a mile a minute. Then she looks away. "Fine. Facing the river."

I grin at her before turning back to the wheel to line up the small trailer just right. It doesn't matter, though, because I don't think she'll be living there for long. She'll give in and move over to my place.

And then I won't have to be alone.

"And stop calling me sugar tits," she adds with a stubborn lilt to her voice.

I don't mind at all, because it's a hell of a lot better than hearing her cry.

"Sugar it is."

11
Bailey

"Should we practice before we go in there?"

My hands freeze on the seat buckle, and I turn to stare at Beau.

The man who moved my trailer and helped me reorganize everything inside.

The man who stayed with me all night when I was scared, who walked through dirty water when I needed him. Who is way older, way more experienced. And who asked me if I was *wet* like we were just having a casual conversation.

The man who is my new fiancé and is about to introduce me to his family. His *nice* family who loves him and wants the best for him.

"Practice what?"

"Well, I don't know. You're looking at me like I terrify you."

I scoff. "You don't terrify me."

"Why do you have that deer-in-the-headlights expression all the time, then? You could barely get through telling Gary. You gonna flinch when I touch you? Kiss you?"

"Why would you touch and kiss me at a family dinner?"

"Because we're engaged?"

I shake my head rapidly. "No. Just tell them we're not into PDA."

Beau glares at me. "We're going to have to convince them a little bit. This is going to blindside them."

I'm about to reach for the door handle to get the hell out of here, away from the super soldier who is turning this into some sort of top-secret mission shit, but I stop in my tracks.

"Hang on a second." I turn back to face his chiseled jaw and stupid face. "Have you not told them *at all*?"

His expression is impassive. "No. I decided it would be best to just rip the Band-Aid off. They're less likely to give me the third degree if you're there. Which is why we need to sell it."

"Are you fucking kidding me? *This* is your plan? How many years in the special forces . . . and *this* is your plan?"

He blows out a breath and leans his head against the rest behind him. "Listen, what I want out of this deal is for them to leave me alone. You can use me to get a job, and I can use you to get them off my back. Maybe we're both wrong and this whole thing doesn't make a difference at all. Just act natural."

"This makes me nervous. How am I supposed to act natural?" Because while I've come to feel comfortable around Beau, that feeling doesn't extend to big family get-togethers.

The man beside me goes from agitated to lighthearted as he reaches out and pulls my hand up to his mouth. He kisses my palm so naturally that I almost forget we're faking this relationship.

"Don't be nervous, sugar," he murmurs against my skin, with a coy glance out of the corner of his eye. Because we both know abbreviating that nickname doesn't make it any better. "We've already slept together. This should be a breeze." He chuckles, and it vibrates through the bones in my hand. Lips and stubble brush against my skin, and I bite down on the shiver that racks my body, tugging my hand back and rubbing at it like I've been burned.

"Okay! Fine. Let's go," I reply brightly, hopping from the truck with a bounce in my step that's not a match for the dread growing inside me.

I barely spare Beau a glance. He overwhelms me. Looking at him will do nothing to quell the way my heart is racing in my chest.

I can feel him beside me, strong and tall, hovering just at my shoulder like a bodyguard.

He links his fingers through mine and casually opens the front door.

The show begins.

When we walk onto the back porch, everyone freezes. Conversation comes to a screeching halt. Eyes volley between me and Beau, then drop and stall on our linked hands.

To say I know everyone here would be a stretch. I've served drinks to most of them, or I've heard *about* them in the roundabout way you do as a bartender in a small town.

That is to say, I've overheard gossip here and there.

Harvey Eaton, the family patriarch, breaks the silence as he relaxes in an Adirondack chair on the wooden deck, beer in hand. "Bailey Jansen, how lovely to see you." He stands up to greet me. "Beau didn't mention you were going to be joining us. But there are so few true surprises left in life, you know? This is a nice one." He winks at me, eyes twinkling with mirth.

My cheeks flame and I drop my eyes to my sandals. The pale-yellow sundress seems ridiculous on me now, as though I'm trying to fool everyone into thinking I'm the type of girl Beau would bring home.

At least the flowy skirt is useful for hiding my left hand, since concealing a diamond the size of the one Beau put on my finger is no easy feat.

"Thank you," I murmur, feeling like I could collapse in on myself under the weight of their stares.

Everyone is here. Rhett and Summer, Cade and Willa, Jasper and Sloane, Theo and Winter—even Sloane's mom, whom I've heard some whispering about. There are babies in arms and a little boy kicking a soccer ball in the field out back.

I'm going to kill Beau for doing this to me later.

He leans in close to my ear, lips brushing against the shell, and whispers, "You look fucking beautiful."

Then he straightens, all casual and carefree, like he didn't incinerate me with one simple sentence. "Well, I'm glad you're in the mood for surprises," he announces. "Because I have another one for you."

Beau glances around, gaze snagging on the single free seat they must have saved for him. In the blink of an eye, he's folding his massive frame into the sturdy wooden chair ... and taking me with him.

I am sitting on Beau Eaton's lap at a family gathering, with everyone watching. I feel made of stone.

I'm supposed to be selling this, but I'm having a mental freak out. Sure, I spent the night curled up against him, but that didn't feel like pretending.

This does.

My back stays ramrod straight, and fire licks up my chest as I make a show of arranging my skirt to avoid making eye contact with anyone.

Beau hasn't let go of my hand, and then his left lands on my lower back. Right on the waistband of the boy shorts I'm wearing under this dress. His palm drags up my spine, the pressure just enough to distract me. Just enough to relax my posture.

His eyes fixate on me, the weight of his gaze like a heavy foot on my chest. He has no business giving me all this panty-melting focus with everyone watching.

His gaze is so heavy that I barely sense all the others.

When I squirm in his lap, his broad palm squeezes at my neck, more of a warning than a comfort. It forces me to stare at him. It forces my breathing to come out short and labored.

"Is the surprise that you two are going to eye fuck each other while we all watch?" Willa asks casually as her fiancé, Cade, scrubs a hand over his face and groans beside her.

A few other people chuckle, but it sounds to my ears more like nervous tittering.

And me? I officially want to die.

Beau chuckles, deep and raspy, but he doesn't look away. "No. The surprise is that Bailey and I are getting married."

You could hear a pin drop. I swear the birds stop chirping.

Beau's magic fingers massage the back of my head as he releases my hand, wrapping his thick arm around my waist and tugging me tighter against his chest.

I feel like an awkward rag doll.

Being held by a Ken doll.

"Well, no one can say you don't love to keep us on our toes," Harvey ventures, sounding shocked, not angry, like I expected.

The only person I manage to peek up at is Summer. She's married to Beau's little brother, Rhett. She has always made an effort to be kind to me, even going as far as hiring me to bartend at her recent wedding.

"Well," she slaps her thighs and pushes to stand, taking a few steps across the deck toward us. "Let me be the first to say congratulations to you both." She holds her arms out for . . . a hug? "Welcome to the family, Bailey." She shifts to peer around me at Beau. "Let her go. You've already peed on her. No one is gonna take her from you."

Her brown eyes gleam, and her lips are upturned in a knowing smile. I can't figure out why she'd be smiling like that at me. *Can't she tell this is fake?*

12

Beau

Bailey goes rigid when Summer cracks her joke and stands for a hug.

She was right. I should have prepped them. I should have prepped her.

When we're alone together, things feel easy. *Natural.*

I didn't feel the need to prepare. But I've spent a lifetime going undercover, playing a part, diving headfirst into danger.

Bailey has spent a lifetime flying under the radar and hoping no one notices her. So when she makes the move toward Summer, I know it's time to let her go. If she'd stayed frozen to the spot, I'd have kept her right where she is. Summer has that effect on people, though. Sweet and warm and welcoming.

She wraps Bailey in her arms and grins at me over her shoulder. Then Bailey gets lost in a swarm of hugs and back pats, handshakes, and congratulations.

I swear everyone is happier for her than they are for me.

Jasper, my best friend, my brother from another mother, stares at me with furrowed brows while everyone else swarms us.

Deep down, I knew he'd be the hardest sell; he knows me too well. But I also know if he can't be sold, he'll be a vault. He and I have been too close for too long. If anything, he'll understand what I'm doing here and why I'm doing it.

I don't know a single person who guards his peace quite like Jasper.

Cade steps up, tugging me into a rough hug. If I didn't know any better, I'd say he's a little choked up. "Was gonna give you shit for no-showing on me today when we had fences down and broken waterers. But if you were celebrating this, I'll let it slide. Back to reality tomorrow, though."

I grunt, slap his back, and roll my eyes. Only Cade, the grumpy workaholic, could turn congratulations into both a scolding and a reality check. "Fucking buzzkill," I grumble back at him, laughing when I see his lips twitch.

"Beau-Beau!" Rhett moves in front of me, a shit-eating grin on his scruffy face, long brown hair dusting his shoulders. "Is this why you keep taking off on us? To hide away with the missus?"

I scrub at my beard. I knew my brothers would razz me, and I knew Rhett would be the worst after all the shit I've given him over the years. Fake hitting on his girl, ditching him at the scene of a crime, tattling on him every time he gets into trouble.

Yeah, his eyes are alight with all the possibilities for payback right now.

However, it's Bailey who throws me under the bus. She has my head spinning like a top when from beside me she says, "Yeah, Beau-Beau likes to sit at my bar and watch me work all night."

Rhett's eyes glimmer even more with delight. I didn't think it was possible, but here we are. He grins at Bailey, who wears a tentative smile and a light blush. The soft summer breeze moves her hair, stray strands whipping against the deep tan on her cheeks.

"That's fucking adorable," my brother says, disbelief seeping into his tone as he glances between us.

I reach for her hand without even thinking. And it's not for show. Or not in the way I thought it would be. It's not like I feel the need to convince my family I like Bailey—I already *do* like Bailey.

I want to show her off. I want to prove to her that life can be a little lighter than what she's experienced. That not everyone looks at her and sees what she thinks they do.

I squeeze once, twice, and when she finally tilts her head my way, it's with a saucy expression on her face. A look she's comfortable giving me. Because I'm not sure what she expected. Everyone to freak out? Be mean? Call her trash and try to rescue me from her?

No, that's not my family.

"God, look at you two. How did I miss this? Bailey's been our server at The Railspur for the last couple of years now." Rhett still can't get over it.

Jasper takes a swig of his beer and regards me carefully. Not judgmentally, as if he's trying to work things out. "Well, he has always jumped to her defense," he says. "And he stood at her bar for your entire wedding reception." I think that might be as much as I'll get from him tonight. I can tell he's suspicious.

Rhett's brows furrow at me. "You did? I didn't even notice. You've been such a grumpy bitch lately, kinda got used to ignoring you. But, dang, I did not see this coming."

Summer elbows Rhett and gives him a scolding, wide-eyed

warning, signaling him to be quiet. It's a prime example of how everyone has been walking on eggshells around me. Treating me like I might break if they nudge me too hard.

The ribbing feels good.

"What?" Rhett gives his wife the same look back. "He has been a grumpy bitch. And now he rolls in all *surprise we're Beau-Bailey now*! Sue me for not seeing this coming."

Bailey giggles and coughs to cover it.

"Beau-Bailey." My dad laughs, stepping close to sling an arm over my shoulders. Everyone watches him with bated breath. He has a knack for saying inappropriate shit at the most awkward times. I suppose it's part of his charm. "Sounds like a Disney movie about two golden retrievers who fall in love. Happy for you, son."

Jasper holds a fist over his mouth, and Willa bites furiously at her lips, trying not to laugh.

"Sorry, what was that, Dad?" I choke out.

"Beau and Bailey. I mean, don't get me wrong, they're nice names, but together they sound like good pet names. If you have a kid, let's avoid naming it Comet, yeah?"

I groan and tip my head back. Compared to my brothers, I'm rarely on the receiving end of the Harvey ridiculousness they get.

I'm about to apologize to Bailey, but she laughs.

Not fake awkward laughter. Laughter the way it sounds when Gary says something stupid to her. Laughter the way it sounds when I test the waters with a ridiculous nickname.

Then she steps into my side and buries her head against my ribs. Like she feels at home with me.

People crack jokes around us, and their attention shifts. We're still standing in the middle of the deck, but people seem to be

114

retreating to their corners, back to their conversations. They're set-tling back into the pre-dinner vibe as if nothing out of the ordinary happened here tonight.

I suppose if Winter can announce her baby daddy at dinner, this might not seem so interesting after all.

When I curl an arm around Bailey's petite frame, her doll-like face tips up to mine. Eyes round, lashes long, lips distractingly plush. "Did I do okay?" she whispers, hand fisting the back of my shirt.

I lean down over her, granting us some privacy. She doesn't pull away. Our eyes lock, breaths intertwined. My muscles bunch as I force myself to resist lifting her up and carrying her the hell out of here to have her all to myself.

"You were perfect." Our lips graze—barely a touch—as the words leave my mouth. I move mere inches to the left, pressing a very real kiss to the corner of her mouth, missing her lips entirely.

Some people might consider it a mistake.

Some people can't tell what's real and what's not.

But I did it on purpose. I did it to plant a seed.

I did it because I don't think I want the first time we kiss to be fake.

"What are you doing?"

My head snaps toward Bailey's trailer as I drop to sit on the steps that lead off my back porch and down to the river. "Sitting on my deck." I don't need the sun to be out to know from here that she just rolled her eyes at me. "How about you?"

She hikes a thumb over her shoulder. "It's hot in the Boiler tonight."

I snort. *The Boiler.* "Cute play on Boler. My house has air conditioning."

"Couldn't sleep?" she volleys back.

I guess me sitting on my back porch in the middle of the night makes it obvious. But I don't add that the second my clock flicks over to 2:11, my body violently wrenches itself from sleep.

"Nope."

"Why not?"

"Are we just going to yell at each other from across the yard?" I prop my elbows on my knees, my body looking more casual than how I feel inside. "Seems kinda weird for an engaged couple."

She snorts this time, then stands and pads across the dew-soaked grass toward me. I watch her feet, the way they roll against the ground. The red polish on her toes. The smooth skin that flows up over toned calves.

I'm still staring at her feet when she plops down beside me. "It's rude to stare, Beau-Beau."

My lips curve as I lift my gaze up to hers. "A man can stare at his fiancée, can't he, sugar tits?"

Her hand darts up to tuck the curtain of dark hair behind her ear. "Fake fiancée," she clarifies, glancing down at my feet.

All I respond with is a low hum. I don't know Bailey all that well, but I know the agreement we reached. Still, I find myself agitated by the word *fake*.

But I'm easily agitated these days.

Sleep would help.

"Can I touch them?"

I start, yanked out of my spiraling train of thought. "Touch what?"

116

Bailey juts her chin at the step below us. "Your feet."

I gaze down. Next to each other, my feet look so fucked-up where hers are so … perfect. Aesthetically, I don't care. Kinda figured being a soldier would scar me along the way.

It's the contrast that strikes me, though. And it's more than just our skin.

"You want to touch them?"

"Yeah." Her dainty fingers brush over the tops of her own feet, and it's like she's too nervous to even look at me. Sometimes I wonder what goes on in her head. What she keeps locked up tight, followed by the things she blurts out.

"Okay."

It takes her a few beats to gather the courage, and I wonder if she'll back down. Decide they're gross. Laugh and tell me she was just kidding.

But she doesn't.

Her left hand moves off her foot and hovers over mine before the pad of her finger trails over the raised ridges and puckered skin. Hunched over, she traces the scars—every line, every divot.

She doesn't seem at all put off. In fact, she seems almost entranced.

I hiss when she hits a tender spot.

"I'm sorry, did that hurt?"

"Got rubbed there," I bite out, annoyed because doing the things I used to has become a different sort of challenge.

She leans down, peering closer, hand drawn away. "Rubbed how?"

My jaw works. "When I couldn't sleep the other night, I just stuffed my bare feet into my sneakers like I would have before the injuries. But everything chafes and rubs now. They were already

117

sore from wearing dress shoes at the wedding. Can't even wear sandals. Walking through the water didn't help."

"That sucks," Bailey replies matter-of-factly.

I almost want to laugh. It does suck. And it's refreshing to have someone admit that rather than tell me it will get better. Or tell me how sorry they are.

Little things she does—without even trying—make me feel like it's okay to not be okay in her presence.

"Yeah." I don't want to be a martyr. I know things could be worse. But admitting this sucks feels good. Being *allowed* to admit it sucks without everyone rushing to patch me up is a weight off my shoulders.

A second and third finger join in her exploration of my damage. What I'd normally register as a slight touch feels electric. The newly healed skin is more sensitive, and I know she's not trying, but the sensation of someone touching me in a way that isn't medical has my dick swelling.

"Have you ever had a threesome?"

Yep. That'll do it.

A strangled noise lodges in my throat, and she finally turns her face up to mine. She is so damn pretty, eyes twinkling in the dark, the warm light of the back porch shining on her dark hair.

"What?" I ask.

Her fingers pause as I stare back at her. "A threesome. Sex with two other people. Have you ever had one?"

"I know what a threesome is, Bailey. I'm having trouble figuring out why this moment is connected to that thought for you."

Her eyes blink down to her hand. "The three fingers, I guess?"

"Three fingers on melted skin made you think about a threesome. Life is certainly never boring in your head, is it?"

118

"Well, no. I was thinking about sex." When she blurts the last part out, she finally looks a little embarrassed. But not *that* embarrassed.

"You were touching my feet ... and thinking about sex?" Disbelief bleeds into every syllable. She's the most entertaining blend of innocent and curious.

"Yeah. I mean,"—her head wobbles—"to be fair, I think about sex a lot."

I scrub a hand over my face, covering my eyes. "Jesus fuckin' Christ."

She scoffs playfully as she traces my feet again, not the least bit uncomfortable touching me. "Don't be such a prude, Beau."

A laugh lurches from my chest. God, I am so unprepared for this woman. "I just don't know how I ended up engaged to a girl with a foot fetish who blurts out personal sex questions at the drop of a hat."

"Well, you are my fiancé. Maybe I should ask another guy instead," she muses, the tips of her fingers now twirling over my skin as though dancing across the scar tissue.

Jealousy hits me hard and fast. I have no right to it. I can't rationalize it. All I know is I don't want her sharing moments like this—quiet and unfiltered, safe and trusting—with some other jackass.

I want to be the only jackass who gets this version of her.

"I've never had a threesome, Bailey," I grit out as I push to stand, needing to put some space between us before I do something stupid.

Her gaze follows, brown eyes staring up at me like I'm the moon in the night sky. "Why not?"

Bailey, sitting at my feet, full attention turned my way, is doing nothing to stop my hard-on from making an appearance.

"Not a big fan of sharing something once I decide it's mine."

Her lips part.

And fuck. I should stop, but the side of me that sees danger and runs straight toward it has made an appearance tonight.

So I reach out and run my palm over her silky hair, cupping her head. "I'll start leaving the back door unlocked for when you decide you want to find out if I'm a prude or not."

Her eyes widen, and I can't help but imagine this is how she'd look as I slid my dick into her pretty mouth.

I was the one who told her we wouldn't have sex, and it's taken only a few days for me to be fighting off the thought of it. After a quick shake to clear my head, I turn away. Hand burning, feet tingling, dick rock fucking hard.

"What if I just come in for the air conditioning?" Her voice is smooth, surer than it has any right to be after what I just said to her.

I laugh, but it lacks humor. There's an edge to it.

A promise.

I don't bother looking back at her when I say, "Sure, Bailey. Call it whatever you want."

13

Bailey

Beau: I can pick you up.

Bailey: No, it's fine. I'll take a cab. You're working.

Beau: You don't need to spend your money on a cab.

Bailey: I actually don't need your permission, sergeant.

Beau: I'm not a sergeant.

Bailey: Captain?

Beau: Not that either.

Bailey: . . . Sir?

Beau: Watch it, Bailey.

Bailey: If it's all the same to you, I'll be taking a cab. Thank you for your help, sir.

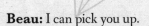

Being engaged to Beau Eaton was supposed to be helpful. Except I'm pretty sure it's my own special brand of torture. *I'll start leaving the back door unlocked for when you*

decide you want to find out if I'm a prude or not is the one-liner that had me rushing back to my trailer to pull out my box of vibrators.

I didn't even bother pretending one of them was Jensen Ackles.

Every single one is now Beau Eaton.

Despite my lack of sleep, I had to wake up early to clean the bar this morning. Beau drove me there in relative silence while I clutched my travel mug with both hands. I figured keeping my fingers latched on would prevent me from crawling across the center console and mauling a man who is only going along with this charade to be nice.

Or because he's bored.

Or something.

I hitched a taxi back out to the ranch when I finished, and now I'm sprawled in a fold-out chair next to my trailer. An iced coffee in hand. A sun beam on my face.

I'm trying not to stress about my tires. Or my money. Or if making myself come while thinking about my fake fiancé was a bad idea.

I want to check out and just—

Tires grind against the gravel road leading to Beau's house. I don't bother opening my eyes, even when they hum onto the paved driveway on the other side of the house. Regardless of any external influences, I don't budge, safe and protected by my trailer. The one thing I still have that's mine.

I know Beau is gonna come here, guns blazing about me saving my money. I hear heavy footfalls, and my lips tip up as I imagine him towering over me like he did last night.

But the voice that interrupts my peaceful moment isn't his. "You seen Beau?"

I startle and shoot straight up to see Cade Eaton, Beau's oldest brother, with his hands on his hips, looking really bitchy.

"No," I breathe, one hand slung over my chest because he surprised me and I'm trying to catch my breath.

Cade glances between the house and me. "Why are you sitting over here when there's all that patio furniture up on the deck?"

I shrug, trying to play it off. "Lacks a certain charm, don't you think?"

The man nods at that. "Gotta say, I'll agree with you there. House looks like it belongs in the city."

I stare at the house, all straight lines and modern shapes.

It suits Beau—or some version of him, maybe—but it doesn't suit the setting. And I find myself wondering if Beau suits the setting.

"Anyway, he took off in the middle of the day," Cade says. "Not a fuckin' clue where he went. Not answering my calls or texts, as usual. So if you hear from him—"

I give Cade a salute. "I'll let you know."

Cade turns to leave but then swivels back, uncertainty painting his features. "You think he's doing okay?"

I weigh the question, torn between being honest and protecting Beau's privacy.

Okay? The sleep, the way he's set off so easily, the alcohol intake. He's not okay, but he's aware of it, and it strikes me that might be half the battle.

A sip of cold coffee hits my tongue, an ice cube slipping into my mouth. It slides around as I consider my options.

I choose Beau.

"Yeah, I think he's doing alright. Better all the time, you know?"

Cade nods again. His movements are harsh, lacking the

predatory, almost feline edge of Beau's. What you see is what you get with Cade. He's straightforward, handsome enough, but he doesn't consume space the way Beau does.

With Beau, I can sense the tension radiating off him, the energy, see the chaos that hums through his veins. He covers for it well, but I see it. I'm drawn to it.

I'm just fucked-up enough to find comfort or familiarity in that type of unhappiness.

It's like we're kindred in our dissatisfaction with life. And at peace with one another because of it.

I want so much more than what I've had.

And it seems to me Beau has had a taste of *more* and is wallowing in the *less*.

"If he acts like an asshole, let me know." Cade is all gruff, protective vibes. It makes me smile against the rim of my glass as the ice melts in my mouth. "I'll set him straight."

I cross my legs and lean back just a little. "That's okay. I'll set him straight myself."

Now Cade grins, pointing at me as he turns to walk away. "And *that* is exactly what he needs."

"Your brother is looking for you," I call out when Beau pops his head out the back door. Thirty minutes have passed since Cade left, and I haven't moved from my chair.

"You better not have taken a cab back here." He points a finger at me like I'm in trouble.

But all it does is make me squirm against the canvas fabric of my chair.

"Or what?" I quirk my head in challenge, my iced coffee taking effect and perking me up a bit.

The carefree expression he was wearing melts from his face as he steps fully out onto the porch. A zing rushes through me as I force myself not to sit up and straighten under the weight of his gaze. I've trained myself to appear casual when I don't feel it for years now. It should be easier than this where he's concerned, but my skin prickles and my legs squeeze together.

There's a sinful twist to his mouth, one that could be mistaken for playful—but I know better. It only lasts a beat and then it's gone, washed away by the shake of his head. "Or you might find yourself stuck being fake engaged to me longer than necessary."

That has me shooting up out of my chair. My instinct is to rebel against that line of thinking, tell him I'm not *stuck* with him at all.

I think I feel freer in his presence than I have . . . ever.

"Shhh!" I whisper-shout at him instead, finger held against my lips, eyes wide. "Shut up! Cade was here sniffing around for you like thirty minutes ago, Mr. Undercover."

A broad palm runs through his freshly trimmed hair. "Great. Nothing like being babysat by my big brother."

"Did you ditch work to get a haircut?" His haircut stands out to me because I'm actually taking him in rather than being overwhelmed by his presence.

He rolls his shoulders back and looks away. "I was due."

"Beau. You can't just ditch work to get your hair cut, especially when your family is relying on you."

"I needed one."

"Yeah, but—"

"I hate working the ranch," he blurts, cutting me off. "Bailey . . . I

125

fucking hate it. I made a promise to my family and now they depend on me to follow through. But I don't feel like myself. I don't care. I stand in a field, and I stare at those fucking cows, blinking back at me stupidly with their too-long eyelashes,"—I stifle a laugh—"and I am just monumentally *bored*. Bored to the point of misery."

I go from almost laughing to rubbing my sternum, trying to push away the heavy ache that's taken up residence in my chest.

"Like, no one even knows the shit I've done. The importance of the things I was doing. My missions? They saved lives, they changed the world. And now? Now I'm supposed to . . . fix fences?" He sighs, his tall frame shifting down incrementally. "It makes me . . . "

"Angry?" I provide, because I can feel it. I know the way the air tastes when someone is angry, can feel the surrounding oxygen thicken with it.

I know an angry man. I grew up in a house full of them. But with Beau, even when he's angry, I feel safe.

"Yeah." His hands link behind his head and he watches me, gray eyes almost shrink-wrapped in tears. "And it's fucking depressing."

My tongue darts out over my lips as I consider his outburst, try to put myself in his shoes—his head. I don't know a single thing about what it's like to feel that way. And who am I to tell him he's wrong?

"It is," I agree, slapping my bare thighs as I push to standing. He seems startled, either by my sudden motion or my words. I'm not sure which. "I know all about living a depressing life, so, like, high five on that. Now let's go do something fun."

"Fun like what?" His suspicious expression almost makes me laugh out loud.

I give him a once-over, from head to toe. My gaze catches on his bright white Adidas Superstars, now smudged with dirt and grass.

"Like getting you some shoes that don't rub you raw." I wave a finger back and forth between his feet. "And maybe not so white. Doesn't suit you."

"What suits me?" He asks me like he doesn't know. In fact, I get the sense that part of Beau's problem these days is that he hasn't reconciled the *before* version of himself with the *after* version.

It turns out, going missing in the desert for days on end changes a person. I'm not sure why this surprises anyone. And I'm not sure why anyone expects him to be the way he was before it happened.

I guess that's why I shrug and say, "I don't know. Let's go find out."

14
Beau

Beau: Hi. Bailey said you were looking for me.

Cade: At least you talk to someone.

Beau: Probably because she isn't up my ass like the rest of you.

Cade: Must be terrible having a family who cares about you. I feel just awful.

Beau: Care a little less.

Cade: Okay, no problem. Keep cutting out on work to do god knows what and I'll fire you.

Beau: You can't fire me. I'm your brother.

Cade: Yeah, and I sign your paycheck. I think you're gonna need it to pay off that ring. Or did you skip work to go mine it yourself?

Beau: Worth it. Looks good on her.

The minute we open the door to the shoe store, Bailey changes. The girl who chatted away in the car, hands gesturing around as she explained her plan to become a chiropractor, evaporates like a splash of water on a hot griddle.

The bell chimes on the door as I hold it open, but she stalls. "You go first." Her teeth worry her bottom lip.

"Bailey, I'm not walking through a door ahead of you. That's just rude. I'm pretty sure it would summon Harvey. He'd pop out from behind a shelf and cuff me in the head."

"I went to high school with her," she hisses, subtly nodding toward a girl chatting with another customer.

"Okay, and?"

"And she was awful to me. Let's just . . . " Bailey's head swivels, and she glances back at Rosewood Street as if she's considering taking a running leap into a getaway vehicle.

It hits me hard that she's scared. This poor fucking girl.

She's dreading walking into a store because someone was so mean to her several years ago that she still can't face them.

I slide an arm around Bailey's rigid figure and lean down over her again. She curls into my body the same way she did the other night, like she can hide behind me.

Like she feels safe with me.

I rub her back as I whisper against her ear, "You're walking in here with me. That was the deal, yeah? Let's give them something to talk about, sugar tits."

She snorts a totally unladylike laugh, head tilting in toward my chest, her long hair falling over her beautiful face. Hiding herself when she shouldn't.

I tug her against my side and drape a possessive arm over her shoulder, pressing her tiny frame next to mine.

She stiffens as we walk, rigid as a plank of wood.

"Relax, Bailey," I whisper, turning us to face a wall of shoes.

"I *am* relaxed," she bites back, staring right through the shoe display like she's somewhere else entirely.

"You look like I kidnapped you and forced you to go shoe shopping with me. This was your idea. Sell it."

Her eyebrows drop, eyes narrowing as she shoots me a dirty little scowl. Then she turns her face back to the wall of shoes and slides her hand into my back pocket.

My body pauses only for a beat as surprise flashes across my face. That's not what I was expecting, but I'm not mad at it either.

"Hi!" The bright voice makes me flinch. It's how everyone talks to me now. Too fake. Too upbeat. "What a treat to have Beau Eaton in the store today with—"

I turn to face the girl with bright blonde hair styled into loose waves. She's pretty, but not beautiful like Bailey.

"Bailey *Jansen*?" The girl is so incredulous I have to bite down on the inside of my cheek to keep my lips from twitching.

It's a struggle, so I turn, drop my lips to the crown of Bailey's head as I squeeze her firmly against me. "Future Mrs. Bailey Eaton," I correct, dragging her hand up over my hip bone.

Bailey's fingers splay over my belt, massive rock on display.

Way too fucking close to the zipper of my jeans.

The girl blinks for a comically long time. Her mouth opens and closes like she's trying to find the words, but nothing feels right.

Bailey's other hand moves, skimming up my back—almost like

she's hugging me—until her fingers fist in my shirt. There's something desperate about the motion.

I reassure her by sliding my hand under the curtain of her hair, propping it on her neck, right where it meets her shoulder. "Do you know my Bailey?"

That comment has my girl's head whipping up to face me, but the salesgirl cuts our eye contact short. She laughs. *Laughs.* Right to my fucking face. "Yeah, I mean, everyone knows Bailey."

I feign ignorance and smile down at Bailey. The woman with pinched eyes and flattened lips who is gazing up at me with a *get me out of here* expression on her face.

"Well, anyone who is a friend of Bailey's is a friend of mine." I grin at the other girl, but she's too stupid to tell it's not a friendly grin. "Maybe you can help us with some shoes?"

She looks confused but replies with a bright, "Of course!" all the same.

I glance at her name tag and decide on the spot that I hate Lily. But I play the long game. So, I offer her a bland smile before I turn away and march Bailey up and down the length of the store, assessing my options. It doesn't take me long to realize that I don't give a fuck about my shoes as long as they don't chafe.

When I get bored with staring at the sea of footwear, I whisper, "Sugar, put your hand back in my pocket."

Bailey doesn't even move her eyes my way when she says, "Why? I think she's buying it just fine."

My lips dust over the shell of her ear. "I don't give a fuck about her. I just like it."

Bailey's hip bumps against mine, a silent reprimand for what she thinks is a joke.

But I'm not joking. I take her hand and shove it back into my pocket, smirking at the snarky look she shoots me. Even the vicious little revenge pinch she gives my ass before carrying on makes me smile.

"What about these?" She points at a pair of brown suede sneakers. They're a mix of white and chestnut with a gummy sort of sole.

They're fine.

"Sure, let's try them." I have no idea what I like, or if I even care about my shoes, but I do like being here with Bailey. The thrill of the mission has me feeling more myself.

"And these?" She steps away and holds up a sportier sneaker. Black on black on black. "Very tier one undercover operator who could break into someone's house in the dead of night."

My lips twist on a chuckle. "Never going to live that one down, eh?"

"Never," she murmurs with a smile as she moves away from me, picking out more shoes and lining them up on a bench.

She runs the gamut, and I say yes to every pair. Every time I do, she stands a little taller, seems a little less concerned about Barbie watching her from the till, like she's about to steal all the shoes on display.

When she finally comes to stand before me, slightly flushed, she props her hands on her hips and says, "So I did some reading."

"So proud of you. I knew you weren't just a pretty face," I quip with a wink.

She blinks away, muttering, "Dick," so quietly that I barely hear it. Eyes back on mine, she tries again. "I did some reading about socks and blistering. Ways to reduce friction." She pulls a plastic bag from her purse and shakes it at me. "We've got some options to try for that too. So sit down and start trying on some combos."

I swallow, staring down at this pint-sized powerhouse, wondering how no one else sees the compassion oozing from her pores. She's not all frilly and sugary. There's a refreshing get-shit-done kind of practicality about her. She's faithful.

Her fingers snap in front of my face. "Earth to Beau Eaton?"

Then we get to work trying on shoes and socks. It's a lot of work for Lily because I decide to be extra thorough. I try half a size up and then request half a size down for every pair of shoes, sending her back and forth every time.

Just to be sure.

I don't miss the suspicious look Bailey eventually shoots me.

It's almost like she's onto the fact that I know exactly what size I wear.

"Were you sending her back and forth on purpose?" Bailey asks when I slam the driver's side door of my truck.

I avoid her eyes as I busy myself with buckling my seatbelt. "No, I was just trying to make sure I got the right size. You saw my feet, gotta be sure."

"Mm-hmm." My gaze latches on Bailey's arms, squeezed tight beneath her breasts. "Petty."

"How is asking her to do her job petty?"

"You know. Don't stoop to their level, Beau. It's unbecoming."

Leave it to the twenty-two-year-old in this fake relationship to be the mature one.

I train my face into a blank expression as I twist the key in the ignition, looking forward to the blast of cold air the vents promise. "Listen, she worked hard. All my respect to Lily."

"Uh-huh." I can feel the disbelief in her voice, sense it in the way her eyes work over me.

"She'll sleep well tonight. I always do after physical labor. And maybe when she wakes up in the morning she'll be less of a bitch. Good sleep does wonders for a person."

Bailey scoffs at that, covering her face with her hands. Eventually she removes them, rolling her head along the back of the seat to stare at me. "Speaking of sleep. How has yours been?"

I shrug and shoulder check vigorously to avoid letting my eyes rest on her. "Fine. Speaking of trucks . . . " I trail off as I pull off onto Rosewood Street, desperate to change the subject. "Let's go get yours."

"I don't feel like facing my brothers, thanks. It can just rot there."

A grin stretches my mouth. Who knew doing nice things for Bailey would become the thing that gets my body humming after months of numbness?

"Do you really think I blew my brother off just to get a haircut?"

"What?" Her voice bleeds confusion.

"The barbershop is next to the auto shop. Your truck is all fixed."

Her fingers press into her chest. "My truck is fixed?"

"Correct. Brand new set of tires."

"How did you get it?"

"Ordered a tow truck."

Several beats of silence pass as I revel in the feel of the cool air blowing against my face. It's fucking sweltering today. The kind of day that ends in a killer storm. The kind of day that has heat waves rolling just above the asphalt of the roads.

"I can't afford this."

"You don't need to," I reply. "I told you I'd take care of it. And I did."

She just stares at me after that statement. Deep brown irises bouncing around my face, a light furrow to her brow, like I'm a puzzle she can't quite figure out.

Because no one has ever taken care of Bailey Jansen before.

But I think it's about time she got used to it.

Jasper's name flashes across my console screen as I follow Bailey out of town and toward the ranch on her fresh set of wheels.

"Hey!" I shout as soon as I press the button.

"Hi." I can hear the suspicion in his voice. "Why are you avoiding me?" He's not a big, dumb hockey player. He's a big, smart hockey player.

"I'm not avoiding you."

"You are. You're a terrible fucking liar for someone who supposedly worked undercover on matters of national security."

"Jesus, did Bailey tell you to crack those jokes?"

"No. I haven't spoken to your *fiancée*."

I bristle. "Why are you saying it like that?"

I can practically hear him shrug through the phone line. I know him so well. And he knows me so well.

"Dunno, man. Just seems weird that you completely failed to mention your engagement to me until you were announcing it everywhere."

"Aw. Jasper, baby, don't get all up in your feels."

"Beau, take that shit somewhere else. My feelings aren't hurt. What I'm telling you is I don't buy it."

The whoosh of air conditioning is all I hear for a few seconds as I consider my options.

"Why not?"

"That's offensive."

I snort. It is. "I'm sorry. I shouldn't have tried to pull one over on you."

"For fuck's sake, Beau. What are you up to?"

I sigh, palms twisting over the steering wheel. "Bailey needed some support. She's trying to get outta here, and people are so damn mean to her."

He hums.

"You can't fuck this up for her. You need to keep your mouth shut."

"You know I'm a vault." He sounds annoyed that I even had to say it. We've been best friends, practically brothers, since we were teenagers, and I don't know a more trustworthy person than Jasper Gervais.

I sigh. "Yeah. I know."

"You guys have a plan? How long you doing this charade?"

"As long as it takes." My words lead to more silence. Jasper isn't a big talker. But he's a sensitive dude. A deep thinker. And I can almost hear him thinking right now.

"But what's in it for you?"

My head tips from side to side as I consider my answer. "A friend. I like her."

"I can tell. And that's what's got me worried."

15
Bailey

"Why not?" The little boy crosses his arms and stares back at Cade, looking like a tiny version of his dad. Dark hair, set jaw, narrowed eyes. He can't be more than seven or eight, but he carries himself a lot older than that as he glares at his dad from across the dinner table.

"Because they make a huge mess and are hard to contain. And I don't need another living thing to take care of and clean up after."

"I'll feed it and take care of it."

All heads swivel back and forth between the two. No one says a thing, but I can tell every single person sitting around the Eaton family dinner table is invested.

"You're only bringing this up here so people will take your side," Cade grumps.

"Willa already took my side. She said she'd back me up when it came to it."

Willa groans and tips her head back. "Luuuuke. You can't just throw me under the bus like that. We're supposed to be a team."

I stifle a smile, rubbing my fingers over my mouth as I focus on staring at the empty plate before me.

"Shit, sorry, Mom."

Beau's hand lands on my bare thigh. It's casual, natural. He's doing it to brace himself against laughing, but I can't peel my eyes from his broad palm and calloused fingers, the way the size of him almost swallows me. The way my flesh gives beneath the firm squeeze.

It sets me ablaze instantly. I pull my stare away from the sight that's got me hot and focused on keeping my breathing even, just in time to see Cade's eyes bug out.

"Luke!" It's clear the cuss word is not approved, but based on the hushed chuckles from around the table, it's not exactly new ground.

"Dad, come on. What's one little goat?"

"No."

The boy's eyes go big now, wide and pleading. "But Dad, they butcher all the boy ones because they don't produce any milk. They practically give them away."

Luke is really taking his shot here; he's gone from tough and driving a hard bargain to trying the sensitive approach.

Smart kid.

"So what you're telling me is that I'd be better off investing in a female goat and making you milk it so it produces something useful rather than work and mess?"

"Dad, please." His voice cracks. I swear his eyes fill with tears. "Consider it a rescue goat."

"Cade, come on. Live a little," Harvey pipes up. I've been watching his keen gaze take in the entire exchange. I can tell he's a great dad, loves his kids—his grandkids. I don't know Harvey Eaton well, but I know he's unlike any man I've had in my life.

Cade shoots his dad a dry look. "Of course you'd side with a child. What am I supposed to do with a male goat?"

As Harvey stares at his son, it seems like everyone is holding their breath. Beau's hand tightens on my leg. I hope it leaves marks. I chance a glance over at him, noting the way he's lifted a fist up over his mouth.

Bracing.

Harvey makes a contemplative grumbling noise while scrubbing at his beard. "Well, you could try milking the male goat. But that might get weird."

The most unladylike noise I've ever made leaves me in a flurry of trying, and failing, to breathe deeply. Finally, I focus less on Beau touching my bare skin as giggles overtake me at the absurdity and inappropriateness of the older man's joke.

Willa loses it. I'm talking sprays water from her mouth. She gets up and walks away, swiping furiously at her mane of red hair.

Rhett groans.

Jasper gets a wildly amused, shit-eating grin on his face.

Beau turns toward me, huffing a soft laugh against the curve of my neck. It's so hot out, so stagnant, that I lean into the rush of air on my hot skin.

And Cade? Cade just sits there, glaring at his dad. "You're getting worse the older you get. You know that?"

I can see Harvey biting at the inside of his cheek, trying so hard to keep a straight face. "What are you talking about?"

"Dad. You just made a joke about ..." Cade swipes a hand through his hair and looks at his son before deciding to forge ahead anyway. "Me jacking off a goat."

A high-pitched gasp lurches from Beau, who is now rubbing at his eye sockets.

"Cade, watch your mouth at the dinner table. And get your head out of the gutter. Male goats have nipples too."

Cade gapes at his dad. "You fucking serious right now?"

Harvey shakes his head. "I think. They might. Okay, fine. I wasn't talking about their nipples." And then he bursts out laughing along with everyone else while Cade drops his head down on the table. His shoulders shake, so I'm pretty sure he's laughing too.

"Okay, enough about Cade and his goat handjobs," Harvey announces.

I hear a, "There is no me and my goats," from Cade, but Harvey ignores him and turns his attention to Beau and me. "Let's talk about the new love birds."

All my laughter comes to a screeching halt, and a heavy pit of dread drops into my stomach. I don't want to talk about Beau and me.

For the past several days, we've worked well together. As in, we see each other in passing. Beau heads out on the ranch every day with his brother, and I work at the bar. At night, I sleep in my excruciatingly hot trailer while thinking about whether I should chance going into the air-conditioned house.

To find out if Beau is a prude or not.

My money is on not, but every time I get up and almost make it there, I stop. I'm too chickenshit to find out.

"Set a wedding date?" Harvey's perceptive eyes bounce between Beau and me curiously.

Beau lifts his hand from my leg, and the skin feels clammy

without his touch. It's too hot to be close to someone, yet I wish he'd put it back.

Like he can read my mind, he slings his arm over my shoulder, fingertips drawing casual lines over the bare skin on my shoulder.

If it wasn't so fucking hot out, I'd cover myself from head to toe so I could avoid the distraction of his skin on mine. Alas, this is the heat wave that never ends.

"A long engagement, I think." He cants his head toward me as I turn my face up to him. Our lips are so close. Uncomfortably close. It takes me back to that morning at the river.

Beau's metallic irises drop my gaze and fixate on my mouth.

I wonder if he'll kiss me.

Our first kiss, at a table full of his family. Part of me wants to dig a hole and hide from that kind of PDA. The other part of me wishes he'd just do it.

We'll have to kiss at some point. We both know.

A shiver runs down my spine as he stays focused on my lips, moving incrementally closer.

But Beau just smirks down at me. It's a carnal smirk, one that says he senses me leaning into him, sees my chest rising more rapidly, knows I crossed my legs just to stem the ache between them.

"Yeah." He turns his face back to everyone sitting around the fancy-style table on the back patio. "Long engagement. Nothing set in stone yet."

I clear my throat and offer the general vicinity a forced smile. "Taking our time," I add stupidly, voice sounding all dazed.

"Well, that's fine. I didn't put a date on the announcement."

"Announcement?" My voice cracks when I pose Harvey the question.

"Yeah, for the *Chestnut Springs Herald*. Did it for all my other kids. You two aren't getting off scot-free. Plus, it'll keep all the lady callers of Beau's away if we get it out there. Some of them are relentless."

"What?" Beau sounds genuinely confused.

He waves a casual hand. "Ah, yeah. I can't even go to the grocery store without some woman walking up and inquiring about you like I'm a pimp or something."

I bristle, shimmying my shoulders taller. I shouldn't care—I *don't* care—it just seems rude that Harvey can't even get his food in peace.

Sloane's mom, Cordelia, pats his hand, giving him an amused look. "Harvey, I think that's enough for one night."

Somehow, that changes the entire vibe at the table. It's like everyone's attention latches onto that one motion. Her hand on his. His eyes on hers. The way he takes her hand, turns it over and links his fingers with hers. I watch the sentimental way he squeezes her hand, an expression of pure adoration on his face.

Then their eyes snap up.

Then they pull their hands back and scoot away from each other.

The table instantly becomes awkward.

Now, I wonder if this is what it was like watching Beau and me staring at each other.

"I got new shoes," Beau announces, attempting to grab everyone's attention. "Bailey took me shoe shopping. Ditched the dorky white runners. Got some black runners, suede sneakers, even a pair of leather boots."

No one talks, wide eyes still moving around the table. Harvey's ears have turned pink, and he's gulping water down as though that might save him from having to talk right now.

"New socks are making all the difference. Got some of these double-lined ones to reduce friction and a super thin wool pair. See?" He stretches a foot out toward the end of the table, but his monologue about shoes and socks is barely registering. "Come onnnnn."

I think it's sweet how he's trying to save his dad from this moment. For a guy who wanted his family to stop paying him so much attention, he sure is happy to throw himself center stage.

Beau crosses his arms and gazes away from everyone dramatically. "Why is no one asking me how fast I can run in my new shoes? Being an adult sucks."

And it's Luke who comes to his rescue, drawing a few chuckles. "I'll race you, Uncle Beau!"

"Do you really think my dad is hooking up with my dead mom's little sister?"

It's the first thing Beau says to me when I pull up beside him at his house and step out of my truck. We met at the main house for dinner and drove back separately.

"Yes."

"But like … how?" He slams his door and rounds his truck, meeting me at the front grill of mine. His eyes are wide, and he looks … adorably naive.

"I—" My head quirks at him. "Well, I don't have any first-hand experience with how it works, but I've done extensive video research. I think the basics are that he would put his—"

His hand covers my mouth. "Whatever you do, never finish that sentence. We're talking about my *dad*."

I laugh against his palm and nod my head.

When he removes his hand, I hold his gaze and shrug. "I think it's nice he has someone."

Beau scrubs at the back of his neck, clearly trying to work his brain around the familiar way Cordelia and Harvey had held hands at dinner.

"I guess. Kinda weird that it's my mom's sister."

"Is it? Maybe it makes perfect sense it wouldn't threaten her. Maybe it's okay for your dad to still love her because they both love her? Or like," I shrug. "Maybe it's nice for them to have her in common?"

Beau winces. "She died a long time ago. It's just weird. He's never brought someone around. And he hasn't told us anything."

"It's almost like you don't need to tell your family every single thing that happens in your personal life, huh?"

He points at me and says, "Fair," while walking closer.

I thought the heat coming from the front of my truck was uncomfortable to lean against, but the way Beau is stalking toward me has me pressing back against it like it's the more comfortable option.

His black sneakers come almost close enough to stub my toes through the tips of my sandals.

"Nice shoes, soldier. They look fast." I toss him a wink and cross my arms, trying to be casual.

Probably failing.

"They are." His eyes assess me. "How's the trailer treating ya?"

I swallow. "Great. Wonderful. I love my trailer."

"Pretty hot these days."

Again, his breath is a cool breeze.

"Sure is."

"Still holding out on my AC offer?" He quirks a brow and mirrors my crossed arm position. And he oozes . . . promise.

I don't know how else to put it. He's not even touching me, and in this moment, I know exactly what he's promising.

Touch. Pleasure. Experience.

He said he wouldn't have sex with me, but what about everything else? It seems improbable. Looking at him, he's like a big, cocky Adonis.

It seems like a bad idea.

But he's also your fiancé. You trust him. He's so damn good to you.

I'm ovulating. That's the only reason my brain is rationalizing this to me.

I let my gaze slide down his thick body and land on the crotch of his shorts. They're fitted . . . ish.

Maybe that's why I can see a bulge so clearly. The really big bulge.

It's just the clothes. Not a real boner.

That would be absurd.

"Please let me know what I owe you for the set of tires."

He ignores me. "Just you alone, up sweating all night. I can imagine it."

"I'm climatized," I squeak, actually spinning and rolling myself against the hood of my truck to escape him.

"Bullshit." He chuckles, watching me flee.

"Love the heat," I toss over my shoulder, dreading how hot my trailer will be when I open that door. I'm exhausted from poor sleep and easily agitated from being so hot for so many days.

"Why are you running from me?" he calls, and I can detect the smug note in his voice. He knows what he does to me. How could he not? I showed him my hard nipples the other day. What am I supposed to do now? Deny it?

"You scared, sugar?"

Dick.

"Have fun doing more extensive video research."

Fucking dick.

"Might do some of my own tonight too."

I trip. My flip-flop jams into the grass, and my cheeks flare as I finally reach for the door handle, fiddling with the keys.

"Back door's open if you need some AC! Or live inspiration!"

I throw myself into the most unbearable heat I can imagine.

But somehow, even the unbearable heat is more bearable than having to face Beau after that toe-curling invite.

16
Bailey

Beau: Back door is open, sugar.

I regret running away. I hate being so stubborn.

If I were smarter than I am stubborn, I'd be in Beau's blissfully cool house, sleeping like a baby. Instead, I'm in the Boiler. I can't sleep, I'm restless, and I hate my life. My skin is damp and clammy, and my internal temperature gauge is totally shot. I'm not sure I'll ever be cool again.

Sure, we get hot spells on the prairies during the summer. But this? This is next-level.

"Fuck it!" Even though I'm beyond tired and barely want to move, I flip myself out of bed and put on the tiniest pieces of clothing I own, planning to go for a swim. Again.

Agitation lines my every movement as I step barefoot down the narrow hallway of my trailer.

Living in a trailer might make me sound like trash, but the fact of the matter is I take a lot of pride in this trailer. I've lovingly cut and glued black-and-white checkerboard linoleum to the floor and repainted all the cabinets, even sewn my window coverings to match.

It's mine, and I made it into one of those that belongs on Pinterest. I'll never get rid of it.

One day, I'll have a cute house and I'll still spend weekends and vacations traveling in this thing. Maybe I'll even be able to afford an exterior paint job and air conditioning for it in the future.

As it stands, for the few days of truly sweltering heat we get, I can't justify it.

I shove the door open and let my eyes flutter shut, waiting for a gust of cooler air. But it never comes. That fresh mountain air I know and love is staying up between the peaks, letting us all suffer down here on the prairies with oppressive nights.

"Uhhh," I moan, but it borders on a cry as I flop down on the spot, feet propped on the metal step of my trailer.

I'm so miserable I could cry.

I sit with my head in my hands, and I think.

I trust Beau, and I know he won't hurt me. He likes to joke around—that's just how he is—and I don't feel threatened by him at all.

So why am I so averse to going into his house?

Because you know you'll never want to leave.

My brain is a smug little bitch, throwing that in my face.

I peek up at the impressive house. It's beautiful and truly unlike any house I've ever seen. For me, where I'm from, it looks like it belongs in a movie. It looks like the type of house I'd close my eyes and envision myself in when my reality became too much to bear.

Where there'd be some cute, wholesome boy hosting a party. Our eyes would meet from across the room. We'd be high school sweethearts, and he'd whisk me away from my shitty life.

Then the sound of my dad's drunken shouting would filter in, and I'd get up and prop a chair under my door.

Fantasy and reality, so close yet still so far apart.

Yet here is that house, that man. They're right there. And they're real.

And here I am, trying to convince myself I don't deserve them.

Teenage me would be horrified.

I guess it's with her in mind that I get up off the step. Teenage Bailey would have run to him days and days ago. She was a romantic at heart.

Young adult Bailey? She's not convinced the back door is open.

But when I try the latch, it clicks, and the door gives way to a rush of blissfully cool air. I sigh and let the flow pull me into the space.

As I stand here, I feel a bit like I'm intruding. After all, I ran away from him today to hide in my trailer.

He just stood there, chuckling.

Fucking dick.

I shut the door behind me, wondering what I'm supposed to do now. Should I call him? Text him? Just shout his name?

It doesn't matter. I know he won't mind.

My gaze lingers on the black leather sectional in the living room that overlooks the riverbank. The thought of laying myself out on cool leather and drifting off is too tempting to resist.

So that's what I do. I plop myself down like a tired burglar. In

149

my tiny cotton shorts and loose crop top, the chilled leather on bare skin is heaven. I'd lay myself out naked if I thought no one was here. I'm at the point where I'd happily lie on the floor just to take my temperature down.

I sigh and stare at the vaulted ceiling with a skylight, so different from the top of my trailer. The light above the stove in the open-concept kitchen is on, which means it's not as dark in here as you might hope.

But I don't care.

As long as it doesn't feel like a frying pan, I'm happy. A simple girl with simple needs.

When I start to doze off, I hear feet padding against the polished concrete floors. Casual and unhurried—unlike my heart rate, which is through the fucking roof.

He whistles a tune, and I debate whether I should sit up and announce myself. That seems like the least weird thing to do, but as I settle on it and sit up, I freeze.

My gaze has just cleared the back of the couch and landed on Naked Beau.

Fully naked.

Head-to-toe naked.

He's whistling and gazing into the fridge. The door covers his head and shoulders but leaves every other inch of his side profile bare.

Narrow waist, round ass—

My eyes go wide when they land on his dick. It's like a porn dick. But flaccid. I stare, trying to figure out if it's just the angle or if it's the fact I haven't seen a penis in real life. Maybe the scale is different.

I duck down, hiding behind the back of the couch but refusing to look away. I'm officially doing my best imitation of that simple line drawing with the head poking up over a wall, little mitted hands curled over the top.

Wide eyes because that little cartoon person is a voyeur. I just know it.

Beau carries on humming to himself as he turns and pulls out all the makings for a sandwich. I dip down, hiding and internally berating myself. Any normal adult would just have announced herself by now. Taken an eyeful. Glanced away politely. Laughed it off.

But I've royally fucked myself because I've waited too long. Now he'll know I was peeking, and I'll never live it down.

I decide I'll stick to my guns and stay hidden, pretend I slept through it when he finds me sleeping on his couch in the morning.

Resolved, I decide there's no harm in peeking again. I've already seen it all. What's one more glance? I'll save it in the brain cam for a rainy day.

Easing up like a stealthy ninja, I let out a quiet sigh when I see he's facing away from me. But the back view is just as good as the front. Or side.

I don't think Beau Eaton has any bad angles.

But his ass? I could die. Everything about the man is big and coarsely muscled. Scars pepper his skin, but they only add to his appeal. The lines in his back and shoulders ripple as he, I don't know—spreads mayonnaise on bread?

Never knew spreading condiments on bread could feel sexual, yet here I am experiencing spontaneous ovulation because of naked sandwich making.

It's making me hungry. But not the food kind. So I stifle a groan

151

and drop back down. Horniness wars with my guilt for drooling over him while he thinks he's alone. It's an invasion of his privacy, but my brain cells packed up and left town the minute I got that side shot of him.

I listen to the sounds of him putting everything away. Shutting the fridge. Footsteps leaving the open living space. I might finally be able to breathe again.

But not before his voice cuts through the silent house. "Sugar, there's a spare bedroom upstairs on the left."

I have never wanted to keel over and die as badly as I do right now.

Of course, he'd figure out I was here. He probably heard me breathing.

I'm startled enough that I shoot up and watch him walk away, round ass bunching with every step.

"And if you want to see me up close, just knock on the door across the hall and ask."

And I officially want to die even more than I did a few seconds ago.

I'm embarrassed enough that I skip the guest bedroom and lie on the couch, silently berating myself until I finally fall asleep.

"Hey! Hey!"

Beau's shouts have me shooting up off the couch. I frantically look around myself, trying to figure out what might be wrong. But the entire house is as he left it when he waltzed out of here on full display.

"Hey!"

I realize he isn't anywhere close. He's just shouting at the top of his lungs. In my dopey daze, my first thought was an intruder, but the more my head clears, the more I think an intruder wouldn't start out on the second floor.

I get up and rush across the smooth stone floors, almost chilled by their coolness. Or by the sound of Beau calling out, "Hey!"

Over and over again.

It starts off loud but becomes more distraught, more defeated the longer it goes on.

I don't knock on his bedroom door. I push right through to find his large, naked body thrashing on the king-sized bed across the room. The digital clock in the corner shows 2:11 a.m.

The pained moans spilling from his lips make my stomach drop.

He's having a nightmare. A painful, stressful, frantic nightmare. And I have no idea what to do.

The feeling of helplessness pricks at my eyes as I watch him struggling against thin air, reliving some sort of horror.

And my heart can't take it.

I might get knocked across the room by a stray limb, but I don't care.

I approach his bed, calmly chanting, "Beau. Beau. Beau." I reach out with caution and touch his shoulder. He stills almost instantly but doesn't wake. "Hey, Beau. I'm here."

"You're here." His voice cracks and he reaches for me. His clammy palm clamps around my arm.

"Yeah. It's Bailey. I'm here. You're okay."

"You're here," he says again. This time, his tone bleeds relief. This time, he tugs me toward him.

And I go. I don't have it in me to resist him right now. As I climb on his bed, my chest aches from his expression—pinched forehead, eyes squeezed shut, and no trace of the humor that painted his handsome features mere hours ago.

With one hand on my arm and one at my waist, he drags me to him, gathering me against his chest.

And very naked body.

But this isn't sexual.

I'm not sure he recognizes who I am right now, but he holds me like I'm a comfort to him. He holds me like I held my sadly departed stuffed horse.

His thick arms wrap around me as I sprawl over him, head tucked under his chin, listening to the sound of his heartbeat.

I can feel the bulge of his cock, firm but not hard, against my inner thigh where my shorts have ridden up.

I can feel his chest hair against my bare breasts where my flimsy crop top has been displaced.

I can feel his deep breaths, his lungs filling and emptying, making me rise and fall in time as though I'm riding a wave while he catches his breath.

"What time is it, Bailey?" His voice is all gravel, his hold not loosening.

I peek over my shoulder at the clock. "Two twelve."

One of his palms slides up the column of my spine to cup the back of my head. "Good."

Then I feel him kiss my hair.

17

Beau

I shouldn't have dragged her into my arms. Not when we're here, alone, in the dark.

Not when I'm unraveled the way I am right now.

Not when I can't blame it on being for show.

Not when I want to do so much—

Bailey's head turns and her lips dust across the hollow at the base of my throat. I swallow, Adam's apple working as she kisses just below it again. Puffy lips press against my chest.

Awareness trickles in as her nipples harden and point against my chest.

I should stop.

My hand slides down her firm back, toned from long hours spent working, and my fingers dust over the thick elastic waistband that they meet.

I should stop.

She kisses me again. Same spot. But her tongue darts against my skin this time. Her back arches, pushing her tits down and her ass up.

155

"Fuck," the word is a breath, a hushed curse marking me, knowing I'm about to go too far.

I should stop.

My hand travels further, and I grip her ass. It's more than just fabric. The shorts have shifted, and it's smooth skin. My fingers dig in, the tips of them dangerously close to where no man has gone before.

It's her fucking moan as she presses herself back into my grip that nearly undoes me.

"Bailey." I'm too keyed up. She's too close. Feels too good. Smells too delicious.

She inches down, strands of her hair slipping through my fingers as she kisses lower on my chest. My hand is still kneading the flesh of her ass when she whispers, "Are you okay?"

"No," I grit out. My dick swells at the nearness of her, the smell, the weight. The way she's just *here* in the wake of me totally freaking out.

"Me neither." Her hot breath fans against my chest.

I realize I'm holding her in place, one hand gripping her ass, the other with a fist full of her hair. My cock goes rock-hard faster than I can fight it off. The thought of filling her with it is more present than ever.

"Tell me how to make you feel okay," I say, my voice rumbling across the top of her head. She hasn't lifted her face, hasn't chanced looking me in the eye.

I think we both might think more clearly if she did.

"Don't stop touching me."

My head tips back and I groan. The things this girl says.

Her lips move over my chest again. "How can I make *you* feel okay?" Her ass lifts higher, knees pushing into the bed on either side of my body. Begging me to explore her.

While I turn her question over in my mind, I let my hands roam along the smooth skin down the back of her thigh to the crook of her knee that she's pushed up onto while straddling me. My nails rake over the skin of her inner thigh, tiny bumps crop up in their wake.

"Bailey . . . I should stop." I say it out loud, the warning sign that's been flashing in my head for the past several minutes.

Stopping feels like it would be pure torture right now, but I'd do it. I should do it.

"No. Please." The words rush from her, breathy and desperate. "Please don't stop."

My breathing grows labored, and all I'm doing is lying on my back. I trail my fingers over the gusset of her shorts, tracing the seam. I could reach beneath the fabric so easily.

Her head turns, cheek pressing against my chest. Face down. Ass up. Hands on my shoulders. Bailey begs me again. "Please . . . tell me how to make you feel better. But don't stop."

My fingers curl around the strands of her onyx hair, and I give a firm tug.

She whimpers and grinds herself against my fingers.

I don't know how we got so far past the line of appropriate, so far past the line of *faking*. But the 2:11 version of me lacks control, and he's the only version of me that's here right now.

"I'd feel okay if you started sleeping in the guest room, Bailey."

She nods, dragging my fist along with her head as she does. My dick juts up, bumping against her stomach.

"And I'd feel even better if you let me reach into these flimsy fucking shorts and make you come on my fingers."

A breath rushes from her lips and sweeps across my chest.

I should stop.

"Yes," she replies breathlessly. Her stomach presses into my length while my fingers curl around the curve of her ass, teasing that line between her thigh and her pussy. "Yes."

"Fuck," I mutter again, because no matter how many times I tell myself I should stop, I won't.

My hand inches forward until I feel her wetness. I swipe through gently, my body almost shaking under the strain of holding back. The dark part of me wants to flip her over and fuck her. Impale her and listen to her scream my name.

But that's not what this is. That's not who she is. I want to handle Bailey with care.

Her hips push back, and the tip of my finger slides in.

"Oh god." She rolls her forehead over my chest, and I'm pretty sure I stop breathing as she rocks herself against my finger.

"Bailey." I groan her name and pull out to spread her wetness over her clit. Her legs tremble on either side of my waist as I do. "Fuck."

Her lips land back on my chest, and one hand grips my shoulder while the other braces above my head on the bed frame.

I press in again, further this time, and feel her clamp down around my finger. "You're fucking soaked."

She nods once more.

With one finger inside her, the others explore between her legs. Lips, clit, sliding up and down her slit. "If it's too much, you'll tell me?"

"Yes, yes." She chants the words, hot shaky breaths against my skin. "Do it again."

"Do what?" I murmur against her ear as she writhes above me.

"Finger fuck me." Her words are languid, not shy at all.

"Like this?" I slide in and out, setting an even and torturous tempo.

She lifts her head to peer over her shoulder. No doubt trying to see the way her body fits against mine, the way I have angled my arm around behind her. "Yeah, like that."

My muscles burn, but I don't give a fuck. It's nothing compared to the way my dick is throbbing from feeling Bailey all tight and wet, riding my fingers.

"What about this?" I slow my motions and add a second finger to join the first, toying with her entrance before easing into her slick heat. A gentle twist of my hand has her crying out, and her head drops back down to my chest.

"You like that, Bailey? Are two fingers better than one?" I push in further, spurred on by the needy mewling noises she's making.

A soft, "Yes," spills from her damp lips before she drags them over my collarbones, up the side of my neck—while still avoiding my face.

"In and out only? Or with a twist? I want to know." My utmost desire is to know absolutely everything that drives her crazy. We can learn it together.

"Twist." She's gone monosyllabic, and I take a perverse sort of pleasure in stealing her pleasure and her words.

I work both fingers in and out, slowly twisting, her wetness surging around me.

Her body trembles.

Her hips rotate.

Her body pulses.

Our breaths come out sharp and choppy.

"Look at me, Bailey. You gonna come for me, Bailey? Just like I told you to?"

"Yesss," she hisses, now bucking against me as she draws back just enough to meet my eyes.

I shove in hard a few times, getting off on the throaty noises she makes. Then I pull out, sliding back and forth over her clit. It only takes a few times until she shatters.

"Fuck! Beau!" She yanks my hair, and her teeth clamp down on my neck. The soaked insides of her thighs spread as she tumbles down on top of me, chest to chest. Her knees give out and she loses purchase on my sheets, slim legs slipping as they clamp my sides.

Her pussy pulses and slides over the edge of my cock. Down the vein, right to the base, where she stalls, trying to catch her breath with my full, round head pressed to her navel.

The worst fucking tease.

It's a temptation so fucking strong I gasp for air and extricate myself from her soft, needy body.

Away from the bed at last, I stand and run my hands through my hair, needing to step away from her so I don't go any further than I just did.

Way too fucking far.

I promised her I wouldn't fuck her. I promised to help make things better for her. And I meant it.

She's young and sweet, and has her entire life ahead of her. I'm the last thing she needs complicating her situation.

This arrangement? It's a glorified bet. And she deserves better.

I should have stopped.

18
Bailey

Bailey: Take tonight off. Go to bed early. I'm fine.
Beau: No, thanks.
Bailey: Seriously, you can't stay up late with me and then wake up an hour later doing your thing.
Beau: My thing?
Bailey: 2:11
Beau: Bailey, you do your thing, and I'll do mine. And mine includes sitting at your bar, so you aren't alone.

The knife slices through the lime, and a fresh wave of pain hums through my veins as the citrus juice hits my paper cut. But I don't even flinch.

I can feel Beau's eyes on me from where he sits at the end of the bar, and I'm sure if I show an iota of pain, he'll call 911 to have me airlifted to the nearest hospital. We may be on tense terms right

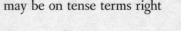

now, but he's still here, guarding me like a German shepherd, ready to leap to my defense.

I'm also not oblivious to the fact Gary is watching us, drunken interest all over his face.

My head shakes as I recall the conversation Beau and I had the morning after ... whatever that was. The morning I'd woken up alone in his bed and gone searching for him.

"I'm sorry I took advantage of you."

Those were his first words when I found him in the kitchen.

My eyes bugged out at hickey I'd left on his neck—the one that's still there today, although more yellow and less purple. I didn't know what to expect him to say in that moment. Because the night before he'd looked down at me, hands on his head, with the most confusing mixture of lust and rage on his face. Then he left without a single word, and my heart dropped. I wanted to follow him, and yet I knew he needed space and control.

"You didn't."

"It's my job to keep you safe. And that includes from me."

"It's literally not."

"We agreed we wouldn't cross that line. We laid everything out. I want you to stay in the house, but if you hear me in here ... you can't come in."

I tried not to stare at the way his back strained against the T-shirt he still wore from the night before as he bent down and slid his new double-walled socks into his new Blundstones. *He expected me to just lay there and listen to him panic?*

"I'm not going to stay here." I lifted my chin, forcing myself to appear prideful in a way that was a complete mismatch for how I felt inside.

And he didn't even bother glancing at me when he said, *"You can stay in the house, or I'll pay to have your trailer equipped with air conditioning. Your call."* Then he slapped the door frame and left the house.

That was two days ago. Two nights of me waking up at 2:11—exactly—and walking across the hallway. Two nights of me wrapping my hand around his doorknob because I couldn't handle listening to him shout.

And then stopping.

We made a deal, and I know all about people not respecting your privacy. This last incident wasn't the first time my brothers ransacked my space searching for something.

For the last two nights, I've reminded myself that Beau is a grown-ass man, capable of making grown-up decisions and setting grown-up boundaries.

And my job as a fellow grown-up is to respect those boundaries.

Which is why I go back to my room, pull my pillow over my head and try not to hear him. But it's impossible. It's stressful. And even though the heat isn't keeping me awake anymore, the anxiety of knowing he's *right there* and all alone is worse than sleeping in the Boiler.

I slice through the next lime and cut a line through the middle of the wedge so it can rest on the edge of a cup. I'm just exhausted enough that I don't stop the knife in time before it continues its motion right over my finger.

"Fuck!" I toss the knife and instantly lift my finger to my mouth.

"You okay?" I can hear the alarm in Beau's voice as he shoves his stool away and pushes through the small wooden doors that divide the space between patrons and staff. He looms over me and reaches for my wrist, rotating my hand to inspect the damage, which is limited.

"I'm fine." I try to tug my wrist free. "It's not the first time I've cut myself, and it won't be the last. Go sit back down." I yank again, avoiding his gaze as I bring my finger back up to my mouth. As I stem the light trickle of blood, I turn away to grab the first aid kit we store behind the bar.

With it laid out in front of me, I rifle through the contents, looking for the correct Band-Aid size.

"Let me," Beau says in a soft voice. It's a fucking punch to the gut. When he's all stoic and removed, it's easier to be irritated with him.

I let out a heavy sigh and finally tilt my head, gazing up at him. Genuine concern fills his silver eyes, along with something else. Paired with the way his tongue darts out over his lips, he appears almost nervous.

His gaze searches my face as his hand wraps around my wrist again, this time more gently, guiding my finger from my mouth. It strikes me this might be the first time we've made eye contact in the past couple of days.

Since Harvey put the announcement in the paper, all eyes have been on us, but our eyes haven't been on each other.

I blink away, not wanting to stare for too long. Because if I do, my body will react. I'll step closer and—

"It doesn't look too bad." Beau furrows his brow as he assesses the world's most inconsequential cut.

"That's what I told you," I reply through gritted teeth.

He seems amused by my annoyance, which just annoys me more.

Deft fingers pull the Band-Aid from its wrapper, and he places it with meticulous care. I can't help but be entranced by him—so big and gruff yet so gentle.

He wraps the sticky ends together and delicately presses my hand between both of his. Making a little Bailey hand sandwich. "There."

Despite all my self-talk about being an adult, I can't bring myself to meet his gaze, so I mumble, "Thanks," and turn away to resume work.

He lingers for a moment, then slowly moves away, back to his seat.

Back to his tea.

Back to watching me like a hawk.

And when Gary slurs, "Trouble in paradise?" I reply with a perky, "Never," and go back to cutting limes. Because after a week spent applying for other jobs, I'm still getting nothing more than a pitying look and a polite, "We're not hiring right now," even though the job is listed online.

When we made this bet, I knew my reputation might be beyond saving. I knew that he was wrong and I was right. I knew I'd probably "win"—whatever that means.

But winning has never felt worse. Because I know my place in Chestnut Springs, and spending time pretending it's at Beau Eaton's side just makes it hurt more.

The quiet buzz of my phone vibrating beside my mattress wakes me.

It's 2:00 a.m. and the urge to shut my phone down, roll over, and go back to sleep is strong. But the extra eleven minutes won't make a difference. No matter how I spin it, I'll be tired tomorrow.

It's agonizing to hear Beau struggle only a few feet from where I'm lying.

At 2:11, we're both haunted. Me, by the way I felt captured in his hold, coming apart above him while he whispered my name against my hair. Him by . . . well, I'm not entirely sure. But I can guess.

Either way, I want to rewrite 2:11 into something different for us. We're stuck together in this little arrangement, and it doesn't need to be this awkward.

Or maybe it's just me being awkward because I can't masturbate without thinking of that night.

"Okay," I grumble to myself and shake away the arousal that sweeps through me every time I recall the way he gripped my hair while he kneaded my ass. I've never felt so *needed*. "Let's do this."

I roll from my bed, grab the bag I set near the door, and pad across the hallway, checking my watch.

2:02.

I knock on his door firmly but with a measured pace, wanting to wake him up while avoiding any sense of urgency that will freak him out. Beau doesn't need any extra freaking out—he already does that on his own.

It occurred to me today, as he tended to my finger and then sat vigil while I finished out my shift, that he's become hyper-fixated on taking care of me.

But who is taking care of him?

I hear rustling and knock again.

2:03.

"Beau, get up." I keep my voice light and airy.

"Bailey?" He's up and at the door like a shot, ripping it open.

My mouth goes dry when he towers over me, wearing nothing but his boxers.

I secretly hoped he'd be naked again. No one has ever looked as good naked as Beau Eaton.

"What's wrong?" His hand lands on my shoulder, drawing me close as he leans out the door and checks both directions of the hallway, assessing for danger.

I place a gentle palm against his chest and give it a reassuring pat. "Nothing. Let's go."

His chin drops now as he looks me over. "Go where?"

"Swimming."

His face scrunches in confusion, hand still branding me where his fingers curl over onto my back. "What time is it?"

I check my watch. Again. "It's 2:04."

"Why would I want to go swimming now?"

My head tilts as I consider what to say to him next. "Because it seems a lot more fun than hitting 2:11 and screaming in your bed. For both of us."

His hand drops from my shoulder and his eyes trace my features in the darkened hallway. His gaze is steely in both color and intensity, more than I can withstand.

I turn and wave a hand over my shoulder. "Let's go, soldier. I'm not even planning on wearing a bathing suit."

19

Beau

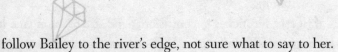

I follow Bailey to the river's edge, not sure what to say to her. And not strong enough to say no.

I'm not even strong enough to look away when she casually undresses. Instead, I admire the smooth curves of her bare skin highlighted by the soft glow of the moon.

She doesn't spare me a glance as she slips into the black water. The gentle sound of it bubbling and rushing creates a sense of privacy. It seems strange to think we just happened upon each other in this exact place not so long ago. That she's been swimming naked in front of my house for who knows how many years.

"You gonna come in?" she calls once she's submerged enough to cover just over her nipples. She's like a goddess with the swells of her breasts on display, the tips of her long hair plastered over her collarbones.

I have no idea what I'm doing. I feel out of my element. Out of control around her.

Consumed by that night, by the guilt of going too far, and

by the knowledge that it plays on repeat in my mind twenty-four seven.

I still wake up at 2:11, distraught. Except now, by 2:15, I'm fisting my cock and dreaming about sliding it into her.

Skinny dipping with her might be a bad idea, but I can't stomach the idea of telling her *no* again, so I start undressing. I kick my shoes off and face her full on, half expecting her to turn and shy away from me exposing myself.

But she doesn't.

She watches with rapt fascination, a blatant level of interest as I slide my boxers down over my hips and let them fall at my feet. I toss them onto the log where she discarded her pajamas and make my way toward the water. My eyes stay on her face, while hers focus on my dick.

"Is your penis normal big? Or like ... " She worries her bottom lip before holding her hands up in that twelve-inch spread again. "*Big* big?"

"Bailey." I shake my head, my voice disbelieving and gruff all at once. "You can't just ask people things like that."

She presses her lips together and blinks away from my cock before moving onto her back to float. "Why not? You just stripped in front of me. And we're engaged. And I practically sat on it the other night. It seems like a reasonable question to me."

I groan as I slip into the water. "Trust me, Bailey. If you sat on it the other night, you'd still be feeling it today."

She jolts back upright as I approach her, eyes wide and dancing with interest. "Does that mean it's *big*, big?"

A deep chuckle rumbles in my chest. Being able to laugh any-where around 2:11 is a fucking treat. "Yeah, Bailey. It's *big*, big."

She slaps the water. "I knew it! I was trying to compare it with porn. You know? But, like . . . the scale seems off on my phone screen, and it was dark in your room, so I didn't get a good look—"

"Bailey." I close my eyes, sink down, and pull a few handfuls of water up over my face.

"Sorry."

But she doesn't sound sorry. I can hear the smile in her voice. The water swishes as she spins in place like whatever innocent but filthy mermaid she's portraying.

It really is the most charming combination. Old enough to not be freaked out by sex but inexperienced enough to be flat-out curious.

She's going to be the death of me.

And my restraint.

We float in silence for several minutes. Me, trying to rid myself of the insta-boner she gave me, and her . . . I don't know, just swishing around.

It's peaceful.

"I think you should tell me about 2:11," is how she shatters the peace.

I knew this was coming when she referenced the timestamp before. She's a bright young woman—perceptive—so it shouldn't surprise me she put it together.

Deep down, I might be ready to talk about it. There's no shrink couch here. She's not holding a notepad or assessing me like I'm an experiment.

I am one of the lucky ones who has ample access to therapy, but one of the dumb ones who won't go. I know I should, but it fills me with dread. And I've had enough of that to last me a lifetime.

Several minutes pass as I consider her question and replay that night in my head. The days that followed.

"It was 2:11 a.m. when I walked out of that bunker with Micah draped over my shoulders."

The swishing stops, and she pushes upright. I opt to look at the moon rather than the dark orbs of her eyes.

"I checked my watch and could see the helicopter taking off. And I knew what time I needed to be back at our extraction point to get on the transport back out. I knew that if I kept going further back into that tunnel system, I wouldn't make it out in time."

I hear her sigh.

"But I kept going anyway. I could hear him screaming. And I—" I swipe an agitated hand over my mouth. "Fuck, I just couldn't leave him there, you know? He was our mission, and I could hear him. He was right *there*. I couldn't leave."

"Would you do it differently if you could go back in time?"

"No." My response comes instantly. I repeat myself to drive the point home. "No."

"Then why do you sound like you're beating yourself up about it?"

"Because everyone treats me like I did something heroic by refusing to turn back, and that's . . . that's not what it was."

I cup my hands and splash my face.

A few beats pass as I wait for Bailey to ask me what I mean, but she goes back to turning in the water, arching her slender neck back to dip her head into the chill.

"They train us differently for JTF2. Choose us differently. It's more psychological, not just physical. We're prepared differently. I have this strategy, a way I break things down in my head, and it works. I mean, of course, some of the shit I've seen has fucked me up, but it's mostly manageable if I'm being honest."

Bailey hums thoughtfully, trailing her fingers through the water. I don't feel like she's psychoanalyzing me, or judging me, or even trying to help me. She's just here, listening.

Actually, as she picks a twig up off the surface of the creek and tosses it to the shore, I'm not even sure if she's listening. But it's better this way.

"I would lie in bed and force myself to think about all the worst outcomes while falling asleep. Like, the first time I would kill someone. I'd look at it, force myself to wallow in it for a minute, really feel it. And then I'd shift to thinking about how I'd cope with those feelings, where I'd tuck them away when it was time to move on. So many times I felt like I'd already faced something when it actually came. I think it desensitized me."

"Shit, and here I was counting sheep."

I huff out a laugh. *Only Bailey.*

"So I had this plan for myself. I programmed it in. Set it and forget it. I knew what I'd do if we found Micah Lane. I'd stop at nothing. I analyzed what I'd do—the actions I'd take—if I became a POW. I mean, shit," I scrub at my hair, glancing around the peaceful riverbed. "I even made peace with dying. The prospect of death doesn't bother me anymore. I don't fear it. The cave—sure, it haunts me some days. But not the way people think. The worst part of it all is that for all my obsessive mental preparation, I never let myself analyze what it would feel like to be *out*, living life as a civilian. To be . . . "

"Famous?" Bailey says it with a light giggle. Even she knows that's a stretch.

I snort. "I doubt that's the word for it."

A grin stretches her lips. Only Bailey would smile after that story. "Infamous."

I grimace. "Isn't that kind of bad?"

Her finger shoots up. "Notorious!"

"Not that one either."

"I got it . . ." Her hands make a sweeping motion. "Legendary."

I submerge my head underwater to keep from bursting out laughing.

When I come back up, she adds, "Fabled."

"Jesus, Bailey."

"Renowned. Famed. Celebrated!"

Now I do laugh. "I'm engaged to a thesaurus."

The white of her teeth flashes at me. "Merriam-Webster is a way better nickname than sugar tits. Just saying."

"Sorry, sugar. That one's sticking."

I see a shiver rack her body as she glances away for a beat. Maybe she's cold, but this is nice, and I'm being greedy. I don't want to get out of the water.

Bailey makes 2:11 better.

"So . . ." Her attention is turned away, so I let myself soak her in. The elegance in the way she carries herself, the curve of her neck, the little divot above her upper lip. "You wake up at the same time every night because . . ."

A heavy sigh rushes from me. "Therapist told me it's because 2:11 is the visual representation of the choice that forever changed my life in ways I wasn't prepared for. Every night I wake up and feel the fire on my feet. The burning is so hot it almost feels cold. I hear the rhythmical whipping sound of the Blackhawk blades overhead, and I feel

173

a deep sense of knowing settling in my bones. Knowing that I'm not going to make it back on that transport. And even though I know it, I turn around to go get Micah, but when I do, all I see is endless, thick black. The kind that swallows you, the kind you get lost in forever. Every night I try to turn around and call out for them to wait for me, but it's already pure darkness all around me. My purpose is gone."

I turn my gaze down and breathe slowly. I've never told anyone about that dream before.

My hands sluice through the water. The river is dark, but not as dark as everything feels at 2:11. I don't feel terror looking at the inky liquid, but it does echo the bleakness I often feel.

Then I lift my head and my eyes catch on Bailey.

And I feel a spark of hope.

With a fist to my mouth, I clear my throat and forge ahead. "I guess it signifies the end of the job I've loved forever—my identity in every way that I've come to know it. The beginning of a life that . . . well, I never envisioned what I'd do when I got out. Didn't want to, so I never faced it. Kept telling everyone I'd leave the military soon, but in my head, that wasn't the plan. I think that's what haunts me. I never saw a different career, or a relationship, or having to act gracious to people who are congratulating me just for doing my job. It's weird. I promised my family for years I'd come back and work on the ranch, but it's boring."

"Only boring people get bored," she replies, flipping herself up to float. The peaks of her nipples crest the water as she does.

"Okay, harsh." My voice cracks and I lick my lips, willing away the urge to reach out and palm her breasts.

"Those are possibly the only words of wisdom my dad ever imparted on me."

"Sorry, taking advice from Mr. Jansen isn't on my bingo card this year."

She doesn't react; she just keeps floating, staring up at the velvet night. "You're a good guy, Beau. But you're kind of out of touch."

"Come again?"

"Do you know how many people out there do jobs they don't like? Or are bored with their profession? They get up and go do a job they hate with every fiber of their being because they depend on that paycheck to live. They don't have a supportive family and a beautiful house to fall back on. That's real life. Being a shitty employee and unreliable at the job you said you'd do because it bores you . . . " She moves to standing, reaching up to push her hair away from her face. "That's a privilege. Recognize it."

My molars clamp down as I swallow. For all my internal monologuing about liking how Bailey doesn't treat me like everyone else, this feels rough.

Because she's right.

"Maybe you wake up at that time every night because you know you need to make a plan. If that's what brought you comfort before, why stop? If you hate working at the ranch, don't. But have the balls to tell the people who've been supporting you. And then *do* something rather than wallowing around in misery."

A dry, disbelieving chuckle bubbles up from my chest. "You really have no filter, huh?"

"You have too big of a dick to feel this bad for yourself. Literally, everything is at the tips of your fingers. Try a little gratitude, Beau. It will change the way you see things. Plus, someone needs to give you a dose of reality. Might as well be your fiancée."

It's my turn to push back into the water and float, looking up at

175

the night sky. I'm hit with an intense wave of déjà vu. Floating here as a boy. I've always loved the river. The sound, the smell, the sensation of being weightless in the water. I'm not sure when I stopped going in and opted to just stare at it instead.

"Okay, fiancée, what do you think I should do? You're the best example I can think of for a person who is taking charge of their life."

Bailey comes up close before flipping on her back to float next to me. Her fingers brush against mine, sending a jolt of awareness through my limbs.

The two of us, in the water together, stripped down in more ways than one.

One of my biggest struggles is going from feeling so needed, so important, so integral to a mission to . . . not.

But with Bailey, I feel like she needs me, and I need her.

"I don't know, Beau. I can't make that decision for you. But I can hang with you while you figure it out."

"I'd like that."

20
Bailey

Bailey: See you at two, soldier.
Beau: See you at two, sugar tits.

M y knuckles rap against the door. "Another night, another swim. Let's go, soldier!"

This is our new normal. Every night, I set my alarm for 2:00 a.m. and come to wake him. And every time Beau yanks the door open, my breath comes to a screeching halt in my lungs.

Like now.

Big, golden, dopey. I want nothing more than to push him back into his room and crawl on top of him like we did a week ago. I want his big, warm palm sliding down my back and gripping my ass, but we seem to have mostly moved past that.

Or maybe just Beau has. Me? I still obsess.

I try to cover for the way I'm ogling all eight of his abs by snapping, "You know you could set your own alarm, right?"

He follows me out, and I can hear the smile in his voice when he says, "But I prefer to be woken up by you."

I roll my eyes, in frustration. I try to be nice to Beau, a confidante, a support to him, and honestly, it feels like I really am his fiancée in all the ways except the sex way.

The further we get from that night without him addressing it, or touching me, or flirting with me, the more it feels like it never happened.

We swim, and some nights we talk a lot.

Tonight, we don't. I don't know if it's because we're both beyond tired or if something has shifted between us.

"You're quiet tonight," he says as we slip naked into the water.

I suppose by now we could start wearing swimsuits, but we don't. I don't even feel like I'm being a creep now when I stare at his body.

In fact, I stare longer. So does he. Neither of us seems to be uncomfortable with the staring. I don't know if it's because he likes what he sees or doesn't particularly care about what he sees.

And I'm too chickenshit to ask.

"So are you," I reply, pushing out to the deepest point of the river where I can't touch. This is where I force my legs to cycle and work so that when I get back to the house, I'm tired enough to crash back out.

"Been thinking," Beau replies.

"Thinking is exhausting." I chuckle softly, feeling the swell and pull of water as he moves close to me.

Super close.

So close our knees bump.

"It is. I went back to it lately. After our swims. I imagine all the things I could do and how I'll handle it. How I'll tell my family."

I watch him, nodding slowly. He's been more reliable around the ranch, helping Cade and his dad. I guess that bit of unfiltered tough love did him some good after all.

"Part of what wakes me up is the sensation of my feet burning. I scorched them when I walked through that fire to get back through the tunnels. They were so mangled, so infected that I was sure the infection would kill me. I may have saved Micah, but in the days that followed, when we holed up in that cave? He took care of me."

"You ever talk to him?"

Beau nods. "Yeah, we email now and then. I think I'd like to visit him sometime."

"You should," I agree.

The hush of the quiet night stretches between us.

"How's the job hunt going?" His unwavering gaze never leaves mine. I'm not dumb enough to think he doesn't know how it's going. I'd tell him if anything came of it and me never bringing it up is a dead giveaway.

"It's going." I refuse to be all woe is me about it.

"I think we need to go out. Be seen together more. We kinda hide out at the bar and at our house."

Our house startles me.

"It's not enough. We need to sell it."

"But you'll win the bet if I don't get a job."

"What bet?"

My eyes roll. "The one where you bet me that being associated with you wouldn't help me get a new job. You knew then I was a lost cause. It's looking like you were right."

"I don't remember that."

His intentional ignorance irritates me, and my hands swish through the water, pushing a wave of it at him. "The bet? The deal? The fake engagement? The *we're not having sex*? I'll take you to a hospital if you keep floating there, pretending you don't remember."

"I remember it differently. I remember thinking that you didn't need my name or my association to get a job because you were smart and capable and qualified on your own. I remember thinking there's no way people would hold your family name against you that thoroughly. Now I know that this town is a lost cause and you're too good for it."

My chest goes tight, and a prickling sensation takes root beneath my eyelids. No one has ever said anything like that to me.

Ever.

I clear my throat. "Okay, well, be that as it may, you must still want to win the bet."

He waves me off casually, even though the words he says next feel anything but casual. "I've never wanted to lose a bet so badly in my life. Is it even a bet, Bailey? What were the terms? What did I get if I won?"

I blink, trying to think back. Was there really nothing in this for him? That couldn't be.

"Well, you said you wanted your family off your back."

He laughs wryly, looking away as his big, strong hand combs through his wet hair. "They're gonna be right back up in my shit the minute you break up with me. Possibly worse, actually."

Panic surges in me, and where I was borderline cold, I'm suddenly very, very hot. "So this is just . . . a pity arrangement?"

"No, Bailey. It's not that." His voice went from cool and collected to rough gravel with a hint of steel.

"What is it then? You playing hero with my life?"

"I'm here because I want to be."

My head shakes. "There isn't even sex in this for you. You made it clear you didn't want any more of that, so—"

He cuts me off. "I wanted more."

My heart goes from thudding loudly, drowning out all other sounds, to still and silent. "What?"

"You shouldn't lose your virginity during a bet. I don't want that for you."

"I thought it wasn't a bet."

His jaw works. "It's a glorified bet."

"If you hadn't known I was a virgin, would you have fucked me?"

He fidgets now, hand scrubbing at his beard as he groans. "Jesus, Bailey."

"Would you?"

He looks away, down river, before turning back to me. Slowly. There's a sudden predatory vibe in the way he carries himself, in the way he moves. "Thoroughly."

Maybe I should be flattered, but I'm not. I'm irritated.

With a disbelieving scoff, I move toward the shore, trying to hide my offense that a man I barely know is telling me what I should and shouldn't do with *my* body.

"Well, I broke my hymen with a toy some time ago. So I'm not sure what's so sacred to you. It's *my* virginity. Feel free to take that benchmark of mine off of *your* pedestal anytime now."

I reach down, grabbing my clothes, barely taking the time to wrap myself in a towel before sliding my feet back into my sandals.

"Bailey—"

I don't want to hear from him right now. I want him to be as uncomfortable as I am, so I guess that's why I toss back, "Besides, if you weren't so lacking in creativity, you'd know there's lots we can do that isn't sex."

Then I leave him there without taking a single glance back.

21
Beau

Beau: You at home?

Bailey: Yes.

Beau: What are you doing?

Bailey: Edging.

Bailey: FML. I am *EDITING*.

Bailey: My resume. Polishing it up. Changing a few things.

Beau: We really just going to skip over the edging part?

Bailey: Yes. It was an autocorrect.

Beau: Why does your phone assume you mean edging though?

Bailey: Guess my phone knows you.

"What is *that*?" Bailey points at the shiny black and chrome Harley I just pulled up on.

I bought it to give myself something to do that isn't holding my dick while thinking about you.

I don't say that, though. Instead, I say, "My new motorcycle," like the Neanderthal I am around her.

"But why?" She lifts her sunglasses off her eyes, pushing them back on her head. I know what she looks like, but I study the movement. She's painted her nails a pretty peach color that pops against the tan tone of her skin. Her lips glisten with gloss, and a bead of sweat trails down her chest, right between her breasts. The ones propped up in a creamy orange triangle bikini top.

I assume she's wearing matching bottoms, but I refuse to let my eyes trail that far down.

Today I'm in control. I won't ogle the twenty-two-year-old propped on a lounger, sunbathing on my back deck.

"Because I wanted to."

"Is this a thing you've always wanted?"

My head quirks as I rip off my helmet. "No. Does it need to be?"

Her gaze peruses me all the way down and then all the way back up. She's blatant. And it makes me wonder why I keep thinking of Bailey as innocent or treating her like she's made of glass.

The girl flat out told me we could do things that aren't sex, like I didn't know that was an option.

But I've always known it was. And I've always known it wouldn't be enough.

She crosses her legs tightly and glances away. "Just seems kind of unsafe."

I take a couple of steps closer to my back deck, even though I dread coming that close to her.

Proximity to Bailey has an intoxicating effect.

"We could all die tomorrow, Bailey. Gotta do what makes us happy today."

Now her gaze is back on me, and her brow rises. She's silently rubbing my face in what we talked about just last night.

Would you have fucked me? She threw the words at me like weapons, didn't lower her volume or dance around the subject.

I glare at her until her plush lips tip up in a knowing smirk. She lowers her sunglasses and settles back in her lounger as though dismissing me. "If I didn't know you were a total stick in the mud, I'd say your new personality trait is impulsiveness."

I puff up with a bit of defensiveness at that. After years of special forces training, my impulse control is something I pride myself on.

You can't be impulsive on missions. It'll get you killed.

Or stranded.

I shove that thought away as quickly as it springs to life. "I am not impulsive," I mutter and glance at the creek, wondering if I should grab my fishing gear and head out for the afternoon. It's Saturday after all. Normal people do things like going fishing on Saturdays.

"Could have fooled me." She glides a palm over the length of her slender arm, as though rubbing more sunscreen in.

"Bailey." I sigh out her name. In a lot of ways, I appreciate her candor. In a lot of ways, she tests my patience.

"You decide to pick up a short-lived drinking habit at my bar." She holds her hand up, lifting her fingers as she prepares to list all the ways I am out of control. "You look for fights in said bar."

"I don't—"

185

"You get engaged to a girl you barely know, mostly for shits and giggles. You buy an absurdly expensive ring for her." She flips that finger up and waves her hand in my direction.

A grin stretches across my face. I don't regret that ring, not for one fucking minute. "Don't see you complaining, sugar."

Bailey shoots me a saucy glare, and, fuck, she looks her age when she does. Ponytail high on her head. Silky, lithe body sprawled on my chaise lounge. Nails painted obnoxiously bright.

"And now you buy a motorcycle? Apparently, I'm the only one you're terrified of being impulsive with."

She sounds bratty. The tilt of her head makes me want to fist that thick ponytail, give it a tug, and tell her to watch her fucking tone.

I shove my fists into the pockets of my jeans, it's far too hot standing around in leather and denim under the scalding sun. Or maybe she's the one I should blame for feeling like I'm suffocating.

"Felt pretty impulsive when you came that hard on my fingers, Bailey."

Her sunglasses cover her eyes, but she's glaring at me. I can tell by the way her lips purse, by the way she crosses her arms under her pert breasts and her shoulders creep up.

"Put some clothes on. I'm taking you to the town fair."

"No, thank you."

"Yeah? How's the job hunt going, Bailey?"

She tips her chin up defiantly. "Great. I dropped off a bunch of resumes this morning."

"And this week?"

Her jaw ticks. "You know I did."

"Hear anything back?"

"Fuck you," she murmurs with a shake of her head, clearly frustrated.

"You can't keep letting those assholes see that you're scared of them."

"I'm not!" she snaps, and I know I've hit a sensitive spot.

"You're better than them, Bailey."

We have a silent staredown. I know she'll never respond to my statement. I suspect, deep down, she doesn't believe the words.

But I do.

"Get dressed. We leave in"—I lift a wrist to check my watch—"two hours. I'll take you to dinner first."

"No."

"Fine. I'll take you wearing that." I wave a hand over her orange bikini. "Since I'm so impulsive, I'll probably break the wrist of every fucker who so much as looks at you."

Her jaw drops, mouth opening so daintily. The speechless reaction fuels me, so I prop my helmet on the new bike and bound up the stairs to get showered.

But not before I stop at her chair, fist her ponytail, tug her head back to drop a kiss to her forehead, and say, "Let's go give 'em something to talk about, sugar tits."

"Everyone is staring at us."

"No, they aren't," I reply while regarding the check.

"They are."

I don't bother glancing up. I know people are gawking. Talking. Whispering. I don't especially care, but Bailey does. She's kept her eyes downcast, and she's spent most of our dinner with her left hand hidden beneath the table.

"They're only staring because we're sitting on the same side of this booth, which is fucking weird."

Her head snaps up as she hisses, "You're the one who yanked me in here beside you!"

I smile at her because I like when she's feisty and shit. Normally, I'd hate the sensation of being boxed into a corner where there's no view of the door and no easy escape. It's a terrible defensive position. But it was worth it to not leave her alone on the other side, exposed to prying eyes—worth it to feel Bailey so close for an entire meal.

I reach up and drape an arm over her shoulders, pulling her stiff body into mine. Then I drop my head, dusting my lips over the shell of her ear. "Fuck yeah, I did. And I'd do it again."

When she tilts her face up to mine, her breath whispers against my lips as her eyes move around my face.

We're seated in the fanciest steakhouse that Chestnut Springs offers. It's booked solid, full of people, on a Thursday night that coincides with the kickoff of our weeklong town fair.

But when she looks at me with this intensity, our surroundings melt away.

I don't know how no one else sees it. Sees *her*. It's like we're all staring at the same painting and every other person in this town is missing the point.

Without thinking too long about it, I drop my head closer and let a sliver of light through the door of our arrangement. An opening for her to kiss me.

"We should go," she whispers, tilting her head ever so slightly. Her soft lips graze my rough stubble, and I'm transported back to that night at 2:11 when she came into my room. Those same lips against my chest. Her tight heat around my fingers. My utter lack of control to stop myself where she was concerned.

"Thanks for dinner." The words filter back to me as she turns to slide herself out of the booth. Another delicate, feminine summer dress, this time in blue, trails behind her on the leather bench.

I swallow hard and follow her, muttering under my breath, "You're going to be the death of me."

With a stiff back, she twists the engagement ring on her finger while people stare. She's uncomfortable. It's written all over her body, which is why my arm is back around her in no time.

I hug her against my side as we walk through the restaurant. "Do it, sugar. Put your hand in my back pocket. You know you want to," I murmur before pressing a soft kiss to her hair.

Someone gasps, followed by a trail of harsh whispers.

He's been through a lot.

War changes people.

I'm sure it's just a phase.

It makes me furious. It makes me want to lay Bailey in the middle of their table and kiss her senseless just to prove a fucking point.

But that would be impulsive.

So I don't.

I kiss her hair again, and though I know she must have heard their cruel sentiments . . . she slides her hand into my back pocket, and we push out into the sunny summer evening.

The sounds of the fair filter down from the end of Rosewood Street. Buzzers buzzing, bells ringing, children screaming. The air smells like popcorn and cinnamon mini donuts. We follow that tantalizing scent down the sidewalk.

My arm slung over her shoulder, her hand in my pocket.

And all the way to the fair, neither of us draws away.

22

Beau

Harvey: Haven't seen you lately.
Beau: Haven't seen you lately either.
Harvey: Been busy.
Beau: Yeah? With who?
Harvey: You know.
Beau: No, I don't. You haven't told me a single thing.
Harvey: Rich coming from you.
Beau: So, anything you want to tell me, old man? About you? Your life? Any news to share?
Harvey: Nope. Not a thing. Mind your business.
Beau: Chicken.

I swing the oversized hammer over my shoulder one final time, bringing it down with every bit of power I can muster.

I channel every ounce of frustration that bubbles inside of

me—that constant feeling of this life not being enough. Of never being satisfied.

I'm realizing I am deeply unsettled and constantly peeking around every corner for that little bit extra. That one *thing* that will give me some sense of peace.

I thought a good old-fashioned fair game would do the trick.

The hammer hits the pad, and the weight flies up to the top. The sharp ding of metal rings out around us, and the surrounding people watching cheer. I turn, all puffed up like a teenager showing off for his crush.

Except today it's for my fiancée. I flex and kiss a bicep like a total tool. But I don't care. The girl laughing at me makes it worth the embarrassment.

I grin at her. Bailey bites down on a smirk and rolls her eyes.

"Alright, kid," the rough-around-the-edges carnie says. His mullet, which ends in a scraggly gray braid, sways as he waves at the wall of stuffed animals behind him. "Pick of the litter for you and your muscles."

Some girl shouts my name, asking me to pick something for her, but it's not Bailey's voice, so I don't bother giving her a glance. Instead, I analyze the wall of stuffed toys.

"The horse!" Bailey calls out to me.

I check it out, but it's too small. I'm not letting her walk around the town fair with a tiny prize when I just made this game my bitch.

I'm not replacing her ripped horse with some cheap fair prize, either.

I take a step toward the end.

"Beau Eaton, don't you dare pick something huge."

I turn to face her now. She shakes her head at me as I walk

backward, straight into the waiting arms of . . . a giant stuffed raccoon. The biggest toy they've got.

"Why not, future Mrs. Eaton?" I call back, grinning so hard my cheeks hurt. "You love that massive rock I put on your finger, don't you?"

"Beau." I guess it's her turn to use my name as a single-word scolding.

"You also like my massive—"

"Beau Eaton!" She rushes forward, clamping a palm over my mouth. Her eyes sparkle while her loose hair dances in the breeze—she's fucking *glowing*.

"I was going to say motorcycle, sugar," I mumble behind her hand. Then I turn out of her grip to the carny. "I'll take the massive raccoon, sir."

"Sir?" The man chuckles as he unclips the oversized stuffed animal. "Not sure I've ever been called a 'sir' before."

When he hands me the raccoon, I instantly pass it over to Bailey, amused by the way it reaches from beneath her chin down to her knees.

"This is ridiculous," she says, peeking around a furry shoulder.

"Utterly," I agree.

"Am I supposed to carry it all night?"

I throw an arm over her shoulder, getting more and more comfortable touching her. I don't even think about it. I just draw her close. "It? Kinda harsh. He deserves a name, don't you think?"

"Who said it's a male?" she volleys back, smiling up at me. Even with an oversized raccoon in her arms, she finally seems at ease.

So it kills me when I hear someone say in a stage whisper, "Bailey

Jansen carrying around a trash panda is the only thing that makes sense about that relationship."

How fucking dare someone say that loud enough for her to hear?

My eyes narrow and I go to turn, instantly ready for a fight, but Bailey is just as fast.

Her hand shoots up and wraps around my wrist, giving it a sharp tug. "Don't bother."

"Bailey, people aren't allowed to talk to you like that."

"She wasn't talking *to* me." Bailey tugs again, urging me forward. "She was talking *about* me. And that's not new. Let it go."

I can't let it go.

"Don't be impulsive," Bailey adds as I turn abruptly.

My eyes land on the girl, and she flicks her long blonde hair over her shoulder like her cruelty might impress me.

Fuck her.

I slip into that eerily cool, calculated zone I know all too well. My gaze cuts through the crowd, and I swear I'm seeing at them all through the crosshairs of a rifles cope. I point at the girl, singling her out, and project my voice, enunciating every word very carefully.

"Talk shit about my fiancée again. I fucking dare you."

Bailey shrinks, but the girl who said it just looks . . . confused.

I stare hard, not at all uncomfortable in the awkward silence. And when no apologies come, I shake my head at all of them and lead my girl away from the confrontation.

"Beau, you shouldn't have done that just now," Bailey whispers tersely.

"You're right. I should have started doing it a long time ago," I grit out as I set my sights on the Ferris wheel.

Bailey doesn't respond, and she stays silent as we wait in line.

When we step onto our square and open-air capsule, Bailey instantly dives for the bench across from me. She seats the massive raccoon beside herself so that I'm forced to sit facing her.

I stare at her profile. The feminine line of her jaw, accentuated by the way she's turned her head to gaze out over the town. The slope of her nose. The unnatural way that she avoids blinking.

She'd be terrible undercover. She looks like a deer caught in headlights, frozen and unmoving.

Our unit moves jerkily, stopping and going as they load other riders into the seats. Bailey still doesn't look at me, even when we reach halfway up one side of the massive circle.

"Bailey."

"Mm-hmm." She crosses her arms as though that could keep me out.

"Come here."

"I'm fine. My trash panda and I have heard worse. It barely hurts anymore." She turns now, giving me the stiffest smile I've ever seen on her face. "Gets easier to brush off every time."

Her eyes peek up and to the right. A dead giveaway that she's lying.

In fact, I get the sense this shit is getting harder to brush off all the time. And I'm not sure if our arrangement is making her feel better or causing her more distress because people still seem to think it's open season for insulting her.

"Come. Here." I fold my hand, ushering her forward.

"No, thanks," she replies, not taking her eyes off the horizon.

"For crying out loud, Bailey," I grumble as I stand, grab her by the waist, and fall back into my seat with her straddling my lap.

"What are you doing?" Her expression is one of shock as the pod swings back and forth wildly. They mentioned not standing, but fuck that. She needed to be held.

"Holding my fiancée." I settle my hands on her hips, fingers splaying dangerously low over the top of her ass. We both glance down, acutely aware of the way we're lined up right now. Her thighs on either side of mine, the hemline of her dress edged up over them.

She swallows, hands on my shoulders. "I said no."

"Okay." Her chest rises and falls as her breathing picks up. I know what I do to Bailey. I'm just so fucking torn about whether or not I should be doing it. "Then go sit back over there, if that's what you want."

She clears her throat and stares at the view like there's something fucking interesting out there when we both know it's just a lot of flat farmlands. "We're not supposed to stand up."

I almost laugh. We both know what's going on here. Age difference be damned. Bet be damned. Bailey and I like each other. We want each other. But we both know we shouldn't complicate things when this agreement has a pretty firm end date. There's a pretty obvious part-ing of ways on the horizon. One that doesn't feel very amusing at all.

So, I don't laugh. I dip my head forward and press a soft kiss to the center of her chest, just beneath where her collarbones meet.

She sucks in a breath, arching in toward me. "What are you doing?" Her fingers fist the collared shirt I put on just for her tonight.

"Kissing my fiancée." I drag my close-cut stubble over her chest, dotting her collarbones with kisses as I go.

"Why?"

"Because I want to."

Her fingers extend over my shoulders, sliding up my neck as a shiver racks her body. "But no one's watching."

I flick the flimsy strap of her dress and watch it fall away, dangling limp over her bicep. "Why does anyone need to be watching?" I kiss the spot where her strap was and glance up at her. With the low sun behind her, her silky hair blazes like a dark fire.

Her tongue darts out over her full bottom lip as her mouth parts on a shaky breath. "Because this is meant to be for show. Right?"

I watch her watching me. Her question hangs between us like a line I know I shouldn't cross. A line *she* knows I shouldn't cross. A line that is becoming consistently less stark the more time I spend getting to know Bailey.

The more time I spend with my hands on her.

"Well, Bailey." Her face dips closer, as though she's struggling to hear me over the noise of the fair. "We can give them all a show when we're at the bottom and just enjoy ourselves when we're at the top. We can walk off this ride looking a little tousled. How does that sound?"

She flushes, cheeks bright pink, just like her parted lips. Her body hums in my hands, and the surrounding air is downright electric.

"Sounds good," she whispers.

"You tell me if there's something you don't like, okay?" I slide my palm over her elbow, wanting nothing more than to give her pleasure after the earlier altercation made her crumble. She went from vibrant and happy to locked down and wounded.

I never want to see that look on her face again. I want to patch her back up and send her out into the world with confidence, knowing she deserves respect and is strong enough to demand it.

"Okay," her voice cracks, and her thumb swipes over the bone behind my ear as she settles her weight on my crotch.

I give her a stern nod, willing my cock to not go full mast. But that's a losing battle.

When I drop my lips to the soft tops of her breasts, the twanging sound of that one flimsy thread of my control snapping echoes in my ears.

Impulsive.

The word repeats in my head as my hands roam her body. And I don't give a fuck.

Being impulsive has never felt this good.

My tongue darts out, leaving a trail of glistening saliva over her cleavage. Her head tips back and she moans, all breathy and scandalized sounding.

That fucking moan.

All hope of not walking off this ride with a raging hard-on evaporates in an instant. *Poof.* Gone.

I move back up her chest, her thighs snug against mine as she squeezes herself closer. Tighter against me.

Her fingers dive into my hair as I work my way back up her sternum. I take my time and savor every inch of her. Every little huff of breath, every whimper.

But the closer we draw to the ground, to the line of people who will no doubt see us, the more she tenses up. She's not a showy person. She's perfected flying under the radar, and straddling me in public is definitely not that.

"Bailey."

"Yeah?"

My lips brush over the expanse of skin where her neck meets her shoulder. I haven't kissed her lips yet.

I'm still not sure I should. Not sure I'll recover.

Not sure I'll be able to walk away after that.

"Ignore them." I rake my fingers through her hair on the side where people congregate, trying to break her line of sight.

We stay locked in a tense, quiet moment. My hand in her hair, my arm over her back, caging her in.

"Ignore them," I say again as we trend back up again.

"It's hard," she whispers against my ear, sounding a little broken.

When we've passed the crowds and head back up into the evening sky, I ask, "Do you mean this?" I guide her hand between my legs to my cock.

She sucks in a breath but doesn't pull away. Her hand grips me through my jeans almost instantly, like she just can't help herself.

"Or do you mean how hard I'm going to bite you for the hickey you left on my neck last time?"

I don't give her a chance to reply before I latch on to the tender flesh of her neck. One hand travels under her skirt, gripping her ass hard enough to leave marks there too.

The sharp gasp that rushes from her sifts through my close-cut hair and over my neck. I pull away and stare at the red spot blooming on her neck before meeting her sultry gaze. Bailey's previously worried eyes are now full of fire.

"Impulsive looks good on you, Bailey," I rasp before lifting her strap back onto her shoulder, then opting to hold her against my chest for the rest of the ride.

Holding her seems safe enough. Safer than kissing her again, than biting her again. Better to pull back now before we both lose our minds and go altogether too far.

23

Bailey

I can't sleep. I've tried.

When I close my eyes, I see Beau.

I smell Beau.

I taste Beau.

I hear Beau.

I feel Beau's hands touching me like I'm his for real. I feel his cock hard for *me*.

My brain is all Beau, all the time. I feel like I've got a song stuck on repeat. One I can't get out of my head.

My brain keeps missing the memo that this thing between Beau and me is fake.

It's cute how I thought getting out of bartender mode to fall asleep was hard.

But this is worse than the sensation of going around in circles all night long that usually follows me to bed.

So much worse. I'm spinning alright, and it's a downward spiral that I'm too horny to stop.

I check my phone. It's 1:54 a.m. and I have my alarm set for six minutes from now. So, there's no point in trying to sleep. I'm mentally preparing myself to walk across that hallway and slap on a cheery facade. One where I pretend I didn't grope his dick in public, at a family-friendly event.

I'm not even sure if Beau is here. After the fair, he walked me to the house, ushered me inside, and said he was going to Cade's house. Then locked the door behind me.

So, I've been alone and left to my devices. To my vicious thoughts.

My head took me down the rabbit hole of how the town will spin what we did. They'll chalk me up to being a cheap whore. And Beau will be the poor, sad soldier just trying to find his way. *Rightfully blowing off some steam*, they'll say.

I can just hear the way the old biddies who meet for morning coffee at Le Pamplemousse will talk about it.

That filthy Jansen girl mauling poor Beau Eaton.

Bless Beau. Bless his good fucking heart. For a man who has seen so much, he's sure got rose-colored glasses on when it comes to me and my reputation.

Maybe we both underestimated how deeply this town hates me, because I don't think the promise of his last name is helping at all.

It might actually be making things worse.

Before this engagement, I moved around town like a shadow. Now I move with a big freaking target on my back, followed closely by a bunch of envious eyes that seem to track me everywhere I go.

I flop onto my back and press the heels of my hands against my eye sockets, preparing myself to get out of bed. My hands fall away when the sound of an alarm filters in from across the hall. The shrill, repeating beep shatters the silence for a few moments. It's followed by a gruff, "Fuck," then heavy footsteps.

I lie flat on my back, alert and listening.

The quiet click of a door. Softer footfalls. And then ... silence.

I check my phone. It's 1:59 a.m. on the nose. One minute before my alarm.

I swear I can *feel* Beau standing outside my door. We're holding our breath in time. These 2:11 meetings take a toll on our sleep and our ability to think straight.

A light knock. Butterflies in my stomach.

"Bailey?"

My heart pounds. This isn't the routine. I'm the one who sets the alarm. I flip my legs out of bed, oversized T-shirt falling mid-thigh as the cool floor seeps into the bottoms of my feet. With my hand on the doorknob, I pause. I don't know why. Beau doesn't scare me or make me uncomfortable. Quite the opposite, in fact.

Yet my throat is dry, and my body is coiled up tight like a spring. If I didn't have my fingers wrapped around the metal lever, my hand would shake.

"Yeah?" I ask.

"You up?"

My lips curve. "That's an awfully dumb question for a tier one operator."

"Open the door," he grumbles, clearly exasperated by my response. But who could blame me? That was a dumb question.

I open the door to face my big, dumb soldier. His body practically fills the corridor, consuming the space, the air. He's a silhouette in a darkened hallway, lit by the soft glow of his room behind him.

Beau's enigmatic presence sucks all the shadows in from around him, straight into his darkness.

Me included.

"You set your alarm?" I inch toward him, fingers curled around the doorframe to keep myself tethered, as though holding onto the molding might keep me from reaching for him.

"Yeah, but I didn't need to. I keep waking up at two every night now."

"But not 2:11?"

"Well, I don't know. Haven't made it there."

I worry my bottom lip. "Then why do you keep letting me set an alarm and come wake you up for a swim?"

He shrugs and drops her gaze. "I enjoy going swimming with you."

"So you just lie there waiting for me to come knock?"

His lips twist in a mischievous smirk. "Yeah."

A disbelieving laugh bubbles up out of me. "Beau. Eaton. Do you know how fucking tired I am?"

He looks so boyish right now, only mildly chastised. He doesn't offer an apology.

Instead . . .

He offers a wordless thank you.

His thickly corded arm extends into the space between us, and my eyes need a minute to adjust to what I'm seeing in the dim light.

"Is that . . . "

I reach out, fingers brushing against the matted, almost woolly texture of my stuffed horse's coat.

"I stitched it."

I let go of the doorframe and take the toy in both hands. My fingertips run over the line of perfect stitches down her side. "You stitched *her*."

He scrubs at his beard. "Right. Her. Well … she's Franken-pony now."

Tears well in my eyes and I blink rapidly to push them away, not risking a glance up at Beau. I'll sob if I do.

"I found her in a park, forgotten on a bench." I trace the thread lines again and laugh dryly. "I know now I probably stole some other kid's toy. But, man, in that moment? God. It felt like the universe gifted me something that was meant to be just mine. I didn't get Barbies or toys, but I had Princess Peach."

"Princess Peach?"

I sniff. "Yeah. That changed into just Peaches somewhere along the way. But I'm not going to lie and say I didn't feel like a princess walking around with this stuffy for a long time." I smile at the little beige horse. "I thought she'd be in a landfill somewhere by now."

"Had to dig through three bags of garbage to find her."

The bridge of my nose stings.

"And then go get a mending kit from Willa."

"Is that why you went to Cade's?" I finally force myself to glance up at him, his rugged features appearing darker in the night.

He shrugs. "Yeah. Willa has all sorts of craft shit. Including extra stuffing. She's gone full Martha Stewart mom."

I smile sadly. *What must that be like?* Having a mom who does crafts with you?

"Thank you," I whisper, stroking the fuzzy, pilled mane. Touching the threadbare faux leather that covers her hooves. "Thank you so much."

I launch myself at him, hugging him almost violently. My body flying toward his like a magnet that can't resist the pull. My arms clamp around his torso, Peaches pressed to his back, as a surprised whoosh of his breath breezes over the top of my head. I feel like I've squeezed the air out of his lungs. And yet I continue clinging to him, and after a few short beats, his arms wrap around me, and he hugs me back.

I sigh. I melt against him. The protective shell around my heart softens. I don't think anyone has ever done something so thoughtful for me.

"You're welcome." His voice is gritty. It scrapes across my skin, down the side of my neck, and summons gooseflesh over my forearms.

Then he steps back, hands on my biceps. Holding me at a distance when I wish he'd go on touching me.

"Let's go swimming," I say brightly. Trying to cover the emotion, the confusion in my voice. Unable to continue facing him, I turn to place Peaches on my bed.

But his voice stops me.

"Nah, Bailey. Get some sleep."

When I swing back around, he's propped his hand against the top of the doorframe. Like it's holding him back. The same way it did me. Until he gave me the sweetest gift and knocked away all my restraint in one fell swoop.

"But I thought you liked swimming with me?"

The way his arm is slung above his head has his bicep bulging and his shoulder tugging at the fabric of his T-shirt. I remember the way he clamped me against him with that exact arm. The way I felt wrapped up safe in him.

"I do."

"But—"

"But you're tired. So am I, and it's probably past 2:11 now. We could both use some sleep."

I nod, pressing my lips together and taking another step toward the doorway. Toward him.

For all the nights I've begrudgingly dragged myself out of bed, I find myself feeling ... wounded. Even though I logically understand his choice not to swim tonight isn't a big deal, I can't shake the irrational emotion.

I reach for the door handle, offering him a wan smile. "Yeah. Totally," I say lamely. "Have a good sleep."

His gaze drags down my body, then slowly back up, settling on my lips for a beat.

Then he taps a flat hand against the frame twice—so casually—before drawing away. For some reason, this exchange is painfully awkward. The humor we usually compensate with is notably absent tonight.

"Is everything okay?" I blurt, foot stepping out into the hall as he takes his first step away.

"Of course, Bailey." He gives me a reassuring smile over his shoulder and then takes another step.

"Why haven't you kissed me?" My question rings out in the empty space. I swear it echoes through the entire oversized house.

Beau freezes, going eerily still. He doesn't turn to face me when he says, "What do you think that dark red mark on your neck is from?"

I reach up, pressing my fingers to what I knew would be there in the morning. "That's not what I meant."

He sighs, shoulders rising and falling heavily. He still doesn't turn my way. "I've kissed you plenty. As much as is needed to sell this. I don't want to blur any lines."

Sell this. My stomach drops. It makes me feel like there's something dirty and undesirable about me.

"Right." My voice is breathy. "Do you think people will find it weird if we never kiss normally?"

He turns now, hands propped on his hips.

"Like a real couple?" I add.

"Do you see lots of real couples out there kissing on the lips all the time, Bailey? Cause I don't. It's more just familiar touches in public, don't you think?"

I nod, swallowing. He's not wrong. I'm just tired. And confused.

"To be fair, I don't see many couples full-on making out on the Ferris wheel while avoiding each other's lips, either."

He stares, eyes narrowing.

"Is there a reason you'd be okay with kissing my shoulder but not my lips? Is it me? I know people talk a lot of shit about me, but did I do something that—"

"Bailey, don't finish that fucking sentence," he grinds out, back to scrubbing a hand over his mouth.

He sounds angry, and it makes emotion well up in me. In my eyes. In my voice. Fuck, I'm about to cry. I can feel it coming, but I forge ahead anyway in a thick, rasping voice. "If I'm doing something wrong, you'll tell me, right? So I can do this for real with someone one day and not make a total fool of—"

"Fuck it!" His hand rips away from his mouth, like he tore off a piece of tape that was keeping him from talking, and with two long steps, he's here.

In front of me.

Cupping my head.

Backing me up against the doorframe.

And kissing me.

The edge of the molding bites between my shoulder blades as Beau devours me. Firm lips, soft tongue, rough stubble, big hands.

He *consumes* me.

And there isn't a soul here to see it. This is just me and him in a dark hallway. This is . . . I don't know what this is.

The hickey he gave me pulses on my neck, the pads of his fingers rake down the back of my head, his thumb strokes at my jawline, all while he kisses me senseless.

A swipe of a tongue.

A moan.

The press of a body.

My hands on his abs. His chest.

For however long we kiss, I don't feel like dirty Bailey Jansen. I feel like a woman kissing a man who wants her. Really wants her. He can't fake this. No one could fake this. No one is *that* good.

Eventually, the fever between us ebbs. Hard, heavy kisses turn to slow, languid ones. He melts against me, hips on hips. My calf rubs against his, and my hands lay flat on his pecs, no longer searching and tugging. Just settling.

"Bailey," he murmurs against my damp, swollen lips. "You are doing nothing wrong. You have done nothing wrong. Anyone who talks shit about you is cruel and small-minded and not worthy of your attention. You are fucking perfect."

Beau presses a kiss to my cheek and then pulls away to dive into my eyes. Long, strong fingers brush through my hair and then curve as they tuck it behind my ears. His hands settle around my neck, and he stares me down so seriously that I can't help but stare back, can't help but listen and hear what he's saying.

I nod, eyes fluttering shut as he rubs his thumbs over the tops of my cheekbones, wiping away tears he never let fall.

"Go to bed, Bailey."

My eyes snap open, my body whining. *This is it?*

"Get some sleep."

I don't know what to say. I've never had a hot older man kiss me stupid and then tell me to go to bed.

So I just nod.

He nods back at me and steps away, hands falling from my cheeks. I want to yell at him to put them back. I want his hands on me. All over me. Inside me.

I stay slumped against the doorframe, boneless and stunned from his kiss. It wasn't my first kiss, but it was my first kiss to feel like *that*.

Like the house could crumble around us and we wouldn't notice.

Like I was safe.

He's stepping back into his room when I finally drum up the will to form words again. "Hey, Beau?"

"Yeah?" He turns, gripping his door handle.

"Why'd you kiss me with no one here to see it?"

The subtle smirk that plays across his lips makes my stomach flip. It's full of promise, and sensuality, and *experience*.

"Because I wanted to."

And with that, he shuts the door.

24
Bailey

I worry my lip between my bottom teeth and then force myself to stop fidgeting.

Then I tug at the bottom hem of my blazer.

The woman behind the counter eyes me, but not in an appreciative way like Beau. It's judgmental, noting my flaws with every inch her eyes roam. They catch on my oversized engagement ring.

"I can work weekends. My shifts at the bar don't usually start until five."

The woman still says nothing, the sheet of paper in her hand crinkling beneath her grip. Based on the name tag attached to her shirt, her name is Mary. As I would expect from someone who owns a hair salon, Mary has perfect hair. It's a warm gold color, with shades of blonde laced throughout.

I wipe a clammy hand down my locks as she peeks at my resume. My hair may be plain dark brown, but I consider it one of my better features. Thick and falling past my shoulders—mostly because I go as long as possible before springing for a haircut. I drive to the city every time because I love my hair and I'm too paranoid to let anyone in Chestnut Springs cut it.

Maybe if Mary got to know me she'd be okay with—

"We're not hiring." She smiles in a way that looks painful to her as she hands the paper back to me. I'm too stunned to even lift my arm and take it back.

"But there's a sign in the window. It says you're looking for a receptionist." Emotion bleeds into my voice. Anger? Frustration? Pleading? It's some combination of them all.

Her head flips toward the window and the plastic sign leaning against the glass. "Oh." That *oh* is all it takes for me to know Mary is full of shit.

"I must have forgotten to take that down." On platform sandals, she totters over to the front window, swipes the sign, and brings it back to the front desk. "There," she finishes brightly.

I can barely make eye contact with her, but I force myself to do it because I refuse to be anything less than kind, level-headed, and professional. That way, people can say anything they want about me, but they'll never have proof.

They can say my family is rotten. They can refuse to hire me. But the onus will always be on them, because they're the ones who have to live with knowing they hate me for no good reason.

"Thank you for your time," I say evenly as I turn toward the door. It's when my palms press against the cold metal push bar that I turn back and add, "You'll want to take the online ad down too. Since you filled the position." My lips tip up, but my head tilts in a way that tells her I can smell her bullshit from here.

I push out the door, and as soon as I hit the street, my smile falls away.

The sun is bright. The pavement is hot. And for some stupid reason, I thought wearing a pantsuit I bought at the thrift store would make me appesar more hireable.

Sometimes I'm adorably naive, even to myself.

"Ugh!" The noise comes out angry and sharp as I tug at the top buttons of my blouse. I buttoned it to my throat—as though that would make me look less like a harlot—to cover the hickey from the man who was already up and gone to work on the ranch this morning.

Someone walking by literally flinches as I undo three fucking buttons so I can breathe, get a little airflow.

I'm tired and frustrated and on the verge of tears.

Had I been tired the night before?

Yes.

Had the most electric kiss of my life been the magic ticket to put me to sleep?

Hell no.

I'm more tired than I already was, and I need a coffee. I shove into Le Pamplemousse, the quaint Parisian café. Ellen, who owns it, is always kind to me. I'm sure she'd hire me, except she doesn't need anyone. She works the place exclusively with her husband. I think it's adorable they can work together all day and not want to kill one another.

I feel flustered as I enter the bustling space. My skin heats to volcano levels as I get in line and sense eyes on me, but I keep my chin up, staring ahead, pretending to be oblivious.

" . . . dad is back in town." When I hear the whisper from a table beside me, I absorb a full-body flinch.

My dad is in town? Not that it matters. He's never paid much attention to me, other than blaming me for shit that wasn't my fault as a child. In adulthood, though? Hasn't had much use for me. The only useful thing he does is keep my brothers in check.

Someone cuts in front of me. As if I'm not in line at all. As if I don't even exist. I shift my focus away, as though the art available for purchase on the wall has suddenly piqued my interest. If I were someone else, I'd tap this guy on the shoulder and give them a piece of my—

"My dude." My head snaps toward the voice I recognize. Willa, Cade Eaton's fiancée, is standing beside me. She has her baby slung on her hip, wild red mane flowing around her stunning face, and indignation rolling off of her in *waves*. "I know you did not just cut my sister-in-law off and pretend like you didn't see her."

Her voice. It's loud. And everyone hears it. I swear a pin could drop in the place. I want to fold in on myself, like a tidy little piece of origami. Transform into something else entirely. Something that no one can see or recognize. Maybe even with wings so I could fly away.

"Seriously?" The guy gives Willa an annoyed look. "She's a Jan—"

"She's an Eaton. But further to that, she's a human. A woman. And you, my friend, are an asshole."

The man's brows shoot up on his forehead. First Mary and now him. It never fails to impress me that in a small town big enough for me to not know everyone's name, they all know mine.

The man still doesn't move. To be fair, I think she's shocked him into stillness.

Willa's arm shoots out, pointing behind me. "Back of the bus, dickhead. Who's your mama? I'd like to call her and ask how she raised you so I can file it away under *what not to do*."

I glance down at the floor, hoping a hole might open beneath me. A rocky maw that swallows me whole. I've been kissed by Beau and now rescued by Willa, and this is all so fucking embarrassing that now might be the time to go.

But Willa just links her baby-less arm through mine and walks me ahead, cutting the *dickhead* off the way he did me. Then she turns and grins at me conspiratorially, looking a little unhinged and a lot pleased with herself. "Good morning, Bailey."

At first, I stare at her blankly, and then I blurt, "You're nuts."

"I know." She grins wider. "Cade says it's one of my best qualities. Well"—her head tilts in consideration—"and my tits."

I can't help it. All my tension bubbles over and I laugh.

"There we go. That's what we like to hear, isn't it, Emma?"

The little girl with a mop of dark hair claps her hands with excitement and it's impossible not to smile.

"She's adorable."

"Yeah, thanks. I agree." The expression on Willa's face as she stares at her baby is pure wonder. Pure love. It pinches a spot in my chest.

The line moves, and so does Willa, arm still linked with mine as we step forward. "So, did Beau manage to fix your stuffed horse?"

I flush, thinking about the sweet gift he gave me last night. Or regifted? Upcycled? I don't know what to call it. But he sewed it meticulously. When I crawled back into bed with Peaches, I squeezed her to my chest and took a huge inhale. She didn't smell musty or like the garbage she no doubt spent some time next to in that black bag.

She smelled like Beau's citronella soap. I'm almost positive he washed and dried her after restuffing and mending her.

She smelled like home.

I clear my throat, realizing I checked out for a minute. "Yeah, he did. She's pretty much good as new. Just a cool badass scar and a wild story to tell."

The smile that touches Willa's lips now is soft, not the maniacal grin from before.

"Kinda like Beau."

"I mean, he speaks in these superior dirty looks that he's been giving me since we were kids. But then he turns around and does nice things for me. Like bringing Skylar Stone to perform at our wedding?"

Willa walked me all the way to the till, chatting my ear off, even though Summer and Sloane were already waiting at a table for her. I ordered my coffee, and she ordered me a mimosa. Now I'm sitting at a table by the window double fisting with them all on a Friday morning.

Life is a wild ride.

"Ford is so extra." Summer laughs.

"Wait, so he's not ... insane like you?" Sloane smirks from behind her champagne glass, still dressed in a tank and tight shorts from dancing this morning.

"I resent that," Willa volleys dryly.

I'm having some sort of out-of-body experience. It feels like I got invited to hang out with the cool kids at school. And now they're sitting here, talking about personal stuff, razzing each other, like there's nothing weird about me being here at all.

"But it's true." Willa sips her mimosa. "We are opposites. I think my mom's body saved all the personality for me and gave all the nerdy, overachiever drive to Ford. He probably ran numbers and created business plans in the womb. If he ever meets someone, she's going to have to speak bitch. Because he can be a real bitch. Sometimes I miss working for him. Driving him nuts was the best."

That gets a round of chuckles from the table.

"But he is a good guy," Summer says. "I think you're giving them the wrong impression. You two have the whole sibling thing going on. And I know you go out of your way to annoy him."

Willa just shrugs, a mischievous glint in her eye.

Summer turns to Sloane and me now. "You'll meet him at the wedding and realize Willa is exaggerating."

The way they talk about me is just ... like it's a given I'll be there. These women don't make me feel like they're doing me some huge favor by having me along. They act like it's perfectly normal to include me, and I let myself sink into that.

After all that's transpired today, it's nice to be wanted.

"Another round?" Willa glances around at us, already nodding her head.

"Another?" Sloane doesn't sound quite so sure. Her mimosa appears to be completely untouched. "It's a Friday morning. Just get me an orange juice."

"It's boozy brunch, Sloane. It's tradition. Put your big girl tutu on and chug that. You got somewhere to be? Or are you wussing out because your new bestie Winter is busy with her new boy toy?"

A pout forms on Sloane's lips. "No, Jasper is at training camp in Rose Hill and so I'm pretty much just dancing to pass the time."

"Perfect!" Willa slaps her leg, plops her baby into Summer's lap, and says, "I always dance better when I'm drunk." She stands and waltzes toward the counter without a care in the world.

There's something inspiring about Willa.

"I want to be her when I grow up." I didn't mean to say it out loud, but the words slip out in a moment of wonder.

"I think we all do," Sloane says softly, nodding.

"Speaking of when we grow up," Summer ventures in, "what are your plans? You don't strike me as a lifer at the bar, Bailey."

"Ha!" The champagne has me feeling loose and a laugh bursts from me loud enough that people turn to stare. I've mostly stopped caring about judgmental eyes on me. But Summer has always been kind to me, so I know she means well with the question. She's probably looking out for Beau. "How could you tell?"

She smiles at me but offers nothing. She's always treated me normally, the way any stranger who doesn't know a person would treat someone new. But now she's been in Chestnut Springs long enough to know the stories about my family, and she still hasn't changed her tune.

Maybe I want to be Summer when I grow up.

"Yeah, my ultimate plan is to get outta here and go to school in the city. Probably kinesiology and then chiropractic school."

"Oh my god, I would love to be related to a chiropractor." Sloane moans the words. "I could ask you to fix my back any time I want."

Summer's chocolate eyes stay on mine. "You'd be great at that."

"Thanks." I smile and lift my mimosa.

"How does Beau feel about you moving to the city?"

I freeze as it hits me how thoroughly I've stepped in it. Why the hell would two newly engaged people be planning to part ways so soon? Or does she think Beau is planning to move with me and hasn't told his family?

I cover by finishing the sip and then smiling as I carefully place the flute back on the table. "We're going to cross that bridge when we get there. It's not that far to commute. Right now, with his hours plus mine at the bar, we're sometimes ships in the night anyway." My head wobbles. "And if I ever pick up another job, I imagine our schedules will be even more chaotic."

Sloane shrugs while Summer analyzes me, far too closely for my taste. "Makes sense to me. Jasper and I are always busy during hockey season. School semesters would be the same."

"What do you mean if you ever manage to pick up another job?" Summer asks.

I sigh, averting my gaze out the window to hide my embarrassment. "No one in town wants to hire me, thanks to my dad and brothers. The bar is the only place I've been able to hold down a job. But I need more shifts, and there aren't any available because everyone who works there loves the money."

Talking about my problems to two women who remind me of Disney princesses feels odd, but I continue. "The manager likes me, but I guess he can't fire other employees to make work for me. He offered cleaning the bar for extra money when I told him I was in a bind, so I do that a few times a week too. I've moved up and into better shifts over time, but it's not enough to save for university."

"Oh, Bailey." Sloane reaches across the table to hold my hand. Everything about her is soft and sweet. I momentarily want to ask her for a hug. I bet she gives superb hugs.

"I'll hire you."

I jolt in my seat, hand turning to clamp onto Sloane's as I stare at Summer. "What?"

"At the gym. I barely have time to do my own workouts anymore. I'm always at the front desk, or answering emails, or ordering this thing or that thing. Why don't you just tell me what time of day is good for you and I'll work with that."

I straighten, my shoulders shimmying as I hold myself tall. "I don't want you to pity hire me. That wasn't what I was trying to do by telling you this."

Summer shrugs and leans back in her seat. "I know. I asked you."

My brows furrow. "Did Beau put you up to this?"

"You kidding me? Beau works all day and then rushes home or to the bar to hang out with you. I barely see him, let alone talk to him. He doesn't even bring you around to the main house that often. He's hogging you, if you ask me. This will be fun. We're going to be sisters-in-law. We stick together now."

A pang of guilt hits me hard and fast. She might not be singing this tune when Beau and I come to an end.

Come to an end.

That has a twinge of pain landing straight in my gut.

But I ignore every sensation and forge ahead with a cheerful smile. "I would love that."

Summer smiles brightly, holding her champagne flute up to cheers me. "You're hired!"

I need this. I need this to get out. I need this to survive, and I'll get over the guilt eventually.

Leaving Beau behind, though?

It feels like I'll never get over that.

25

Beau

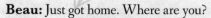

Beau: Just got home. Where are you?

Bailey: How do most guys like a girl to have her pubic hair?

Beau: Bailey, honest to god. You can't just lead with things like this.

Bailey: Can you just tell me? It's hard to know. In porn, it's nothing at all. But I know porn isn't real life. So like, what am I supposed to do? What's the norm out there?

Beau: Whatever you like best. Any guy who holds a strong opinion on how you style your pubic hair doesn't deserve to be between your legs.

Bailey: So maybe a triangle or a strip? I can't decide.

Beau: Decide some other time. When it doesn't involve me.

Bailey: It's the final hour over here. I'm in the bath.
Razor in hand.

Beau: Why do you insist on asking me things like this?

Bailey: Because you've presumably seen a lot of pussies.

Beau: Bailey, just stop.

I thought I was tired when I walked in the door. A sleepless night of mending Peaches followed by a very real kiss with my very fake fiancée means I slept like shit. Then I got up early to work with my very grumpy brother all fucking day.

I'm wrung out. Fried, if I'm being honest. Delirious maybe. I've never been as tired as I am at this moment, and that's saying something for someone who was stranded in a cave in Afghanistan for several days.

But knowing Bailey is naked in my bath, asking for my input on how she shaves?

I pace my house, trying not to think about it. I go to the fridge and eye up a beer because I know it will take the edge off. But I don't know if I can handle it. I thought 2:11 was wigging me out, but I think Bailey might be fucking with my head more than anything else.

I grab a can of kombucha instead. It's beer-like—that's what I keep telling myself—and healthy. The popping sound of it opening is satisfying, but the first sip is not. I'm still jittery.

I need a shower after a long day moving cattle from one quarter to the next. Yes, a shower. I head upstairs and go straight past the door where I know Bailey is in the bath.

"Hi. I'm home. Going to have a shower," I call out loud enough that she can hear.

"Okay." Her voice is crystal clear, so feminine as it echoes back.

Yeah. This shower will have to be cold. And it is. I leave it freezing as I step into the glass box. I take my can of kombucha with me, a million times less satisfying than a shower beer. In fact, almost everything about my life right now feels unsatisfying.

Everything except for Bailey.

She's a breath of fresh air. She's excitement, and innocence, and a purpose all wrapped up in one. I *missed* her today. I couldn't wait to get home and see her. I spent all day sitting on the back of a horse plotting out ways to kiss her again.

And she's down the hall. Asking me how to shave her pubic hair after recently telling me there is so much we can do that isn't sex.

I lather and scrub the dirt from the day off my body. The only contact I make with my dick is to wash it quickly. If I linger there too long, I know what I'll end up doing. And I don't want to be the weird guy who jerks off while the younger girl he's supposed to help is having a bath just a couple of doors down.

Shaving her pubic hair.

Before I have time to overthink it, I'm out of the shower, the can of shitty replacement beer forgotten on the tiled shelf, wrapping a towel around my waist.

Before I have time to talk myself out of it, I'm standing at the door of her bathroom, knocking lightly.

"Yeah?"

"Did you decide which one?"

I hear a light chuckle on the other side.

"No. I'm still considering my options."

"What are the options?" I shake my head at myself, one arm propped high on the doorframe, opposite hand pressed flat on the door. In no time at all, I went from *don't be the creepy guy* to this.

"Are you going to make me shout them to you through the closed door?"

"Are you inviting me in?" I volley back.

There's a beat of silence and then a simple, "Yes."

221

I swallow, assessing myself. My speeding heart rate, the towel tied tightly around my waist, my wet hair dripping down onto my bare shoulders. I probably look just as out of control as I feel.

Not for the first time, the promise of Bailey makes me totally impulsive.

I reach for the door handle, turn it, and walk straight into the bathroom. The air is thick with humidity, coating the mirror in a light layer of steam, and everything smells like lavender. Bailey's tiny head pops up out of a heaping pile of bubbles. The way she has twisted her hair on top of her head matches their shape.

She looks fucking perfect in the massive, oversized bath—rosy cheeks, eyes a little glassy, and her lips tipped up. The earthy tile surround matches the tones of her hair and skin so well. If I didn't know any better, I would say I designed this bathroom knowing how perfect she'd look in my tub.

My eyes snag on the pink razor resting beside a fresh white bar of soap on the tub's ledge.

"I definitely thought you'd be too chickenshit to come in here," she taunts with a smirk. The water shifts beneath the bubbles. No doubt her hands are moving under the water.

"You don't know me *that* well, Bailey," I reply, shutting the door behind me.

Her eyes race over my body, eating up every inch of bare flesh.

"I know you're scared of losing control around me." Her chin tips up as though she's told me something that will make me back down. Run me off.

It doesn't.

"No, I'm scared of you becoming something I can't live without."

She sucks in a breath as I stalk confidently toward her.

"I'm scared of taking something I don't deserve, something we both know will lead to a bigger mess than we're already in."

I kneel beside the bath, propping my elbows on the edge and staring her down.

"This isn't a mess—"

"I'm scared of having to go to work tomorrow and spending all day with a hard-on because I'm wondering if you went for a triangle or strip."

All she does is stare back and breathe heavily as I reach into the hot, soapy water and trail a hand over her thigh to her knee. Leaning closer, I whisper against her ear, "And I'm fucking scared of what I'll do when the day comes I find out some other fucker gets to help you decide these things."

She regards me carefully, arms propped on the ledge, breaths even but shallow, dark eyes sparkling like the river at 2:11. My palm slides up and down her thigh, never going too far.

"Okay, but tonight . . . are you helping me or leaving?"

I mull the question over, telling myself I *should* leave while admitting to myself I'm not sure why I think I need to. Is it because she's younger? Is it because I've become borderline obsessed with helping her and I worry that this will all just hurt her in the end?

Or am I worried it will hurt *me* in the end? I don't know if I can handle being hurt anymore.

She squeezes her thighs together, trapping my hand between them and forcing my eyes from the crackling bubbles up to hers.

We stay like that for a beat, and then I say, "Helping you."

26
Bailey

I thought he'd leave. I thought he'd say my name in that one-word scolding way of his. The one that says *stop, you're testing my patience*.

But he didn't.

And now I don't know what to say back. So I nod, stomach aflutter, words failing me.

I'm scared of you becoming something I can't live without.

File that away under sentiments I don't know what to do with.

I ease off on squeezing his hand between my legs and search his face for any sign he might back out. That he might come to his senses and walk away. I don't want to tie my self-esteem to a man's response, but if Beau Eaton walks out the door telling me this was a mistake, I don't know how I'll look him in the eye again.

"So," my voice cracks on a suddenly dry throat, "triangle or strip, what's better?"

The column of his throat works as his arm moves again. On this swipe, his hand moves higher than before, over that dip just above my inner thighs, painfully close to my core. His broad palm slips over my stomach, skirting the boundary as his fingertips trace the lower ridge of my opposite hip bone.

I buck against his hand, all sensation and foreign twinges. I can't see his hand through the thick layer of bubbles, but, god, I can feel it.

"Neither is better, Bailey. I already told you this. I'm just here to see what you decide."

"But what do men li—"

"No. Don't ask yourself that. What do *you* like?"

He looks incredibly handsome, kneeling beside the tub. I want to drag him in here with me.

"I mean . . ." I lick my lips, trying to form words when every cell in my body is ready to explode over the sensation of Beau's fingers tracing my hip. His eyes on me make me feel exposed, even though soapy white bubbles conceal my entire body. "I don't know what I like. I usually just trim everything. As I'm sure you noticed the other night."

His responding chuckle is deep and raspy. It oozes sex and experience. "Bailey, trust me," he says, palm sliding up and shaping my waist. "That's not what I noticed."

"What did you notice?"

He groans, eyes flickering shut for a beat. "The noises you made," he confesses quietly as his palm slides up over my ribs. "How wet you were." The edge of his hand skims the lower swell of my breasts as he continues his gentle assault on my senses.

I whimper, fixated on the stern expression of concentration painting every feature of his face.

His big, strong hand slides down the center line of my torso and cups my sex. "The way you shook when you came for me." His thumb swipes over the trimmed pubic hair. "So, no, Bailey. I didn't give a fuck about this. I was too busy holding myself back from sliding into you."

Those fingers don't make a single move. They're there, but he doesn't try anything. We're in a standoff, eyes locked, panting more than breathing. His lips are so close to mine that I can't help but drop my gaze to them, remembering the way he kissed me last night.

Soundly. Like he couldn't control himself enough to stay away. Like I undid him, and he undid me too.

"I know what I want," I murmur.

"Yeah?"

He thinks I'm still talking about shaving.

But I'm not.

"I want you to kiss me." My lips part as I suck in a breath on the heels of my confession and watch raptly as his tongue slides out over his bottom lip.

Then his hand on my center moves to cupping my cheek as he angles my face to his and takes my mouth in a searing kiss. One that has me bowing up out of the water, body yanked toward his by forces outside my control. Giving me exactly what I want, like he could never say no to me.

Cool air hits my nipples as his tongue slides against mine. My hand grips his neck, holding him near, not wanting him to pull away and break this moment between us. As his lips move skillfully against mine, the rasp of his stubble sends chilled gooseflesh out over my hot body.

He smells almost sweet, like limoncello.

He tastes like temptation.

He feels so damn real.

When we slow, he leaves his forehead pressed against mine, his thumb stroking over the bow of my top lip.

"This isn't helping me decide," I huff out with a breathless chuckle.

A deep humming sound rumbles in his chest. "Okay, well, let's take a look. Maybe that will help you decide."

"What—"

I don't get to finish my sentence before Beau stands and swings a leg over the side of the oversized tub. He steps right into the water.

"I already started! There's hair in here."

He grins and shakes his head as he tosses his towel to the tile floor, his long, hard cock bobbing between his legs before he sinks into the bubbles. "I lived in a cave for eight days, sugar. I don't give a fuck about a bit of your hair in the water."

The massive hands around my waist lift my body effortlessly. He sets me on the tub's ledge, and with gentle strokes, he removes the bubbles from my skin and hair.

My cheeks flame as he takes me in, eyes focused between my legs before dragging up. The weight of his gaze is like a sharp point gliding over my skin. Like if he stares too hard, he might pierce me.

When I glance down, my skin is rosy, taking on a pink hue, and patches of bubbles slide down different parts of my body, melting away as I bare myself to him.

We've been swimming naked together every night, so this shouldn't feel as stripped down as it does. But the lights are on, and he's looking at me like he's seeing me for the very first time.

The inexperienced girl in me wants to shy away, but the woman who goes after what she wants opens her legs and revels in the look of intensity on Beau's face.

"Bailey." This time, my name is less of an admonishment and more of a plea.

"Triangle or strip? I tried to get the rest, but it was awkward."

He touches me now, calloused palms sliding up the insides of my thighs. Spreading me. Silver eyes burning like hot coals.

"I can clean it up for you," he murmurs, removing one hand to take both the bar of soap and the razor.

"You don't have to—"

"I want to." He silences me with the finality of that statement. I almost get the sense that it's more than just wanting to. He *needs* to.

He wets the bar of soap and rubs it over the mound of my pubic bone and along where the seams of my underwear might go. He's thorough and ... businesslike about it. Which might explain how I'm able to sit here with my legs spread—without combusting entirely—while Beau looks at my pussy really fucking closely.

I'm both relieved by his restraint and aching for his fingers inside me. To feel so full like I did all those nights ago.

But he doesn't cross that line. He lathers the soap, rubbing it back over the same spots with a wet hand. I feel myself clench and release when he gets dangerously close to where I want him. My arousal is only disguised by the fact that we're both drenched with lavender soap and bath water right now.

"Are you sure you're okay with this?" he asks as he places the soap down and dips the razor in the bath.

I gaze back at him, eyes wide, lips parted. His chiseled body kneels between my spread thighs, and the way he handles me is so sure, so caring. How could I be anything but okay with this? "I trust you," I reply quietly. As the words land, he jolts slightly.

Without saying a word, he dips his head closer and uses his

fingers to spread my lips in a way that makes the razor land in flat, even strokes.

My head tips back and my eyes flutter shut. "Fuck," I murmur as he grips me. The pressure of his fingertips, the scrape of the blade, the knowledge that his face is *right there*.

When he finishes tidying one side, he methodically moves on to the next. Large, deft fingers spread and manhandle me as he fixes up the spots I failed to reach. I can feel myself leaking, but I ignore it. There's no way he can tell.

I feel like I could come just from his proximity. But I don't. I focus on breathing, on not shaking. I focus on willing one of his fingers to slip inside me—for him to cross that line.

For him to be even more impulsive than he's already been by crawling into this bath with me.

"There," he announces roughly, voice echoing in the steamy bathroom as he massages the top portion of hair that remains. His jaw is set tight, brow lightly furrowed. "Have you decided what I'm doing up here?"

"Oh, you're doing that part, are you?"

He doesn't even pretend to make eye contact with me when he responds, "When I start a job, I finish it."

"Okay."

"What shape?"

"I don't know. I don't even think I care." All I care about is coming. Based on the way Beau's eyes are eating me up right now, I don't think it matters at all.

"Triangle," he bites out. "If you hate it, you can easily change it to a strip."

"Or you can." My voice sounds thick, deep—not my own. I feel like someone else right now. Someone beautiful and powerful, someone sure of herself and what she wants.

And what I want is him.

He swallows and nods, then moves in closer. My hand grips the tiled edge, the sharp corner digging into my palm. The huge diamond on my ring finger sparkles under the light from above.

"Or I can," he repeats as he glides the razor over the top horizontal line.

"Next time," I add, making his eyes finally snap up to mine.

"Next time," he repeats, and it feels like an agreement. It feels like a moment where we both realize this pull between us is stronger than either of us can resist.

Or maybe in this moment, we both realize that neither of us cares to struggle. We've both struggled enough already.

His gaze drops along with his head, and he gets to work.

Beau is meticulous, hand moving between us, pressing each leg open wider, and then resting on my lower stomach. His face is close, *so* close. He looks like an artist painting at an easel or something. It almost makes me laugh, because what else is a girl supposed to do in this situation? Tossed so far out of her realm of experience by the gruff military man.

I almost don't recognize myself.

After he shaves my pubic hair into a symmetrical triangle with military precision, he scoops up water, washing away all traces of soap and hair.

The pads of his fingers trail delicately over my slit, and I shiver. A moan tears from my lips, loud enough to hear over the swish and trickle of water. My head tips back and I try to hide my embarrassment behind closed eyelids.

I swear he growls. My legs try to clamp shut in response, but he catches them first.

"If I leave this bathroom right now, what are you going to do?"

Heat lashes at my cheeks, spilling down over my chest. My breasts are full, my nipples peaked almost painfully.

"Tell me, Bailey. I wanna hear it. I can see you. You're making a mess on the edge of my tub. If I get up and walk out right now, what am I gonna hear you doing from the other side of that door?"

My mind races. A little part of me wants to clam up on him right now. Tap out. This water feels too deep for someone who hasn't spent much time swimming.

But I'm a survivor. And I want this.

"Probably play with myself until I come with your name on my lips," I admit in a hushed tone.

His hands move up to my inner thighs, one on each side, then his thumbs press up over my outer lips.

He's teasing me.

I arch my spine, teasing right back.

"Seems unfair that you get to play with this pretty pussy when I'm the one who's been down on his knees doing all the hard work."

One thumb goes higher, brushing over my clit.

I cry out.

"Don't you think that seems unfair, Bailey?"

Another swipe.

"Yes!" My voice is a desperate whine.

"Ask me to play with your pussy. Let me hear it."

I lick my lips, glaring down at him through lust-filled eyes. And then I raise him one. "Please play with my pussy."

"Fuck, Bailey," is all he gets out before he buries his head between my legs and his tongue spears into me.

One of my hands flies back to prop up my needy body, while the other shoots to his hair. I brace for what has to be the most overwhelming wave of pleasure I've ever been hit with. Maybe it's the past five minutes of anticipation, maybe it's that no one has ever used their mouth on me.

Maybe it's *him*.

Whatever it is, it makes my vision go black and my brain shut down. It makes my legs spread impossibly wider, and my hips grind forward against him.

"You're fucking delicious," he rasps, then slings my legs over his shoulders.

My whimpers turn to moans when his tongue moves up, teeth grazing my clit before he sucks on it. And my moans turn to cries when he adds one finger—and then two—stretching me so carefully. He soothes the bite of his intrusion with the overwhelming pleasure of his tongue.

"Beau. Beau. Beau." I chant his name as he pushes me higher.

He shoves his fingers into me hard, shaking my body with the force of it while sucking me all at once, and I scream his name. A rush of heat flows from me, disintegrating my bones in the process.

My orgasm rocks my very foundation. Beau stays between my legs as I come back down, softly licking and sucking and telling me how pretty I am, and that makes my addiction to him even more obsessive.

Cool air rushes in when he pulls his head back, and I open my eyes just in time to see him lick his lips. He looks pleased with himself. He's got that devilish smirk on his glistening face, and that cocky glint in his eye.

"New rule, Bailey." He points at my left hand, slung over the edge of the tub, and then between my legs. "So long as you're wearing that ring, this pussy is mine."

My heart thunders at how base he sounds, staking a claim to my body.

"Next time you find yourself thinking you're going to pull that box of toys out and play with it all by yourself, you're going to offer it to me first."

I straighten slightly, trying to appear less boneless than I feel as I nod back at him. I'm buzzing with excitement as my tongue darts out over my lips. "Okay."

He pushes to stand above me, and my eyes bug at what's pointing straight at me from between his legs. He regards me carefully, completely ignoring his raging erection, something I find challenging to do.

I itch to touch it. I wonder how it would feel in my mouth. I want him to tell me in painstaking detail how he wants me to suck it.

"You're fucking perfect. You know that?" Then he leans down, kisses me tenderly, and brushes a thumb over my bottom lip, making me taste the lingering remains of my orgasm.

My eyes catch on his, and the sincerity there stuns me silent.

So silent that I watch him step out of the tub, replace his towel around his waist, and leave me there without another word.

27
Beau

I don't wake up screaming for once.

But I wake up with phantom burning pains. My first thought is that this is an improvement. My second thought is that it's 2:11 a.m. and Bailey didn't come to my room.

I should be happy I seem to be improving, even if my healed feet feel like they're sizzling against a hot grill beneath the covers.

But all I can think about is Bailey. The girl I'm supposed to be helping, not playing games with.

I saw her today. The way she looks at me. How easily she told me she trusts me.

She shouldn't.

And I shouldn't have taken as much trust as I did. Said the things I did.

I thought about marching across the hall and dragging her into my bed. It kills me to know she's right there, yet just beyond my reach. It kills me to know there's an expiration date on our arrangement. But there needs to be, because I've gotten myself in

234

far deeper than I ever should have. I've taken my hero complex to unseen levels.

This mission I backed myself into is beyond compromised, and she has no idea.

I scrub at my face and roll up to sitting, turning to press my feet against the cool floor. It does nothing to stop the burning sensation on my feet or the roiling in my stomach. I basically promised her a next time when I shouldn't have. I know I should keep her at a distance, but I wish she was in my bed, not alone in hers after what we just did. I want the "next time" to be right now.

How fucked-up am I? I'm hot and cold. I say left and go right.

I tell a girl who needs help getting a job that her pussy is mine now, like I'm some sort of over-the-top obsessive caveman.

She makes me feel like I am.

I'm so lost in thought that I don't even hear her approach. She rushes into my room without knocking. Tiny shorts, an even tinier tank top, and totally disheveled hair. "I'm so sorry! You orgasmed me stupid, and I forgot to set my alarm."

Hands propped on the edge of the bed, chin almost against my chest, I laugh silently. My shoulders shake, and the laughter comes out as a soft whoosh of air.

"Oh my god, Beau." She rushes forward, falling onto her knees at my feet. "Are you cry—" Her eyes widen when she gets a read on me in the dark room. "Are you laughing? I thought you were crying!" She slaps my knee.

I bring one hand up, pressing my fingers into my eye sockets. "The shit you say sometimes. I never know what's going to come out of your mouth."

"You scared me!"

"Did you really say I orgasmed you stupid?"

She glances away, biting at her lips, clearly to keep from laughing too. "Well," she says primly, glancing down to brush at her shorts. "It's true. You did. And I was sleeping like the dead because of it."

I go to reach for her, but drop my hand back down on the bed. "I shouldn't have just walked away after that. I'm just not used to . . . I haven't done this before."

She smiles, turning big, dark eyes up at me. Giving me a flash of how she might look on her knees, staring up at me with a mouth full of my cock.

I shake my head and blink the image away.

"Been engaged? Yeah, me neither." She waves a hand dismissively through the space between us. "It's okay. I didn't expect you to stick around."

There's no trace of hurt in her voice, no thread of a lie. She didn't expect me to stick around after being intimate with her, and that realization is like a steel-toed boot to the gut.

"Did you have the bad dream?" She carries on like what she just said to me isn't infuriating.

"Bailey, don't let men take advantage of you and expect nothing in return," I grumble.

She leans back a little, taken aback by the abrupt change in my demeanor, no doubt. "Is that what you did, Beau? Take advantage of me? Sure didn't feel like it. Felt like I asked you for something and you gave it. And then we high-fived and parted ways."

"We didn't high-five."

"If I'd been able to move, I'd have high-fived you."

"Good god, Bailey."

"Listen, I know you're hung up on treating me like a porcelain doll because I'm a virgin, but I think you're mixing up my expectations with your expectations. What happened tonight was consensual. I don't feel taken advantage of just because we're doing this thing for show."

"I wish you wanted more for yourself."

She barks out a quiet laugh, and I realize the words are cheap. They make what happened feel cheap.

I reach out and run a palm over her silky, mussed hair. "I'm sorry, that came out wrong."

She looks back up at me now, sadness shimmering in her eyes. "I want plenty for myself, Beau. I am single-mindedly making that *more* happen. It's why I'm here. It's you who believes he isn't more of what I want." Her hand covers mine. "You *are* more. But I've become accustomed to wanting more and not getting it. I don't let myself *need* more. That's a luxury I can't afford. I just keep moving toward my end goal. But you'd be a fool to think that means I don't want things for myself."

Her fingers pat against mine, and she pushes up to standing, turning to walk away like I did to her earlier. I thought I was doing what was best for her.

For me.

I felt cocky and amped up, ready to tease and play games. But now, my feet hurt, and with every step she takes away from me, so does my chest.

"Bailey," I croak her name in the quiet room, and she stops but doesn't turn. "Stay."

It feels like the world stands still for a moment. Like I just poured myself out there and am waiting to be judged. It's a strange sensation, waiting for another person to choose when I've always prided myself on being a person of action. A rational decision-maker.

This isn't rational, though. I'm operating on instinct, which is something I've done before, just not with a woman. Usually, I prepare for women in my life the same way I prepare for anything else. I let myself imagine all the outcomes—the worst outcomes—and then I decide if it's worth the risk.

I've done this exercise with Bailey in my head.

And I think that's what holds me back.

I won't let myself think of the worst-case scenario. It hurts too much.

After one moment turns into several, she slowly rises up on her toes and rotates, like she's trying not to startle me. "Stay?"

I say nothing. I feel laid bare enough right now, hunched over on the edge of my bed, asking her to stay while my feet continue to burn.

"Like, you want to go swimming?"

I swallow and shake my head.

"Stay here? In your bed?"

I nod, biting at the inside of my cheek and kicking myself for coming off all Old Beau before. I acted confident and commanding when *this* is what I feel like inside. Panicked, and sore, and lonely.

I must be giving Bailey whiplash. It's not fair to need her like this. It wasn't the deal we made. But I care less about that deal all the time and more about keeping her close.

"If this is you offering some sort of pity sex, I don't want it."

I scoff and hang my head. *This girl.*

"I'm serious, Beau." She walks toward me. "If I'm going to lose my virginity, it's going to be hot. Not sad."

I bark out a dry laugh and swap to staring up at the ceiling as she approaches. "Dear God, send help. I'm so far out of my depth with my fiancée."

She points at the ceiling as though adding to my fake prayer. "Same for me, big fella. Send help. I'm engaged to the most confusing man in the world."

Then she moves past me and crawls onto the bed.

"You're going to stay?" I turn to ask.

She tugs back the covers and wriggles in with a grumbled, "I can't believe our military thought you were cut out for special ops. Get in. I'm tired." Her hand pats the mattress matter-of-factly, and she flops back on the pillows like she owns the place.

I thought she might be awkward, but I should have known better. Bailey might get uncomfortable around other people.

But not me.

"Why do I get the mouthy version of you and everyone else gets the agreeable version?" I ask as I stand up, flick the bedside light on, and head to my ensuite bathroom. Once I grab the body lotion, hoping it will help the sensation in my feet, I head back to the bed.

Bailey shrugs, wild dark mane tumbling around her shoulders, a web of creases on her cheek from where she was clearly passed out against a crinkled pillow. "I've thought about that. I think it's because I know you won't hurt me."

I suck in a hissing breath like I've just been sucker punched.

"What are you doing?" she asks, carrying on with her stream of consciousness as I take a seat beside her on the bed.

"Rubbing some lotion on my feet."

"As one does in the middle of the night," she replies dryly.

I snort and carry on, propping one foot over my quad to spread cool cream over the mottled skin.

Bailey watches without speaking.

I glance at her and her eyes flick to mine but drop back to my foot. I swap to the opposite foot and start rubbing. I wish I could say it was making them better, but my hands just feel like chafing on raw skin. I growl in frustration, refusing to look up at her.

The silence between us is almost awkward.

And then Bailey says, "It rubs the lotion on its skin," in the softest, most sugary voice.

I crack up.

My feet burn like I'm stuck in that fucking cave, but I didn't laugh then. "Bailey!" I wheeze her name and tears prick at my eyes. "Please tell me you did not just quote *The Silence of the Lambs* right now."

Her melodic laughter caresses my ears and the bed shakes beneath us as we both laugh over the creepiest fucking quote she could have pulled out.

But that's Bailey. Saying random shit at random moments.

"Woman, you're out of control." I wipe at the corners of my eyes, smelling the non-scented lotion that smells like a hospital to me.

"Come on. You gotta tell me why we're silently sitting here side by side, rubbing cream onto our feet in the middle of the night."

I'm still chuckling when I offer her an explanation. "Phantom burn pain, according to Google."

"And your doctor?"

I grunt.

"Beau."

"I haven't asked. Not a big doctor guy."

"Therapist?"

I give her a wry look. "You saying I need therapy?"

"I'd go if I could afford it. Gotta take care of yourself, Beau. If you don't, who will?" As she scolds me about taking care of myself, she crawls out from under the covers, moving down toward the end of the bed. Then she peeks up at me, folding her hand in a come-hither motion. "Give me a foot."

"Apparently, you will."

She yanks my foot into her lap, hands wrapping over the sensitive skin so gently. The burning sensation instantly soothes under her touch. Her dainty fingers trail over my limbs with a feather-light touch. She spreads the moisturizer up over my ankle, pressing more firmly at the back of my calf.

"Someone's gotta do it."

"Might as well be my fiancée," I say, eyes fixed on her face.

When she looks at me, I wonder if she'll correct it to *fake* fiancée. I've used the term twice tonight. I'm testing our boundaries, waiting for her to put me back in line.

But she doesn't.

"Might as well be," she agrees softly.

Her hands work and we both get lost in watching until she asks, "What did you eat in that cave for eight days?"

"Rations from my kit. A sip of water here and there. It wasn't much, but just enough for us each to have a bit each day. We ran out the day before they rescued us. Micah was starving, so he got more of the dried rations."

"So you just didn't eat?"

"I didn't say that. I had to at least stay strong enough to get us out when the time came."

"Alright. So . . . "

241

"Cockroaches." I grin as I say it, ready for her to get all squeamish. But I should know better by now. She doesn't.

And she doesn't offer me sympathy for it either, which is something I constantly brace for when I talk about those days. I don't want sympathy; I want to feel normal again.

I want to feel something again, and with Bailey, I do.

Her hands keep working, and her lips part and close. Like she was about to say something and then thought better.

"Were they good?"

That's what she comes up with. She is priceless.

"They kept me alive. Not gonna be ordering them at a restaurant anytime soon."

She smiles, switching to my other foot and propping it over her thighs.

"Speaking of delicious foods." I chuckle at her transition, my eyes fluttering as the burning sensation slips away. "I had brunch with Willa, Sloane, and Summer today. Well, yesterday, I guess."

"Terrifying. But go on."

"It was nice. I wasn't having a very good day. Applied at the hair salon and got told the position had been filled. Spoiler alert: it hadn't."

I scrub a hand over my face. "Jesus fucking Christ."

"And then some guy was a dick to me at Le Pamplemousse."

"Bailey—"

She waves me off. "It's alright, Willa swooped in and . . . " She pauses, smiling while staring off into space. "Willa fucking lost it on him."

That makes me smile too. "Good." In my book, Willa is one of the best. Actually, all those women are.

"They seemed a little confused when I told them I was saving up to leave town. I probably shouldn't have said that, but I just—"

"You're an honest person. It's okay."

She nods. "And then, Summer offered me a job."

I sit up straighter at that. "Yeah?"

She nods, lips rolling together, looking a little bashful over it. "Yeah. But Beau . . . " Big brown eyes flick up to mine. "You didn't ask her to do that, did you?"

"No."

"Because it seems like a bit of a handout, and I already feel like a welfare case. It would embarrass me if you were maneuvering like that behind my back. You're already doing enough. I need to achieve some of my successes on my own."

"I didn't." I swallow, my body taut.

Her eyes are wide, earnest, searching. "Promise me you didn't create a job for me."

"I promise I didn't create that job for you with Summer."

She sighs a deep sigh, shoulders softening as she releases the breath. "Okay, good."

"I—" I start to talk and then . . . stop. Switching gears, I blurt, "I think I want to become a fireman."

She stops rubbing my foot as her head quirks. "Yeah?"

"I thought a lot about what you said that night. About doing something I want to do, and I don't want to spend the rest of my life working this land. It seems weird to switch careers and start something new at this age—"

"It's not weird at all. You'd be incredible at that."

Leave it to Bailey to support me more than I care to support

243

myself. "I think a lot of the skills I learned in the military could be applied there."

She bites at her lip in the most distracting way. "Yeah, I don't think firemen do any stealthy undercover work, so you'd probably be fine."

I gently shove a foot at her, toppling her back, and we both laugh. Always picking on me.

"Beau Eaton, tier one operator." She waves a hand in front of herself like my name is the title on a movie poster. "Asker of obvious questions. Shaver of pussies."

I lunge for her with a laugh. "Bailey, get your snarky ass up here." Arms around her waist, I haul her to me and soak her laughter in, letting it soothe what's inside me the way her hands soothed my feet. She squirms and squeals as I cage her in, leaning over to click my bedside light off.

I turn, flopping down and wrapping my body around her the way I did that night on the riverbank. Been dreaming of holding her like this since then, so I might as well capitalize on it while the opportunity is still here.

With my arms around her torso and my leg slung over hers, she finally settles. Her laughter eases into a light, contented sigh.

"How are your feet?" She pushes back into me, pressing her back flush against my front, and I drop a kiss to her hair.

"Better. Thank you."

"You're welcome," is her soft reply.

I shut my eyes, assuming now is the time we go to sleep.

But I should know better than to assume anything where Bailey is concerned.

"Hey, Beau?"

I sigh raggedly. "Yes, Bailey."

"Why didn't you let me put your cock in my mouth earlier?"

Good fucking god. "Bailey."

"I thought that was coming next. Ya know? You stood up, and it was *right there*. Pointing at me like I was the chosen one. And I was ready to practice. But you took off before I could make my vocal cords work again."

Any trickles of relaxation that were taking over in my brain are washed away in an instant. Rapidly replaced by images of shoving Bailey back into those white lavender-scented bubbles and letting her practice putting my cock in her mouth.

"Ready to practice?" I grumble, annoyed by how uncontrollable my urges are around her.

"Yeah, some instruction would be good, so I know what I'm doing out there."

Out there. That means *after this* and I don't like that thought at all.

So I squeeze her tighter, not letting my head go there. Not letting my brain plan for that worst-case scenario. The inevitable case scenario.

I can't handle facing it, so I just say, "Go to sleep, Bailey."

And I spend all night dreaming of teaching her all the things she wants to know.

But only here and only for me.

28
Bailey

Beau: Cade called me out early. You were out cold, so I didn't wake you. But I didn't want you to think I just ditched you either.

Bailey: You left me breakfast and a note on the kitchen island. Why would I think you ditched me?

Beau: Thought you might see this first when you checked your messages. Didn't want you to think I'd do that to you.

Bailey: I just didn't check. You're the only person who messages me. Thank you.

"Where's Beau this morning?" Summer looks up at me from behind the front desk of her athletic club. She's fresh-faced, sporting a topknot with damp hair by her temples, and she's wearing a branded Hamilton Athletics tank top stretched tight over her chest.

"He said Cade called, and he had to run out and help with something at the ranch." I try to keep my voice bright, taking in the wide-open gym with high ceilings and perfectly polished mirrors.

Truthfully, I wasn't sure what to make of the fact that he was gone when I woke up. Couldn't tell if he really had work or was making an excuse. This all started out as a show, but the things that are happening behind closed doors make it feel like a hell of a lot more.

There's something fractured about Beau. About his spirit. Like he's torn between so many versions of himself and doesn't know which one to pick.

I wish he knew it's okay to be all of them with me.

He swaps from solemn and brooding to playful and flirtatious, to sensual and domineering, to introspective and sensitive. Frankly, it's becoming difficult to keep up with which version he's going to give me each day.

It's becoming difficult to not want them all.

We're intimate and he walks away like nothing happened. I'm unfamiliar with how to navigate relationships with men, and I'm realizing I picked a complicated one to get my feet wet.

"Okay, well, I'll show you around and get you acquainted with everyone and the space." She takes a swig of water and smiles at me. "When do you want to start?"

"Anytime. Literally any time. Today?" Am I coming off as desperate? Maybe, but I don't care. I *am* desperate. "Monday?"

Her head tilts in question. "I thought you worked at the bar on weekdays?"

I shrug. "Yeah, I do." But that makes no difference. I'm used to working hard. "I don't mind, though."

Elsie Silver

"You're going to work both jobs on those days?" She seems slightly alarmed.

"I need the money," I confess.

"You don't have to explain yourself to me." She twists the cap back onto the bottle. "I just . . . I figured Beau would give you a bit of a leg up."

I keep my face blank.

"He's done well as a single guy with next to no expenses. Invested well. He's—"

I scoff and wave a hand. "Oh, totally. I just don't want to rely on him, you know? I've been forced to be super independent my entire life, so it's hard to escape that." My explanation really isn't much of a reach. I pride myself on how hard I work, on busting my ass to be different from the people who raised me.

"Well, why don't we work your shifts around your current schedule so you can still have a couple of days off? Be with your man." Summer winks at me, like we're two girls who know what the other is up to.

I feel instant guilt. She's been so kind to me, and I'm lying to her face and using her brother-in-law to get ahead.

My brain cycles back to where it did earlier, and I wonder again . . .

"Did Beau ask you to do this?"

Summer rears back. "Do what?"

I shift on the spot, suddenly nervous. Asking that was probably a bad idea, but I don't back down. I asked, and I meant it. "Hire me."

The other woman eyes me speculatively, and we stare at each other, but not for long. She catches me off guard when she laughs. "That's funny, because Beau would absolutely do something like

248

that. Those Eaton boys are a protective bunch, but no. If I started letting those meatheads make my business decisions, they'd take over the damn place. Beau hasn't asked me to do anything for you, Bailey."

My eyes skim over her face, and then I nod. "Okay."

She mimics the motion and replies back with her own, "Okay."

Then I spend the next couple of hours learning the ropes at Hamilton Athletics.

My new job.

"We're going out," Beau announces as he struts into his modern marbled kitchen. His jeans and V-neck T-shirt have no business clinging to his body the way they do.

I want to be that shirt.

I glance down at my cropped tank top and oversized sweats, rolled over and over at the waist. "We are?"

"Yeah. I'm taking you out."

I look down again, wondering if he's blind, because I am definitely not ready to go anywhere. I've got a celery stick in one hand, a jar of peanut butter in the other, and I'm leaning up against the kitchen counter having a snack.

"I'm good." Going out in this town is a constant exercise in humility.

"Oh, yeah?" His eyes peruse me, licking over every inch of my body. Flicking every switch. Like electricity zipping through a circuit, I go from relaxed to highly aware of him in an instant.

I guess tonight I get the sexed-up version of Beau.

"Yeah. Every time we go out, it's a huge spectacle with drama and whispers. I started at the gym today with Summer and worked a bit, so I'm all set."

My sentiment hangs in the air between us, and his gray eyes flash. *I'm all set.*

We can both see that means we might not need this arrangement anymore. We can both see the point I just made flashing like a neon light between us.

We both pretend it's not there.

"I'm not taking you out in Chestnut Springs. We're heading into the city."

That has me straightening, my eyes snapping to his.

"Why?"

He smirks. "For fun."

His expression drips with promise, and I don't know what to make of it.

"Just us?"

He nods. "Just us."

"Why?" I ask again, mostly because I'm trying to figure out what this means. Where we stand. Beau has me all twisted up inside, and I should have known we'd end up confused. I should have seen this coming.

Once again, he gives me the same simple answer. "Because I want to, Bailey."

"Well, I can't go out like this." I sniff and twist the lid back onto the peanut butter.

"Why not?" I detect his teasing tone, and the motion of him propping a hip against the kitchen island and crossing his arms, making his biceps bulge, draws my eyes.

Fuck, he's hot.

"Because look at you." I wave a hand over him. "You look like that, and I have to try to match you."

"You do match me. And it has nothing to do with what you're wearing."

I have to turn away because I don't know what to make of that sentence. All I know is I can't meet Beau's eyes in the wake of it, so I opt to put the peanut butter back into the pantry and give him my back.

I sense his gaze burning between my shoulder blades.

"What if I tell you I still don't want to go?"

I feel him prowling closer, his voice dropping an octave as he adds, "Then I'll have to do my best to be even more convincing."

A shiver races down my spine. I'm talking a big game, but the prospect of going into the city with Beau, where no one knows us, where he's not an Eaton and I'm not a Jansen . . .

It's really appealing. Fun is a rare commodity for me, so I'm willing to give it a try.

Large hands land on my shoulders and he turns me around to face him. Then his fingers slide under my chin, forcing me to meet his eyes.

"Bailey, I don't give a fuck what you wear. You can wear that if you want. Won't stop me from taking you out."

My cheeks flush. He's not Aloof Beau tonight. He's . . . almost aggressive in saying what he wants. It has my chest fluttering and my stomach flipping.

"Not a chance. I'll go change." I force myself to sound unaffected, but I'm not sure it works. I would guess that my pink cheeks are a dead giveaway.

"And don't wear a frilly little dress, Bailey. We're taking my bike."

The thought of spending an hour pressed up against Beau makes my cheeks burn brighter. Still, I hold my head high as I walk away, through the spacious house and toward the stairs that lead up to my room.

I've started keeping all my clothes there, even though my trailer is pretty much on his front lawn.

That's another thing we haven't talked about. The heat wave is over, and yet here we are. Still living together.

It feels a little like the straw house we built is starting to tumble.

I don't need the air conditioning, and yet I'm still here.

I don't need another job, and yet I'm still here.

I don't need to go out with Beau tonight, and yet I do.

I hold him close, the wind whipping against us as we race down the highway into the city.

At every stoplight, he reaches back and rubs my calf until it turns green again.

And nothing about any of it feels fake.

29

Beau

Willa: Talked to my dickhead brother. Just drop your names at the door. His name is Ford Grant Jr., and you can ask for him if you run into any problems.
Beau: Junior?
Willa: Yeah. Emphasis on the junior. It's his favorite.
Beau: For some reason I don't believe you. But thanks, Wils. I owe you one.
Willa: Cool. Actually, you can pull the little hairs at the back of his neck and say it's from me. He loves it.
Beau: I will not be doing that. But I'll tell him you send your love.
Willa: Lol. Yeah. Tell him that. That's even funnier.

It's dark out by the time we hit the city. I got caught up with work today and didn't make it back home until later than I thought I would.

Bailey presses against my back, her arms wrapped tight around my waist. She squeezes tighter every time we take off from a standstill, and it makes me want to stop and go all night.

I know she wasn't super keen on the bike. In fact, her words were, "Don't get us killed, soldier. Things are finally looking up for me."

And then she swung a leg over and hung on for dear life.

I revel in the feel of her against my body, in the knowledge that she trusts me with her life. Cocooning her in my bed last night stuck with me all day, and I'm not above admitting part of the reason I wanted to do this tonight was to have her close again.

I want her to sleep with me again too. But asking for that with the way we designed our relationship feels too forward.

Getting into her bath and making a meal out of her was probably too far too.

So maybe Bailey is right. Maybe I *am* impulsive. But only where she's concerned. And I don't regret it.

We stop at another red light. The bar I want to take her to is just ahead. I reach back, trailing a hand from her knee down over her calf. Hoping I haven't freaked her out too badly with the bike, I squeeze her reassuringly.

I turn over my shoulder, my helmet bumping against hers. "You okay, sugar?"

She nods.

"Almost there."

The light turns green, and within minutes, we pull up in front of Gin and Lyrics. Owned and operated by the one and only

Ford Grant—world famous investor slash record producer and Willa's older brother. Which is the only reason I got our names on the VIP list.

This bar offers music of all kinds. Different genres on different nights. Concerts for slightly bigger bands, talent nights for newbies. Tonight, there's a DJ playing. I don't know shit about them, but I figured a night in the city for Bailey to have fun without constantly having to look over her shoulder would be a good gift. She's still so young. She needs some fun in her life.

I want to give that to her.

"We're here," I say as I pull my helmet off and run a hand through my hair. Bailey's hands trail over my back and my ribs as she extricates herself from the bike. Music thumps from inside, and when I glance back, she looks excited.

Her eyes sparkle like dark gemstones as she straightens her hair, only slightly flattened on top from the helmet, then curling in little swoops around her arms. Long and loose.

She looks carefree for once.

Platform sandals prop up her wide-leg, loose jeans, and the skin on her chest shimmers from the reflection of the lights out front. She's wearing a black leather jacket with a little tear in the elbow and a corset-style tank top that has me fighting not to stare at her breasts like some basic asshole who sits at her bar every night.

Even though I am one.

"I've heard about this place," she murmurs, combing her hair out with her fingers. There's a soft smirk on her lips. A flash of anticipation in those chocolate depths. "Have you been here?"

I shake my head no, struck speechless by how different she seems in the glow of the city lights.

She's standing taller.

Her eyes aren't darting around.

It seems as though just getting her past those town limits has given her a boost.

Even her voice sounds different—less sugary and fake. More sultry, like she isn't trying to be someone else.

She can be *herself* here.

And I can't stop staring at her.

"Beau?" Her head flips in my direction, hair whipping over her cleavage, hip cocked out.

I shake my head to clear it. It doesn't help, though. I'm fully distracted by her, and I don't think I'll be getting over that anytime soon.

"Yeah, sorry. No, I haven't been here."

A flash of white teeth grates over her full bottom lip as she considers my answer. "I heard it's hard to get into."

I toss her a wink, deciding I need to get back in my confident mode and leave this starstruck version of myself out here in the parking lot. "Not for us. Willa got us onto the VIP list."

Her eyes widen. "Seriously?"

I pop our helmets on the bike and step toward her, hand outstretched. "Seriously. You ready? Date night?"

My breath stills, a little part of me wondering if she'll correct me. We had an agreement. This shouldn't be a date night.

But I want it to be.

She eyes my hand with a smile that makes my chest ache, then she links her fingers with mine. "Ready."

I underestimated how claustrophobic I would feel in the midst of this crowd. It hits me that I haven't been anywhere truly busy since getting out of the military. I've been hiding on the ranch, in that town, not living my life the way I should.

I feel intensely free and deeply terrified all at once.

I cling to Bailey's hand like she's my lifeline and push into the bar. The thrum in my body gives me a thrill, the burst of dopamine I only get when I buy something dumb, do something impulsive, or anytime I'm near Bailey.

Bailey's dark eyes glance over her shoulder as she leads me in. "You good?"

She looks like a different person. With a little over an hour between her and her childhood home, and a face no one recognizes, she *becomes* a different person. I adore every version of her.

But this?

Suddenly, I want nothing more than this for her. Excitement dancing in her eyes, a warm blush on her cheeks, a casual smile on her lips.

Conversation hums and bass thumps around us, and all I can do is nod. Because I don't know if I'm good, but I'm realizing she is. It's hitting me she can't stay in Chestnut Springs, and I would never want her to. How could anyone want to keep her there when she blossoms into this vibrant woman the minute she's away?

"Where to?" she asks.

"Not sure," I reply, tugging her back, not wanting her too far ahead. Not wanting to lose sight of her in the crowd.

Not wanting to lose sight of her ever.

My eyes catch on a roped-off section that is only a couple of steps up from the main floor. It's similar to what Willa described, but the man talking to a security guard beside the entrance isn't quite an exact match for how she depicted her brother. Though I can see the relation clear as day.

Hair almost like mine, but scruffy, dull, and boring, just like him.

This man's hair is more of a copper brown than Willa's bright red.

Tall, so he can glare down his nose at you.

Okay, he's about my height. Six-foot three or so, which I guess is tall enough to "glare" down his nose at Willa.

Green eyes like mine, but darker like money—his favorite thing.

I chuckled at that, but I can't see his eye color in the dim club. He's got a green V-neck T-shirt on, though.

Decent fashion sense but clearly trying to dress like he's salt of the earth when he's actually a stuffy billionaire.

Jeans. Scuffed boots. Some bracelets adorn his wrists. Leather strap on one side. Beads stacked over a Rolex on the other.

I can't help but chuckle to myself at Willa's description of him. It's so . . . Willa. And yet, I feel like it helped me pick him out.

"This way," I murmur against Bailey's ear as I move us toward the two men who are deep in conversation.

The man's head turns as we approach, and up close I can tell that he does, in fact, have an unusual eye tone. More jade-like than Willa's golden moss.

"Ford?" I ask, inclining my head slightly while squeezing Bailey's hand.

He looks me over swiftly before doing the same to Bailey. I have to stop my brain from going feral every time a guy lays his eyes on her. But I'm not above admitting there's a suave energy around Ford Grant that I'm pretty sure I don't possess. And I wonder if Bailey likes it.

His gaze doesn't linger, though. There's nothing inappropriate or rude about his gaze.

"You must be Beau." We stick our hands out, giving each other a firm shake. "And Bailey," he says, turning to her. She looks startled when he shakes her hand, like it's alarming to her that someone would want to shake her hand at all.

"Nice to meet you both." Ford smirks. It's not a relaxed, laid-back kind of smile, but it's not the scowl and grunt Willa prepared me to expect. "I'm sure my sister only sang my praises to you," he says as he turns and unhooks the red velvet rope. "She's got a real knack for that." He snorts and gestures us through.

I chuckle. "A special way with words, for sure. But I know she means well. Still, makes me wonder what she said about us."

He grins now, pointing at a table for us along the dropped dance floor. "I believe the text message I received mentioned her *GI Joe brother-in-law and his jailbait fiancée.*"

Bailey gasps and covers her mouth to stifle a giggle, the massive engagement ring on her finger sparkling as she does. I just shake my head.

Fucking Willa.

"For what it's worth," Ford continues as Bailey and I slide into our seats across from each other, "I think you make a lovely couple and my sister belongs in a straitjacket."

Now it's Bailey's turn to bark out a laugh.

Ford winks at her. "And you can tell her I said that." Then he knocks a couple times on the table and says, "You two have fun. Need anything, just let me know. I'll probably be hiding in my office, so I don't have to listen to fucking dance music all night long, but you can ask Karl there at the entrance to ring me."

"Thanks for—" I stop because Ford is already walking away. I chalk him up to being abrupt and all business, but not quite the raging asshole Willa made him out to be.

"Wow, the genes in that family are something else," Bailey says appreciatively while watching Ford walk away.

It rankles me more than it should. I straighten and give her a pouty glare.

She gives me wide eyes back. "What?" She lifts her left hand, waving her fingers to show off her ring. "I'm engaged, not dead. And you'd have to be dead to not notice that—"

"Bailey." I stare at her flatly, and she just smirks.

"Jealous?" Her lips curve up, and I know she's teasing me.

I swallow and hear the crackle of it in my ears. "Yes."

Her already big eyes go wider. "Really?"

It annoys me she thinks no man could be jealous over her. That she's learned to view herself as so undesirable I wouldn't feel threatened by someone else.

To be frank, it's a new feeling for me too. And I can't help but wonder if it's rearing its ugly head because of the nature of our relationship. The fakeness. Because I've never been insecure in this part of my life.

But I don't tell her that.

I lean over the table, elbows pressed to the flat surface with my forearms crossed, and say, "If you want someone to eye-fuck, I'm right here."

I expect her to be taken aback, but she's not Chestnut Springs Bailey tonight. Instead, she leans in closer. "And what if I want someone to actually fuck?" She spits the words out and they land on me like *rat-at-at-at* from the spray of bullets in combat.

Of course, an unwanted intruder approaches the table. "Hi! I'm Dani! I'll be your server tonight. What can I get started for you two?"

Bailey and I stare off for another beat or two before we both give into our polite instincts and turn our attention on the girl.

"I'll have a margarita on the rocks," Bailey answers smoothly, like she didn't just challenge me to fuck her.

"I'll have a Coke," I bite out, not looking away from the woman across from me as I make my order.

The server leaves and Bailey gives her head a slow shake. "No need to be snippy at her just because your panties are twisted up over nothing."

I clear my throat and lean back a bit in my chair, snapping out of whatever intense headspace I was just in. Of course, Bailey is right. She's the only person with a big enough pair to call me out when I'm being a dick.

"You're right," I grumble, regarding the bustling dance floor.

"Have you decided which version of yourself you're going to be tonight?"

Her question startles me, and I sit up straight again to look at her. "Pardon me?" I almost have to shout it across the space for her to hear me.

"You. You're inconsistent. I'm gonna need a neck brace to keep up with all the different personas."

I stare at her. Really stare. Being anonymous in a busy bar has emboldened her in more ways than one.

The truest thing I've ever said to her pitches up out of my throat unbidden. "I don't know who I am anymore, Bailey." I shout it across the table, listening to every syllable get swallowed up by the thumping bass.

"Who do you want to be?"

The question is so simple, but it bowls me over.

"I don't know. I was so tied up in my job. Now I don't even know. A rancher? Part of my community? Around for my family? A good uncle? A good son?"

She shakes her head at me slowly. "No, those are all things that you think other people want you to be." She reaches across the table, index finger poking me in the center of my chest. "Who do *you* want to be? Be selfish. You already told me you want to be a firefighter. Why are you pretending that's not on the table now?"

I don't know what to say, but she forges ahead.

"Me? I want a job I can't wait to go to every day. One that isn't dependent on how I look, one that I'll have worked impossibly hard to get. I want to walk into a store or a cafe and have people be happy to see me. I want them to wave hello at me. I want a fancy-ass truck with leather seats and all the bells and whistles. I don't want to work at going unnoticed constantly. I want to look respectable, but I also want to *be* respectable. I want to *be* respected."

Vitality courses through her and I want to soak it all up. Just being around her makes me want more for myself.

I want to answer her question with the same kind of fervor and surety, but the only thing I can think is, "*I want to be yours for real.*"

"Wanna dance?"

Bailey has had two margaritas now and I can tell she's feeling good. Loose. She seems . . . relaxed.

I chuckle and take a sip of my Coke. I'd kill for a beer right now, and I think I could handle one, but I still have to drive us back to

Chestnut Springs, and I have precious cargo. "I'm not a big dancer, Bailey. Or not this type of dancing." I gesture at the DJ, lifted on a podium across the dance floor. Bodies bounce and writhe in the pit between us.

"More of a two-step kinda guy?" She grins at me and pats my shoulder as she stands up, jeans hugging her hips, breasts full and on display over the neckline of her top. She's totally oblivious to her sex appeal.

As I watch her walk away from me, weaving through the crowd toward the dance floor with her head held high and her shoulders rolled back, she doesn't look young or inexperienced. She looks like a woman who could bring me to my knees.

I can't help but note that other men are noticing her too.

My eyes never leave her. Her hair shines, reflecting the flash of blue and purple lights from above. When she finds an open spot, her toned arms slide up over her head, her eyes flutter shut, and her hips sway in time with the sultry beat of the music.

It's a punch to the gut.

She's fucking stunning. And confident. I can't peel my eyes away. I can't believe this is my Bailey Jansen.

Quiet, nervous, borderline mousy, Bailey Jansen.

But that's not who she is today. That's not who she is at all.

She's someone else entirely and her transformation is something to behold. It feels like a gift to sit here and watch her be herself.

And it's a gift I only get to savor for so long before I see a hand slide around her waist. One brush of another man's fingers over the single inch of exposed skin between her waistline and shirt, and her eyes snap open.

Her gaze latches onto mine from across the room.

The guy shouts something in her ear from where he stands behind her and she smiles, still staring directly at me.

Then she holds her left hand up.

I see her palm.

But he sees her ring.

I see the guy chuckle and say something else before patting her shoulder and moving away. Which is perfect because he just freed up my spot.

I'm out of my seat and moving across the dance floor toward my fiancée within seconds. We don't drop eye contact even once. When I get to her, I skim my hands over her waist, that inch of skin, as though washing away the other man's touch.

"Bailey," I growl against her cheek and press a brief kiss there as she wraps her arms around my neck.

"Beau." She says my name like a sentence, as I do hers, and returns the one simple kiss to my cheek.

I tug her close, lining our hips up, reveling in the feel of her swaying against me, the vibration of the loud music that rattles in our bones.

Dropping my lips to her ear, I confess, "I have no idea what I'm doing."

The dancing, my life, this deal with her—I mean all of it. I have no idea what I'm doing. And for a man who's had a plan for so damn long, it terrifies me.

She sways against me, fingers raking through the closely trimmed hair at the back of my head. "You're just being here with me. That's all I want."

She turns and leans her back against my chest, ass brushing against my cock. I let myself settle into the thought that maybe it's okay to have no idea what I'm doing.

That being here with Bailey is enough.

That maybe she wants more than this arrangement, impossible as it might have seemed originally.

I spend all night on the fucking dance floor, swaying to the beat, while Bailey dances against me with a heart-rending smile on her face.

"Beau, take me home," she finally asks.

Of course, I'm more than happy to do that too. But this time, I don't just hold her leg at red lights. I reach back and grip her thigh for the entire wordless drive back to Chestnut Springs.

And I swear she holds me closer than she ever has before.

By the time we make it home, I've realized that I'll probably give this girl anything she wants.

A ring.

Sex.

Forever.

30

Beau

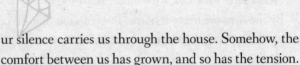

Our silence carries us through the house. Somehow, the comfort between us has grown, and so has the tension. She's slipped into an oversized vintage Madonna T-shirt that hits her mid-thigh and casts curious glances my way through the mirror when I bring my toothbrush into her bathroom to brush my teeth next to her.

Did I take one look at my empty bathroom and then opt to brush my teeth in hers instead?

Yes.

I don't want to be far away from her, and I'm too tired to fight it right now.

We spit our toothpaste simultaneously, and both of us awkwardly reach for the tap. Our hands bump, and we yank back like the brief touch electrocuted us.

Her eyes snag on my naked torso as I mumble, "Sorry."

She clears her throat, blinking away. "Don't be. What are you—"

"Where are you—"

Our words collide with each other clumsily. After a fun night spent yelling at each other over the blare of electronic music, the house is too quiet.

Too private.

We're out of places to hide from each other.

"Can I stay with—" I start, right as she says,

"I need to masturbate."

My earlier sentence dies on my lips. "Come again?"

"You told me I should offer it to you first." She straightens with pride, staring at me through the mirror. "The next time I was planning on doing it."

I stare back, hating myself for saying those words to her in a moment of weakness. Hating that I meant them, and she's throwing them back at me when I'm already feeling so vulnerable around her.

"Listen, you can't just maul me all night on the dance floor and expect me not to have needs. I'm not a robot like you, apparently."

I keep staring, grappling for some semblance of control, but it's slipping through my fingers like sand I have no hope of containing.

Bailey turns to look at me directly, forcing our gazes away from the reflective glass. Our eyes clash as the tension pulls taut between us. "I felt you hard against me, Beau. You gonna tell me that didn't happen?" Her voice takes on a venomous tone, frustration humming at the back of her throat. "You got some big, mature, paternal words of wisdom for me about what I should and shouldn't do with my body? Because so help me g—"

My hand shoots forward, fingers curling into her hair. Until I'm fisting it, tipping her face up to mine while I step up close, toe to toe with her, cutting her off. "Bailey, stop running your mouth or I'll find another creative way to keep it busy."

Her tongue darts out over her puffy rosebud lips. Her eyes are furious flames. "Good. Do it."

My jaw pops as I squeeze a fistful of her thick, silky hair. I want to flip her over and take her hard and fast and wild. I know she'd rise to the challenge.

But I'd never forgive myself. It bothers me that what we're doing here can be filed away as fake when it's the most real thing I've felt in my life. And Bailey's been picking up the scraps of what she can find for far too long.

No, when I take Bailey, there's not going to be a single *fake* thing between us. She's not going to need me to stay afloat to pay a bill—I won't take advantage of her that way. I want her to need me for no other reason than she can't stand the thought of not having me.

"Where's that box of toys you're always going on about?" I growl.

"Under my bed." Her voice is breathier now, laced with nerves and anticipation.

"Good, now you're going to show me."

"Show you?"

I drop her hair, reach beneath her thighs, and hoist her into my arms. Her legs wrap around my waist as I march us out of the bathroom straight to her sprawling king-sized bed.

When I drop her down she steps back, the backs of her thighs butting up against the bed, breathing heavily, just like me.

"Who do you want to be?"

That question again. Like she can see straight into me through the confused haze.

Be selfish, she said. So I respond with the first thing that pops into my head. "The man who watches you come tonight."

It's true, but it's also not enough. I want to be so much more than that.

Bailey's eyes dance across my face, flitting from eye to eye as she rolls her lips together. Finally, she nods slowly as she lowers herself to sit on the edge of the mattress, the warm glow of the bedside lamp making her smooth skin shimmer.

"The box is under the bed, Beau."

I crouch and reach, feeling the cool edge of a small plastic box. When I pull it out, it resembles something you might store old keepsakes in. I open it and find about ten different toys. Various colors, shapes, and sizes.

I swallow.

My fingers trail over the edge as my brain flips over into a place where I'm functioning only on instinct. Images of Bailey using these, squirming, moaning—in the room next to me or in her trailer just across the lawn—flash through my head.

I consider my options. Slender with a second arm. Hot pink. Another that looks like—

"Listen, if you're going to back out, why don't you just—"

My hand wraps around the one that looks like a real dick, thick and heavily veined. I push to stand and cup her cheek with my other hand, running my thumb over her plush lips. Pushing them to the side and watching them pop back into place. "Bailey, what did I tell you about running your mouth?"

A demure smile curves her lips as she says, "That you'd find something creative to do with it."

Her smile may not be so demure after all.

I lean down and whisper, "Brat," just before I press my lips to hers. When I swipe my tongue into her mouth, she makes this happy little humming noise and tips her head back. Tangling her tongue with mine, her hands go from gripping the edge of the bed to wrapped around my neck. Pulling me closer. Kissing me deeper.

I let her. And for several seconds, I kiss her back. Taking pleasure in the feeling of being so wanted. So needed.

So *alive*.

When I eventually pull back, she drops her arms from around my neck, and I chuckle, deep and raspy. "Is that what you thought I meant by creative, sugar?" Her eyes widen when I trail the head of the silicon cock over her lips. "Open, Bailey."

She does.

"Tongue out. Nice and flat. Like you're begging for it."

Her fingers dig into the mattress as her thighs squeeze together. Then her mouth opens wide, and she sticks her tongue out, just like I instructed.

I feel like I'm going to burst right through my fucking boxers as I slide the toy over her extended tongue while she stares up at me. Ready. Nipples pointed against thin cotton.

I push it back, watching the fake cock fill her mouth, lips thinning as she wraps them around its girth.

Fuck, I wish it were me.

It will be me.

I drag it back out, her saliva coating it, and then glide it in again. Further this time, but not too far. I'll save that for another day.

"Can I go further?" I ask, working it in and out.

She nods, and I pump it into her again.

"Suck, Bailey. Move your tongue. But no teeth. Open wide for me."

I watch her adapt. Her cheeks hollow out, and I almost blow in my fucking shorts.

Saliva coats her lips, a string of it stretching between the toy and her mouth when I pull it all the way out and go back for more. Easing back in. I watch her lips part around it again.

"You're fucking perfect, you know that?" I look her in the eye when I say it.

A little whimper lodges in her throat, and she reaches for my hips, bracing herself. Bracketing my cock. My palm on her hair gently paces her motion.

"You're doing so well, Bailey," I murmur in the quiet room, easing back out just a bit.

And then she does it. Mouth stuffed full, she moves one hand and lets it roam over my rock-hard dick.

"Fuck," I groan. Eyes fluttering shut.

She adds a second hand, tugging my shorts down and gripping me. Soft, tentative hands roam my body.

There's an innocence to it. It's exploratory. And I let her go on the adventure. My hips buck forward without even meaning to.

Her eyes flit to mine as one hand moves down to cup my balls while the other works up and down my length.

"Careful, Bailey."

She draws back, the rubber cock leaving her lips with a wet popping sound. "Why?"

"Because my control is shot, and it's been a long fucking time since anyone other than me has touched my cock."

"So, you're going to come on me?" I swear to god her lashes flutter as she asks me that.

This girl. Her questions. I can hardly keep up. It doesn't help

271

that her hands haven't stopped working me. I tip my head back and groan.

"I'm fine with that. I think I might like it."

My body coils tight, muscles bunching beneath her touch. "Bailey."

She hums in response, and there's almost a laugh to the noise. She knows she drives me insane and gets off on it.

"What? I'm on birth control. You can come wherever you want, and it would probably be—"

"Jesus," I bite out and reach down for her. With my hands gripped around her ribs, I lift her easily and toss her back against the pile of pillows that protect her from the headboard as I scramble up on my knees.

"You're a little cock tease. You know that?"

Her eyes are like saucers, wild and sparkling, and this girl . . . this girl fucking smirks at me.

Her shirt has lifted high enough that I have an easy view of the red lace shorts she's wearing. The sight of her—legs splayed, cheeks flushed—makes me feral.

"Lose the shirt. I'm not staring at Madonna while I watch you fuck this toy."

Her mouth pops open, and I consider shoving my dick in to watch her try to keep up with the real thing. But she's never done this before, so I can't do it all at once. I have to pace myself. I have to go slow with her.

She deserves every one of the bases. She deserves all the angsty *almosts*.

Bailey rips off her shirt, tossing it carelessly to the side. I move forward and kneel between her legs, using my eyes to trace every curve.

I want to memorize exactly how she looks right now. Dusky nipples, heaving chest, goddamn triangle tan lines from that bathing suit she's always laying out in.

My fingers trail the scalloped top edge of her red lace underwear, hooking under but not pulling yet.

"Can I take these off?"

She nods, eyes now fixed on where my hands are. She looks so tiny beneath them. I peel the fabric away, inch by delicious inch, bending her knee to free one side.

I decide I like the look of them haphazardly still stuck on one leg, wrapped around one thigh, like we didn't care enough to take them off completely.

It makes her look a little disheveled. A little undone.

I smirk at the sight, glancing up at her. "You okay, Bailey? Gonna need you to keep talking to me."

She nods, an edge of panic in the movement.

"Sugar." I move forward, leaning over her sprawled body, the one I had my hands on in the middle of a stupid dance floor mere hours ago. I grasp her chin gently between my thumb and forefinger. "Any time you want to stop, we stop. You got that?"

"Oh my god. Please don't stop." The words come out on a sharp exhale. "Just ignore me. I'm having an out-of-body experience."

"Bailey. I'm not ignoring you."

She licks her lips. "You should."

"Impossible. I'm memorizing you," I reply softly before kissing her again and feeling her naked body bow up into mine as I settle down over her.

Her hands tangle in my hair before running over my shoulders, trailing down my spine. I lose track of how long we spend like this.

Elsie Silver

My body draped over her. Her lips fused with mine. My fingers pinching her nipples. Her hips rocking desperately against mine.

I don't stop her when she reaches for the waistband of my partially removed boxers. "These are driving me crazy," she mumbles against my lips as she tugs at them frantically. "I want them off. I want to feel you."

I pant against the crook of her neck as she leans up just far enough to shove them away. And then her hands are back on my cock, gripping me. Her touch is clumsy and unfettered. Warm and firm.

"Beau," she moans my name and my hips flex toward her, into her grip. Her legs wrap around me, her heels digging into the backs of my calves. "More."

She draws me close.

"Bailey ..." My swollen head bumps against her inner thigh. "Careful."

I dig my teeth into her shoulder, wanting to leave another mark on her.

"I ..." She breathes that one syllable, and it's so full of longing that I almost lose it. "I don't want to be careful."

I bite her neck. Her skin is hot, a match for mine as we slide against one another. It's intoxicating. Her smell. Her feel. Her words.

We're both impulsive right now.

I rear up above her, eyes catching on the red mark I left behind.

Her legs are splayed over my thighs. Pussy on full display. Pink and wet as her hands draw me closer.

"Bailey," I grit out as she lines us up.

A pearl of pre-cum glistens at the tip of my cock. She fucking wipes it against herself, right through her wetness. Her eyes shut and her tits tilt up at that first contact.

"Bailey," I say again, reaching forward to fist my base, pushing her hands away in the process. They end up on her tits, pinching, squeezing—that big diamond flashing at me like a warning light to slow the fuck down.

She's mindless right now, for *me*.

And me? I'm mindless for her.

But she's depending on me. Depending on me to take care of her. To not be *too* impulsive.

"Beau." Her eyes flip open, searing me with the heat dancing in their depths. "I want it."

"I know, baby. But we're not rushing this."

I swipe myself through her folds again, because I am a glutton for punishment. "I want to make it so good for you, Bailey."

She squirms and moans. "It already is."

"Not yet." I barely rasp the words out, seeing the head of my cock come away all wet with her.

She whines, actually whines, and spreads her legs further. "When?"

Fist around my dick, I press it against her pussy again. "When I say so, Bailey. Didn't I tell you this pussy is mine now?"

She moans in response.

And god, I'm so fucking weak. My hips defy me. They edge forward, and one inch of my cock disappears inside her.

We both freeze.

"Fuck." I groan, feeling her pulse around me.

Her head rocks slowly from side to side on the pillow as she chants my name.

I'm standing at the edge of a cliff. One half of me says *jump*. The other says *maybe grab a parachute first*.

I pull out and press that same inch back in, watching her spread for me.

God. It would be so easy to just—

No. I don't want to be careless with her. It's not just her body. Her first time. It's her heart.

It's my heart. It's my hang-up on faking it. It's my control in question.

Which is why I pull out and reach for the toy that's lying forgotten on the mattress beside us.

I replace myself with it and watch her writhe.

"Fuck!" she cries out as I work it into her.

It's not as large as I am, but she still shakes when I push it all the way in.

My fist is painfully tight around my girth, like I can somehow cut the blood flow off and keep myself together by squeezing tighter.

"Bailey, baby, use your hands. Show me what you do."

Eyes on me, she trails her hands down her torso until she's holding the silicon base.

She presses somewhere, and the thing hums and vibrates. Wetness leaks out from where her body grips the skin-toned toy as she cries out instantly.

"You like that?"

She nods in response, and I use my free hand to graze a finger over her lips, stretched tight around the vibrator.

"You look so fucking pretty like this." I wrap my hand around my cock and pump once, and she moves in time with me, easing the toy out and back in.

It's the worst tease in the world, watching her fuck herself and wishing it were me. My body aches with it. Low on my back. Behind my hip bones.

"What do you think about while you do it?"

"You." *Fuck.* She doesn't even hesitate. Lips parted, both hands working between her legs.

I swipe a thumb over her clit. Her legs shake, and she moves the toy in a more even tempo.

"You pretending I'm fucking you right now, Bailey?" I can't look away. We're a jumble of limbs and wetness.

"Yes," she whispers and licks her lips.

I keep at her clit, palm sliding over my dick as I imagine what it will be like to fuck her how I want to. Rough and messy. Claiming her.

"I don't know, Bailey. I'm bigger than that toy. You think this tight little cunt can take me?"

She gasps as she shoves the toy in harder. "Yes, Beau. Fuck. Give it to me."

"Give what to you?" Our words are choppy. Breathless. So is every movement. Every muscle and tendon strung up tight. Everything about this moment is ready to snap and crumble down around us.

"Your c-cock," she stutters slightly, doing her best to keep up.

I don't miss the deep blush on her cheeks. Listening to her say things she probably never has makes me harder. I'm the lucky fucker who gets to hear her try them all out.

"What about my cum, Bailey? Would you settle for that tonight?"

A strangled groan catches in her throat as she shuts her eyes for a beat. Then her lashes lift lazily, and she takes a quick bite on her full bottom lip before she says, "Yes, sir."

That's all it takes. I blow.

One hard jerk and I'm coming, hand now braced on her inner thigh, spreading her open. The first rope lands on her toy, the one she doesn't stop fucking herself with even as I mark her. The next on her clit, dripping down onto her lips.

She works my cum into her pussy with the vibrator. And I watch her do it.

"Oh god," I groan, losing it over how fucking good she looks. Another rope hits the freshly trimmed triangle, the next her hand.

She doesn't stop thrusting her toy. She watches, lips parted, legs shaking against mine, as I make a mess of her in the basest way possible.

She's hot and pink and trembling. All it takes is me wiping the slick of my cum off her hand and pressing it against her hard clit, rubbing it in one firm circle, for her to fall apart right before my eyes.

Bailey screams my name as her head falls back, exposing the elegant column of her throat.

"Oh god, oh god, oh god," she repeats. Her body goes impossibly taut, then impossibly slack.

She tosses the toy away before slinging an arm over her face, but otherwise doesn't move to cover herself.

I press her clit once more before my hands explore more of her exquisite body. Palms over her inner thighs. Her stomach. I shape her waist. Gently cup her breasts. Then kiss each one.

And she lies there, letting me. A stillness rolls over us. A peace.

"You're perfect," I murmur as I kiss my way down the valley between her breasts. "Every inch. Every look. Every word."

Her hands move to my hair, fingers trailing over the shell of my ear. The back of my skull.

"I'm so fucking hung up on you, it's not even funny," I confess quietly, and then press a kiss to her belly button. She shivers, fingers gliding down the back of my neck.

I don't expect her to say anything. Or to feel the same way. I'm too old. She's too young. Too good for me when it comes down to it.

Which is why it sends me reeling when she whispers, "Wherever you're hanging from . . . I think I'm on the same hook."

31
Beau

Beau: I need to talk to someone.

Jasper: No shit. Been telling you that for a while now.

Beau: No. Dick. I need advice.

Jasper: Have you considered Harvey? His advice is always the most entertaining.

Beau: Jas, I'm serious. I can't handle Harvey's insanity right now, and you're the only one who knows about this.

Jasper: Oh. Beer?

Beau: Beer.

Jasper: Pick me up. Sunny will drive me home when she's done practice.

Beau: I can bring you back.

Jasper: You could, but you'll prioritize sitting at the bar like the lovesick puppy you are.

I swing by Jasper's house to pick him up. He's back from summer training camp in Rose Hill and getting ready for pre-season with the Grizzlies. Which means we're heading into the time of year where I hardly see him at all.

Especially now that he has Sloane.

Not that I'm one to talk with the amount of time I've been spending with Bailey.

I put my truck in park and wait. This fucker is constantly running late. Has been since we were teenagers, since I picked him up and made him move in with us. Made him an honorary Eaton.

My mind drifts back to this morning. To waking up with Bailey, naked, cradled against me, my nose nestled into her coconut and sugar-scented hair. My arms wrapped over her body while her hands held my biceps, as though I would let go if she didn't hold me against her.

After our orgasms, I used a warm, damp cloth to clean the mess we made and crawled into bed with her.

We didn't say anything.

At 2:11, I woke with a gasp rather than a yell.

She reached for me before padding to the bathroom and returning with lotion that smelled like her. In the dim light, she gently rubbed my feet until the burning sensation subsided and then crawled back under the covers with me.

We didn't say anything. Didn't need to.

Until morning, when I realized there were things I needed to say to her. Things that shouldn't go unsaid.

And for all my heroics, I took one look at her peaceful, sleeping face, felt my body come alive from watching her lie there, and I crawled out of bed before I could do anything I shouldn't.

I worked all day, found things to fix just to keep myself busy.

Then I texted my best friend—my almost-brother—and told him I needed to talk.

Movement at the front door draws my attention. Jasper jogs down the front steps of his and Sloane's new house. He's dressed like he's been to the gym. Hair curling around his ears, Calgary Grizzlies hoodie stacked up around his neck, shorts, and sneakers.

When he yanks the door of my truck open, he smiles at me. I've known Jasper for the better part of our lives, and I've never seen him look as happy as he does lately. He's lost so much, been alone in so many ways. He was moody and quiet and shy.

But now he has Sloane.

I smile back at him. "Hey, man."

He hops in, slamming the door. "Hey, dumbass," is his reply as he buckles up. "How's it going?"

I roll my eyes and pull out of the driveway. "Fine."

"That's it? You text and tell me you need to go for a drink when I know you're basically living some sort of deep-cover mission and what you give me is *fine*?"

"I'm waiting until we're on the road."

"Why?" He's literally laughing at me now.

"I don't fucking know, Jas. I'm paranoid about anyone hearing. I don't want to betray Bailey."

"You think Cade has some sort of special microphones planted around the ranch?" He peers around us dramatically.

"Fuck off."

He does not fuck off, though. Instead, he claps his hands together and then points at me. "Nah. It's probably those new supersonic hearing aids Harv got."

"Dad got hearing aids?"

Jasper chuckles, flopping back in his seat. "Goddamn, dude. You ask some seriously stupid questions for someone who was supposed to have been a super soldier."

I can't help but crack a smile now. "That's what Bailey always says."

I expect Jasper to laugh, but he doesn't. In fact, he goes so quiet I glance over at him as we turn out of the ranch and head into town.

He stares at me.

"What?"

He tips his chin at me. "You."

"Don't be Mr. Mysterious with me. That's not our jig, and you know it."

"Okay, well, that rule goes both ways. Yeah?"

I shake my head. Can't ever pull one over on Jasper. He's too smart. Watches everything too damn closely.

Including me, apparently.

"Fine. Sure."

"I've been in your company for like two minutes and you've brought Bailey up twice."

"And?"

"Just making an observation. Once per minute is a pretty solid clip."

"You talk about Sloane all the time." I sound defensive to my own ears.

"Well, we are married. Were *actually* engaged at one point."

I straighten and twist my palms on the steering wheel. "Well, so are Bailey and I."

I don't need to turn my eyes on Jasper to know the look he's giving me right now. It's blank and impassive. He does it well.

"Really, Beau? We're gonna play that game?"

"What? We are. For all intents and purposes, we are."

"Do you know what the word 'intent' even means?"

My molars grind. "Yes."

"Okay, good. Cool. Thought you might have been confused." He chuckles as he props one foot over his knee.

"I'm not. We're engaged."

I refuse to glance over at him and keep my eyes on the road as silence blankets the cab of my truck. Five seconds stretch into ten. Into twenty. I'm ready to snap at him about the silent treatment when he finally says, "Oh shit."

"Oh shit, what?"

"You're into her."

Into her.

That seems like it's vastly understating whatever it is I feel for Bailey.

Invested.

Possessive.

Obsessed.

I scrub a hand over my face and decide not to use any of those words in case Jasper thinks I'm insane. "Yeah," is all I reply with.

"So, the fake part of this fiancée thing isn't very fake anymore?"

"I don't know. It's changed."

"I thought you didn't want to be tied down?"

I grunt. "I don't. Okay, I *didn't*."

Jasper lets out a low whistle, like he's impressed. He knows all the reasons why I haven't wanted to tie myself to anyone. But now I'm not taking off at the drop of a hat. Now my chances of dying are significantly lower.

Now I'm here to stay.

"But you guys haven't talked about it?"

"No. Not yet."

"Then why are you talking to me about it?"

"Because I don't know who else to talk to about it," I bite out.

"Maybe try the girl who it involves?"

"Rich coming from you. How many years did you pine after Sloane before you came clean?"

From the corner of my eye, I see Jasper shake his head. "That was different, and you know it. But even if it weren't, I have enough perspective now to tell you I wish I'd told her sooner. I wish I hadn't counted myself out or convinced myself I didn't deserve something happy."

I flinch at his words, covering it by pretending to swat at a fly. *Didn't deserve something happy.* He's a little too on the nose today.

"Nobody just waltzes around telling their lifelong friend they're into them, Jas. Not anyone with a modicum of survival instinct anyway. Imagine she turned you down. Oof. That would have been rough. Kiss that friendship goodbye."

I look both ways before pulling out onto the main highway that will lead us into Chestnut Springs. The tires go from crunching over gravel to humming over asphalt. The radio from slightly crackling to clear sound.

Finally, Jasper speaks. But it's in that quintessentially Jasper way, quiet and introspective, like he's thought out every single word before they even leave his lips. "Right. But it would have been worse to spend my life wondering what would have happened if I told her. Or wishing I had."

I swallow as the horizon line in front of us changes. Buildings crop up as downtown comes into view. As we draw closer to the bar. To Bailey.

To the girl I might spend a lifetime wishing I'd told this thing isn't fake to me anymore.

32

Bailey

Beau: Jasper and I are coming to hang out for a drink.
Bailey: Oh, a sign of life. Thanks for the heads up.

I should be Beau Eaton's biggest fan today. He made me see stars last night and then held me against him like I was his favorite stuffed toy all night long. Then, when I thought he was getting up to go to the bathroom or get a drink of water, he disappeared on me. If it were for work, he'd have gone earlier. But instead, he slept in and then left without a word when he thought I was still asleep.

He told me he was hung up on me. Then fucked off. And I was too chickenshit to go after him.

I grab another fork, spoon, knife combo and angle them across the paper napkin, rolling the cutlery up like it's done something to offend me. I toss it into the bucket beside me, glance up and down my mostly empty bar to see if anyone needs topping up, and start all over again.

I've spent all day trying to make heads or tails of it, and it's become clear to me I have no clue what I'm doing where Beau Eaton is concerned. I'm officially a basic bitch with a massive crush on the same person as every other girl in town.

And I know I'm leaving. Which is a hilarious combination.

Do people masturbate together all the time and then just carry on like nothing happened? I don't even know! Worse, I have no one to ask.

Except for Beau. Which just comes off kind of pathetic in this case. So I've stewed all day. Lying in the sun, pretending to read when I'm fairly sure I just read the same page over and over again while waiting for him to show up.

Then I got ready early for work, taking extra time to look really fucking good. Glowing from an afternoon spent in the sun made it easy to go light on my makeup. I scrubbed and moisturized my skin until it freaking shines when the light hits it. Wanting to showcase the goods, I picked a floral tank top that ties at both shoulders and tucked it into skin-tight black jeans. Jeans I know make my ass look great.

And then I spent a painstaking amount of time blowing out my thick head of hair, section by section, with a round brush. It tumbles down my back like a mane, heavy and voluminous.

I'm counting on Beau actually showing up. For all his mixed signals behind closed doors, he's been nothing but steadfast and dependable where safeguarding me at my bar is concerned.

And sure enough, the door swings open at 8 p.m., and in he walks, all bronzed skin, tight T-shirt, and sun-bleached hair. His brown locks are now highlighted with streaks of blond and warm chestnut because he refuses to wear a hat at work. He insists he's not a cowboy while simultaneously burning his ears working the ranch all day long.

My stomach flips over on itself, butterflies erupting as he approaches.

He doesn't belong here.

The thought pops up and I swipe it away. Write it off as wishful thinking. Of course he belongs here. He's the prince of Chestnut Springs.

"Boys." I smile stiffly and toss two coasters on the bar as Beau and Jasper saunter up, pulling stools out for themselves and greeting Gary. Beau reaches across the bar, avoiding my gaze, and grabs my hand. He presses a kiss to the top of it, his usual bar greeting for me since we got engaged. His lips brush my skin and electricity sizzles their wake as I tug my hand away.

Gary slurs some sort of greeting and I shake my head at him. He tosses his keys up on the bar without argument and gives me a watery smile.

Attention back on Beau and Jasper, I finish with, "What can I grab ya?" My eyes meet Beau's briefly and his gaze scorches me. It licks over my body, hot and intense. Tongue darting out over his lips when he gets to my breasts. The ones propped up in my very best bra, because fuck him for leaving me this morning.

"Hi, Bailey," Jasper says kindly, eyes bouncing between Beau and me. "I'll have a Rose Hill Red, please."

Beau's brows furrow as he turns to his friend. "Not a Buddyz Best? I thought that was yours and Sloane's favorite."

Jasper laughs, caramel locks shaking around his ears, skin beside his eyes crinkling. "Truth is, I don't really like it. But Sloane does, so I drink it with her."

Beau seems confused. "You drink beer you don't like because your wife does?"

Jasper shrugs, offering me a knowing wink. "Yeah. Makes her happy. It's our thing. I'll sit around and drink watery Buddyz Best with Sloane for the rest of my damn life if it makes her happy."

I swallow and blink away. Fuck. That's really cute.

Meanwhile, I've got the emotional equivalent of a rock sitting across from me after hightailing it out of my bed this morning like he couldn't get away fast enough.

And I wasn't even asking him to drink watery beer with me.

"I'll have a Rose Hill Red, too." Beau's long fingers rap against the bar top, and I slice him an *are you sure* kind of look.

He nods.

"You'll like it, man," Jasper carries on, unperturbed. "There's a little brewery in Rose Hill where we just had training camp. The best craft beers, patio right on the lake. Can't beat it." Then he launches into a conversation about hockey, and I instantly zone them out.

While I pour the pints, I mull over all the alcoholics I've known in my life. I peek over at Gary—all the alcoholics I've served here. I know Beau isn't one of them. I saw Beau at a down-and-out moment in his life, and he quit without a backward glance.

Peeking up over the reddish-brown beer accumulating in the pint glass, I watch him. And he catches me. Our eyes lock for a beat, and another. My heart rate quickens.

And just like last night, dancing with his hands all over me, everything around us melts away. Until the only things that exist are him and me and the air between us that feels thick enough to trip on.

Cold liquid hits my hand as the beer overflows. "Shit! What the hell. This tap always pours slow and then today it magically works." I shake my hand off, but all that does is flip a sizeable spot of beer foam right onto my cleavage. I watch it there, white and dripping, then my gaze flits up to Beau's, which is plastered on the same spot.

Only me.

After last night? This would only happen to me.

With one finger, I wipe the foam off the rounded top of my breasts and shake my hand off again. The splatter falls to the rubber mat beneath my feet, wetness dotting my sandals.

"Jesus fuckin' Christ, can you two not? We're in public right now." Jasper groans and scrubs a hand over his face.

I decide now isn't the moment where I'll start cowering around these guys. I'm a bartender. I'm paid to banter with creepy old men. My fake fiancé and his best friend should be a breeze.

"I don't know what you're talking about, Jasper." I force my eyes to go comically wide, staring at the man like I'm genuinely confused. "It's just beer."

Poor, sweet Jasper Gervais. His neck turns pink first, right at the edge of his stubble. I watch it creep up his throat and spread across his cheeks. "It's just that you two were all"—he makes googly eyes and sort of shakes his hands beside his face—"and then it looks like . . . well, you know."

I blink a few times, channeling my inner Bambi and leaning into the fact that I look younger than my age. "What does it look like? I don't follow."

Jasper blinks back at me and tugs at the neckline of his hoodie like it's choking him. But I know better. It's the awkwardness that's choking him.

"It . . ."

"It looks like beer foam?" I tilt my head innocently.

Beau laughs. "Jesus, Bailey. Give the guy a break. He's as wholesome as they come. He can't even say it out loud."

Jasper straight up chokes, a fist hitting his chest as I hand him his beer. "Here. Wash it down. Breathe through your nose." I wink at him, and he shakes his head, doing his best tomato impression. I turn back to Beau. "Say what out loud?"

"You two have the same fucked-up sense of humor, that's for sure," Jasper murmurs against the rim of his pint glass.

Beau's eyes stay pinned on me, a knowing smirk tugging at his lips. When he stares at me like this, I forget why he annoyed me in the first place.

"That it looks like you have jizz on your tits."

Jasper sprays beer into his hand, a sad attempt to cover his mouth foiled by his inability to keep it together right now. But Beau and I just smirk at each other.

When I push, he pushes back. When he pushes, I push back. We keep ending up right in the middle.

Together.

It's with a light shake of my head that I get back to work. I silently hand Beau his beer and proceed to mostly ignore the two of them. They speak in muted tones, and I hear the odd name I recognize. Beau's eyes watch me all night long, while Jasper peeks between the two of us curiously.

He scrutinizes with a curious intensity. It makes me wonder what he knows.

It makes me feel like they're talking about me.

Beau nurses his single pint and switches to tea. Sloane comes in, hair in a bun. She wraps her arms around Jasper's neck, and he turns on his stool to kiss her soundly. When he pulls back, the look he gives her makes me think he's a lot less wholesome than Beau might realize.

Shortly after she arrives, they leave together.

But not before Jasper whispers some parting words in his friend's ear, squeezes his shoulder, and gives him a stern nod. "You need to tell her."

I don't know if I hear it or if I read his lips. All I know is that one sentence lands in my gut like a boulder at the bottom of a lake.

Tell me what?

33
Bailey

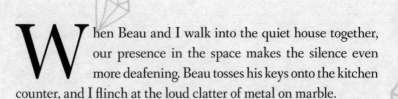

When Beau and I walk into the quiet house together, our presence in the space makes the silence even more deafening. Beau tosses his keys onto the kitchen counter, and I flinch at the loud clatter of metal on marble.

There's clearly an elephant in the room and neither of us knows how to talk about it. At thirty-five, he should know what he's doing with all this shit. Apparently not. In his defense, it's not like he didn't warn me he doesn't do real relationships.

But here I am, falling for him anyway.

I start toward the stove, needing to do something with my hands to combat the awkwardness blooming between us. "Want me to make us some tea?"

"We need to talk."

I freeze. That boulder is so damn heavy in my gut while everything else spins around me. I force myself to keep walking. Every movement feels like a struggle, like I'm walking through molasses up to my knees.

294

"Sure. About what?" I keep my voice airy as my fingers wrap around the kettle.

"Bailey, I don't want tea. Come here."

The rush of my heart pumping blood sounds like a heavy drum in my ears, but I turn and walk back to him, like a marionette on strings.

He's taken a seat on one of the stools on the island. His brows dip low, and he crosses the massive arms I slept in last night. They felt so warm and welcoming.

But I'm seeing them differently now. Big, foreboding, perfect to crush my heart with.

Propping a hip against the island, I mirror him and cross my arms as a shield against what I seem to know is coming. "What's up?" It sounds more petulant than I intended, but I'm feeling a little petulant right now. "You ghost me and barely acknowledge me all day, and now you want to talk? Lucky me."

I guess I'm all in on the petulance tonight.

"I didn't ghost you. I went to work."

"Right." My lips press together, and I glare at him.

Beau sighs, broad chest rising and falling as he reaches back and grips his neck. "Look, I needed some time to wrap my head around things after last night."

The urge to berate myself is overwhelming. I shouldn't have told him I was hung up on him too. I'm sure I freaked him right the fuck out.

"So help me, if this is some moment where you decide to admire my virginity again, I will walk out that front door."

"I'm not admiring it, Bailey. I'm telling you it means something to me. I'm telling you there are only so many firsts in your life before every day just turns into a blur of more of the same. I'm telling you that, whether or not you realize it, it might mean something to you one day. And I hate the thought of you living with any regrets."

I gnaw at the inside of my cheek, feeling more childish and inexperienced by the second. Beau isn't staring at me like I'm childish at all, though.

I can't put my finger on what's there in his gaze. All I know is I'm quite certain no person in my life has ever looked at me the way Beau is right now. My chest warms under the intensity in his eyes.

But he squashes that in its tracks.

"I think we should stop."

Stop.

That's what my heart does. Stops right in its tracks.

"I can't do this anymore."

My lungs no longer pump air as I stand in the too-quiet kitchen, staring at the too-handsome man before me.

"You've got a job now."

I nod, but I don't really hear his words. I keep repeating to myself: *don't let him see you cry.*

"A secure one. You'll be able to save up to get out of town, no problem."

"Mm-hmm," is all I can manage to choke out. I'm certain that if I open my mouth to say something, only a sob will come out.

Every word feels like he's tearing away a piece of my heart I swore I wouldn't give to him. I thought I hadn't.

" . . . so we can probably safely end this arrangement now."

He was talking, and I wasn't listening. It's one of those moments where you know it's happening, but it doesn't seem real. Everything happens in slow motion.

I blink hard, forcing my lips into a smile that leans more toward a grimace. Beau is a nice guy. I don't want to make him feel worse than he probably already does. I don't want to be the naive girl who was foolish enough to believe in something that was never meant to be.

I'm so fucking hung up on you.

I shake the words away, filing them under "things men must say when they've had an amazing orgasm".

"Yeah, of course." My voice is watery, but I don't think there's any helping that.

Beau's forehead crinkles in concern, and he unfolds one thick arm, reaching for me. When the tips of his fingers trace my hip bone, I recoil and step back.

He just dumped me. Fake dumped me?

Whatever the fuck you call this, I have enough self-respect to not want his hands on me.

In one smooth motion, I pull the diamond ring from my finger and drop it onto the marble between us. "No problem. Definitely don't want to overstay my welcome. You take this—"

"Bailey." He pushes to stand, and I hate that I notice the way the muscles in his legs flex. The line from his quads that runs down to his knees. Down to his marred feet.

The feet that still burn every night.

The feet I woke up and rubbed last night.

How fucking dare he do this to me?

"I'll just head back out to my trailer."

I can't even look at him.

My feet move swiftly across the floor to the front door.

"Bailey, wait—"

297

I hold a hand up over my shoulder to cut him off. "It's all good. Totally fine. Cool, cool, cool." The last *cool* comes out as a sob.

My sandals sit in the entryway, but I don't feel like taking the time to strap them back on. A buckle is just not in the cards right now. I yank the door open, sensing him behind me.

"Fuck," he mutters. He starts to follow me, but then he turns around, moving in the opposite direction, back into his house, while I jog out into the cool night. The dog days of summer are upon us. They hit with startling rapidity. It went from hot at night, to tepid, to refreshing. The minute the sun disappears, so does the heat, the mountain air creeping in as fall approaches.

Dewy grass clings to my bare feet as I fixate on my trailer. If I can just get myself there—across that line, behind that door—I might be safe.

Safe enough to break down.

My palms land flat against the chilled fiberglass exterior, and I reach for the handle, my fingers wrapping around the chipped metal.

Inside, I'll be okay.

I tug, but the door holds still.

It's locked. Because of course it is.

A sob racks my body, and my forehead thumps against the side of my trailer. "Fuck, fuck, fuck."

The back door of Beau's house slams. "Bailey."

This time, my name isn't laced with amused frustration. There's an edge to his tone, a sharpness. It's not casual and unaffected. It's hot and fired up with military abruptness.

His footsteps approach me, and I feel the tension that radiates from his body. For some reason, he seems angry.

"What made you think I was done talking to you?"

I laugh, but it sounds more like I'm crying. I wipe at my cheek and my fingers come away wet. Turns out I *am* crying. "Felt pretty final to me. No need to drag it out, Beau. I'll be okay." I don't turn to face him. "Just leave me alone. I'll be fine by morning."

"Bullshit. You won't be fine in the morning."

I start at the harshness in his words. Okay, probably not, but it seems cruel to rub my face in that fact. "Fuck off, Beau."

His palm lands on my shoulder, and when I go to shrug him off, he flips me around, pressing me up hard against the exterior of my trailer. He gets right in my face, one hand cupping my cheek. "No. You're crying."

His head drops, and he kisses a tear that streaks down my face. "I can't fucking stand the sight of you crying."

Oh god. My heart twists and it fucking hurts.

I knew it would be painful, but nothing could have prepared me for the searing, intense ache.

I need space. I need to breathe.

I shove him, but it's no use. He's too big. Might as well run around trying to push trees over at this rate. "Please." My voice cracks as I look up into his face. "Fuck off."

"Not until I finish what I was trying to say back inside the house."

"You dumped me. What more do you want to say?"

Intensity paints every inch of his stupid, handsome face while his eyes dance back and forth between mine.

I wait for him to say something.

But he doesn't.

"Did you forget what you wanted to say, Beau? Because I think *I can't do this anymore* sums things up, don't you?" I spit the words out, steeling myself. Trying to inflict pain. Though I think repeating his words out loud hurts me more than anyone.

His hands tighten on my body, gripping me as he pushes his knee between my legs, pinning me in place. Tears stream down my cheeks, clumping my eyelashes, and my chest aches so heavy and deep that simply breathing hurts.

The hand on my waist moves up, wiping away another tear before pushing back a lock of my carefully styled hair. "What I meant to say, *Bailey* ... " He emphasizes my name in a way that sends a shiver down my spine. His hand cups my head so I can't look anywhere but straight at him. "What I meant to say is ... will you go out with me?"

Everything around me comes to a screeching halt. Not only is the sentence juvenile, but it's also just plain confusing.

"You just broke up with me."

A boyish smile curves his sinful lips. He kisses my temple and goes back to staring me down. "If you had let me finish, I'd have told you I couldn't keep doing it anymore because pretending this thing between us is fake is fucking killing me."

"What?"

God, that's what I blurt out? *What?*

"The only reason you got this far is because I went back into the house for the ring."

He reaches down and pulls the teardrop-shaped diamond from his pocket, holding it between us.

"I'm done pretending to be head over heels in love with you because I'm legitimately head over heels in love with you. And acting like I'm not tears me up."

I grip his wrists, squeezing so I can assure myself that

he's real. That this moment is real. Because it feels distinctly unbelievable.

"Maybe it's too soon. Maybe this is impulsive. Maybe you don't love me back. But I'll wait. I don't care. I'll take my time with you. So long as I know you're really mine, I can be patient."

"Beau . . . " My chest heaves as my brain struggles to catch up.

He doesn't give me a chance to say any more before he's pulling my hand down and sliding the engagement ring back onto my finger. "This belongs here," he murmurs.

"Maybe we should just date for a bit?" God, I'm not firing on all cylinders right now. I should tell him I love him back. I should kiss him.

"Call it whatever you want, sugar. But the ring stays here."

We both stare at the diamond, the back porch lights flitting off every brilliant facet. Our breaths come out ragged. We're both amped up. Confused, excited, frustrated.

"Feels like bad luck to wear it when we're not really engaged."

"We *are* really engaged." His response leaves no room for debate.

"I mean, if we're taking our time, testing this thing out for real, you probably shouldn't waltz around pretending you intend to marry me when you don't."

I swear he growls at my response. A deep rumble in his chest. A narrowing of his eyes. The vein at his temple throbs.

I hate myself. Why am I arguing with him and poking holes in his logic when this should be a dream come true?

It's because it doesn't feel real. Good things like this don't happen to Bailey Jansen. Not with men like him.

"Stop thinking what you're thinking. Stop pretending this isn't real." He bends slightly and lifts me, picking me up easily and carrying me back toward the house. "Stop telling me what I intend to do," he whispers against my ear. "Because I do intend to marry you. And I want you to wear that fucking ring while I show you that it's true."

Then he kicks the door open. Marches me up the stairs to his room. Drops me to my feet at the foot of his bed, and says, "Strip."

34

Beau

Bailey's eyes have widened to unbelievable size, and her lips pop open as she stares back at me. Shocked? Confused? I'm not sure, but I can tell the events of tonight have thrown her for a loop.

"Was there a part of that order you didn't understand, Bailey?"

I step closer to her, chin tipping down to keep my gaze fixed on hers. Her tongue darts out over her bottom lip and my eyes follow it hungrily.

"Okay. So, let me get this straight."

I nod, biting down on a smirk. She's having a hard time accepting this. In hindsight, I should have started this conversation differently.

"We're not faking anymore."

"That's right."

"Because we both want this?"

"It seems that way." A deep chuckle rumbles in my chest as I watch her work it out in those coal-black eyes. A darkness I actually want to get lost in.

"How do we do this? Like, we just carry on? I . . . " One of her hands grips her throat. "Beau, I have all these plans."

I skim a hand up and down her rib cage. "We'll work it out. We don't have to have all the answers right this second."

She nibbles at her lip. "I'm your real fiancée now?"

"Yes."

She slowly nods her head, understanding flaring to life in her eyes. And then . . . something more playful?

Her head tilts, her arms cross, and her mouth takes on a teasing curve. "What if I told you I don't want to be engaged to you?"

I drop my lips closer drawn in by the heat from her skin. We breathe each other's breath. "Then I'd call you a fucking liar, sugar."

I kiss her. I don't give her a chance to run her smart mouth and test my patience with bratty jokes. I take her mouth to shut her up and to claim her.

Her hands fist my shirt and our tongues tangle as my fingers thread through the silky locks of her hair. This kiss feels different. Better. Less tentative and more desperate.

"You're insane," she mutters against my lips between kisses, and she's probably not wrong. But I'm past caring about the way I'm perceived.

I pull back, dotting kisses over her cheeks. Over her nose.

And I confess my truth to her.

"I've been doing impulsive shit, hoping one of those things might make me feel something. And not a single one of them did. Until you. So if this thing with you makes me insane? I'll be happy to wear that badge."

When our eyes meet, all I see is longing and pride. No pity, no uncertainty. We both know this is right. It just felt too unlikely to say out loud.

"Do you really love me?"

Do I love her? God. What a pedestrian question, one that feels like it doesn't encompass all the feelings I have for her. It doesn't seem like enough. But I'll keep telling her, keep showing her, until I figure out better words to describe the way I feel about her.

"Bailey Jansen, I love you," I murmur as our faces dance close to one another, exchanging soft kisses. We're in this kind of lull. Standing on a precipice, ready to topple over the edge.

"How do you know?"

I kiss just below her ear, reveling in the way she tilts her head. My lips move down to her neck. "I just do." I kiss her shoulder, right beside the tied strap.

"I don't think anyone has ever loved me."

I freeze. The pain in my chest is sharp, instant, acute.

She says it like it's a fact.

I've seen a lot of sad shit in my life, but none of it has wounded me the way that one sentence just did. I don't know what to say. What is a person supposed to say to that? Are words enough?

It strikes me that they're not.

A boy might stand here waiting for her to say it back, but I don't need that validation. Bailey might not know what love is, but I do.

Love is telling me I'm acting like an asshole when no one else will.

Love is taking me shopping to find shoes that don't rub my feet raw.

It's waking up every goddamn night for weeks to swim in the river with me, so I don't have a nightmare.

Bailey doesn't need flowery words.

Bailey needs proof.

I lift my head, getting lost in the inky depths of her irises. "Then let me be the first to do that too."

She nods and my fingers curl around the soft cotton. I slowly lift it, dragging it up her body. Her arms raise without resistance as I discard the shirt, leaving her standing before me in a pale pink strapless bra. My hands roam as I take her in, continuing down her back where I unfasten the hooks and let her bra fall away too.

When I drop to my knees in front of her, her hands sink into my hair. Combing. Stroking.

I take my time. It feels a bit like unwrapping a present. But not the way I did as a child, shredding and tearing until I got to what was underneath. No, this is me carefully peeling the tape back, smoothing every crease.

Her button. Her zipper. Her jeans. All gently pulled away until it's just a smooth expanse of skin and a pale pink thong.

I look up at her, meeting her gaze, as my hands slide over her hips, cupping the firm globes of her ass. "I love you."

"Okay," she whispers, like she still can't quite believe it. And that's fine with me. I like a challenge.

"Should I keep going?"

Her nod is fast, slightly frantic. "Yes. Please."

My lips quirk as I work her underwear down her thighs. She's still. Too still. "I like it when you're so sweet and polite, Bailey."

A nervous laugh tumbles from her lips, and she breathes again. "Fuck you, Beau."

My cheek twitches. There's the girl I know.

With her panties around her ankles, I glance up at her, giving her my wickedest grin to cut the tension. "That's exactly what you're going to be doing once I finish eating this pretty pussy."

35

Bailey

I'm pretty sure this is a dream and someone will shake me awake at any moment.

But when Beau licks up my slit, tongue flicking hard at my clit, my back bows off the bed and I know this isn't a dream.

Because I always wake up from sex dreams right when it's finally getting good.

And that was really fucking good. I make some sort of uncontrolled mewling noise and my body trembles against my will.

"You like that, baby?" Beau asks as he drapes my thighs over his shoulders.

Then he does the same thing again. Slow and purposeful, the pressure is just right.

I attempt to stifle another desperate sound coming from the back of my throat, but fail. "Yes," I try to reply, but the word is all garbled.

I feel the rumble of his deep, amused chuckle against my core. The noise I make is something wilder than a whimper—this man knows exactly how to handle me.

He devours me. My legs wrap around his shoulders and eventually work their way up to the back of his head, tugging him closer. His strong arms wrap around my thighs, big hands splayed, holding me open so he can feast on me.

"Am I the first to do this to you?"

I nod, tugging at his hair. Mindless for this man. "Yes."

"I'm going to be the only one to do this to you, Bailey. Mark my words."

My head spins. He's so fucking *sure*. I don't know what to make of his confidence. How to cope with it. In my world, nothing lasts forever, and love isn't even on the table.

Beau gives me so much. I worry I'll never be able to repay him.

He slides a finger into me, working my body in time with his mouth. My back arches and my palms fly up to my face, gliding back over my hair.

"Should I add another finger, Bailey? Get you nice and ready to take my cock?"

"Yesss." I moan the word right as I tug at my own hair.

He does exactly as he promised, slow and steady, sucking at my clit as his hand moves faster. Harder. My body shakes as he works me over—squeezing my ass, fingers curling into me, devilish tongue flicking.

"Fuck, fuck, fuck," I curse. All my hard-won attempts at being a "lady" fly out the window with this man's head between my legs. "Beau, I'm going to—"

"Come for me, baby." He pulls back, watching his fingers pump in and out of me. "Let me see it."

His intimate gaze, his husky words, and his thumb reaching up to rub my clit cause me to shatter. He grips me like a vise, two fingers pushing at that magical spot deep inside me as I call his name. My body is suffused with heat. The backs of my calves cramp. Every muscle braces, clenching on him, before releasing every ounce of pressure. Rocking me to my core.

And Beau never stops. Watching. Touching. Admiring his handiwork.

"Yeah, I'll never tire of this view," he says gruffly, as my limbs go soft.

All I can do is concentrate on breathing, getting my vision back into focus. His fingers leave my body, accompanied by a wet sound. My eyes shut, a trickle of embarrassment finding its way in.

"What was that, Bailey?" he asks, and I feel the bed sink under the weight of him. His knees brace on either side of my naked body.

My eyes flip open to meet his. "Nothing."

"Do you know how fucking beautiful you look, coming with my name on your lips?"

"No," I reply honestly, and he just smiles.

"What about how good you taste? Do you know how fucking good you taste?"

I shake my head, my body thrumming just from the rumble of his deep voice in the dim room.

He smirks, full of promise and knowing, and the fingers that were just inside me trace my lips. "Suck, Bailey."

"Your cock?" My eyes widen with excitement.

"We can save that for another day. I'll be happy to let you practice. But for now . . ." His two fingers tap against my lips and my mouth pops open.

He slides his fingers onto my tongue, and my lips close around them. My eyes lock with his as the taste of what he did to me fills my mouth. "Such a pretty girl," he murmurs, pulling them back out with a pop. "And if I ever see you looking embarrassed about yourself again, I'll leave another mark on your neck to wear around town."

Then he kisses me. Hard. And I taste myself there too. I taste him, that signature scent.

I taste *us*.

In the blink of an eye, he flips us and pulls me up the bed with him so I'm straddling him. He leans against the headboard, looking like some sort of king. Tousled and golden and impossibly broad.

"Undress me, Bailey." He doesn't blanch or blink away when he tells me what to do. His eyes burn hotter, and I want nothing more than to burn with him too. To rise to his challenge and not crumple under the weight of my inexperience.

So with a soft nod, I reach down and grasp his shirt, tugging slowly at first, then more frantically. He leans forward and lifts his arms to help me. I toss it away, and it's just my hands on his skin. Roaming. Memorizing him in a way I haven't been able to until now.

Warm, smooth skin beneath my palms. Thick bulges over his pectoral muscles. Tight nipples. I pinch one and peek up at him. His eyes blaze and he gives me a reassuring nod.

So I pinch again. This time both, noting the sharp intake of breath that follows. My hips grind down in response and his buck up to meet me.

God. I can't believe I'm really here, doing this with *him*.

To cover for the way my hands shake, I keep moving them, roaming down his toned abdomen. A thin scar mars one of his perfect abs.

I trail a finger over its length and whisper, "What's this from?"

"Got shivved."

My gaze snaps up. "What?"

"Let my guard down that day, getting one of my first targets into custody. Learned a valuable lesson. Never letting that happen again."

I smile softly, feeling the raised skin again. "Don't think you're much at risk of getting shivved in Chestnut Springs."

His broad palms slide up my thighs, my ribs, over my shoulders until he frames my face with them and pushes my hair back behind my ears. "Still not letting my guard down. Not when I've got you to keep safe."

A shiver races down my spine as I stare back at him. All I can offer is a nod.

I don't think anyone has ever prioritized keeping me safe.

The weight of his gaze is almost more than I can manage, so I drop it and go back to touching him. My fingertips travel the light dusting of hair along the top of his shorts. I pull at the waistline, then tug harder, wanting them off. Gone. Wanting to explore.

Wanting his skin on mine.

Between the two of us, they get tugged down, slid off his legs, and forgotten.

Forgotten because all I can see is the massive cock laid across his masculine stomach. I take in everything. Muscled thighs. Heavy balls. The vein that runs up the underside of his length, pulsing.

I mean, yeah, I've watched porn, but it's not the same. It's like watching the National Geographic channel and saying you've seen a lion in the wild.

One of these things is not like the other.

I kneel beside him, and my tongue darts out.

"Keep looking at my dick like that while licking your lips and I'll be in your mouth instead of your pussy."

I flush, eyes flashing up to his. "I want both."

"You'll always get everything you want. I promise." The need, the want, the lust radiating between us are downright electric. "Take it."

My eyes widen, brain stumbling through the fog of my hormones. "Take what?"

His tanned hand reaches down, wrapping around his girth. He jerks once, then twice. It reminds me of watching him come on me, marking me while I fell apart under his watchful gaze.

"Take my cock and put it in your mouth. Get it nice and wet for me, Bailey."

I lick my lips again as I glance down at his penis. The darker head looks so smooth.

"Fuck," he mutters, fingers gripping the base of it tightly as a pearl of pre-cum forms at the tip. "Bailey if you don—"

He doesn't need to finish that sentence. I'm salivating for him. I lean forward, wrapping my hand around him for a taste.

I want to know how it feels to hold that part of him in my mouth. To see how he might react.

My tongue darts out, lapping up the liquid, and Beau groans. When I peek up, his eyes are at half-mast and fixed on me.

He moves his hands away, folds them behind his head, and leans back like he's ready to take in some sort of show.

Nerves hit me.

I don't fucking know what I'm doing. What if I do it all wrong? What if he hates it?

"You're perfect, Bailey." His words soothe me instantly. He reads me like a book and knew exactly what was running through my head.

Perfect.

I'm not sure there's any such thing, but I let myself bask in the compliment anyway. I let it encourage me as I slip my lips down over the swollen head of his cock. I feel every ridge with my tongue, every silky-smooth expanse.

I explore, and he lets me.

I lick. I suck. I fill my mouth with Beau, and the noises of pleasure he makes are all I hear.

Fuck, yes.

Just like that.

You're doing so well.

The more he talks to me, the better I feel. The bolder I feel.

I push further down, feeling the blunt tip of him at the back of my throat. I gag when I go too far.

"Easy, Bailey." He swipes a hand over my hair. "You don't have to go that far. Everything you do feels so good."

I pull up, flushing as his praise wraps around me. "It's okay?"

His cheeks are rosy too, eyes a little shiny, like he's had too many drinks. Except I know he's drunk on *me*.

"Best I've ever had. The only thing that's not okay is that I'm going to finish in your mouth if you keep it up. And that would be a waste when we both know what you really want is my cum in your pussy."

My eyes flutter shut as gooseflesh breaks out across my skin. I do want that, but god. Hearing him say it out loud?

His hands pull me up to him as a knowing chuckle rumbles in his chest. "You like it when I say things like that, don't you?"

"Maybe," I murmur, kissing his shoulder as he lays me over him.

"You do. I just watched your nipples get harder right as your cheeks got even pinker." He lifts me higher, sucking one nipple into his mouth. I gasp at the sensation, and jerk when he nips gently. "I can't wait to find out what else drives you crazy." His damp lips drag across the valley between my breasts. "You like it when I tell you what to do?"

I kiss his skin again, trying to act more coy than I'm feeling inside. *I do like it*. "Maybe."

He sucks my opposite nipple, and a rush of wetness pools between my legs.

He smiles against my breast before a sharp nip once again leaves me gasping.

"Well, in that case, quit fucking around and sit on my cock, Bailey."

His massive hands circle my waist, and I rise above him, nipples glistening with his saliva, pink indents from his teeth beside them. My blood thunders through my veins as I gaze down at this beautiful, protective man who's given me everything and more and asked for almost nothing in return.

He says he loves me, and I don't know how to process that, but I want to feel it all the same.

I inch my hips back, hand splayed across his chest as I line us up. I know how it felt to have just an inch of him inside me, and knowing I'll get the whole thing this time sends a thrill through me. He holds me up as I reach down and take him in my hand.

I swipe the head through my wetness, feeling his cock slip so easily through my core. He groans, fingers flexing on my waist like it's taking his all to not shove me down and impale me on his length.

When I notch him at my entrance, our eyes catch. The weight of his gaze is almost more than I can bear. And yet, I don't look away. I can't.

I'm so caught up in him, in us—he's all I see.

The muscles in my legs strain as I carefully lower myself onto him.

One inch, his jaw ticks.

Two inches, his eyes go steely.

Three inches—fuck, he's so thick—his hands shake. Or my body does. I don't even know anymore where he ends and I begin.

With a whimper, I ease down further, and so do his eyes. He's gone from watching my face to watching where he's filling me up.

"Fuck, Bailey."

I only moan, letting my eyes flutter shut and moving my hands to his round shoulders for support.

"You okay?"

I nod, feeling his hands soften and his thumb rub reassuringly against my stomach.

This is nothing like my toys. It's tenfold more intense. I'm full in a way I never have before.

"Bailey, baby, you're doing so good. If you need to stop—"

"I don't need to stop." My voice is breathy as I continue to sink down onto him. My body pulses. "I just . . . god. I feel so full."

I whimper, letting the bite of his size distract me for a moment. But like always, Beau is right there to reassure me. "You're almost there, Bailey. You're so beautiful with my cock inside you. Just go slow."

I nod and moan as I look down at where we meet, struggling to get the last of his length inside me.

His palms slide over my ribs, shaping down over my ass. "I know, baby, I know."

Suddenly, I'm struck by an urgency, like this moment might slip through my fingers if I don't make the most of it. I drop myself all the way down and cry out as I hit the base of him. "Oh god."

"Fuck, fuck, fuck. That feels . . . "

Fingers grip me, and he's everywhere. I'm so full of Beau, I'm so—I don't even know where I am, only that I'm on top of him, he's inside of me, and I've never felt more safe.

I pant, nails digging into his pecs.

"Does it hurt?" he asks, voice all raspy and low.

I shake my head no.

"Bailey, talk to me."

My eyes snap open to meet his silver gaze. "It's just intense. It feels so different."

He nods, smoothing his calloused palms over my back, the tops of my thighs. "I'm following your lead. Tell me what you need."

"I . . . " My vision goes a little blurry. "I need you to move or something."

He tips his chin up. "You first. Lift and come down again. Get a feel for it." His hands swoop up my stomach, palming my breasts almost reverently. His eyes, such an unusual color, glow metallic. They're hard not to get lost in. "You can't do a single thing wrong. Just do what feels good."

"What about you?"

One side of his mouth tugs up, an almost pained expression gracing his handsome face. "Trust me, baby. It all feels good with you."

My teeth sink into my bottom lip, and I flush at his praise. Then, with my hands on his chest, I lift up, feeling in every inch of him as I do.

The outstroke sends a jolt of delicious spasms through my body.

At the top, pushed up on my knees, I look down, wanting to watch every inch of him disappear into my body. As I sink down on him, I can't look away. It's so foreign. So fucking hot.

I do it again. And again. Every stroke is less foreign than the last, more pleasurable than the last. His hands roam, always soothing. Slow and steady. I'm unable to tear my gaze from where Beau and I are joined. Like it's some sort of experiment and I'm completely fascinated.

"See how pretty you look taking my cock, Bailey?"

"Yeah," I murmur absently, because it's hard to disagree with him. There's something entrancing about the sight.

Beau moves a hand between us, tracing his thumb over the tight grip of my pussy lips around his girth. He spreads my wetness up, swiping it over my clit as I continue my slow ride.

Oh.

My eyes widen as he makes gentle circles.

"You like that, don't you?"

I nod, struck speechless. I don't just like it, I—

"Let me hear it, Bailey. Use your words."

"I love it."

He smirks, confident and playful all of a sudden. "I told you I'd make it good for you."

Good? This is so much more than good.

He plays with my clit again and rolls my nipple between his fingers, forcing me to cry out. A surge of wetness coats us as my hips move in a way I never knew they could. I rise and drop more heavily, hips rotating as my muscles relax into the motion. And true to his word, Beau lets me get a feel for it—for him.

"Atta girl. Ride me," he urges as his fingers work me over expertly.

317

A sheen of sweat covers my body as my hands grip and scratch. My eyes flit from one delicious corner of him to the other before they sink into those silver pools.

"You gonna come on my cock, Bailey?"

"I think so," I breathe out. Every corner of my body is warm and sizzling with anticipation. Every muscle coiling as he fills me up.

"That's my girl. Give it to me." His thumb presses harder. His fingers pinch tighter. His bare cock pulses inside me and like a countdown *one, two, three . . .* I'm washed away.

Bowled over by a wave of pleasure so intense, I feel like I've left my body. I topple forward as the exquisite burst claims me. I feel everything.

Him.

Me.

Warm.

Safe.

Before I can even gather my senses, he's flipped us over, his body caging me in. One hand strokes my cheek, while the other hikes my thigh up high. The angle is new and I gasp when he sinks into me from above.

He stops, cock filling me to the brim while my pussy still pulsates around him. "Bailey, baby," he bites out, voice rumbling over my skin, setting it aflame. God, just the vibration of him against me has my nerve endings jumping. "I don't think I can hold back any longer. My control is—"

"Give it to me." I repeat his words back to him, lifting my head just enough to brush my lips over his. "And don't hold back."

"Fuck." He spits the word out and crushes his lips to mine, taking my mouth in a searing kiss as he pistons into me relentlessly.

The bed shakes with the ferocity of his thrusts and my body aches in the most delicious way as he claims me.

"Hottest fuck of my life," he growls, then he shouts my name against my shoulder before biting down hard. His body goes taut, and his cock jumps and pulses as he spills himself inside me.

"I love you, Bailey Jansen," he murmurs, stroking my hair and licking gently over what I'm sure will be a bite mark tomorrow.

And all I can do is smile. Because that was worth the wait.

I have never felt more cherished than I do with Beau Eaton wrapped around me.

36
Beau

Jasper: Did you tell her?

I lather soap over Bailey's body, rubbing her shoulders to ease any tension, running my thumbs firmly over the tight spots. Her head tilts, and she lets out a moan as she leans into the pressure.

After I shampoo her hair, I rinse it under the warm spray, then follow with a generous amount of conditioner. I comb my fingers through her strands to rid them of any knots and turn her, enjoying the way her body moves readily to mine. The way she trusts me is more than I deserve.

Our eyes meet in the steamy space. But we don't talk and she watches me as I carry on soaping her and massaging her body. Her chest, her breasts, gently and quickly before moving over her ribs.

I drop down onto my knees before her, using the bar of soap

to wash her hips, the trim triangle of hair I helped her shave, her thighs, calves. Hell, even her feet.

Her perfect fucking feet.

They go with everything else that's perfect about her.

I'm at a loss for words. For what she shared with me tonight. For what she's shared with me over the past several weeks. I feel unworthy in the most profound way. But I want to be worthy.

I feel desperate to be.

Reaching behind her, I trace the soap over the round globes of her ass before putting it back on the ledge and directing the water to rinse the soap away. I retrace my steps, ignoring the nip of the porcelain against my knees. When her fingers comb through my hair, I drop my stubbled cheek against her stomach and hug her to me.

This girl has brought me back to life without even trying. All that time I searched for someone to make me feel something, and she was right fucking there.

My lips press a kiss to the spot just above her belly button and then I tip my head, dragging my gaze up to meet her dark eyes, swirling with emotion and edged in confusion.

I don't think anyone has ever cherished Bailey.

Not like I do.

And no one else ever will.

"I love you," I repeat to her, not caring I've said it multiple times tonight and she hasn't.

You don't tell a person you love them with the expectation they'll say it back. You tell them because you want to. You tell them because it's true.

I spent many hours in a cave in Afghanistan wishing I'd told more people how much they meant to me. I promised myself I would start, but I've been too hung up on my shit to get around to it.

That ends now.

Bailey's fingers press firmly at my temples before sliding back through my hair. "How do you know you love me?" she asks softly.

"How do I know?"

"Yeah." Her hands don't stop moving, soothing. "Doesn't it seem soon? Fast? Unlikely?"

I hum, a smile touching my lips. "I don't know that there's a prescribed length of time it takes, Bailey. There's not some magical benchmark or test you need to take to see it. Sometimes I think you just know."

"You just know," she repeats thoughtfully, worrying her bottom teeth between her lips.

I kiss her stomach again. "My pain disappears when I'm with you. I get to be a new version of myself when I'm with you. I sleep. I laugh. I have something—someone—to look forward to at the end of the day. I feel . . . " I peer back up at her again, swallowing as I run my hands up the column of her spine. "I feel whole again with you."

Her palms cup my neck while her thumbs brush over the high points on my cheeks. "I don't know what to say to that."

My hands squeeze at her hips, and I know I'm overwhelming her. That I need to lighten the mood. That she's too young and I'm coming on too fucking strong.

So I land a playful slap on her ass that rings out in the shower, then I tease, "You say 'yes, sir' and let me rinse the conditioner out of your hair."

She bursts into a fit of nervous giggles as I stand and flip her around into the spray, watching the creamy-colored water cascade down her back until it runs clear. I wait, and I watch, and I wait some more while she tries to get her bearings.

When she steps out of the water, I take a fistful of her hair, tipping her head back to me, and murmur against her lips, "I didn't hear you, Bailey."

"Hear what?" Her eyes glisten with excitement, and I know she's pretending not to know what I'm talking about.

"Do you know what brats get?"

She bites down on her bottom lip, but she's not worried. She's trying not to smile. "Hopefully spanked."

I groan and let my eyes fall shut as I rub my lips over the apple of her cheek. "You're going to be the fucking death of me."

She chuckles and turns her face into mine as she whispers, "But what a way to go. Am I right?"

Then she kisses me, and I let her. Because she's not wrong.

This would be the way to go.

I wake with a start, shooting straight out of bed, practically shoving Bailey off of me as I go.

A glance at the clock tells me it's 3:26 a.m., which is a refreshing change from 2:11. We must have either slept or fucked through that one.

"What's wrong?" I hear the alarm in her voice and sneak a quick glance at her over my shoulder. She's on her knees in the middle of the bed, both hands held flat over her chest, likely over her pounding heart.

Something is off. It feels like a spider is crawling up my spine.

Call it what you want—a sixth sense maybe. One that has saved my life countless times in the field.

I hold one finger up to Bailey, signaling to her to be silent, as I approach the large window facing the river out back.

I hear it then. Clumsy footsteps. A soft, "Ow!" Followed by, "Shut up! Someone will hear you!"

I roll my eyes. He fucking shouted it. Of course someone is going to hear them. You wouldn't need to be special ops to hear these idiots coming. I pull the curtain back an inch to see two dark figures on my back lawn. With a shake of my head, I turn and stride toward the door.

"Bailey, stay here. On the bed."

"What's wrong?" she repeats, apprehension in her voice.

"Gonna go have a chat with your brothers," I grumble, not bothering with a shirt as I storm out of the bedroom.

"Beau!" she whisper-shouts with such ferocity that I turn to take her in. It's a good thing I didn't go searching for my shirt because she's wearing it. Hair all wavy and bed-mussed, looking so tiny and swallowed up in that plain white tee.

I quirk my head, waiting for her to say what she needs to say.

She sighs and licks her lips before offering a quiet but borderline tearful, "Be careful."

I give her a salute and a wink, which only earns me a watery smile, and then I'm heading down the hallway, straight for my gun safe.

Don't have much use for them now, save for target practice or if I ever happen upon something in my backyard that wants to kill me. But I'm pretty sure I wouldn't need to shoot a bear or a cougar to stay safe.

At the back of the closet near the front door, I enter the safe's code and pull out my old hunting rifle. I prop it under my arm as I make my way to the back.

Tweedle Dee and Tweedle Dumb are trying so hard to pick the lock on Bailey's trailer they don't hear me exit my house. Granted, I'm pretty stealthy about it, even as I plunk myself down in the chair where Bailey lays herself out while wearing that tiny bikini I like so much.

I spread my legs and prop the gun over my knee. It's hard to tell in the dark, but I think they're using a bobby pin to open it. I watch them struggle for more than a few seconds.

Fucking stupid.

Bet they slam river rocks together trying to start a fire too.

"Y'all want some help with that?" I announce, forcing myself not to laugh at how high they jump when my voice rings out, echoing back off the river.

"Fuck you!" the first one to get his bearings says. I can't tell in the dark which is which. "This is our trailer."

I bounce my knee, noting the way their eyes drop to the gun propped on it.

I wouldn't actually shoot them, but I get a kick out of watching them go real fucking still. I feel like the old me. In my element.

"It's not your trailer. It's Bailey's. And it's on my property. So are you. It's time to get the fuck off."

"Where's Bailey? She owes us rent!" the other pipes up and licks almost rabidly at his lips. High as a goddamn kite.

"Bailey doesn't owe you shit. You got something to tell her? It goes through me. Something to give her? You give it to me. You want to so much as lay eyes on my fiancée? You better come crawling asking for my permission."

"She's my sister! Over my dead fuckin' body am I askin' you for permission for shit."

"That's exactly what you'll be if you go anywhere near her or her things."

"Come again?" I can see now that it's the older brother as he takes an aggressive step toward my back deck. He's too high to be properly afraid of me.

I chuckle and scrub at my beard. "You heard me. Harass her again and I'll paint my driveway with your brains. You won't be the first man I've killed, but you could easily be the last."

It's the younger one who pipes up now. Possibly the smarter one. Likely the more sober one. "She owes rent! She pays it and you guys won't hear from us again."

I click my tongue. "You Jansen boys must be as dumb as everyone says if you think that I, of all people, am going to negotiate with terrorists. Get off my property."

"You just—" They start to argue with me, but I don't let them get far.

I pick up the gun and pretend like I'm taking aim, which is when they scramble. I almost want to laugh. These two fuckers are addicts, petty thieves—not criminal masterminds.

But they're just troublesome enough that I know they'll pick on Bailey as long as she's here. They're too lazy to follow her anywhere else. She's just an easy target for them here in Chestnut Springs.

Well, she *was* an easy target.

Not anymore.

"You're fucking insane!" one of them calls back as they run into the dark river valley.

"Yeah, buddy. You have no idea!" is all I call back as I watch them scamper away. Eventually, I hear cussing and splashing as they make their way back across the creek to their land.

Idiots.

I don't like them on our river, where Bailey and I first spent a night together. It seems like an intrusion, so I'll be running electric fencing along that side of my property too. With a labored sigh, I stand and head inside. I check every door and window on the main floor and set my barely ever used alarm system before trudging upstairs to the girl who feels like she's the part of me that's been missing for too damn long.

When I get to my room, she's standing at the window, looking ashen.

"Thought I told you to stay on the bed."

She nods. "You did."

"And yet, there you are, at the window."

"I wanted to watch." She shrugs. "And you're not my boss anyway."

I smirk. "Yeah, I am."

She rolls her eyes before letting the curtain go and making her way back to the bed. I meet her there, lifting the covers so I can tug her closer and cradle her in the curve of my body where I know she's safest.

Silence surrounds us until she whispers, "Paint your driveway with their brains?" A soft snort leaves her, and her shoulders shake on a laugh. "That is so romantic."

I pull her tighter against me and huff out an exasperated breath. "I meant it, Bailey. You asked me how I know I love you? That's how. I've got anyone who wants to hurt you in my crosshairs, and I won't feel bad about taking them down, either."

That statement makes her quiet for a few moments.

She kisses my hand and presses back on me. "Should we call the cops?"

"Nah, I got this."

"Thank you," are her final whispered words before her breathing eventually goes deep and even.

But me? I stay up listening.

Until the sun comes up and I know she's safe.

37
Bailey

We fall back onto the bed in a tangle of sweaty limbs. My head is resting on Beau's quad when he bites my inner thigh, leaving yet another mark I'm sure, since that seems to be his thing.

I yelp and roll off him, pretending I'm trying to get away. But he knows better. He grabs me and hauls me back against his body.

"Starting to think you ask me if I've ever tried something just to make me show you how, sugar. Such a needy little brat."

I laugh against his chest, biting his pec in response. "Sixty-nine just seemed so confusing. I needed some coaching, sir." I can't say it without giggling. I swear I'm giddy all the time now.

Sex with Beau is hot, and fun, and emotional all at once. I can't get enough of it.

"Bailey," he groans in that exasperated way he likes to say my name, but his dick twitches beneath my leg where it's slung over his naked body.

Does it make me a brat that I get a real thrill out of saying things that shock him? I don't know. But I don't care because I get a kick out of it.

I also get a lot of orgasms out of it.

And a lot of feelings. Big feelings that I'm not sure what to do with. Big feelings that make me still wanting out of this town very confusing. I was so convinced that sex was just sex, but with Beau, it's so much more. Everything feels so different now.

We snuggle, me plastered over him and his arms snug around my waist as the morning sun filters in through the window. He woke me up getting ready for work, and I took advantage. I'm tired and want to go back to sleep, but he must be tired too, considering he still sits at my bar four nights a week guarding me.

He hums contentedly and then carries on to make a fake snoring sound that has me smiling against his chest. "I'm sorry. You must be so tired."

A broad, calloused palm slides up and down my back. "All good, baby. It's worth it."

"You can't keep this up."

"What?"

"Staying up all night with me and working on the ranch all day."

"Sure I can. I sleep through 2:11 like a baby with you here."

I roll my lips together, weighing my words carefully. "We need to talk about what we're doing at some point, Beau. We basically fuck, cuddle, and then you watch me work."

"Yes, it's perfect."

"You can barely keep your eyes open."

"It's not my fault you're so horny all the time. You wear me out. I'm old. It's hard to keep up."

I can't help but laugh. "You don't seem to struggle with keeping up. Like, at all."

"Was talking to Mitch Henderson, the fire chief, the other day while I gassed up."

"Oh?"

He nods, his chin bumping up against the top of my head. "Yeah. He told me to come down any time, and he'd slide me into the next training group. Thinks I'd be perfect for the job."

I know he doesn't mean anything by it, but his comment chafes. A casual conversation at the gas pump gets him an in with whatever job he wants. Meanwhile, I struggle to stay afloat at a job where it's taken years for me to work my way up. And truthfully, I don't know how they haven't fired me yet. And now I have another job with a woman who thinks we're about to become sisters-in-law.

It feels unfair, and I go rigid in his arms as I wrap my head around what he's just told me. I'm happy for him.

I am.

I'm not happy for me. He's putting down roots here, and I'm still planning my exit strategy. I'm going to be the first person in my family to attend university. I have plans for myself because I don't want to be Chestnut Springs Bailey. I'll always be a Jansen here, no matter what. The fact Beau thinks he still needs to watch over me constantly is proof. And whether or not he wants to admit it, he can't keep it up.

"You would be great at that, I agree."

"Then when you go off to school, I'll have a regular schedule that we can work around if need be."

"Oh." I don't know why I assumed he hadn't planned for this.

"Long distance. To start with."

331

"Long distance." Even I can hear the surprise in my voice as I repeat his idea. "We could do long distance. And it's not that far. An hour? That's child's play."

But what does *to start with* mean? That he expects me to move back to Chestnut Springs?

"Of course we can."

God, I'm an idiot. He probably isn't even thinking that far ahead. I should just enjoy the moment. Trust that Beau has got this.

I squeeze him and suck in a deep breath of his citronella scent. *Long distance.*

I'll miss this, though. Having him every day. I've only had it for a week, and I already know I'll have a hard time going without.

And that prospect terrifies me.

"Bailey."

"Yeah?"

"I can feel you worrying."

"Yeah?" I snort. "Is that something they teach you as a tier one operator?"

He nips at my ear, always turning a serious moment playful to ease my anxieties. "Mouthy little brat."

"*Your* mouthy little brat," I murmur as I snuggle into him, my ear against where I can hear his heart beating.

"Yes, Bailey, you're my mouthy little brat. And I'll give your mouth something to quiet it down later."

"Cheesy."

"Fine." He unfolds himself from the bed, peeling my spent body off him. "I'll see you at work tonight. And when we get home, I'll watch you try to mock me with my dick shoved down your throat."

I laugh and roll over to look at this beautiful, filthy, funny man who stormed into my life and turned it all upside down.

I think I'm still reeling.

I think I'm overwhelmed.

I think I'm in love with him too.

"See you tonight," I reply with a wink.

Then he kisses me and swaggers out the door like he hasn't got a care in the world.

38

Beau

Beau: T-minus six hours until you're choking on my cock.
Bailey: Lol. But who's counting, right?
Beau: Me. I'm counting.
Bailey: He's hot *and* can count. Really, the whole package.
Beau: Will be giving you the whole package in T-minus five hours and fifty-nine minutes.
Bailey: CHEESY.

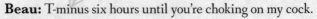

My palm lands flat against the cool door. The brass push bar across it looks a little worse for wear. I make note of that as I walk into the tail end of the Monday night dinner rush.

The low chatter of conversation hums through the air while George Strait plays over the speakers. Pool balls clatter against each other like a chime in the song.

I catch sight of Bailey behind the bar. Shiny, almost-black hair cascades down over her shoulders.

Her tight, drawn up shoulders.

My eyes race over her. Jaw set stubbornly, movements almost jerky, like she's trying and failing to act casual.

She's a terrible liar. Everything about her, from her face to her body language, absolutely gives her away. Something is wrong, and she might as well be a flashing neon sign telling me as much.

The other dead giveaway is Gary, who is sitting up straight with a half-drunk pint in front of him. He doesn't even have his hand on it. Usually, he never lets it go once she hands it over. It bothers me because I feel like the beer must get warm, which is just very unappetizing. But then I always suppose that he drinks it fast enough for it not to matter.

Either way, he's rigid too and watching Bailey with a glint of fatherly protectiveness in his eye that I've seen before. But today it's sharper . . . more sober.

I check my watch.

Seven thirty. He's usually drunk by now.

My eyes scan the room, noting the smiles people toss me as my gaze slips past. I don't smile back. I went from relaxed to high alert, and when I hit the back corner, I know why.

Bailey's shitty fucking brothers and her shitty fucking dad are here. I thought he was in prison somewhere, but what do I know? Truth be told, we don't talk much about her family. I can tell she doesn't like it. I can tell it makes her feel dirty and I never want to make her uncomfortable.

They're happily tossing back beers, laughing, playing pool—like they belong here. Fury races through me.

Have I not kicked them off my property already?

I take a few steps their way, ready for confrontation, when I turn and give Bailey a quick glance. I must have felt her eyes on me because we make a connection instantly.

She shakes her head no.

I bite the inside of my cheek so hard it bleeds, then tip my head harshly toward the door before turning and storming out. Hoping she'll follow. Needing to talk to her.

I march back out into the parking lot, freshly paved, so the place isn't so fucking dusty all the time.

"Beau!" she calls as she clears the door.

"Over here." I wave her back with me, going around the building to the little sheltered shed at the back where we keep the empty kegs. Pickups happen on Mondays, so there's nothing in here right now, and I yank the door open, ushering her in. She scoots past me and I slam it shut behind us.

Light seeps in from between the boards, casting a faint glow.

Bailey's eyes are wide with unease, and she opens with, "I'm sorry. I didn't—"

I cut her off by pressing one finger to her lips. "Are you okay?"

She nods but blinks rapidly. Fuck, my girl is tough. She's saying she's okay, but she's not.

"Bailey," I sigh her name and take my hand back, scrubbing it over my mouth. All the tension in my body pulses to the surface, writhing beneath my skin.

"Beau, please. Just don't make a scene. They're never as bad when my dad is around. I don't want there to be a scene. I want them to finish their shit and get out and to just be the bigger person."

"I'm fucking sick of you having to be the bigger person, Bailey.

They know what they're doing. I told them to get off my property and stay away from you. And yet, here they are, shoving their defiance in my face. You deserve so much better than this."

She rubs at her temples, peering down at her feet. And I wish I could make this all so much easier for her. But I don't know how.

She needs to get out of this town, and soon.

We both know it. We just don't talk about it.

I don't pretend to know how much money she needs to save up to pull the pin, but I suspect there's a level of nerves that accompany her plan. Wanting to leave, but also afraid of starting fresh.

I worry I'm holding her back.

She turns tearful eyes up at me. "I'm so tired, Beau. So fucking tired."

The air in my lungs empties in a heavy whoosh as my chest caves in at her admission.

I don't know what to say to make it better, so I kiss her instead. It starts with a little whimper into my mouth, but then her hands are on the back of my neck. Her nails are in my hair. She's gripping me to her like she might breathe me in and sustain herself on my kiss alone.

My hands start on her hips, but the minute they start to roam, the energy in the shed changes.

Our patience frays.

I want her with a violence I've never experienced, with a ferocity that shocks me.

I shove her against the wall, pressing my leg between hers. My thigh grinds against the apex of hers while I take her mouth and rip at the button of her tight jeans.

"Beau," she whispers between bruising kisses, hands running up under my shirt.

"I want these pants off. Now."

"Beau."

"I want you to walk back in there knowing that you're mine. No matter what happens. No matter what anyone says."

"What?"

"I want you to walk back in there looking freshly fucked so that no one questions a single thing about us. Especially not you."

"Beau, there are customers . . . " She trails off as I yank her jeans down her firm thighs, leaving them stretched there, and run my fingers over her panties.

"Bailey, shut up and let me fuck what belongs to me. We can talk later."

"Yeah," is her breathy response as I rub at the cotton thong that's now wedged between her pussy lips.

"Turn around and bend over." My voice is sharp, bordering on demanding, but she doesn't flinch. She knows me well enough to know there are different facets of me that come out to play, depending on the day.

She tells me she likes all the versions of me, so I haven't bothered hiding even the most vicious parts of myself from her. The ones I've always left overseas or on base. I don't have to pretend those facets of me don't exist with her.

I love her all the more for it.

Bailey spins, palms flat against the crudely constructed wall of two-by-fours. Her bare ass faces me, her head bowed while her body rises and falls under the weight of her panting.

"So obedient, Bailey." I hook a finger under the T of her thong while my opposite hand presses flat on the small of her back to bend her over further.

"Yes, sir," is her rushed reply. But this time she isn't joking. She knows it makes me hard when she says it.

She knows me too damn well.

And yet, she doesn't know everything.

"You need me to fill you up before I send you back in there to finish your job?"

"Yes."

I land a firm swat on her ass that makes her jump. "Ask politely."

Her breathing goes ragged, and I watch the tips of her fingers curl into the wall. "Yes, please."

I spank her again and she moans. "Yes, please . . . "

"Yes, please, *sir*."

God, the way she emphasizes it. I shouldn't be getting off on fucking a twenty-two-year-old at work and making her call me sir.

But I don't let myself focus on it for too long. I quickly unbuckle my belt, pull my cock out, and fist it, slapping it down against the pink hand shape blooming on her ass.

Holding her panties to the side, I run the head of my cock through her wetness. "Fucking soaked, Bailey. Should I tease you until you drip down your thighs, make all your customers wait? Or would you rather be dripping my cum?"

"Your cum." Her hips move back suggestively, and she peeks over her shoulder at me. Eyes still glassy, but not sad like before. "Please. Sir."

"Fuck." I shake my head and grind my molars as I notch myself inside her. "Are you sore, baby?"

We started off slowly, but we haven't been lately.

"No, no."

She wiggles again, and I admire the way my cock looks against her tight little cunt. Then I blink up at her. "Good, because you will be after this."

I shove myself in to the hilt and her body bows to accommodate me. She tries to bite down on a cry while her pussy clenches and flexes, wrapped around me.

"So fucking tight, Bailey," I bite out as I withdraw. "You fit me like a glove. Like you were made for me."

I shove back in, feeling her legs tremble and struggle against the tight denim that prevents her from spreading them wider like she clearly wants to.

A frustrated mewl spills from her lips and she tries to reach down, but I grab her hand, putting it back against the wall. "Hands stay there, Bailey. Flat."

I hold her hand there, reaching above her, while my other hand holds her hip and my cock drives into her repeatedly. Roughly.

The sound of my hips slapping against her ass is accompanied by our mutual panting.

I thrust harder, and she pushes back, meeting my every stroke.

Her fingers lace with mine against the wall above us. I don't know who initiated it, only that it lends a soft spot to our otherwise rough fucking.

Linked. Bailey and I are linked in inextricable ways.

We don't make love, we fuck.

I lay a claim.

She meets me at every turn, just like she has since the day I stormed into her bar in a foul fucking mood.

"Beau. Yes. Fuck me. Spank me again."

I take my hand off her hip and land it on her ass again. Her skin goes rosy, her body shakes.

She fucking loves it.

"Again."

"Ask nicely, Bailey." I bite her shoulder in my favorite spot, hoping it leaves a mark.

"Please." The word is a mindless whine.

It's so fucking hot, hearing her ask for what she wants, getting to watch her try all these new things on for size.

I lean back slightly and land another, louder than it is hard, and her muscles clamp down on me.

"Oh god. Oh god. I'm going to—"

"Atta girl. Come on my dick."

I drive into her hard as she shatters. Her body milks me as we both race past the finish.

She slumps against the wall, and I lean into the hand above us, using it to prop myself up after what might have been the most intense orgasm of my life.

"Fuck," I breathe out against her neck.

"Yeah," she responds, squeezing my fingers against the wood.

I kiss down her neck, and she shivers when my lips drag over the bone at the top of her spine.

"Ready?" I finally ask.

"As I'll ever be."

My cum slips from her body when I pull out, and I take a sick sort of satisfaction in lifting her panties back in place to cover the mess. "I think your panties might be ruined." I nip at her ear before I ease away, putting myself to rights, fixing my pants and stepping back to see how pretty she looks with my handprint on her ass.

She looks really fucking good.

I grunt. "That's a hell of a view, sugar."

It's with a breathless chuckle that she finally finds the where-withal to move again. She slides her jeans up and glances back at me with the most breathtaking smile. "You're welcome." She winks playfully, like I fucked the worry right out of her.

But we both know better. When we leave this shed, it's back to reality.

She smooths her hair, rubs at the corner of her eyes, and shimmies her shoulders back. "How do I look?"

I stare at her for a few beats. What a woman.

What an incredible fucking woman.

She deserves the goddamn world.

And I'm going to be the one to give it to her.

"Like mine," I say with a firm nod.

Then I reach for her hand and lead her back into the bar, straight into the fire. Because the minute we step through the front door, I see her brothers leaning at the bar, impatience practically dripping from them. As though they couldn't wait five fucking minutes for a beer.

"Hey, Bails. If you're done playing the Eaton's whore, we need another round," Aaron, the younger of the two, calls out loudly through the busy bar. He's trying to show off by embarrassing her, and it works.

She tugs her hand from mine and shrinks beside me as all eyes turn to her.

I watch a woman who was so alive and so sure of herself mere moments ago turn back into the girl she's trying so desperately to grow out of.

She didn't want a scene, but I think a scene is what she needs to break free of this place.

I know I'll pay for what I'm about to do, and I should have come clean a long time ago. But if it means Bailey comes out ahead ... then so fucking be it. Haven't left a man behind on a mission so far in this life, and I have no plans to start now.

"You three!" I point in turn at her brothers and then at her dad in the corner, all lean muscle and shrewd eyes.

"Beau," she hisses through her teeth and tugs at my shirt. "Don't do this. It's not your place."

I tilt my head and gaze down at her, memorizing the little freckle beside her upper lip just in case I never get close enough to see it again. "Yeah, it actually is."

Confusion flashes on her face, and I turn back to the now mostly quiet bar where every set of eyes in the place is turned on me. Then I project my voice, so every single person hears me loud and clear. "You three, get the fuck out of my bar! Or I'll have the cops come remove you from my property this time."

Bailey gasps, but I don't stop there. "And anyone else who plans to treat my fiancée and my staff with anything less than the utmost respect, you can get out too."

I turn to the woman I love to see if I can gauge what kind of damage my secret has caused. All it takes is one beat spent in her eyes for me to see the damage might be more than I can repair.

39

Bailey

My bar. My staff.

Shouts ring out around me and a dull song I've heard a million times plays over the speakers, but all I hear is the pounding of my heart, the blood rushing in my ears.

I stare at the polished wood floor. It used to be more scuffed. The chairs? They used to look dated. Brass chandeliers replaced dingy hanging lamps. The Railspur became country chic somewhere along the way . . .

Under new ownership was the town gossip, but I never cared much. I had a job that paid reasonably well. I kept my head down and worked. Management never changed, and the company signed my checks. The story was that there was a silent investor. Someone hands-off.

I pull my eyes back from the floor, catching on Beau. All I can do is shake my head. "No."

His features are stone as he stares back at me, giving nothing away—except the vein that runs down over his temple is pulsing.

One, two, three.

His heart beats.

My heart beats.

He stares at me while I try to catch up.

"Since when?"

"A few years now."

A few years.

God.

The ache in my chest has me gasping for breath. It could take me to my knees if I let it.

"Trouble in paradise, sissy?" Aaron taunts, the stench of his breath filling the air around me as he leans in close.

It's the swat of my dad's grizzled hand that pulls him back. My dad was always swatting us. Sometimes harder than others.

My own father says nothing to me as he passes by; instead, he mutters to my brothers, "You fools trying to get me sent back to the clink? Get out."

I erupt.

"Yes! Get out!" My voice is loud and strong and brimming with years of frustration. My hand doesn't even shake as I point at the door. "Go to jail. Go to hell. Go dig a hole six feet deep and stay there. I don't fucking care. But go *away*. Far, far away from me and my life. I am done!"

I can feel every goddamn eye in the place on me. Like people are confused by the fact that I don't seem chummy with my family.

"Done with all you assholes and all your shit! I am done being treated like garbage. I am done rising above it all with a polite fucking smile. I am done trying to be classy about it. I am done with being related to you when I *hate* you. Go. Away."

A pin could drop, and you'd hear it. The bar is silent. All I can hear is my labored breathing and the blood rushing through my veins.

With a scoff, they leave. I doubt they even care about what I've said to them today. But it felt good all the same.

So I keep going.

"And everyone else!" I turn and face the other patrons in The Railspur. "Stop looking at me like I'm infectious. Stop watching me like this is entertainment. Stop treating me like you're superior. You're all cruel and shitty and bigoted and have made living here my entire life absolutely miserable."

The vast majority of people in the bar look like deer caught in the headlights. I just ran my truck into them full tilt. There are a couple murmured "sorrys" and the odd clearing of a throat.

I just shake my head and prop my hands on my hips as I peer over at the table that my *family* just left. Dined and dashed, naturally.

I used to have to pay for those out of pocket.

But ever since "new ownership" took over, we haven't been on the hook for walkouts. Or, well, I haven't been. No one in this town would walk away without paying, unless I was their server—then it was a funny joke. I used to hear them laughing about it.

Until "new ownership" banned anyone who left without paying from coming back.

Fuck. *Fuck.* How long has Beau been looking out for me? And he let all this go unsaid while we . . .

While I started to feel . . .

"Beau, you get out too. I need to get back to work," I whisper as I lift my chin and drop my shoulders.

I've held my head high through deeper embarrassments. This will be no different.

"I'm not leaving." He crosses his arms and stares at me down his straight nose as if it's some sort of challenge.

But I'm not strong enough to face off with him right now. Not with an audience. Not at all.

My eyes shutter and I suck a deep breath in through my nose as my hands prop on my hips. I press them in on my hip bones to keep them from shaking. "Then I quit."

His rigid body starts like I've hit him. He didn't see that coming.

I reach back and pull my swipe card for the computer system out of my back pocket and hold it out to him. "Here."

He looks at the card but doesn't take it. "Okay, Bailey. I'll leave."

"No." I shake my head rapidly, tears welling, stinging along the sides of my nose as I struggle to keep them from falling. "I need to leave."

"You can't quit. I'll come—"

"I can. And I need to be alone right now more than I need the paycheck." My voice cracks and I purse my lips together. I shove the card toward him again, silently begging him to take it. The massive diamond ring he gave me sparkles in the warm light from the beautifully updated chandelier above us.

How did I never think more about who the silent investor might be? How did I never question things? How did I not see this?

"Bailey." My name is a sigh on his lips as his broad shoulders sag in defeat.

An angry whimper lodges in my throat, and I drop the card on the perfectly polished hardwood floor before spinning on my heel and getting the fuck away from Beau.

The fuck away from my fiancé.

The fuck away from my boss.

When I get home . . .

I shake my head as I walk up the concrete front steps.

When I get to *Beau's* house, I walk in the front door, enter the alarm code, swipe my Boler key from where all our keys—*his keys*—hang. I don't even bother taking my shoes off as I walk straight through the main living space and out the back door.

He can wash his stupid clean floor with a toothbrush while he thinks about what he's done, for all I care.

And what he's done is lie. Lie so deeply, so thoroughly—even if it was well-meaning—he made me believe something was real, and it now feels as though maybe it isn't. Now it feels like I was just a pawn in some stupid game for him. Like he got home and made my life his new undercover mission.

Except he failed to tell me about it and made me fall in—

"Ugh!" A tear spills down my cheek and I swipe at it angrily as I storm up to my trailer. Key in the lock, I yank the door open and shove myself inside, swiftly bolting the door behind me.

I need to be alone.

I need to think.

And I can't think in a house where everything reminds me of *him*. Everything smells like *him*.

Tears fall freely now, and I don't bother wiping them away as I plop woodenly down onto the bed at the far end of what used to be my house.

Maybe it's my house again?

The thought of that, of leaving him, makes me feel like my bones are cracking under the weight of such a heavy burden.

I try to calm my breathing, but it just gets to the point where I feel like I can't breathe at all.

I'm hurt.

I'm embarrassed.

I feel foolish that I let myself believe someone could love me so honestly.

And yet, I ache for him. I only want him. His arms. His words. His smell.

I know it's the only thing that will make me feel better, but . . . I'm furious.

Moments pass and I watch the silent tears land on my jeans, staining the light denim dark as they soak in. The spots start small and seep out into bigger, rounder ones with softer edges.

Suddenly, I hear his panicked voice calling my name from the house. I close my eyes and listen to him.

"Bailey!"

His voice—it hurts. I can sense the pain in it, pain that would match my own if I could even find any words to say.

"Bailey!" He's in the kitchen now, I can tell by how close he sounds, and I know that hiding from him like this is hurting him. It makes me feel like I could throw up.

But I need this moment. I need this space. This trailer may sit on his land, but it's still mine. Simple and plain and run-down, but mine.

I thought the bar was mine. I thought that was the one place people appreciated me and my hard work. I thought I earned that place in the world.

The back door crashes open, and I know this man would tear the world apart to find me. To save me.

But I'm so tired of needing saving.

"Bailey!" His palm lands flat on the door of my trailer. I can hear it slap.

The childish part of me wants to keep hiding from him and not respond.

But the part of me that's in love with him is being shredded, strip by strip, as I listen to him frantically search for me.

"Yeah?" I sniff.

There's a thump on the door and I feel like I can perfectly envision him, forehead tipped against the plain matte-gray exterior of my junky little trailer. All golden and perfect.

"Bailey."

"Why didn't you tell me?" The words are a sob. I thought I'd hold it together, but I'm not. I'm fucking crumbling.

He says nothing, and it infuriates me, so I get up and shove the fiberglass door open, sending him stumbling back. "Why didn't you tell me? For a guy who desperately didn't want our relationship to be founded on a lie, you sure doubled down on this one."

He licks his lips, the golden light behind him glowing over the silhouette of the house. "I didn't lie."

I bark out a harsh laugh. Tears still mar my face, but I don't care. "Oh, fuck off. It was a lie of omission, and you know it." I shake my head, looking away at the yard. "And it came out in the most humiliating way. In front of everyone, Beau."

"I know." He braces his hands behind his head and stares at me, totally forlorn. "I'm sorry."

"I don't want your apology! I want an explanation. Have you spent all these nights sitting at my bar because you're protecting your investment or because you wanted to be with me?"

"Bailey, how can you even ask me that? I've been totally hands-off with that place for years. It's *always* been about you."

My chest. It hurts.

"Explain."

His hands scrub over where the hair is shorter at the back of his head, an expression of concentration on his face as he rifles through his head. He's clearly trying to pick his next words carefully.

He paces. "One night when I was home and heading in there to meet Jasper for a drink, I overheard the owner and the manager talking outside."

I prop a shoulder against the doorframe and cross my arms. A silent instruction for him to keep going.

"They were talking about how the place was getting run-down. There wasn't enough money to fix it up. Fred, the guy who owned it, told Jake that firing you might bring more people down."

I try to cover my flinch, but my cheek twitches and I know he sees it. I look away. *Fucking Fred.* That guy was such a creep.

"But Jake refused. Said you were a good employee and needed the job. He went to bat for you and lost his job for it."

"Jake?"

Beau nods.

"But he's still the manager." Jake is from the city and has always been nice to me, didn't know or care much about my background.

"I hired him back, but I've done it all through a lawyer to keep myself anonymous. I'm totally hands-off. Except when I go in and fix the odd thing. I fixed that tap for you the other day. But I still wanted to be able to go to my favorite bar with my friends and family and just be a regular joe patron. A regular small town guy in a regular small town bar."

"I ... I don't even know how to make sense of this. Why buy it at all?"

The smile that touches his lips is sad. "I watched you that night. I saw how hard you worked. How nervous you were. And I ..." He scrubs his hands down over his face. "I don't know, Bailey. I guess I've always been impulsive where you're concerned. Because I walked into the back and made Fred an offer on the place that he couldn't refuse. It just didn't feel right. Knowing what he was going to do to you."

"That's insane. Of course it's not right! For a man who's been through some shit, you're awfully idealistic, Beau. Bad things happen to good people. You don't need to be a hero every time. You don't need to save everyone."

He shrugs. "You're not everyone."

I stare at him, slack-jawed. I want to hug him, and I want to hit him. All at once. He is infuriating. My teeth grind as I watch him. "I'm so fucking mad at you."

His eyes drop, but not before I see the shame there. "I know."

"Why didn't you just tell me?"

"I wanted to. Fuck." He wipes at his mouth and paces. "I wanted to. Jasper told me to. He's the only person I ever told. But I knew we were too far down this path for it to not hurt you or make you feel like I was maneuvering behind your back. And, god, Bailey. The very last thing in the world I ever want to do is hurt you."

My throat aches, constricts on itself until I'm almost nauseous.

"I actually felt like I was your partner, Beau. Like you respected me. I really felt like I was integral to you somehow. I wasn't a project. Not some deep-cover mission. Not a pawn in you playing super soldier to scratch an itch or fool your family."

352

"I do respect you. And you are integral to me. I fucking love you, Bailey."

Love.

Whoever said love hurts wasn't fucking lying.

"And that job? That job has always felt like proof I did something for myself, despite where I come from. Proof that I don't need anyone's pity. That I'm strong enough to rise above it all. That if I had the chance to show people how hard I work, they'd reward me. And you just tugged the one thing I thought I'd done with my life right out from under me. I'm utterly dependent on you, and that terrifies me. And it's even worse because first you made me fall in l—you know what?" I wave a hand dismissively. "I need some time to get my bearings so I don't say anything I'll regret."

Beau blinks rapidly, standing tall and proud. Like he's prepared to face the consequences head on. He doesn't tell me it's okay, or that I'm overreacting. "That's understandable."

He takes all my frustration and swallows it. Like a man.

Like the flawed but good man that he is.

Like a flawed but good man who loves me.

Hold onto that.

I nod and go to close the door on him, but he stops me, stepping up and wrapping his hand around the edge of it, his fingers brushing against mine. "How long?"

My gaze bounces between the swirling metallic pools in his eyes. "As long as it takes for me to not be this mad at you."

His lips press into a flat line as he bites down on whatever he was about to say. And then, after a beat, he repeats what he's already told me. "Sugar, I am so sorry."

I smile sadly and draw away from him. "I know," is all I say as I lock myself into my lonely little trailer. And then I head back to the bed, where I lie awake all night long, analyzing my life from every angle and wondering how the hell I got here.

And how the hell I'm going to fix us so I don't spend the rest of my life feeling like Beau Eaton's pet project.

40
Beau

Beau: Gary wants me to tell you he's on your side.
Bailey: He fucking better be.
Beau: I'm on your side too.
Bailey: You fucking better be.

I knock on Bailey's door.

She said she needed time, and I don't blame her. I'd want a break from me too. Unfortunately, I'm stuck with myself—hating myself—and obsessing over how to make this right. Last night, I went back to the bar to help out. Came back just in time to watch her swim in the river by herself from the top of the bank like a total creep. Then went to bed, where I didn't sleep a wink and laid awake despising myself instead.

I see a swish of her curtains. Movement. A sure sign that she's in there and knows I'm standing out here like a sad puppy.

"I'm not done being mad at you," is what she calls from inside.

My lips twitch. She sounds so . . . huffy. And I can take this. I can take her being mad at me. I can wait her out. I will happily wait her out.

"That's fine. I just came to bring you breakfast and your tips from last night. And a little something else."

I glance down at the tray in my hands. Coffee. Scrambled eggs. Strawberries. Cash. Envelope.

Her door swings open and my heart lurches in my chest. Her eyes are puffy, thick hair drawn back in a high ponytail.

"Why are you bringing me tips?"

"Because it was your shift."

"I quit."

"I worked it for you anyway."

She sniffs and her nose wiggles as she glances away. "Didn't know you could bartend."

"I can't, and Gary was really mean to me all night."

Her dark eyes laser in on me and I can see her fighting her lips into a downward curve at that tidbit. "Good."

"Here." I hold the tray out to her and sigh with relief when she takes it and I see my ring still on her finger.

"What's in the envelope? Why does it say #teambailey on it?"

I shrug. "Some people from town dropped by with cash to help with your new unemployment status. Gary wrote the hashtag."

"People from town? Gave *me* cash?"

"It would seem you going off on them had an effect. You may have inspired some . . . remorse?"

She sniffs. "I don't want their cash. Don't need it."

"Well, good luck returning it. There's a lot in there. From

multiple different people and businesses. I don't think they know how to say sorry to you, and this is the best they could come up with."

Her irises widen as she stares down at the tray, lips lightly parted like she's ready to say something but can't find the words. To be fair, I was surprised too.

"Fuck me," is what she settles on.

"I know." I agree with a light chuckle, which just earns me a sour glare.

"Stop agreeing with me. We're still fighting."

I hold my hands up in surrender and start backing away from her. "Sorry. My bad. It's just that I am also hashtag team Bailey."

She shakes her head at me. "You're relentless, you know that?"

And I just give her a salute and a wink. Because yeah, I am.

No one has ever showed up for Bailey, but she's about to get the full experience.

"No, sugar. When it comes to you, I'm downright hopeless."

"What is this?"

I smile because Bailey doesn't look as disheveled today. No, my girl looks stronger. Like she slept.

Her oversized crew neck is loose on her petite frame, long tan legs stretching out of her sleep shorts, stacked fuzzy socks on her feet as she holds the trailer door open with a scowl on her face.

She's got a pen stuck behind her ear.

I imagine this is how she'll look when she's cramming for final exams at university.

I'll be bringing her breakfast and coffee then too.

I stare down at the tray. "Food. And caffeine. Thought you might need it before you head to the gym again today."

"How do you know I work at the gym today?"

"I asked Summer. She didn't know that anything was amiss between us."

"Why would she?" Bailey crosses her arms and quirks a hip. Ring flashing on her finger.

I shrug. "Thought you might have told her while you were there yesterday."

She rolls her eyes, looking her age. But what comes out of her mouth is wise beyond her years. "No, Beau. I'm not going to run to your family wagging my tongue about what a shithead you've been because that's our business, not theirs."

Our business.

That sentiment gives me hope.

I clear my throat and offer her a nod, not wanting to overstep. She's clearly still miffed with me.

Bailey's finger points down at the tray. "What's that?"

"Cash."

"Why?"

"Because I worked your shift at the bar again last night. Gary stiffed me. Said he wasn't paying someone as stupid as me to pour his beers and then threw his keys at me."

Her hand comes up to cover her mouth as her eyes flit away. I know she's trying to smother a laugh.

"You should keep it—"

"Bailey. Take the cash. You deserve a fresh start. You deserve a fair chance at what everyone else gets. Take the money and make it happen. I don't need it."

"Beau . . . " Her head tilts, confusion painting her features.

"No, listen. You need out of this town. For a while there, I thought you didn't. For a while, I thought I could make it better here for you. But the truth is, you made my life better, so much fucking better, and I worry I made yours worse."

She looks stricken by my words.

But she still takes the tray before turning back into her trailer.

"So you're just going to keep making her breakfast? And sending her on her way?"

I flip the bacon with my phone wedged between my ear and my shoulder, trying to ignore what a smug prick Jasper sounds like on the phone.

"Yeah. She was up late. I could see the lights on in her trailer. And she needs to leave. It's what's best for her."

"Dude, I told you to tell her. I hope she makes you bring her breakfast for years."

"Fuck you."

Jasper laughs. "You could use a little humbling. It's good for you. Builds character."

"I'm full of character!" Bacon grease splashes me on the hand, and I pull it away, shaking it out.

"You're full of shit, is what you are. And she figured you out."

"Jas, what the fuck? You're supposed to be my brother from another mother. What is this tough love garbage? I thought you were on my team."

"It's a kick in the pants. Wake up, Beau. You're not the same person you used to be. The class clown, the shiny, happy hero.

Now you're a mere mortal, like the rest of us. One who makes dumb mistakes. One who doesn't get everything handed over to him easily."

"Hey, I—"

"I know, I know," Jasper placates me. "Not everything has been easy. But your path has always been clear cut. The decisions you make are obvious. Did you even think twice about going back into that bunker to get Micah?"

"No," I grumble. "I already knew I was going to."

"Yeah. Exactly. So what's your plan for this? You gonna keep working a job you hate in a town you clearly feel uncomfortable in because of your misplaced sense of duty while she leaves and lives her life? You've got a choice to make, and I'm not sure you realize it. You going with her or not? You keep saying that leaving is what's best for her, but what about what's best for you?"

"I have a plan," I mumble. Because I do. I have for quite some time. I just haven't told anyone. Haven't given anyone the honest truth about my plans in years, and the only person I'm going to change that with is Bailey. Truthfully, I don't want any input. I trust my judgment where she's concerned. I haven't felt such a single-minded purpose since before my accident.

And her comment about not sharing our business with everyone hit home.

She and I.

We started out as a secret but turned into so much more. Even though we're both doing our own thing right now, it always feels like we're . . .

Alone together.

"She'll probably meet someone a lot less old than you in the city,"

Jasper prods me and jealousy lashes at my stomach even though I know he's joking.

"You and I are the same age, dick."

"Yup." He pops the P, and I hear the clatter of him doing something in his kitchen. Lazy fucker could have just driven over to see me. "Old enough to know better."

"Good lord, man—" I stop when I see Bailey step out of her trailer. She's wearing a pretty white dress and a denim jacket, and her hair is all silky and freshly brushed. I know she's been showering at the gym. Summer told me so with a piercing glare that dripped with *don't fuck this up.*

I glance at my watch, realizing it's pretty early for her to be leaving already. I don't want to miss her.

"Gotta go, Jas. Bye." I hang up on him before he can get another word in and toss the bacon in the waiting bun, complete with tomato, lettuce, and mayo. Then I wrap it in a paper towel and race to the front door, where I know the path around the side of the house will take her.

"Bailey. Wait!" I call right as I rip the door open and bound down the stairs. "I made you breakfast."

She stops in her tracks and turns to look at me. "You don't need to keep making me breakfast."

"You were up late."

Her head tilts, and she regards me with a confused expression on her face. "How do you know?"

"Lights were on. Checked on you."

Bailey clears her throat and reaches forward to take the bun. Ring still on her finger. "Thanks."

"Sure," I say, tucking my hands into my pockets. "Where are

you off to so early?" I kick at the driveway, feeling like a teenager talking to his crush.

She's quiet just long enough that it has me looking up at her to see what's wrong.

"To the city."

"Oh, yeah?"

She nods, teeth sinking into her bottom lip.

"Can you wait five minutes?"

She sighs.

I can't stop cataloging every move she makes. Like it gives me some insight into what she's doing. What she's thinking. When she's going to let me come close enough to kiss her again. Leave a bite mark again.

"For what?"

"I'm heading in too. Can I catch a ride?"

It's a moment when she could say no. There's zero reason I couldn't drive myself. Truthfully, I'd rather be the one behind the wheel, but I also just want to be near her. And if sitting in her shitty little truck while she gives me the cold shoulder is what I can get, then so be it.

I can also tell by the way she's peeking at me that she's curious about why I'm heading into the city. And the feeling is mutual.

Maybe if she's stuck in a vehicle with me, it will force her to talk.

If nothing else, it will force her to listen.

41

Bailey

Summer: Have fun today! Send pics of the places you look at. And tell me which neighborhoods. I want to know literally everything.

Bailey: Okay. Thanks.

Summer: You alright?

Bailey: Yeah. I just wasn't expecting you to text me.

Summer: Why not?

Bailey: Beau is the only person who texts me.

Summer: Well, now it's Beau AND me.

Bailey: Thought you might be annoyed about me moving.

Summer: Why would I be annoyed at that?

Bailey: Uh, because I just started working for you?

Summer: I know a thing or two about going after what you want. I love to see it. Make that world your oyster, girl.

Beau pulls himself into the passenger seat and the air in my truck instantly gets harder to swallow.

He looks delicious. A plaid shirt, a mixture of greens and creams, with a khaki tee beneath. I can see the silver chain of his dog tags disappearing beneath his layers. Jeans. The leather boots I helped him pick out.

It's cool this morning, and the nip of fall creeps across the flat fields around us. It gets hot midday, and then the temperature plummets in the evening.

I love this time of year.

Shifting into drive, I pull away from the house, trying to keep my eyes on the road rather than on him.

I miss him.

For three days, I've missed him. For three days, I've forced myself not to walk back into his house.

And not because I'm trying to punish him. I realized that on day two. This isn't even about him.

It's about me. It's about my fear outweighing my desire. It's about taking my own first steps to start fresh. Being able to know I did it on my own, without anyone holding me back, and without anyone giving me a leg up. I've been a victim of my circumstances for too damn long.

First, I got mad at how unfair my life was.

Now I'm getting even.

"What are you doing?" he asks after we've left the limits of Chestnut Springs.

"Driving." My hands twist on the wheel.

"No shit. In the city, Bailey. What are you doing?"

My tongue darts out over my lips as I consider what I want to tell him. He's so . . . overbearing, overwhelming, overprotective, and I don't want him barging in on this day for me. He made it very clear the other morning that I need to leave town. That he *wants* me to leave town.

And him? He's got a family. A home. Any job he wants—that he can casually pick up at the fucking gas station.

No, doing any of these next steps with him in tow would hurt too damn much.

"You can't come with me."

"That's fine." He settles back in his seat, thick biceps straining against plaid as he crosses his arms. "I have something I need to do anyway."

Curiosity tugs at me. "What are you doing?"

I peek at him, and he grins. My stomach does this nauseating little flip. *God.* He's so beautiful.

"Asked you first, sugar."

My eyes roll. How a dumb joke about calling me sugar tits has turned into a term of endearment is beyond me. And yet, it makes me smile.

"Going in to check out the campus. I finally activated my enrollment to start in January."

The grin he hits me with is downright blinding. I blink away, like he's too bright to look at directly. It hurts.

"Gonna check out a few rental places too," I mumble. Talking about these things with him feels awkward in the wake of everything that's happened between us. Fake, to real, to a little too real.

I guess I'm just inexperienced enough to not know where I stand with him, or how to even broach the subject, even though I know I have to.

All I know is he lied. My feelings got hurt. He brings me breakfast every morning and gives me every bit of space I asked for—possibly too much space. And he told me I should leave town.

But then he smiles at me like he loves me.

And I go right back to being confused.

"Good for you."

I scoff. *Good for me.* It's like a pat on the head, and that's not what I want from him. I want him to toss me over his shoulder and drag me back to his house.

But I don't want to be in Chestnut Springs.

I am so fucking lost.

"What are you going in for?"

"Work," he replies simply. All that does is make me think he's doing something with the bar, which reminds me he's been lying to me out of some misplaced sense of duty.

Heroic motherfucker.

We fall into silence once more as the fields whip by and the skyscrapers over the city come into view.

"Where am I taking you?"

He shifts in his seat, grabbing the overhead handle and looking out the window. "I'll direct you."

Cryptic motherfucker.

We head straight into the city.

"Left here."

I turn.

"Right up ahead."

Again, I turn, following the road into a cozy, tree-lined neighborhood. Older houses. Some infills. A one-level brick school with a brightly colored playground out front.

I was expecting something different when he said "work". I have no idea what we're doing here. At least it isn't far from campus.

"One more block up."

My brows furrow as I watch a stream of children make their way down the sidewalk, too-big backpacks slung over their shoulders.

"Just here. On the left."

I stop on the opposite side of the road and look across at another brick building.

A fire hall.

"What's this?"

"Kinda figured the big red truck out front might be a dead give-away," he replies on a chuckle.

I hear him unbuckling his seatbelt, but I can't seem to peel my eyes away from the building.

"Right. But why?"

"Job interview." He tugs the handle and opens the door to exit the small cab.

As he gets out, I ask the same question again, not quite comprehending what's going on. "But why?"

Beau turns, and his eyes sweep over my face, like he's trying to memorize my every feature. Then he shrugs, a nonchalant motion in contrast to the intensity of his gaze. "Told you I love you, Bailey. And I meant it." He gives me a wink and hits the truck roof twice, like I'm a fucking cab driver or something. "Make sure whatever house you pick has room for us to host family dinners. You know the Eaton clan will visit more than we want them to."

Us. We.

I sit here slack jawed, at a loss for words. Is he getting a job in the city just so he can be with me?

But I don't get a chance to ask because he strides off, calling back over his shoulder, "Text me when you're headed back. I'll keep myself busy until you're done."

Then he's across the street. Going for a job interview.

And me? I'm an emotional puddle.

I wander the campus in a daze.

I drink a coffee that tastes bland and watery. The ones Beau makes me are better.

I walk, checking for any cafes or restaurants that might be hiring. I drop off a resume at two that I like the looks of. Both times I'm met with smiles and enthusiasm. People who seemed excited by the prospect of hiring me.

It's nice, but . . . I don't feel that good about it.

The first rental I have an appointment at is a condominium on the twelfth floor. The woman showing it to me seems nice enough as she leads me through the space, which has big windows and lovely views. But when she says, "And there's room for a small dining table right here," while pointing at a practically non-existent space, I burst out crying.

Because that's not nearly enough space to host the Eatons. And I want that. I want Beau, and I want that life, and I—god, I wish he was here with me.

Looking at places to live without him here feels wrong. Especially after that smug little bomb he dropped on me right before leaving my truck. So casual. Like he's known all along what I don't.

I press my palm against the center of my chest to press away the ache there as I ride the elevator down to the lobby. I'm pretty sure this isn't the spot for me. Not only because I'm almost positive no one wants to rent their place to a girl who cries over a dining room, but also because that dining room is simply not big enough.

I miss Beau more intensely in this moment than I have in the past three days.

I wonder what he's doing.

I wonder how he's feeling.

I wonder if he knows what he's doing.

I wonder if he'll regret changing his life for me. And the weight of that is downright crushing.

I don't go to my next appointment. I don't think I can handle looking at another dining room and wondering about Beau. What I want is to crawl into bed with him and have him hold me.

I don't text him. I just drive back to the fire hall, prepared to wait for him if I have to.

But I don't have to.

When I pull up, he's seated on a bench in the sun, knees slung open, phone held low while he scrolls the screen.

You'd think for a tier one operator he would notice me across the street, but he doesn't. So I watch him. He smiles and his shoulders vibrate on a laugh.

I wonder what he's watching.

I wonder how his interview went.

I wonder how long he's been waiting.

I wonder if he's hungry or if he ate lunch.

I wonder if he'd be okay with me coming to sit beside him.

It feels like my brain is just an ode to Beau Eaton. I think about him all the fucking time. Worry about him. Crave him.

I'm staring at him when he finally glances up, like he finally felt me here, soaking him in. Spellbound by him.

Not for the first time today, he hits me with a smile that makes my entire body warm. It's genuine and soulful, and so damn boyish.

I love that smile.

With no further overthinking, I turn the key to stop the ignition and step out of the truck. After a quick glance in both directions, I'm walking to him. Okay, more like jogging.

"Hi," I whisper as I stand in front of him, my eyes getting lost in his.

"Hi," he says, patting the bench beside him.

I take a deep breath and sit down next to him. The wooden slats are warm beneath my bare legs, and I feel safe next to Beau's strong body. "How was the job interview?"

"I got the job." His voice brims with pride, and my eyes sting. "And not because they knew who I was. They'll put me straight into a training group because of my JTF2 experience. And that . . . I earned that. I worked really hard to get into that unit. It's a big part of who I was, who I'll always be. I miss it. But I was offered a chance at a job today based on that merit. It's not a favor from a friend or a built-in job from my family."

He turns now to look at me, shoulder bumping mine lightly. "Been sitting here thinking about today. It feels good to be wanted because you bring something to the table. I'm really proud about this possibility, Bailey. It feels like I earned it. And I'm sorry I took that away from you."

I hum, or sob. I'm not sure which, but it lodges in my throat, and I blink my lashes wildly to keep from crumbling in front of him.

"Thank you," I whisper, and then I reach across the sun-baked wood and take his hand in mine. Calloused fingers envelop my own, and I sigh, enjoying his touch.

I close my eyes and soak up the moment.

"Did you find us a nice place to live?"

"No. I couldn't look without you."

His fingers pulse.

"Actually, I went to one. She showed me the dining room, and I started crying."

"Why? Was it nice?"

"No." I sniff, feeling the tears slip out past my lashes. "It was too fucking small for our family dinners." I finish the sentence with a true sob, one that he hears loud and clear.

"Oh, Bailey." His voice is so tender, and his grip is so firm as he gathers me against him. Strong arms encircle my shoulders. "Baby, please don't cry. I'll do anything to make you not cry. I'm so fucking sorry."

I bury my face in the crook of his neck and breathe him in. "Don't lie to me again. Ever. Don't pull the rug out from under me again. Ever." I draw back, gripping his handsome face in my hands, searching his eyes. "I fucking missed you. God. Even when I'm furious with you, I want to be with you."

He grins.

"It's not funny. I think I'm obsessed with you. Like every other starry-eyed girl in that godforsaken town."

He laughs.

"Don't laugh. It's diagnosable. I'm mad at you, and I lay awake all night wondering if you were sleeping. Or if you'd eaten. After years of holding it together, I've finally lost it." I try to pull a hand up to swipe away my tears, but he's holding me so tight, so close that I can't.

I opt to wipe my face on his shirt instead.

"You haven't lost it. Or if you have, so have I. Because I was wondering all the same things. Shit, I don't know how many times I got up to check the perimeter of the house. So the answer is no, I wasn't sleeping." He chuckles, like that's funny.

I gaze at him in wonder. "But why?"

"You ask an awful lot of questions some days, Bailey Jansen."

"I don't understand, though. You. This. The breakfasts. None of it makes sense to me."

His smile is different this time, tinged with sadness, brimming with reverence as he touches me urgently, brushing my hair behind my ears. "You're not used to anyone showing up for you, Bailey. This is what that looks like. I told you I love you. I've never loved a woman before. Wasn't sure I ever would. But now I do. And you and me? We're a team. You don't quit on your teammates. You don't leave a man behind. So now you're stuck with me. I'm just being patient. Waiting for you to come back."

My tears fall freely as I listen to him pour his heart out to me.

"It's like I've been searching for something, something to tie me to this new reality. I wasn't looking for love; I was looking for a purpose. I just didn't expect my purpose to be you."

I say the only thing I can say in the wake of his words, in the wake of everything he's done for me. "I love you, Beau."

That blinding smile is back, but this time it's matched with glassy eyes. He nods at me, every motion swimming with love. Admiration. I can feel the affection in everything he does.

And it feels so foreign. It feels so good.

"I told you once that I don't think anyone has loved me before. But . . . " I nibble at my lip. "But I don't think I've ever really loved anyone either."

His thumbs swipe at my cheeks, brushing away the tears that slip over my skin.

"That's okay, baby. I can be your first," he says.

And then he kisses me.

The first, last, and only man to love me.

And I'm okay with that.

42

Beau

Beau: Everyone better show up tonight.
Harvey: YES, SIR.
Beau: You can't say that. Like, ever, Dad.
Harvey: Why not?
Harvey: ... Sir?
Beau: You just can't. It's off the table now.
Jasper: REPORTING FOR DUTY, SIR.
Rhett: SEE YOU FOR DINNER, SIR.
Cade: WHY AM I RELATED TO SO MANY IDIOTS, SIR?
Beau: I hate you all. See you tonight.

"Everyone is coming?

"Yes." I casually slick my hair back in the mirror like nothing in the world is wrong—because it's not.

"Like, everyone?" Bailey hovers behind me, her hands tucked into the sleeves of the camel-colored sweater she's wearing. She's got one arm crossed over her stomach, the other brushing at the bottom of her chin in a steady rhythm.

"Of course. You told me to invite everyone."

When I peek at her standing behind me, she's worrying her lip between her bottom teeth and looking a little frantic.

"Right. Of course."

She's nervous and scans the bathroom, like there might be something to distract her from her thoughts.

The bathroom is small but freshly tiled by yours truly. White squares with little black diamonds at each corner. A claw-foot tub in the corner. A pedestal sink. This house on a cozy, tree-lined street is full of vintage, old-world charm.

As much as I love my house at the ranch, I have to confess . . . it felt less *me* since Bailey came into my life. The hard lines and echoey spaces felt cold. At odds with her there.

This house, though? Warm hardwoods and big windows that the light spills through. The oak trim around every wall reminds me of her tan skin in the summer. And the crystal doorknobs that adorn the French doors that lead into the dining room remind me of the way her eyes sparkle when she's excited.

Nah, my house at the ranch is the old me.

This one? This is the new me. The me with her. And like I told her, it's a great investment. Every investment I've made in this woman will always be.

I turn to her, trying to hide my smile. It's become downright impossible not to look at Bailey without smiling. Even when she is a ball of stress. "Come here, sugar tits."

Her eyes roll, and she lets out a beleaguered sigh, but she steps into me anyway. She keeps her arms where they are and drops her head right to my chest. "You need to come up with a better nickname."

"Absolutely never." Her forehead rolls back and forth against my chest as I wrap my arms around her. "Bailey, stop stressing."

"I can't. I don't want them to hate me."

That gives me pause. "Why would my family hate you?"

"I don't know. You all are Chestnut Springs royalty. It's like you're with the banished pariah, and are choosing to live in exile with me over staying with your family."

My chest shakes with silent laughter, and she slaps my shoulder. "It's not funny! What if I change? What if we change and you've given everything up for me?"

I squeeze her tighter. "Bailey, Bailey, Bailey. You *will* change. You're . . . ugh. Saying your age out loud makes me feel old."

"You are old," she quips, but I can hear the smile in her voice.

"You're twenty-two. You start university in six weeks. Of course you're going to change. Nobody stays the same at your age, and in my case, thank fucking god, cause you'd have hated twenty-two-year-old me."

She laughs and I carry on. "And we'll change. And we'll have difficulties. Because that's life. You don't recognize the highs without the lows, sugar. I've changed too." I grip her shoulders and nudge her away from me to look her in the eye. "That's how I knew you were it. That's how I know I'll love you in every version of yourself, because we're all constantly changing. Growing. Becoming."

"I'll register for a philosophy class if I want one, soldier," she says, swiping at her big, glittering eyes.

"Bailey, shut up and listen to me." She chuckles softly with another eye roll before giving me back her full attention. "You fill me with purpose. Lifting you up gives me a reason. Seeing you smile makes me feel whole. And I'm never going to apologize for that. We're symbiotic, you and me. Without you, this version of me doesn't exist. Without the next version of you, the next version of me doesn't exist either. We're going to grow together."

"You're fucking my makeup up, Eaton," she murmurs dryly, wiping a stray tear off her face with the sleeve of her sweater.

I just smile. She needs to hear these things so badly, be reassured of them over and over. And I'm happy to do it. "You asked me who I wanted to be once, and it's this. Me. Right here. Right now. With you."

All she can manage is a nod and a sniffle. "Okay. I have no poetic response to that. Other than yes, please, sir."

Now it's my turn to roll my eyes.

Her hands land on my cheeks, and she rises on her tiptoes to kiss me. "I love you, soldier," she whispers as she pulls away.

"You fuckin' better." I kiss her back now, lifting her against me and giving her a tight squeeze. The tension seeps out of her. And when I put her back down, we stare at each other. It's been a wild couple of years in my life, but worth every hardship to be standing here looking down at this woman.

"Ready to host our first Eaton family dinner?" I ask.

She nods, appearing stronger already. "You ready to tell them you're moving here permanently?"

I snap my feet together and give her my best salute.

It makes her laugh.

And that makes me feel whole.

The house is full. Bustling. Loud. Warm. Chatter fills the space with life. Long, dark, quiet days spent in a cave, thinking I'd never make it out, feel so far away they hardly seem real. Even in my childhood home, I felt like I was stuck in a cave. And now it's like a trippy dream I once had.

The mind works in mysterious ways.

Bailey sits on one side of me, hand on my thigh, chatting away with Summer. But it's Winter, to my right, who watches carefully. Her fiancé, Theo, holds their daughter, Vivi, on his lap, chatting with Harvey and Cordelia.

I barely hear the woman beside me when she murmurs, "I'm really happy for you, Beau."

I lean over slightly toward Winter. "Is that a medical diagnosis?"

Her lips curve up, but her face remains mostly impassive. "No, I'm not your doctor. Just a friend who's been worried about you."

"I didn't know we were friends."

All she offers back is a cool shrug as she picks up her glass of wine and takes an unaffected sip. "Family, I guess. Kindred spirits? We're not so different, you and me. I like to see us fucked-up people pull ourselves out of our own shit."

"We probably need therapy," I joke quietly.

Winter nods. "Not probably. Definitely."

"You're not nearly as mean as everyone made you out to be, ya know?" I lean over just enough to bump my shoulder against hers.

Her lips curve up as she takes another sip of her white wine. Then she bumps my shoulder back. "And you're not nearly as dumb as everyone made you out to be."

I snort. She is kind of mean, and yet I'm charmed. Theo turns to glance at us, and when his eyes catch on Winter, they soften. They warm.

I know how that look feels, but seeing it is something else entirely.

I turn back to Bailey, loving the way she thrives in this environment. My family has become hers. And hers has gone radio silent since she left town. Which is a good thing. Bless them for being the perfect combination of too dumb and too lazy to bother harassing her if it requires any effort on their part. Out of sight, out of mind, I guess.

Stirred to action by that thought, I clank my knife against my glass. "Everyone shut up! I have an announcement to make."

Winter scoffs beside me, but everyone else quiets down.

Except Rhett—leave it to him to make it into a fight. "This isn't the military, bonehead. I don't take orders from you."

Summer groans and gazes up at the ceiling. "Why are you like this?"

"Should we take it outside like when we were kids, then?" I quirk a brow at my little brother. Shit disturber that he is.

Rhett laughs. "No chance. You'll kick my ass with your James Bond shit. I'm wild, not stupid."

Winter scoffs again, but just keeps drinking. I see Theo stifle a laugh behind his fist.

"Take Cade with you," Willa whispers as loudly as possible to Rhett from across the table while bouncing a baby on her lap. "A tag team situation. And I'll watch. Or referee. Whatever you call it, I don't care. It's hot when he gets mad, so I'm all in on this idea."

"I'm on Uncle Beau's team!" my nephew, Luke, announces.

I point at him. "Smart, kid."

"At this rate, we'll just be a bunch of skeletons sitting around the table by the time he makes his announcement," Jasper says. "We'll die never knowing what it is he meant to say because you all were planning a Royal Rumble in Bailey's new house." His eyes dance with amusement from across the table as he takes a swig of his shitty, cheap beer with a dog on the label.

"I hate you."

Jasper grins at me, reaching to take Sloane's hand. "Hate you too, bro."

"Listen, I'll be the first of us to turn into a skeleton," Harvey pitches in. "Out with it."

Silence descends, and Bailey goes tense beside me.

"So . . . this isn't just Bailey's house. It's mine too. I'm moving here and starting a new job with the fire department." I glance over at Cade. "Sorry, man, this is my two weeks' notice."

He just grunts. "That's fine. You're the worst employee I've ever had."

I roll my eyes and forge ahead. "So I—we—won't be living on the ranch anymore. We'll come hang out sometimes, but this is home base now."

Everyone is quiet. Watchful.

My dad speaks first. "*That's* your announcement?"

My brows furrow. "Yeah."

"That's the stupidest announcement I've ever been fool enough to get excited about."

Jasper wheezes a laugh and tries to cover it with his hand.

"No, listen. Winter announcing her baby's secret paternity at a family dinner? That was an announcement."

"Gotta win at something sometimes, I guess," she mutters from beside me.

"Me telling you all that Cordelia and I are together? That's an announcement."

A table-wide intake of breath sounds out. Cordelia covers her face with her palm, but Harvey ignores it all.

"But you and your fiancée buy a house—a damn nice house—in the city, where she's going to be spending the next, what? Seven years, at least? And you're announcing this to us like it isn't the most obvious thing in the world? Y'all are a bunch of attention seekers. Or dumb. I'm not sure. Either way, just wild." He shakes his head.

Winter scoffs. Again.

Bailey leans in close and whispers, "I knew it."

"Harvey," Jasper starts, fingers rolling against the brown bottle in his hand. "Since you're not an attention seeker . . . " He can barely get the words out without losing it. "Care to elaborate on the 'you and Cordelia' bit?"

Harvey shifts in his seat.

"It just sorta happened, you know? She was all up in my space when she left her husband. And we, well, it's been a long time since your mom, you guys. Thirty years, and I've never stopped loving her. And . . . " He trails off, staring at Cordelia with a twinkle in his eye. One I'm glad to see because he really has been alone for a long time. Lonely for a long time. "Cordelia never stopped loving her, either. And we bonded over that, I guess. It feels like another lifetime, one that people are often too uncomfortable to bring up. But we can talk about it all. Laugh. Reminisce. I'm happy."

She smiles at him, skin crinkling around her eyes as he folds a hand protectively over hers, right on top of the table. "Me too."

"I'm so happy for you both!" Summer claps her hands together, looking genuinely excited. Everyone else follows suit, offering their congratulations and love.

"And quite frankly, if Sloane can marry her cousin, I figure I can—" Harvey starts up again, and I groan.

Jasper's head drops, his palms pressing into his eye sockets while Sloane bursts out laughing, rubbing soothing circles on his back.

"Then I can be with Cordelia."

"She's not my cousin," Jasper huffs through a laugh.

Harvey elbows him playfully. "Sure, sure. And Cordelia isn't my sister-in-law."

"Well, if we're all laying things out on the table," Sloane says. "Since Harvey brought up Jasper and me . . . " She places a small black-and-white photo on the table. "I'm fourteen weeks." She glances at Harvey, so happy that she's fucking glowing. "Brought the sonogram so you can see there is indeed no tail."

Everyone laughs, recalling my dad's never-ending jokes about Sloane and Jasper having tail babies because they're related—even though they aren't.

After that, the table breaks out into happy chatter. More ribbing. More laughter.

Bailey turns to me, eyes bright, smile wide, cheeks rosy. "This is . . . this doesn't feel like alone together. This just feels like *together*-together."

With one hand, I grip her chin, watching her eyes dance between mine. I kiss her hard. My better half. My other half.

"That's us, sugar. Together-together."

Epilogue
Bailey

Cade and Willa's wedding belongs in a country lifestyle magazine. Willa's softly curled hair cascades down her back over the tight lace dress she chose. Cade went with a brown suit and a bolo tie. They look stunning.

We're all seated in the massive white tent, sparkling with string lights, set up in the field behind the main ranch house. It has a black-and-white checkered dance floor, and there's even a stage where Willa's brother has arranged for Skylar Stone to perform later.

Right now, he's wrapping up his toast to the bride, and his dry humor has everyone in stitches. I've watched Rhett wipe tears of laughter from his eyes at least three times.

Ford Grant stands at the podium, chestnut hair just a little too mussed to be accidental, wearing a tuxedo that fits like it was created specifically with him in mind. He's suave. And cutting. The way he looks at his sister with so much love in his eyes has my own brimming.

"In closing"—he clears his throat—"I'm relieved that I'm no

longer the only person on the receiving end of all your most annoying text messages. In fact, their occurrence has decreased dramatically since Cade came into your life. Or you blasted into his, and—let's be honest—knowing you, that's the more likely scenario. Which leads me to believe you've made him the target of all your unhinged harassment, and I couldn't be happier for myself about that."

Chuckles ripple through the crowd.

"Most of all, I'm happy my little sister found someone who loves getting those obnoxious messages as much as I do. And if seeing her this unbearably happy means a few less chances to mock her mercilessly via text, then that's a sacrifice I'm willing to make." Willa's eyes roll, but I see tears well in the wake of that motion. "Because I'm selfless like that." Ford tosses her a wink and a killer grin.

She mouths *you're an idiot* back to him.

"Willa, if you ever stop making fun of me, I'll know you're not okay. So check in now and then. Tell me something mean so I know you're still well. But since we're not texting right now and I don't see you that often, I'll take this opportunity to tell you I love you and I am wildly proud of the woman you've become. It takes a special man to keep up with a formidable person like you, and I'm so glad you dropped your panties in front of one who can."

Everyone laughs. Everyone knows Willa. *Everyone* knows the panty story.

Ford holds up a glass of champagne by the stem, tipping his chin down at the happy couple. "Cheers to you, baby sister. I wish you a lifetime of unhinged happiness."

Now there are sniffles, followed by polite clapping and a few whistles.

Beau's warm hand squeezes my thigh through my silky dress. "You good?"

I smile up at him. "I'm good," I reply, watching him look out over the crowd of people gathered. Locals—townspeople—who don't glare at me with contempt anymore. That treatment came to a fairly abrupt halt as word of my rant that day at the bar spread. I have to confess, it makes Chestnut Springs a far better place to be. Which is nice considering we still like to spend the odd weekend at Beau's ranch house.

"We gonna do this one day, sugar tits?"

I shake my head with a smile. "We fuckin' better."

"Soon?" His lips dust over the shell of my ear. Living in the city with Beau has been like existing in some sort of dream world. He finished his training. I'm in school and loving it.

"Yeah, soon."

"What kind of wedding do you want?"

He keeps getting closer, turning in his chair, long legs wrapping around where I'm sitting. Mauling me, basically.

"Something small. Not quite like this."

"Okay."

He kisses my neck.

"Maybe down by the river," I whisper, confessing what I've envisioned for some time now. "Behind your house. Like, where it all began kind of thing." I shrug, feeling suddenly shy.

"Where we spent our first night together?" His laugh rumbles over my skin as he kisses my shoulder.

"Where you came across the water to save me."

"Where we struck a deal." Another kiss, beside my mouth this time.

"Where we spent so many 2:11s together," I whisper.

He nuzzles into my neck now. "So what you're saying is . . . where I fell hopelessly in love with you?"

"Yes, soldier. *There*."

"When?" His hands grip my hips just a little too low.

"Yesterday."

He laughs at that. "Wanna go scope out the location?"

"Right now?"

"Yeah. Let's sneak out. I'll show you what I was thinking about doing that morning with the boner."

"Life's always an adventure with you, Beau Eaton."

He grins, drawing away ever so slightly. "It is."

And I grin back, twining my fingers with his.

"Let's go."

Hopeless
playlist

▶ **Fall Into Me**
Forest Blakk
03:45

▶ **Heat Waves**
Glass Animals
03:58

▶ **Wicked Game**
Chris Isaak
04:48

▶ **Mine (Taylor's Version)**
Taylor Swift
03.51

▶ **Feel Like This**
Ingrid Andress
03.15

▶ **Collide (Feat. Tyga)**
Justine Skye, Tyga
04:19

▶ **Any Man of Mine**
Shania Twain
04:06

▶ **Stay A Little Longer**
Brothers Osborne
05:34

▶ **Change Your Name**
Brett Young
03:32

Acknowledgements

If you're wondering how I know I know about third degree burns and skin grafts on feet . . . it's me, hi, I'm the one with burned feet. It happened when I was very young and while they're obviously totally healed now, finding shoes that are comfortable and don't irritate that thinner grafted skin is *still* a struggle.

All that said, giving Beau this little piece of my own story was a huge help in me finding a thread to connect with him and his struggles, because in a lot of ways he was the most challenging hero I've ever written. He will also go down as one of the most memorable (and asked for!) and I hope you all loved his and Bailey's love story as much as I do.

I told Mr. Silver that I needed to write my acknowledgments and he had some sarcastic comment about that I better thank him. Turns out he's never read any of my acknowledgements. This is my ninth book, and he is in every single one. I literally just watched him stand in my office and flip through every one of my books searching out his little note. So I feel like he's probably had enough praise for one day. But still, thank you for everything babe. I love you to the moon and back.

To my son, who makes me laugh every day. Who hugs me every day. Who tells me he loves me every day. You recently told me that you'll snuggle me *forever* and I feel like that will be an awkward conversation with any future girlfriends, but honestly I'm holding you to it. No takesies backsies.

My parents, who are my biggest cheerleaders. Thank you for always believing in me, even when I haven't believed in myself.

A very special thank you to my agent, Kimberly Brower, who has believed in this series (and me!) from start to finish. I probably don't say it enough but, *thank you*. You are truly incredible. Your advice and your wisdom are so appreciated. I would not be where I am today without you in my corner.

To Rebekah West, my editor at Piatkus. Meeting you and spending time with you this year was a true highlight. Working with you is a privilege. Thank you for cheering me on and loving this series the way that you do. Cheers to more bubbly and maybe even a football match next time I'm in London.

Catherine Cowles, I wouldn't have finished this book without you. Bless your organized persona and supportive spirit and incredible heart. I'm so damn fortuante to have a friend like you. I love you.

Kandi and Lena, my Spicy Sprint Sluts, I love our little tribe. You're stuck with me forever. I love you both.

My assistant, Krista . . . sorry, you're actually the executive assistant now. Keeper of my schedule. Organizer of my life. The only person I can randomly text and ask, "Would it be hot if her shaved her pussy?"

Stephanie and Kody who both make #teamelsie complete and help me balance all my socials. I'm so fortunate to have you both in my corner. Thank you for all your support and hard work.

Paula, my editor since my debut novel. I can't believe we've been at this for NINE books together. Here's to nine more, my friend!

My developmental editor, Júlia. You are talented and wise. And watching you eat a banana is one of my favorite past times.

To my proofreader and beta reader and signing assistant (!!!) Leticia, thank you for lending your brain to my books. You're stuck with me now.

To my beta girlies who never fail to crack me up as they read. Trinity, Josette, Amy, you are all so wonderful, thank you for gifting me with your time and opinions. I so appreciate you all.

Finally, to my ARC readers and street team members and influencers who shout about me and my books and this series ... cheers. Your work is always appreciated. Your creativity is valued. This career is a dream come true and I will never forget the way you've rallied around me to make it possible. From the bottom of my heart, thank you.